"Well, well." Luke Jacobs gave her a lazy smile. **"We meet again."**

Mary's hands curled into fists. "Yes, Mr. Jacobs, we do."

"Will you tell me where I can find the livery?"

The cocky grin he wore infuriated her. And he knew it.

"Have you a remedy for horses? Or looking for some manure to add to your spiel?" That ought to wipe the smirk off his insufferable face.

He chuckled. "I need to bed down my horse. You wouldn't want an innocent animal at risk."

"True, but I wouldn't mind putting a guilty beast at peril." She eyed him, making no secret which beast she meant.

Instead of leaving, he took a step closer.

"I can see my presence in this town unhinges you. I assure you, I'm quite harmless."

Mary pulled her five-foot-two frame erect. "Nothing unhinges me, Mr. Jacobs. Not even the prospect of a charlatan in town."

Janet Dean
and
Janice Thompson

Courting the Doctor's Daughter
&
Spring Creek Bride

HARLEQUIN® LOVE INSPIRED®CLASSICS

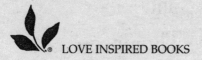 **LOVE INSPIRED BOOKS**

ISBN-13: 978-1-335-45451-5

Courting the Doctor's Daughter & Spring Creek Bride

Copyright © 2019 by Harlequin Books S.A.

The publisher acknowledges the copyright holders
of the individual works as follows:

Courting the Doctor's Daughter
Copyright © 2009 by Janet Dean

Spring Creek Bride
Copyright © 2009 by Janice Thompson

www.Harlequin.com

Printed in U.S.A.

CONTENTS

Janet Dean grew up in a family with a strong creative streak. Her father and grandfather recounted fascinating stories, instilling in Janet an appreciation of history and the desire to write. Today she enjoys traveling into our nation's past as she spins stories for Love Inspired Historical. Janet and her husband are proud parents and grandparents who love to spend time with their family.

Books by Janet Dean

Love Inspired Historical

Courting Miss Adelaide
Courting the Doctor's Daughter
The Substitute Bride
Wanted: A Family
An Inconvenient Match
The Bride Wore Spurs
The Bounty Hunter's Redemption

Visit the Author Profile page at Harlequin.com.

COURTING THE DOCTOR'S DAUGHTER

Janet Dean

If any of you lacks wisdom, he should ask God,
who gives generously to all without finding fault,
and it will be given to him.
—*James* 1:5

To Andrea and Heather, fine women, wonderful
wives and mothers, precious gifts from God.
No mother could be prouder of her children.

To my dear brothers, Michael and Philip
without you, my childhood would have been dull.

To the Seekers, prayer partners, forever friends,
a daily dose of delight.

Chapter One

Noblesville, Indiana, 1898

Mary Graves couldn't believe her eyes. And the gall of that man. A stranger stood on the seat of his wagon holding up a bottle and making ridiculous claims for its medicinal value with all the fervor of an itinerant evangelist. His Eastern accent grated on her Midwestern ears.

She slipped through the gathering crowd to sneak a closer look. Gazing up at him, Mary pressed a hand to her bodice. The man didn't resemble any preacher she'd ever seen. Hatless, the stranger's dark hair lifted in the morning breeze. He'd rolled his white shirtsleeves to his elbows revealing muscled, tanned forearms. He looked more like a gypsy, a member of the marauding bands tramping through the countryside stealing chickens and whatever else wasn't nailed down—like the Noblesville residents' hard-earned dollars.

Well, she had no intention of standing by while this quack bilked the town of its money and, worse, kept its citizens from seeking legitimate treatment.

Not that her father needed more work. Far from it. Since Doc Roberts died in the spring, her father often worked from sunup to sundown—and sometimes through the night. With the exception of those folks who'd profited from Noblesville's natural gas boom, most patients paid with produce or an occasional exchange of services.

The peddler raised the container high above his head. "Just two capfuls of this medicine will ease a nervous headache and an upset stomach. It'll cure your insomnia, but most importantly, this bottle holds the safe solution for a baby's colic."

This charlatan attempted to take money out of her father's all-but-empty pockets with a potion no doubt containing nothing more than hard liquor or flavored water. Imagine giving such a thing to an infant. But her neighbors nodded their heads, taken in by his nonsensical spiel.

"Imagine, folks, getting a good night's sleep and waking refreshed to tackle the day," the peddler went on.

Around her, John Lemming, Roscoe Sullivan and Pastor Foley, of all people, reached in their back pockets for their wallets. Even her friend, Martha Cummings, a baby on her hip and two of her youngsters clinging to her skirts, dug into her purse. And everyone knew Martha could squeeze a penny until it bled.

Mary clenched her jaw. Such foolishness. Why couldn't these people recognize a sham when they saw one?

"Step right up, folks, for the sum of—"

"Whatever you're charging is disgraceful," Mary called, the words pouring out of her mouth. She turned to her neighbors. "Have you forgotten the swindler who came through here last year, promising his tonic would do all that and more? Not one word of his claims proved true."

The townspeople stilled. Her gaze locked with the fraud's. Suddenly cool on this sunny October morning, Mary tugged her shawl tighter around her shoulders. "You're preying on these good folks' worries, knowing full well what's in that bottle can be found for less money over at O'Reilly's saloon." Her deceased husband, Sam, had hidden his drinking behind the pretext of using it for medicinal purposes.

The man shot her a lazy grin, revealing a dimple in his left cheek, giving him a deceptive aura of innocence. Then he had the audacity to tip an imaginary hat. "Pardon me, Florence Nightingale, but without testing my product, you've no cause to condemn it."

Florence Nightingale indeed. No one in the crowd chuckled as the man had undoubtedly intended. They all knew her, knew she lent a hand in her father's practice. Knew what had happened to her mother.

Mary folded her arms across her chest. "No right? I've seen your kind before...." A lump the size of a walnut lodged in her throat, stopping her words. She blinked rapidly to hold back tears.

Though his smile still remained, the stranger's eyes darkened into murky pools and every trace of mirth vanished. Good. Maybe now he'd take her seriously.

He leaned toward her. "And what kind is that?"

She cleared her throat, determined not to be undone by this rogue. "The kind of man who instead of putting in a hard day's work, earns his living cheating others.

That nonsense in your hand isn't worth the price of an empty bottle."

His eyes narrowed. "Your assessment of my remedy—of my kind—is hardly scientific."

He jumped to the street, and bystanders stepped back, giving him a clear path—a clear path leading directly to her. He stopped inches away from her skirt, his features chiseled as if from stone, his dimple gone. The starkness of that face put a hitch in Mary's breathing. Her hand lifted to her throat.

"This isn't a bottle of spirits as you've alleged." He unscrewed the cap and thrust it under her nose. "It's good medicine."

She didn't smell alcohol, only peppermint and honey, but couldn't make out the origin of another scent.

"Let's hear what he has to say," Roscoe Sullivan said.

Roscoe's rheumatism had been acting up, and he probably had trouble sleeping. The poor man dreaded the onset of winter, and no doubt hoped to find a miracle in that bottle. But miracles came from God, not from a peddler with a jarring accent.

John Lemming, the owner of the livery, waved a hand toward the remedy. "Our baby cries all evening. I'd give a king's ransom for something to soothe him."

"*If* it worked." Mary exhaled. How could these people be so easily fooled? "Don't you see, John, he's in this to fill his pockets and then move on before you folks discover his claims are meaningless. Just like last year's peddler."

The stranger smiled, revealing even, white teeth. "Since you're so sure of yourself, Miss Nightingale, why don't you pay the price of this bottle and investigate the medicine yourself?"

Lifting her chin, she met his amused gaze. How dare the man poke fun at her? And worse, ask her to pay for the privilege of disproving his claims? "And line your pockets? Never!"

He stepped closer. If he intended to intimidate her, she wouldn't give ground, though her heart rat-a-tatted in her chest.

"Well, then, stand aside for those folks who are open-minded enough to give it a try." He pushed past her and lifted the bottle. "For the price of three dollars, who wants a bottle of my remedy?"

"Three dollars. Why, that's highway robbery!" She grabbed his arm, then watched in horror as the bottle slipped out of his hand and hit the ground, shattering the glass. Her neighbors' gasps drowned out her own.

The man pivoted on a booted heel. "I believe you owe me three dollars," he said, his voice low, almost a tease.

The liquid trickled between the bricks. She lifted her gaze to lock with his. "I'll pay your price—if you'll move on to another town."

His mouth thinned into a stubborn line. "I'm not leaving."

Perhaps she had a legal way to get rid of this menace. She planted her hands on her hips. "Do you have a permit?"

With that lazy grin and irritating dimple, he reached inside his shirt pocket and retrieved a slip of paper, waving it in front of Mary's face. Her hands fisted. This rogue had thought of everything.

Nearby, Roscoe and John exchanged a glance, and then both men ran a hand over their mouths, trying to bury a smile and failing. Apparently, her neighbors found the exchange entertaining.

Mary dug into her purse and handed over the money. "You've made a handsome profit on this bottle alone, so move on to fleece another town and leave us in peace."

"I like it here." He tossed her a smile, as arrogant as the man himself. "I'm staying."

Though he deserved it, she had no call to give this scoundrel a sharp kick to his shin, but oh, how she'd love to give in to the temptation. Mary closed her eyes and said a quick, silent prayer to conduct herself like a God-fearing woman, not a fishwife. "Well, I don't want you here."

John Lemming pulled out three dollars. "If it works, it'll be worth every cent."

The peddler gestured to the knot of people crowded around them, opening their purses and wallets. "Looks like you're in the minority, Miss Nightingale."

He returned to his wagon, and the good citizens of Noblesville started forking over the money, purchasing the worthless stuff the man had undoubtedly concocted out of peppermint and honey. How could they trust him?

Why had her mother befriended such a man? Her stomach knotted and tears stung her eyes. Even five years later, grief caught her unaware, tearing through her like a cyclone. She bit her lip, forcing her gaze on the hawker.

Surely he didn't mean to stay. If he did, everyone would discover the worthlessness of his remedy. No, he'd depart in the middle of the night, having a good laugh at the town's gullibility.

Handing out bottles of his so-called remedy, the stranger glanced her way, shooting her another grin. Obviously, he took pleasure in swindling her friends and neighbors right under her nose. Like a petulant

child, she wanted to stomp her foot—right on his in-
step. That ought to wipe the grin off his haughty face.

As if he read her thoughts, he turned to her. "Best
remember the exhortation in the Good Book to love
thy enemy."

How dare he mention the Bible while he duped her
neighbors? Still, she had let her temper get the best of
her. *Love thy enemy* was a hard pill to swallow.

Then of all things, the man gave her a wink, as bold
as brass. A shimmer of attraction whooshed through
her. Aghast at her base feelings, Mary turned on her
heel and stalked off.

Behind her, the man chuckled.

Cheeks burning, Mary strode down Ninth Street and
then turned right on Conner. Permit or no permit, she'd
find a way to run that peddler out of Noblesville. He
represented the last thing she and this town needed—
trouble.

Opening the side door leading to her father's office,
Mary's nostrils filled with the smell of disinfectant, a
scent she'd grown as accustomed to as the honeysuckle
fragrance she wore. The waiting room chairs sat empty.
A stack of well-worn *Farmers' Home Journals* and *Ladies' Journals* cluttered the top of a small stand. She
took a minute to clear out the old issues before the whole
heap tumbled to the floor.

Finished with the task, she strode through the office
and found her father in the surgery, filling a basin with
hydrogen peroxide. Henry Lawrence, his hair falling
across his forehead, looked tired, as he frequently did of
late, even a tad peaked. She believed doctoring weighed
him down physically and mentally. Yet he kept work-

ing, seeing to the sick, rarely taking time off except to attend church on Sunday. He should take it easy and eat better. His grandsons needed him. Didn't he know how much they all loved him?

Earlier that day, she'd taken action she hoped would ease her father's load. And free her to pursue her dream. Thanks to an unexpected inheritance from her late father-in-law, she had the money for medical school. If God wanted her to practice medicine, she'd be accepted at the Central College of Physicians and Surgeons. But she couldn't leave her father to handle the practice alone.

"Hi, Daddy."

Her father looked up and smiled, the corners of his gentle hazel eyes crinkling in his round face. "Hello, kitten. Got the boys off and now you're checking on your old man?"

"Exactly." She gave him a peck on the cheek. "It's such a pretty day. Want to take your grandsons fishing after school?"

"Wish I could." He screwed the cap onto the bottle of antiseptic and tucked it into the glass-front cabinet, banging the door shut. "I've got office hours all afternoon."

"Well, at least come to supper tonight."

"Sounds good. Six okay?"

Nodding, she laid a hand on his arm. "You look tired."

"I spent the biggest part of the night at the Shriver place, bringing their firstborn into the world. A howling, healthy, eight-pound boy." He gave a wry grin. "They named him Quincy. Imagine tagging a child with such a name."

Normally Mary loved to hear about a new baby, sharing her father's joy of the miracle of birth. But she shook her head, only half listening, thinking about her father's lack of sleep. "Daddy, don't you think it's time to bring someone into the practice?"

Henry's head snapped up and his gaze met hers. "Now, why would I do that?"

"Well, for one thing, you're not getting any younger. And for another, you work too hard."

"I'm fifty-one, not ancient, and I don't work harder than any other small-town doctor. Besides, I have your help."

"Doc Roberts didn't have any warning before his fatal heart attack." She sighed at the stubborn set of her father's jaw, then bustled about the room, emptying the wastepaper can, checking and laying out supplies, doing all she could to ease his burden. "You're handling his patients and your own. You're not getting enough rest."

"Babies come when they decide—not to fit my schedule."

"True, but your days are so full that you have little time for the boys. They need a man's influence."

Her father's brow furrowed. "I know they do, honey," he said, gathering the instruments out of his bag. "I'll try to spend more time with them. If no one gets sick, maybe we can go fishing Saturday afternoon."

How likely would that be in a town this size? Then her heart squeezed. She shouldn't pressure her father to do more, even if the "more" involved relaxing with his grandsons. "Let me clean those for you."

"Thanks." Her father dropped into a chair.

"Oh, I almost forgot to tell you." Mary gave a wide smile. "I heard from the placement committee. The Willowbys relinquished their guardianship and asked to assume the role of Ben's grandparents, instead of his parents."

"From the look on your face, I'd say the news was good."

"The committee gave me permanent custody of Ben." Her vision blurred with tears of gratitude. Ben, the little boy she shared a bond with, was now her son, just as much as Michael and Philip. A wave of tenderness rippled through her. She'd do everything in her power to give her boys the happiness they deserved.

"Even before his apoplexy, Judge Willowby told me they could barely keep up with a four-year-old boy. Since the stroke, he's naturally troubled they won't live to see Ben grown." He frowned. "What about the Children's Aid Society's rule against giving custody to a single woman?"

"As a widow with two sons of my own, the committee felt that qualified me to raise another child." She swiped a hand at her tears. "That I'm already taking care of Ben for the Willowbys worked in my favor. They didn't want to move him again."

"Thank you, God. With your brother-in-law sitting on the committee, I felt reasonably sure of the outcome. Still, a couple of those members adhere to rules as if Moses himself brought them down from on high."

Laughing, Mary gave her father a kiss. "I can always count on your support."

She returned to the counter to wash, soak in hydrogen peroxide and then dry the equipment her father had used to deliver the Shriver baby. Her father kept his surgery and office immaculate, while his quarters lay in shambles. She tried to keep up with the cleaning, but he could destroy her efforts faster than her boys put together. When she finished, she stowed the instruments in his black leather case then set the bag in its customary spot on the table near the door, where he could grab it on the way to the next house call.

Mary turned to say something to her father. He'd nodded off in his chair. As she prepared to tiptoe out of the room, he roused and ran a hand over his chin. "Guess I'd better shave. Don't want to scare my patients."

In the backroom, she filled the ironstone bowl on the washstand with hot water from the teakettle, and then sat at the small drop-leaf table to watch her father shave. He lathered the brush and covered his cheeks and chin with soap. Since Sam's death, she'd missed this masculine routine, a small thing, but small things often caught her unaware and left her reeling.

If her father didn't slow down, she could lose him too. Yet, Henry Lawrence was as stubborn as a weed when it came to helping others. No point in beating a dead horse…for now.

She'd tell him about the peddler. Surely he'd share her concern. "You won't believe what's going on downtown, Daddy. Why, it's enough to turn my stomach."

"Let me guess." He winked at her in the mirror. "Joe Carmichael organized a spitting contest on the square." He scraped his face clean with his razor and rinsed the blade in the bowl.

Mary planted her hands on her hips. "I'm serious."

"Your feathers do look a mite ruffled." He patted his face dry with a towel. "So tell me, what's wrong?"

"Some fraud is selling patent medicine. He's making all kinds of claims. Says it'll cure upset stomachs and headaches, a baby's colic. People couldn't buy it fast enough, even after I warned them the bottle probably held 90-proof."

"My precious girl, you've got to stop trying to protect everybody, even from themselves."

She lifted her chin. "I don't know what you mean."

Her father crossed to her, touched her arm, his hand freckled with age. "Yes, you do. You've always been a caring woman, but since you lost Sam, you're on a mission to save the human race. Trouble is you're not God. You don't have the power to control this world, not even our little piece of it."

Mary covered her father's hand with her own. "I know that. But I worry about you."

"Yes, and about the boys getting sick or hurt, about their schoolwork." He gave her a weak grin. "Why, your worrying worries me, Mary Lynn. Remember the scripture that says we can't add a day to our lives by worrying."

"You're right. I'm sorry." *Forgive me, Lord, for not relying on You. Not trusting You. Give me the strength to change.*

These past two years, widowed and raising her sons alone, and now Ben, hadn't been easy, even with her brother-in-law pitching in with the heavier chores. The money she'd inherited from Sam's father had made a huge difference, meant she might live her dream, but the added financial security hadn't eased the constant knot in her shoulders. Hadn't eased the loneliness. Hadn't eased the empty space in her heart.

Not that Sam had filled it.

Trying to alleviate the tension of her thoughts, Mary tapped her father playfully on the arm. "Besides, the topic isn't about me. It's that traveling salesman. Don't you find his claims upsetting?"

Her father sat beside her. "Most of those tonics and remedies are worthless, but until I give his a try, I can't condemn it."

Her father prided himself on being impartial, as if the past meant nothing. "Think about it, Daddy. How could just anyone concoct a remedy with real medicinal value?" She leaned toward him. "Can't we do something to protect the town from a quack?"

Her father rubbed the back of his neck. "Does he have a permit?"

"Yes. He's too cunning to be tripped up that easily."

"Well, then there's nothing to be done."

As if on cue, they both rose. Her father put his arm around her shoulders and they walked into the surgery.

"Doesn't it bother you that half the town owes you money and they're squandering what they have on a worthless tonic? If you could collect, you'd have a nice little nest egg for retirement."

His gaze roamed the room and then returned to her with a smile of satisfaction. "What I do here is important. I have no desire to retire." Her father snorted. "Besides, I can't leave this town with one less doctor."

From the stubborn set of her father's mouth, she could see her argument fell on deaf ears. "There's got to be doctors from one of the Indianapolis medical schools who'd be interested in entering your practice." She took his hand, bracing for his reaction. "I'm so sure of it that I put an advertisement in the *Indianapolis News Journal*. The ad should draw inquiries from graduates seeking an established practice."

Her father's mouth tightened, his displeasure at her actions unspoken but palpable.

Sudden tears stung Mary's eyes. "I'm sorry you disapprove."

He walked to the window and rolled up the blinds, letting in the morning sun. "You've already admitted there's no money in doctoring here. That's not going to draw many applicants. Besides, I'm doing exactly what I want to do. I know these people. Know their ailments, their struggles…their secrets."

When they had troubles, the folks in this town turned to two people—their doctor and their pastor. She respected and admired her father and the preachers in town who had a knack for listening. Knew how to comfort, and knew how, when necessary, to admonish.

Henry Lawrence not only made a difference in people's lives but he'd saved quite a few. He had a purpose she admired more than any other and wanted to follow. And once she was a doctor, she'd be dependent on no one.

Her father returned to her side and tweaked her cheek. "If you want to help and can find your way around that pigsty I call a kitchen, then please, darling daughter, make me some breakfast."

Glad to be useful, Mary smiled. "It won't take but a minute."

He hugged her. "You're like your mother. Susannah could make a feast out of an old shoe."

Pleased by the comparison, Mary laughed. Even five years after her mother's death, she missed Susannah Lawrence every day, wanted to be like her serene, unflappable mother. But failed. In her mother's north-facing kitchen, the walls painted the hue of sunshine,

Mary's spirits lifted. Her mother always claimed she never had a gloomy day working here, but she'd surely be amazed by the condition of her workspace now.

Mary might not know how to fix the problems around her, but she knew what to do here. She donned one of her mother's bibbed aprons and tackled the mess.

Once her advertisement brought in the ideal doctor to help in the practice, she could go to medical school, knowing someone young and capable would help her father oversee the health of his patients. That is, assuming she got accepted. No guarantee for anyone, especially a woman. Months had passed without word. At twenty-eight, would her age work against her?

She finished clearing a spot on the counter, washed it down and then poked around in the icebox, emerging with a slab of bacon and a bowl filled with eggs. Once she'd fed and helped her father with his patients, she'd complain to Sheriff Rogers about the dark-eyed stranger. Maybe he could find a way to retract the permit. Surely he didn't want that swindler taking advantage of people's worries.

Taking advantage of her.

Her hand stilled, and a wave of disquiet lapped at her. The dark stranger *had* thrown her off balance with that outrageous wink…but only for a moment.

She wouldn't let that happen again.

Chapter Two

Luke Jacobs snapped the padlock into place on the back of his enclosed wagon and gave it a yank. The last straggler had gone about his day, leaving Luke alone, that meddling woman who'd opposed him heavy on his mind. He'd run into do-gooders like her before.

True, Miss Nightingale happened to be more attractive than most, with glinting green eyes, chestnut hair and a stubborn jaw—shoving into something she knew nothing about. A royal pain who fought what he'd worked hard to achieve.

The remedy stashed inside this wagon had taken him months to formulate. He'd spent untold hours experimenting in a small lab in his house, using himself to test his product. He took pride in what he'd accomplished. The remedy contained good medicine, meant to help people, not to separate them from their money.

That sassy woman probably wanted to drive him back to New York herself. Well, he had no intention of going. Not yet. Not until he learned if the boy lived here.

A band tightened around Luke's throat, remembering the guilt and shame of his misspent life. If only he could go back and relive all those wasted years—

His eyes stung. Sin brought consequences. He'd gotten off scot-free. Lucy had paid with her life.

His son might still be paying.

Without question, he wasn't cut out for fatherhood. He had no experience at the job. No stable home. No hope of having one. But he couldn't leave the boy's survival to chance.

If only he'd find the boy here.

Amongst thousands of children, somehow his son's guardianship paperwork had been lost. All Luke knew for certain was the child had ridden west on a train full of orphans. He'd followed the trail for weeks, first riding the train, then buying this wagon and moving from town to town, selling his medicine and searching for the boy. Every lead had come up empty, every clue pointing to another town until he'd landed here in Noblesville, Indiana.

Another town. One more out of dozens. Would this town hold Ben?

If not, he'd move on tomorrow, though the prospect pressed against his lungs. He was tired, bone tired.

But his comfort didn't matter. Finding his boy did.

God, help me find my son.

"How's business?"

Luke whirled to face the sheriff, a big man with a friendly face and keenly observant eyes. From his trek across the country, Luke had learned the importance of getting on the right foot with the local lawman. It appeared Rogers had decided to keep an eye on him. "Can't complain, Sheriff."

Rogers patted his midriff. "That remedy of yours is easing my touchy stomach."

Luke smiled. "Glad to hear it."

"I'll want to stock up before you move on."

"I'll set some bottles aside."

The sheriff thumped the side of his wagon. "You drove this clear from New York City?"

"I rode the train as far as eastern Ohio, bought the rig and then followed the route of the Erie line."

The sheriff shoved his Stetson higher on his forehead. "Same route that brought them orphans last year."

Luke's pulse leapt. "Orphans?"

"Yep, I'll never forget the sight of that train. Youngsters poking their heads out the windows, squeezing together on the platform. Why, some had crawled on top of the cars."

"How many stayed?"

"Twenty-eight. Eleven of 'em live in town. The rest are scattered 'cross the countryside."

Luke hoped one of the eleven was his son. If so, he'd likely come across the boy without having to make inquiries that would raise suspicion. Or force him into an action he didn't want to take. "Finding them homes must've been lots of work. Did you have to do it?"

"Nope. Fell to a committee."

Luke forced himself not to push for information. Fortunately, the sheriff was in a chatty mood.

"The committee did its best, but the guardian of two of those orphans physically abused 'em." Sheriff Rogers shook his head. "Ed Drummond will spend the rest of his days in state prison."

Luke's blood ran cold. "Did the children survive?"

"Yep." The sheriff smiled. "Emma and William Grounds got themselves a fine home now."

A gentle breeze carried off the breath Luke had been holding. "Good to hear. Sounds like a brother and sister."

"Yep."

Which meant Luke's son wasn't one of the abused orphans. Thank God.

The sheriff gave him a long, hard look and then slapped Luke on the arm. "Don't forget to save me them bottles."

"Sure will." Luke hadn't missed Roger's piercing stare. Had he unwittingly revealed too much interest in the orphans and raised the sheriff's suspicions? "Say, can you suggest a place to stay while I'm in town?"

"The Becker House's food is second to none. Classy accommodations, too."

"Sounds expensive."

The sheriff rubbed his chin, thinking. "Last I knew the room over the Whitehall Café was empty. Try there."

"I will. Thanks."

Whistling, Sheriff Rogers moseyed off, hopefully overlooking Luke's concern about the orphans. Early on, Luke had learned asking too many questions made folks wary, even led them to ask some questions of their own. He'd have to be more careful.

Pocketing the key to the padlock, Luke headed for the Whitehall Café. Someone waved to him; it was probably one of the morning's customers. Along the way, he passed prosperous brick buildings, gas streetlamps, paved avenues. Trees on the lawn of the impressive three-story courthouse had changed to hues of gold and orangey-red. A crispness to the air hinted at the approach of winter, but on such a sunny day, winter appeared a long way off.

Noblesville looked like a good place to pause. He'd had an arduous trip, exposing him to the elements—rain, cold, heat. It was hardly his existence back East. In most ways, he'd found the journey good, even pleasurable. The towns where he'd stopped in the past weeks may have blended in his mind, but he'd enjoyed seeing the middle part of the country, meeting everyday people living everyday lives.

Mostly he'd found hard-working, good people who understood what mattered. He'd been glad to give back, to offer them a medicine he believed in. And yet, always searching, seeking that one last piece of his family puzzle.

No matter what that aggravating female thought of his remedy, of him, she wouldn't thwart his quest to find the boy.

He wasn't here to ruin a child's happiness, or get involved. Life had taught him to hold people at arm's length. He'd learned the lesson well.

If Ben had a good home and was happy with a family, Luke could return to New York and his lab.

Yet he couldn't help questioning how it would feel to leave his flesh and blood behind. To forsake his responsibility to Ben as his parents had to Joseph.

Could Luke leave and repeat the family history he despised?

Geraldine Whitehall was dying. *Again.*

Mary bit her tongue, searching deep for a measure of patience, then greeted the café owner with a smile. All afternoon, the office had a constant parade of patients. Hoping to leave when the Willowbys arrived, Mary sighed, resigned to the delay.

Geraldine leaned close, her eyes wide with fright, her face creased with worry. "I need to see Doc."

"He's with a patient."

"I have this cough. It's worse at night. I'm sure it's consumption," she said, her tone hoarse like the words scraped her throat raw on their way out.

Mary patted the woman's hand. "Have a seat. I'll get you in as soon as I can."

The patient collapsed into a nearby chair. Within seconds she flipped through a magazine, stopping at an article. Even back at her desk, Mary could read the title, "Tumors of the Eye." Soon Geraldine would find enough symptoms to keep her tossing tonight with yet another worry. Awareness thudded in Mary's stomach. She had no right to criticize.

Mary rose and eased the magazine out of the woman's clutches. "How's your daughter?"

"Oh, my poor, darling girl." Tears welled in Geraldine's eyes. "What will Fannie do without a mother to help plan her wedding?"

"Fannie's engaged?"

"No, but she and James are madly in love. It can't be long until he asks."

Frances Drummond walked into the waiting room. Another woman saddled with a man who'd hurt her. Fortunately Ed would spend the rest of his life behind bars for the years of abuse he'd heaped on Frances. Not nearly long enough for murdering Frances' mother last year and all but killing Frances and Addie too. The short time the children lived in the Drummond house had taken a toll on Emma and William. Thank God those orphans were out of Ed's clutches—and thanks to Frances—in the loving hands of Addie and Charles. God had shown there was hope, even amongst all that pain.

Frances paid her bill, exchanging a few words with Mary, who struggled to keep her mind on the task with Geraldine hovering nearby, coughing into her handkerchief and then examining it, most likely looking for the telltale blood of consumption.

With Frances out the door, Mary led Mrs. Whitehall into the examining room. The woman shadowed Mary so closely she could feel Geraldine's breath on her neck. At any moment, Mary expected to feel tracks on her back.

Her father greeted Geraldine, keeping his expression blank and emitting only the faintest groan. After his short night, Mary admired his self-control.

"What can I do for you, Mrs. Whitehall?"

Mary ducked out the door and returned to her desk. Her father could handle this latest malady alone.

Within minutes, Geraldine returned, having regained the spark in her eyes and the spring to her step. "I'm not dying! Hay fever is giving me this cough. It'll disappear with the first hard frost."

"I'm glad to hear it," Mary said, but wondered when the café owner would be back wearing a panicked expression, ticking off new symptoms on her fingers.

Geraldine dug through her purse. "With these doctor bills, it's a good thing I've got a renter for the room over my café."

Mary smiled. "Oh, to whom?"

"To that traveling salesman. He's taking his meals at the café, too." She beamed, then paid the fee and scooted out the door.

Mary's mouth drooped. That peddler was staying, as he'd said.

The door opened and the Willowbys entered. Mary gave them a hug, then gestured for them to follow. Judge Willowby leaned heavily on a cane, his gait unsteady and shuffling. Although it was still a huge improvement from when he'd first had his apoplexy.

In the weeks since the stroke, Mrs. Willowby had devoted herself to her husband's recovery. If anything, his illness had brought out her gentler side. An outcome appreciated not only by Mary and her father but by everyone who had dealings with Viola Willowby. Mary had come to admire the woman—something she couldn't have expected a few months ago.

"How's our...grandson?" Judge Willowby asked.

The Willowbys had wanted Mary to have custody of Ben, but the judge's tongue still tripped over calling Ben his grandson, rather than his son. Mary smiled. "Fine. No asthma episodes as of late."

Oh, how Mary enjoyed Ben's presence. Shy at first, the youngster had taken a few days to adjust but soon settled into the family. He adored her sons, and Michael and Philip loved playing with him and reading him stories.

Mary smiled. "Ben prays for your recovery every night. By the looks of you, God's answering his prayers."

Viola's eyes misted. "We're so grateful, Mary, for your willingness to raise Ben as your own. Tell Carrie how much we appreciate her watching Ben so you can work in the office. The generosity of the people in this town amazes us. Food brought over, help with chores—we've been blessed in countless ways."

When needed, folks in this town pulled together. Mary loved living here.

Her father appeared in the doorway, scrutinized his patient for a moment and then gave an approving smile. "You're looking spry, Judge."

"I'm thinking of trying the new cure, Doc," the judge said. "Maybe it'll loosen me up."

"You're the second patient to mention that remedy. Guess I'd better buy a bottle."

Mary could understand the Willowbys looking for answers, but surely her father didn't believe that nonsense too. "If you don't need me, I'd like to leave now."

"Sure." Her father turned and handed her a capped bottle. "Would you stop by the livery and deliver this medicine to Mr. Lemming? He's been without it for several days. Make sure he realizes the importance of taking it correctly."

Mary nodded, tucking the bottle in her purse. "See you at supper."

"Wouldn't miss it," he said with a forced gaiety belying the weariness in his movements. He didn't fool her.

Before she delivered the medicine, she intended to talk with Sheriff Rogers. See what could be done about that peddler.

Chapter Three

Mary passed the town square and didn't see that rogue, but his wagon remained where it had that morning. He'd probably gone to the saloon, spending his morning profits on liquor to fill more bottles and, more than likely, himself.

A hand-lettered sign boasted in bold letters: CURATIVE FOR HEADACHE, STOMACHACHE AND INSOMNIA. What some people would do to make a dollar—uh, three dollars.

Though her father's rebuke stung, his words held a smidgen of truth. She did tend to get wrapped up in worry. But didn't the Bible instruct her to help others? Surely that meant protecting them from this bloodsucker.

By the time she'd reached her destination, the imposing limestone structure housing not only the jail but also the sheriff's quarters, she'd envisioned the charlatan tarred and feathered, or at least run out of town.

Inside, Sheriff Rogers turned from tacking up a wanted poster and tipped his hat. The sheriff's gray-streaked hair and paunch belied the strength of his muscular arms and massive shoulders. Not a man she'd care to cross. But then again, she needn't fret; she wasn't the criminal in town.

"Afternoon, Mrs. Graves."

"Hello, Sheriff." Mary walked to the wall and checked the poster to see if it held the medicine man's picture. Not seeing the peddler's face, she sighed and turned back to him.

"What can I do for you?" he asked.

"I hope you know a way to rid the town of a swindler bilking our citizens out of their money."

He chuckled. "Reckon you're talking about Luke Jacobs."

That vile man carried the first name of the doctor in scripture, the follower of Christ? The similarity didn't sit well with Mary. "I don't know his name, but the man I'm talking about is selling home-brewed medicine."

"Jacobs convinced me of his product's value." He gestured to his desk. There, as big as life, sat a bottle of that remedy. "I gave it a try, and it's eased the pain in my gut."

No doubt the result of wishful thinking. Hadn't she seen that outcome before?

"Either way," Sheriff Rogers said, taking a seat behind his desk, the springs whining in protest, "he obtained a permit to sell on our streets, so he's within his rights."

"For how long?"

"Believe he said a week."

"In that length of time, he can filch everyone's money." Still, it could be worse. "At least he'll be gone by week's end, maybe before, if we're lucky."

The sheriff laced his fingers over his chest. "His eyes

lit when I mentioned those orphans who came to town last year. Wonder if he's here for more than peddling."

A lump thudded to the bottom of Mary's stomach, and she sucked in a gulp of air. Ben, along with Emma and William, Charles and Addie's two, had ridden on that train. "Did he ask about any of them?"

"Nope. Reckon I could be wrong, but in my work, I make a point of reading people."

Mary paced in front of the desk, then spun back to the sheriff. "He can't come to town and wreak havoc on our children's lives."

"Now simmer down, Mrs. Graves." Sheriff Rogers rose. "I'm not going to let anyone harm our citizens, much less those youngsters."

Ever since Ed Drummond had beaten Frances, William and Emma, the sheriff took special interest in the orphans, becoming a protective grandfather of sorts. She couldn't discount his well-honed instincts about Luke Jacobs.

Mary shivered. "Did he say anything else?"

"Nope. Jacobs is closemouthed." The sheriff gave a smile. "Don't worry. I'll keep an eye out. But if he's half as good as his medicine, we're fortunate to have him."

Fortunate? The man meant *trouble*. Why couldn't anyone see that?

Mary said goodbye to the sheriff. She hadn't gotten anywhere with him. What reason would a traveling salesman have to concern himself with the orphans? Could he be a relative of one of them? Surely not to Charles and Addie's two blond, blue-eyed youngsters, not with the man's dark looks.

She pictured Ben's impish grin and dark-brown curls—

She bit her lip to quell its sudden trembling, refusing to finish the thought. She didn't like what she'd heard at the sheriff's office, didn't like it at all. She had to make sure Luke Jacobs did nothing to upset the peace of the children, especially Ben, the little boy who'd staked a claim in her heart.

Charles would know what to do. Before she could talk to him, she had to deliver the medicine to John Lemming over at the livery. To save time, she cut across the courthouse lawn and rounded the corner of the building—all but colliding with her adversary.

Luke Jacobs. *Again.* The man hovered over her life like crows over a cornfield.

"Well, well, Miss Nightingale." He gave her that lazy smile of his. For a moment, their gazes locked. "We meet again."

At her side, Mary's hands curled into fists, ready to protect the whole town if need be from this man, his smile and his phony charm. "Yes, *Mr. Jacobs,* we do."

His brows rose to the lock of dark, wavy hair falling over his forehead. Why didn't the scoundrel wear a hat like any decent man? "Appears you've learned my name, but I don't know yours," he said.

A team of horses couldn't pull the information out of her—any information for that matter. "I believe you do, Mr. Jacobs." She planted a hand on her hip. "Florence Nightingale."

"So, *Miss Nightingale,*" he said, mocking her—teasing her, "will you tell me where I can find the livery?"

That cocky grin he wore affected her. It was like waving a red cape in front of a bull. And he knew it. From the gleam in his eyes, he enjoyed it too.

"Have you a remedy for horses? Or looking for some manure to add to your spiel?"

He chuckled, apparently not at all upset by her words. "I need to bed down my horse." He put a hand to his chest, feigning distress. "Surely even you wouldn't want to put an innocent animal at risk."

"True, but I wouldn't mind putting a guilty beast at peril." She eyed him, making no secret of which beast she meant.

A deep belly laugh escaped him. If he'd been any other man, the laugh would've been contagious. "You give me too much credit, dear lady."

Uninvited humor bubbled up inside Mary, but she tamped it down before it reached her lips. She might as well give him directions. He'd find out soon enough, with or without her help. She motioned to the opposite corner. "The livery is at Ninth and Clinton."

Instead of leaving, he took a step closer. Mary inhaled sharply.

"I can see my presence in this town unhinges you. I assure you that I'm quite harmless."

Mary pulled every inch of her five-foot-two frame erect. "Nothing unhinges me, Mr. Jacobs. Not even the prospect of a charlatan in town." She folded her arms. "How long are you staying?"

"Hard to say."

Her gaze darted to the wagon, loaded with his tonic. Could his claims be valid? The sheriff thought the remedy had value. Even her father wouldn't dismiss it out of hand. If so, what ingredients made up his concoction?

No, this man had no training qualifying him as a pharmacist. His bottles contained nothing of worth.

Still, in an unguarded livery, who knew what could happen to his tonic.

He looked at her with an intensity suggesting he could see right through her skull and into her brain. "Planning mischief, Miss Nightingale?"

Mary's face burned with shame. For the briefest moment, she'd actually considered dumping the contents of his bottles and breaking the commandment not to steal. She couldn't meet his gaze.

His laughter lifted her chin. "Sorry to disappoint you, ma'am, but my remedy will be bunking with me."

"Not even a reprobate like you could push me into breaking God's law."

He flashed a smile. "Wish I had more time to chat, but my horse needs water and feed."

Without a backward glance, he walked to his wagon, scrambled up, released the brake and pulled on the reins, backing onto the street. Then giving her a jaunty wave, he turned in the direction of the livery.

Mary let out a gust. The man took pleasure in irritating her. Still, Ben remained her chief concern. At the thought of the little boy, Mary only wanted to pick him up at the Foleys'. Talking to her brother-in-law could wait.

Then she remembered the bottle in her bag. The errand would take her to the livery. She'd prefer to deliver the medicine tomorrow, but her conscience wouldn't allow her to shirk the responsibility. She despised having to be anywhere near that peddler, but more than likely she'd find Mr. Lemming in his office and wouldn't have to set eyes on that no-good.

Or so she hoped.

Outside the livery, Mary waved to Red, the freckle-faced hired hand, dumping a wheelbarrow of manure he'd mucked from the stalls. As the odor reached her nostrils on the brisk breeze, she wrinkled her nose and hurried inside.

Mr. Lemming wasn't in his office. Mary set the bottle on his desk, tempted to leave. But, her father had asked her to stress the importance of taking the medicine. Her heart skipped a beat. Searching for the owner could bring her face-to-face with that peddler. As she hustled past stalls, the horses' gazes followed her progress with large doleful eyes, probably hoping for a treat or a pat.

Up ahead, Luke Jacobs filled a bucket from the trough. Mary skidded to a stop, her heart tap-dancing in her chest. The sight of all those muscles rippling beneath his shirt held her transfixed, powerless to move.

Oh, yes, he most definitely was trouble.

He raised his head and their eyes met. Butterflies danced low in her belly. Slowly, he straightened. "Checking up on me?"

A flush crept up Mary's neck. He had the audacity to imply she'd followed him. "Certainly not. I'm looking for Mr. Lemming, the owner of this livery. Have you seen him?"

The man had the audacity to smirk, like he didn't believe her. Well, she wouldn't give him the satisfaction of explaining her reason for being here.

"Nope, only a freckle-faced youth who offered to see to my horse, but I prefer taking care of Rosie here myself."

Mary raised a brow.

"Rosie's an odd name, I know, but it's the name she

came with when I bought her. I don't believe in changing a gal's name unless—"

"Unless it suits your purposes," she said, spitting out the words, "like trying to humiliate me in front of my neighbors."

"With your overblown interest in the town's welfare, I'd say Miss Nightingale suits you." He waved a hand. "Does your husband have a horse stabled here?"

"I don't have a husband." The words popped out of her mouth before her brain could squelch them.

He carried the bucket into the stall, gave his horse a pat, closed the lower door and then turned back to her. "Are you renting a conveyance?"

Why the interrogation? "No."

He shot her a smug grin. "Hmm, then I've got to wonder if you're following me."

She huffed. "I most definitely am not!"

Chuckling, he headed toward her with a lazy stride. "Then what reason do you have to see Mr. Lemming?"

Rosie craned her neck, turning a stern eye on Mary. To be censored by the man's horse was too much. "It's none of your business."

At Mr. Jacobs's approach, her heart leapt to her throat, but she refused to be bullied and stood her ground. Even though her insides rolled like a ship tossed at sea.

He stopped in front of her. "Sorry I can't be more help locating the owner."

She harrumphed. "I seriously doubt you care a fig."

His eyes sparked. "I admire a woman who watches out for her neighbor—but lashing out at whomever you deem a threat must get exhausting."

Her gaze sought the floorboards. Had she behaved that badly?

With gentle fingers he lifted her chin and looked into her eyes. "Angry or not, you're a caring woman."

Something about the rapt look in his eyes kept her rooted to the spot, trapping her breath in her lungs.

"An attractive one too."

Heat rushed to her cheeks. No one had said such things to her in years and years. She hooted her disbelief. She wasn't some naive, giddy schoolgirl. He'd have to find another target to wile with his charms.

Yet, the compliment clung to her like a terrified toddler during a thunderstorm.

Tentacles of mistrust wrapped around her every muscle and tendon and squeezed. "Why are you really here? What do you want?"

"Isn't it obvious? I'm here to sell my remedy."

"Is that the *only* reason?"

For a moment, she saw a glimpse of hesitation in his eyes. But then he flashed a smile, and despite herself, Mary's gaze traveled to that tiny hollow in his cheek. Inhaling his scent, pleasant, with a hint of spices, she pressed a hand against her bodice, felt the pounding of her heart through the fabric of her dress. "I'll pay you thirty dollars to leave…today."

He whistled. "That's a lot of money, ma'am. You must really want me gone." He leaned closer. She couldn't help noticing his eyes resembled the color of roasted coffee beans. "Why, you make a man feel downright unwelcome."

"Ah, you've gotten the message." She raised her brows. "Finally."

"It's a message I won't be heeding. I'll leave when

I'm good and ready," he said softly, but Mary didn't miss the stubbornness in his tone, like he dared her to disagree. Then he grinned. "Have a pleasant day. If I see the owner, I'll tell him you asked for him." And with that, he returned to his horse.

Mary spun on her heel and left the livery, her head held high, her back ramrod straight and her insides quaking like winter wheat in March winds.

Was Sheriff Rogers right? Did Luke Jacobs have an interest in the orphans?

Luke met his horse's stare. "You're a female, Rosie. Do *you* think she followed me? Or did you believe she had a reason to see the livery owner?"

The mare nudged his shoulder with her muzzle. Mute. Then she dipped to the bucket for a drink.

"Guess you gals stick together."

For some reason he couldn't explain, he admired that half pint of a woman with her sassy mouth and flashing green eyes. Maybe because she stood up for her convictions.

"Don't worry, Rosie. I have no intention of getting involved with Miss Nightingale. Or any woman."

He gave his horse one last pat and then headed for the Whitehall Café, his temporary home. Mrs. Whitehall loved to talk and knew everyone in town. Perhaps she'd offer up additional information that would lead him to his son.

If not, he wouldn't stop there. Nothing would keep him from Ben.

Nothing and no one.

Mary picked up Ben from the Foleys', gathering him close. He grinned up at her, his dark eyes dancing with mischief. "I'm too big to hug," he said then belied his words by squeezing her so hard he squeaked with the effort.

"What did you do today?"

"I played with the baby kittens. Pastor Foley named a kitty Simon Peter like Jesus's dis…disapple."

"Disciple." She brushed a lock of hair off his forehead. "That's a wonderful name."

"So is Ben."

"Yes, Ben is a very special name."

For a very special child. A child who'd endured more than his share of upheaval. Could the sheriff have misread ordinary interest in the children for more? Mary worried her lower lip. But if his instincts were right, she wouldn't let that no-good peddler rip apart her carefully constructed, orderly life.

Nor would she let him near this boy.

Michael, his green eyes so like her own, his lanky ten-year-old body outgrowing his clothes faster than she could order them from the *Sears, Roebuck Catalog*, tromped in from school, forcing her mind off Luke Jacobs and his intentions.

Philip, his hazel eyes shining with mischief, followed on his brother's heels. He grabbed Ben and tickled his belly. "We're going to pick flowers, Ben. Wanna help?"

"Yes!"

That morning she and the boys had planned their monthly trek to the cemetery. "Before you do, how about some cookies and milk?" All three boys slid onto the kitchen chairs. "Wash your hands first." They scrambled down, racing toward the sink, jostling for first in line, reminding Mary of playful puppies. If only she had their energy.

Back at the table, they gobbled her molasses cookies and slugged down the milk.

Swiping the back of his hand over his mouth, Michael removed his milk mustache. "I recited the preamble to the Declaration of Independence," he said. "I got it the first time."

Mary smiled at her older son. "I'm proud of you. All that practicing helped."

"I cleaned the erasers," Philip said, then reported the highlights of his school day, none of which had anything to do with his lessons. Philip would rather play than study.

Ben listened, wide-eyed, hanging on to every word. "I wanna go to school."

Philip drained his glass. "You aren't old enough."

Ben puffed out his chest. "I'm four!"

"You have to be six. That's two more years."

The little boy's face fell.

Always the peacemaker, Philip jumped from his chair and put a hand on Ben's shoulder. "But you get to play with the preacher's kittens while we're in school. That's lots more fun."

All smiles now, Ben finished the last bite of his cookie while Michael, always aware of what needed to be done, cleared the glasses from the table.

Mary dug under the sink, retrieved two canning jars and filled them with water. "Michael, get the shears. Cut the flowers for Ben and Philip."

She set the containers on the back porch. The boys hurried past on the way to her garden. Within minutes, they ambled back clutching asters in their now grubby hands, and stuck the stems into the jars.

The boys enjoyed tending their father's and grandmother's plots. Mary encouraged their efforts, hoping the activity would help them remember Susannah and Sam. Not that she wanted her boys to dwell on the past. She'd tried to show them that even after losing a loved one, life went on. Doubt nagged at her, tightening the muscles in her neck. Had she always lived that example?

They set off with Ben in the wagon, two flower-filled fruit jars wrapped in a burlap bag hugged to his chest. The water sloshed over the top, dampening Ben's shirt. His giggle told her he didn't mind.

When they reached Crownland Cemetery, Michael and Philip each carried a jar with Ben tagging along behind. They put their offerings on the graves. Then they gathered the dried, crackling leaves blown against the headstones, their solemn faces eager to help, and stuffed them into the burlap sack to dump on the compost pile at home.

Finished with the task, Michael and Ben leaned against the trunk of a tree, studying the clouds overhead. Philip ambled over to where Mary knelt pulling the tall grass away from her mother's headstone, his mouth drooping.

"What's wrong, sweetheart?"

"Could you…" He studied his hands. "Find us a new dad?"

Mary's heart plunged. She enfolded her son in her arms. "I know you miss your dad, but we'll be fine, Philip. Just fine."

He sighed, then pulled away and plodded to his brothers. His words lingered in Mary's mind, gnawing at her peace. Philip wanted a dad, but she knew a bad choice was far worse than living alone.

Eleven years ago on this very day in October she'd

married Sam. The raven-haired stranger who'd come into her father's office one sultry afternoon in August, his thumb split open from an accident at a factory in town. It'd been his first day on the job. "A dumb accident," he'd said, but then with a smile that captivated her, added, "A lucky one." She'd asked why he called his gaping wound requiring six stitches lucky and he'd said, "If I hadn't torn up my thumb, I might never have met the prettiest filly in these parts."

Samuel Graves had been a smooth-talking, charming man. She'd fallen for him on the spot. They married in a matter of weeks, long before she had any idea of her husband's terrible past. And of his compulsion.

Sighing, her thoughts turned to Luke Jacobs. No matter how hard she tried, she couldn't erase him from her mind. Maybe a dip in White River would cleanse that man from her system.

Regardless, she would not make the mistake of giving her heart to another handsome, persuasive man.

Chapter Four

Mary stepped into the backroom of Addie's millinery shop and the monthly gathering of the Snip and Sew quilters. Five pair of inquisitive eyes lifted from basting the Grandmother's Flower Garden quilt to the frame and focused on her. Mary loved these ladies and they loved her, so why did she feel like a rabbit caught in the sights of a cocked rifle?

Her sister-in-law smiled. "Glad you could make it this afternoon."

Addie's baby girl slumbered in a cradle a few feet away, her little mouth making sucking motions as she slept. Mary placed a kiss on the top of her niece's fuzzy blond head. "Lily gets more adorable every time I see her."

"I can't keep her awake during the day. But in the middle of the night, she's all smiles and coos. Fortunately for me, Charles can't resist walking the floor with her until she falls asleep."

Sally Bender poked Mary's arm. "What kept you? Still trying to chase that handsome peddler out of town?"

Had everyone heard about her encounter with that reprobate? "I wish. How could you call that trouble-maker handsome?"

"What woman wouldn't notice, right, Sally?" Martha Cummings pulled a length of thread from her mouth, her eyes twinkling with amusement. At Martha's feet, her youngest sat on a blanket gnawing on a bell-shaped rattle. "I may be happily married for ten years, and have five children eight and under, but I can appreciate a fine-looking man."

A flash of dark eyes, muscled forearms and a dimpled cheek sparked in her memory. Averting her face, Mary opened her sewing box and took out her needle, avoiding the question, but her stomach tumbled. She *had* noticed and didn't like it at all.

Raising her head, she met Martha's stare.

"By the look on your face, Mary, I'd say you've noticed too."

Once again the women turned toward her, their expressions full of speculation. Heat climbed Mary's neck, but she forced a calm, indifferent tone. "His looks are unimportant. He's pilfering hard-earned money out of our neighbors' pockets."

Martha poked the damp end of the thread through the eye of her needle. "Are you sure you're right about that? I bought a bottle myself, and the sheriff's wife claims that tonic eased his sour stomach after only one dose."

With all this talk about the peddler and his remedy, Mary barely kept her hand steady to thread her needle. "The sheriff's probably getting relief from the peppermint I smelled in that bottle."

"Peppermint never helped the sheriff before. No reason it should now," Martha said.

Successful at last, Mary knotted the end of her thread. "I've read about people believing in something so much the concoction works—for a while."

Sally guffawed, her eyes crinkling at the corners. "Whether his potion works or not, you're wasting your energy, Mary, trying to run that peddler out of town. Men don't have any inkling when they're not wanted."

How could he not? Hadn't Mary made her feelings abundantly clear?

Fannie Whitehall moaned. "More like, men don't have any inkling when they're *wanted*."

Sally patted the young woman's shoulder. "Having trouble hog-tying that young reporter, Fannie dear?"

"James still hasn't proposed. I'll be old and gray before I'm married." Fannie heaved another heavy sigh.

Sally skimmed a palm over her grizzled head. "I'm thankful Leviticus and Proverbs have a more positive view of getting old and gray."

Laura Lawson's silver-streaked hair sparkled in the sunlight streaming through the shop window. "I prefer salt over pepper, don't you, Sally?"

"Yep, every one of these silver hairs represents a lot of living," Sally said. "I'm right proud of 'em."

"Oh, fiddlesticks. Sally, Laura, I'm sorry. I didn't mean getting old and gray is bad. It's just I'm tired of waiting to start my life."

Fannie frequently had to make amends for speaking before thinking, but the girl had a good heart and everyone quickly forgave her.

"Time rushes by, Fannie," Laura said. "Best not waste a minute longing for the future, instead of enjoying the here and now."

Mary gulped. How much time did she spend fretting

about what *could* happen, instead of enjoying the hugs of her sons, who grew as fast as weeds in an untended vegetable garden?

"Besides, James is young. Boys don't become men until they're at least twenty-five," Sally grumbled, then brightened. "Say, Fannie, with three grown sons, none of them married, I'd be beholden if you took one of them off my hands. I could use help skinning and dressing the game they kill. Why, you could move in with us—"

Eyes wide with horror, Fannie gasped.

Sally laughed. "I'm only teasing. Truth be told, my boys have lost their bragging rights as marksmen."

"Your sons are…very nice, but I love James." Fannie's face glowed, verifying her statement. "I don't want to wait forever to be his wife."

An aching loneliness gnawed in Mary's belly. Two years had passed since she'd lost Sam. Years before his death, more years than she cared to think about, she'd spent her evenings alone. To have someone to talk to, to share a sunset with, the small things she'd expected to share with a husband and never had, left a huge void that children, no matter how much she loved them, could not fill.

Still, she couldn't imagine caring for another man. Sam's death had hurt too much. Living with him had hurt even more. She'd never risk a second marriage.

The image of Luke Jacobs flitted through her mind. A hot day. Him on her porch, holding a glass of cold tea with a smile and an invitation to sit awhile. A shared kiss—

Her pulse leapt.

How could she even think of that man? The answer rattled through her mind. Luke Jacobs possessed charm, a way about him that wrapped her around his every word—just like Sam.

But Sam's charm had covered a deep pain from a childhood of abuse, leading him to swig patent medicines. Later when he gave up the pretense, it led him into saloons to forget. She and the boys and endless years of prayer hadn't been enough to keep Sam home.

Best to remember frosting can cover a bitter cake.

"Mary?" Addie said. "You look like you're off somewhere. Is everything okay?"

A pair of dark, piercing eyes reappeared in Mary's mind. With all the strength she possessed, she forced her thoughts away from Luke Jacobs and back to Addie's question. "Fine. Fine. Say, how are William and Emma doing in school?"

"William is at the head of his class. I can't say the same for Emma." Addie rolled her eyes heavenward. "Charles says not to worry. She'll charm her way through life."

Sally snipped a thread. "Nothing wrong with that, is there?"

Mary saw plenty wrong with charm. "Emma may not be a leading student, but she's already designing hats. Mark my words, Addie, one day you'll turn the shop over to her capable hands."

"Whatever path they take," Laura said. "We're all grateful to you, Adelaide, for saving those orphans from a life of terror."

The group quieted, each face growing somber, remembering how Addie's suspicions had led to Ed Drummond's arrest for not only beating Frances half to death but for murdering Frances's mother. Ed had planned to kill Addie and hide the act by starting a fire.

Charles not only saved her life, but he won her heart. Now Charles, Addie and their children lived happily ever after. A storybook ending Mary couldn't imagine.

Laura inched her needle along a gingham petal, adding a white edge to the pink and white design. "I saw Frances at the grocery. Now that she's healed up and that awful man she's married to is in jail for life, she looks ten years younger."

"Ed Drummond should've hung," Martha said. "How could a man go to church as regular as a ticking clock yet kill his mother-in-law and beat on his family? I can't believe how he had us all fooled."

Tears stung the back of Mary's eyes. In his childhood, Sam had lived with abuse—Charles too. This town had suffered more than its share of violence. People's lives had been changed, some for the better, but for others, life would never be the same. "Do you ever wonder…why God allows evil to touch good people?"

Laura reached over and squeezed Mary's hand. "That's a hard one, dear. One of those things we may never understand in this life."

Mary forced a smile, but worry churned in her gut. Laura's pat answer didn't solve a thing. She'd learned in the blink of an eye that life could end. If only she could know what lay ahead so she could keep misfortune at bay. But only God knew, and He wasn't telling.

Then again, she didn't need God to tell her that peddler was up to no good.

With the office closed while her father made rounds in the county, Mary and Ben visited the Willowbys then stopped in at the post office to retrieve the mail.

With a jab of her index finger, the postmistress

shoved her reading glasses up her thin nose. "Morning, Mary. Morning, Ben."

"Hello, Mrs. Hawkins."

The postmistress shoved three envelopes across the counter. "Can't say I've seen these return addresses before."

Mary merely smiled and thanked the postmistress, giving no hint of what she hoped the envelopes contained. Once outside, she sat Ben on the bench. Dropping down beside him, she tore open the flaps. Her pulse leapt. Each envelope held a request for a job interview. Finally, her father would get the help he needed.

She'd hoped for another letter—

Right now she'd give thanks for these answers to prayer.

The three applicants promised to arrive on consecutive Saturdays, the day she'd specified for interviews. Perfect. Within three-weeks' time, her father could interview the candidates and handpick his replacement, then ease the young doctor into the practice until he'd earned the town's trust. But in her heart, Mary knew the hardest citizen to convince would be Henry Lawrence.

"Come along, Ben. We need to get home." Mary tucked the letters into her purse, then took Ben's hand and scanned the street, looking for her nemesis.

Logan Street swarmed with buggies and wagons. A horse tied to a nearby hitching post nickered and stomped a hoof. The door of the Whitehall Café opened and closed as satisfied diners came and went, patting full stomachs and chewing on toothpicks. She didn't see Luke Jacobs, which eased the tension between her shoulder blades.

Ben tugged at her hand, pulling her toward Hudson's General Store window. "Wait, Mary. I wanna see."

The Willowbys had spoiled Ben. Every time he passed a shop, he wanted a new toy or book. Usually Mary didn't give in to his demands, but she'd let him look.

They stood in front, the sun glinting off the top of the glass, reflecting slivers of gold. Her gaze traveled to Ben's reflection. That small, timid boy who'd arrived on the orphan train had become a taller, healthier child with a mischievous sparkle in his eyes and an air of happiness about him that no one could resist.

Ben scanned the display, and Mary marveled at how he'd taken his new life in stride, become part of the town, part of their family. Part of her heart.

Her throat clogged with emotion, and she wrapped a hand around his shoulders, drawing him close. Ben didn't know they shared a connection, but Mary understood what it meant to be unwanted then welcomed into a family. With all her being, she prayed the road ahead would be smoother for Ben than the one left behind.

"Oh, Mary!" Ben pointed toward something. "That big ball's my favorite colors: red and yellow. And it has stars, bright blue stars." Ben tugged her hand. "Can I have it? I could bounce it clear to the sky!" He clapped his hands and glanced up, hope shining in his eyes. *"Please?"*

Listening to Ben's clever reasoning made Mary smile. "You have a ball. Now let's get home for lunch, sweetheart."

Ben's chin lolled toward his chest. "I don't want lunch. I want to go into the store."

Her stomach growled. She tousled his curly hair then

took his hand. "Well, I'm hungry, and by the time we get home, you will be too."

"My tummy doesn't want food. My tummy wants the big ball."

Mary laughed. "We don't eat toys, Ben. But after lunch, you can play with the ball you have. Before you know it, Michael and Philip will be home from school."

A huge smile took over Ben's face. "Michael and Philip want you to get the ball for me."

Biting back a smile, Mary started up the street, but Ben lagged behind for one last look.

"Why, hello again, Florence Nightingale."

Mary's head snapped up, and she stared into the dark, mesmerizing eyes of Luke Jacobs. Remembering the sheriff's words, her heart raced faster than a thoroughbred at the county fair.

Then his stare slid to Ben and stayed.

Ben giggled. "That's not her name. Her name is Mary Graves."

"Mary Graves." Her name rolled off Luke's tongue. "Is this boy your...son?"

Why would he ask such a question? Unless—

Unable to continue the thought, Mary's heart jumped into her throat and wedged there, closing off her speech. Still gripping Ben's hand, she took a step, but the peddler blocked her way, looming over her. "Let me pass," she said.

But he didn't move aside. If anything, he looked more determined. Warning bells clanged in Mary's head.

"Yoo-hoo! Mary!"

Mary whirled toward Carrie Foley, eager for the interruption, for anything that'd take the focus off Ben.

Carrie reached them and chucked a gloved hand under Ben's chin. "Hello, dearest."

The little boy beamed at the woman who cared for him while Mary worked at the office.

Carrie turned to Luke Jacobs. "Aren't you the man peddling that remedy?"

Luke tipped an imaginary hat, all smiles. "Yes, ma'am, I am."

"The sign on your wagon boasts your tonic will cure headaches and stomachaches. Does it work?" She waggled a finger at him. "Now, before you answer, I'll have you know I'm a pastor's wife."

"Yes, my remedy works." He chuckled. "Even for pastor's wives."

Mary shifted her eyes heavenward. As if the rogue didn't grasp Carrie's meaning.

"Did you hear that, Mary? You ought to get a bottle for your headaches."

Luke Jacobs turned toward Mary, flashing the dimple in his cheek. Of all things, her legs turned to jelly, like she didn't have the gumption to stand on her own two feet.

"I'd be happy to give Miss Graves a free sample. She need only ask." Mary started to protest, but before she could, the scalawag gave a nod. "Good day, ladies," he said, striding away.

Ben grimaced. "Ouch, you're hurting my hand."

Mary eased her hold. "Oh, I'm sorry, sweetheart, I…" What excuse could she give? She'd been so unnerved by Mr. Jacobs's presence that she'd wrung Ben's hand like the neck of a Sunday fryer.

"Isn't he the nicest man?" Carrie said. "I should've invited him to church."

Mary wouldn't find Luke Jacobs's name under *Webster's* definition for nice. Nice would be seeing the man drive his rig out of town.

"I've been meaning to ask you about my nephew's rash. Is something going around?" Carrie said and then shot her a curious look.

Heat rose in Mary's face. "Ah, not that I know of."

"It's probably that homemade soap. I told my sister it's too strong for that boy's skin, but it's cheaper than store-bought and…"

As Carrie chatted about the boy's rash, Mary nodded, barely able to concentrate. Luke Jacobs exhibited interest in Ben beyond ordinary courtesy. Instinct urged her to rush Ben home.

Evidently satisfied that lye soap caused her nephew's mysterious rash, Carrie said goodbye, then touched Mary's sleeve. "Oh, look. That peddler's coming back."

Still clinging to Ben's hand, Mary pivoted, almost colliding with Luke Jacobs. Wobbling on her feet, she gasped. He reached out a hand to steady her, then let go. A warm sensation shot through her and fluttered against every nerve.

In his other hand, Mr. Jacobs held the ball Ben wanted. Mary swirled to the store window, to the empty spot where the toy had been.

"This is for you." The rogue bent down and put the ball into Ben's outstretched hands. "I saw you admiring it."

"Thank you!" Ben beamed, clinging to it with both hands. "Look, Mary, look what the nice man gave me!"

Hot anger sliced through Mary. Surely he'd heard her refuse to buy the toy. While she'd talked to Carrie, he'd gone into the store and bought it. She wanted to snatch the ball out of the youngster's arms, but he'd raise a ruckus. Besides, that would be cruel. She couldn't blame Ben that this cad took pleasure in undermining her authority.

The peddler sat on his heels in front of her son. "I'm Luke. What's your name?"

"Ben."

"Ben. *Ben*," the man repeated, as if he couldn't believe his ears.

Mary's heart tripped in her chest. He'd used the gift as a way to obtain Ben's name. She took a step closer.

"Red's my favorite color," Ben said, still smiling at Luke, chattering on as if he'd made a new friend. "I have a red truck, and now I have a red ball with yellow stripes and blue stars."

Under Ben's direct gaze, Luke wavered, as if he didn't know the first thing about children. Well, good.

"Ah, red's my favorite color too," he said.

Ben smiled. "Do you like stars?"

"Yes, 'specially stars in the night sky."

"Mary showed me the Big Dipper." Ben lowered his voice. "I didn't see it, but I pretended cuz Mary is real nice."

The vendor chuckled, his expression exhibiting fascination with Ben, his gaze never leaving the boy's face. "You're a smart young fellow."

Touched by Ben's obvious delight at the man's words, Mary's heart twisted, then unfurled. Luke Jacobs wasn't above using every trick at his disposal to entice Ben, a boy hungry for a man's attention.

Ben nodded. "I know my colors *and* I can count by tens." He took a deep breath. "Ten, twenty, thirty, forty, fifty, seventy, oh, ah, I mean sixty, seventy, eighty, ninety, one hundred."

"Excellent."

"Michael taught me." Beaming, Ben's small chest puffed with pride. "Want to play catch? Mary can't play good cuz she wears dresses. Girls don't like playin' catch."

Luke Jacobs glanced around, as if uncertain how they'd manage a game on the walk.

Mary tugged Ben closer. "We don't have time to play."

The boy's lower lip trembled and his eyes glistened.

Luke ruffled Ben's hair, then dropped his hand to his side. "Maybe next time." He rose and turned his dark gaze on Mary, full of interest, sending a shiver down her spine. "Would you allow me to take you and Ben to lunch, Miss Graves?"

The nerve of that man. Shaking her head, Mary scooped up Ben, pushed past her adversary and hurried up the street, listening for his footsteps, but she heard nothing but her breath coming in harsh spurts.

She glanced over her shoulder. The peddler remained where she'd left him. Still, she couldn't risk letting him know where she lived. Her hands trembled. He could show up at her door, demanding to see Ben.

Instead of going home, she'd go to *The Ledger*. Charles would know how to get that man out of this town.

The sooner, the better.

Realization crashed over Luke, kicking up his pulse like a runaway mustang. The boy's name was Ben. He looked to be around four. The fact he called Mary by name and the resemblance to his childhood pictures left no doubt in his mind. This boy was his son.

Luke's throat clogged. I've found him. *I've found Ben.*

The youngster looked well cared for and happy. He'd give Mary Graves that much. As soon as he determined Ben's condition and sold the rest of his inventory, he could return to New York and his lab, assured the lad would be fine.

The prospect of never seeing his son again twisted in his gut. Odd how he'd found the boy's every word and action enchanting. Ben's innocence and delight tugged at Luke. That pull left him shaken, unsteady, as if the earth had shifted under his feet. He tossed the strong feeling aside, refusing to be drawn into Ben's life.

If he did, he'd only ruin it.

But before he could leave, Luke had to know if the child had inherited the family curse. Only then could he depart in good conscience, knowing he'd armed the child's new family with the proper knowledge, so Ben wouldn't suffer as Luke's brother had.

Yet, something else nagged at Luke. Why did his son call Miss Graves Mary, instead of mother? Did Ben feel unconnected?

Luke knew the feeling, knew the necessity of keeping his distance. Until he could leave, he vowed to maintain his reserve in a town that appeared woven together as tightly as a well-made blanket.

He'd already seen wariness in Mary Graves's flashing green eyes. He suspected she could make trouble for him. How much trouble remained to be seen.

Chapter Five

Holding Ben in her arms, Mary hustled toward The Ledger, greeting the people she knew but avoiding conversation. She couldn't waste a moment in idle chitchat, not after that disturbing encounter with Luke Jacobs.

Inside the newspaper office, Teddy Marshall, Charles's typesetter, ran the printing press. The noise drilled into Mary's aching head until it throbbed. The strong smell of ink hung in the air, as if the printed words hung there too. In her mind, frightening headlines swirled: "Medicine Man Makes Off With Orphan. Local Boy Claimed By Peddler." At the prospect of losing Ben, Mary could barely breathe.

Charles rose from behind his desk, and Mary put Ben down. Still clutching the ball, the little boy ran to his uncle, throwing his free arm around Charles's legs, and beamed up at him. "A nice man gave me a new ball!"

Charles shot Mary a puzzled look, and then smiled at Ben. "That's a great ball, Ben."

Though taller and leaner than Sam, her brother-in-law looked enough like her deceased husband to have been his twin instead of his older brother. Some days the resemblance hurt, fueling Mary's regrets, but today the likeness brought comfort. Since Sam's death, Charles had been her rock. He would help her.

He kissed Mary's cheek. "Are you okay? You look pale."

"I've got a headache."

"One of your bad ones?"

She nodded. If only Charles knew. This time her headache was six feet tall and refusing to leave town.

Without a word, Charles ushered her into a chair, then led Ben into the back where he kept treats and toys for his children. Ben could play freely there while she unburdened herself to Charles.

He returned and gave her a smile. "Ben's nibbling graham crackers and rolling his ball into the wall." He motioned across the street. "You just missed Addie. She finished her column, then walked over to her shop to go over the accounts. Why don't you join her for a cup of tea? I know she'd like a break, and a visit might do you good. I'll keep an eye on Ben."

Charles's wife had become Mary's best friend. She'd like nothing better than to confide in Addie. But her thoughts about Luke Jacobs were mere speculation. Still, they would alarm her sister-in-law, especially after what she'd been through with William and Emma.

"Actually, I want to talk to you." Mary glanced out the window, relieved to see no sign of Luke Jacobs. "Alone."

The crease deepened between Charles's brow, and he took a seat across from her. "Sounds serious."

"Have you heard about the new peddler in town?"

He nodded. "We're always looking for news. Today,

he was it." He smiled. "From what my reporter said, you weren't on the town's welcoming committee."

Mary bit her lower lip. "That man has me in a tizzy, Charles. First selling a remedy he concocted himself, making all kinds of claims about what it can do. Folks can't throw their money away fast enough."

Charles took Mary's hand. "Just because your mother took ill from nursing a peddler isn't a reason to judge them all."

Mary couldn't think about her mother. Not now.

But Charles's words reminded her that the Bible had plenty to say about judging others—none of it good. Still, how could she protect her loved ones if she wasn't alert when problems came knocking?

"Ben and I ran into him a few minutes ago. From the rapt expression on his face, he has a special interest in Ben. He even went against my wishes and bought him a ball."

"I'm surprised he disregarded your authority, but I can't see any harm in being generous."

"I do, if he bought the ball to get into Ben's good graces and discover his name. Why would he do that? What does he want?"

She clasped her hands together to keep them from shaking. Luke Jacobs meant trouble. Not merely for her or this town but perhaps for Ben, an innocent little boy she loved like her own.

Charles rose and crossed to the window, staring out on the street. Her brother-in-law guarded his opinions until he had all the facts, which Mary found both endearing and frustrating. But today she wished he'd drop his editor hat and share her apprehension, instead of refusing to sense a threat when it stared him in the face.

"Other than his expression, did he say something to alarm you?"

"Well, no, but Sheriff Rogers said when he mentioned the orphans, Luke Jacobs's eyes lit."

"I'd hardly call that evidence of a particular interest in our orphans."

"Mark my words, Charles. Nothing good will come from that peddler's presence in our town. I can feel it in here." She tapped the spot over her heart.

Yet, if she hadn't been taken with Luke Jacobs, why did she get lost in his dark, captivating eyes? How could that scoundrel have that control over her?

The man was a magician, pure and simple.

Charles crossed to her and took her hand. "Let's not panic. Still, we should pray about this, asking God to put His shield around Ben."

But even as she heard Charles's words and admitted their wisdom, Mary knew she would not stand by waiting on God and let Luke Jacobs destroy Ben's world.

Saturday afternoon, Luke climbed the stairs to the room over the Whitehall Café, his home in this town whether Mary Graves liked it or not.

His landlords had equipped the space with old, mismatched furniture, shabby but surprisingly comfortable and clean. When he crawled into the iron bed at night, the springs creaked, but a cozy quilt covered the mattress. Quite a change for him, a man accustomed to posh dwellings and elegant restaurants. This trip had been yet another in a long string of lessons on what mattered. With a roof over his head and food in his stomach, he had everything he needed.

When he'd spoken to the café owner Monday, she'd

appeared glad to have him move in, gladder still to get his money, though disappointment he'd rent by the week had clouded her eyes. She'd asked for cash in advance, no doubt seeing him as shiftless.

Not so long ago, her description would have fit him like a glove. If only he'd done right by Lucy. If only he could undo his past. How could he have repeated the family history he despised?

He slumped into a chair by the window, staring aimlessly at the street. No matter how much he wanted to, he couldn't erase those years when he'd rejected God. He'd tried to make up for his past. Spent months searching for Lucy and his child, only to learn she'd died from complications not long after delivering his son. Every piece of the puzzle since that revelation had shaken him to the core.

His eyes stung. That he could never ask her forgiveness for covering his responsibility with a pile of dollars rippled through him. His only recourse now was to ensure Ben was loved and would not pay for his father's sins. Luke's breath caught.

Father. Luke could barely wrap his mind around the word. He didn't feel like a father. He didn't know how to be a father. He didn't want to be a father.

He rose and paced the room. His central goal, to find a cure for epilepsy without potent narcotics like laudanum, had evaded him. He'd interrupted his quest to find Ben. Now that he'd found him, he'd stay just long enough to evaluate his health and make certain he received good care.

He couldn't believe the aggravating woman who'd claimed his medicine contained spirits was Ben's guardian. She'd be surprised to learn his remedy was a concoction of catnip, peppermint, chamomile and honey. Despite what catnip did to cats, he'd found the herb a safe and effective tranquilizer for humans and an excellent treatment for insomnia, colds, colic, upset stomachs, nervous headaches and fevers. This trip gave him the opportunity to test his remedy's effectiveness on a considerable number of people. Its success pleased him. When he returned to New York, he'd expand production.

In the meantime, unless Luke planned to give up eating, he needed money. Setting up his lab had devoured most of his savings. The rest went to producing his medicine and buying his rig. He had no choice but to wire his housekeeper and ask her to close up his house. He could no longer afford to pay her salary.

His sorry financial state was exactly what he deserved, according to his father, who ridiculed Luke's refusal to spend a dime of the family money.

But nothing came without a price and the price of sharing in the Jacobs wealth was more than Luke was willing to pay. First thing tomorrow he'd look for work.

In the meantime, he'd find ways to spend time with his son without raising Mary Graves's suspicion.

Mary shifted in her chair, wishing she could be anywhere but here. Luke Jacobs had turned her life upside down, and she'd let her chores slide. The list grew longer every day: washing, ironing, mending, cleaning. She'd promised to take food to the Shriver family, to make sure Mr. Lemming took his medicine and then tonight she had a Sunday school lesson to prepare. Even with the boys' help, she wouldn't be finished by nightfall.

But her father had pointed out it had been her idea

to find another doctor for the practice and insisted she be present at the interviews with each candidate who'd answered her newspaper ad. She hoped this interview would bring the help Mary sought.

The first applicant sat across from her. The hunched set of his shoulders and the way he twisted his hands gave Mary a bad feeling.

Her father looked up from reading the young doctor's résumé and shoved his reading glasses farther along his nose. "You finished last in your class, Dr. Edgar."

"Yes, but I passed the course."

"I'm not willing to turn my patients over to a doctor who barely passed medical school, especially a regional school like Central College of Physicians and Surgeons." He rose. "I'm sorry, but I have to terminate this interview."

Dr. Edgar's face flushed. "No offense, Dr. Lawrence, but are you in a position to be so selective?"

"Yes, I believe I am, young man, as long as I'm alive and kicking." He handed the paperwork to the doctor, then ushered the red-faced applicant out of the office.

When he returned, Mary said, "Maybe the other two applicants—" Her father's scowl stopped her.

"If a doctor is to take over this practice, Mary, he must be competent, honorable and care about people. If such a man exists, I'll hire him on the spot."

Mary nodded. The first interview hadn't been a positive beginning, but surely one of the other two applicants would meet her father's high standards.

She found the boys in the waiting room playing hide-and-seek. Michael counted to ten, while Ben and Philip scurried for cover. As soon as Ben saw her, he forgot the game and plunged into her skirt. "Is it time to go home?"

"Remember, we're having lunch here with Grandpa."

A hank of dark brown hair tumbled over Philip's brow, covering a hazel eye. He swept it off his forehead. "Ben wants to play ball."

Michael's green eyes fixed on her. "Why can't we take him outside? We do at home."

Mary glanced through the window. The sun shone bright for October; the wind had died. A perfect fall day. But with Luke Jacobs snooping about town, she couldn't bear letting Ben out of her sight.

Ben jumped up and down, his pleading eyes melting her resolve. "Can I? Please?"

If the boys played out back, no one could see them from the street. "All right, just until we eat lunch. Here's your ball."

Ben whooped and trotted alongside her as they headed for the door. She had work to do, but the beauty of the day and the boys' shiny faces pulled her. Chores shouldn't come before her children but sadly often did.

A few minutes later, her father joined them and raked leaves while her sons tossed the ball. As soon as her father gathered a pile, the boys tumbled into it, hollering with delight. Even her father, who saw his efforts undone in minutes, chuckled at their antics.

"Children and leaves go together," he said, resting a forearm on the rake. "When you were young, every fall you collected leaves and pressed them in the pages of my medical books." He smiled then tugged her close. "Daughter, you've brought indescribable joy to your mother and me."

Mary leaned into him, wanting to be that carefree

girl, instead of a woman weighed down by the past and what the future might hold. "You and Mother gave me a wonderful life, Daddy."

Leaving the boys to their fun, Mary and her father ambled indoors arm-in-arm. "I'll clean the surgery before I start lunch," Mary said.

"You have your own chores to do. I can manage here."

"We'll work together."

Her father crossed to the counter where a familiar bottle sat.

Too familiar.

A knot formed in Mary's stomach. Luke Jacobs's potion reminded her of their confrontation in the square. Of his unsettling interest in Ben. And his accusation that she'd followed him to the livery. Every time they met fire or ice erupted in her veins, leaving her reeling. Feeling wrung out. Confused or frightened.

Her father picked up the container. "I decided to give that peddler's tonic a try. He told me the secret ingredient is catnip. Imagine that?"

"How could you purchase that man's remedy, knowing I worry about his interest in Ben?"

"Kitten, I'm a doctor. I must be open to anything that'll help my patients, whether I like the seller or not." He smiled. "I took a dose last night and got the best night's sleep I've had in ages. I plan to buy a couple more bottles."

"I didn't know you had trouble sleeping, Daddy."

"Ever since your mother—" He looked away, blinking hard, then cleared his throat. "I fall asleep in my chair, but by the time I get to bed, I'm wide awake, staring at the ceiling."

To learn the fatigue on her father's face had more
to do with the pain he carried in his heart than the patients in his practice banged against Mary's lungs. She
slipped her arms around his waist and gave him a hug.
"Delivering babies and making house calls in the middle of the night doesn't help either. What you need is
another doctor in here."

He ignored her comment. "All I need is a couple
nights of taking this stuff. That should break the cycle."
He gave her a smile. "That medicine might do you some
good too, with those severe headaches of yours."

She stepped away from her father. "Never!"

He laughed and tweaked her chin. "You're a stubborn woman, Mary Lynn Graves."

In his humorous tone, Mary heard his approval and
basked in its warmth. She laid a soft palm on her father's cheek. "Like you, Daddy. Just like you."

"Goes to show, the Good Lord knew what He was
doing when He brought you to us."

Moisture filled her eyes. Her father always made her
feel special, loved. She'd expected all men to be like
Henry Lawrence.

How wrong she'd been.

She craved the happiness her father had shared with
her mother, happiness she'd never found with her husband.

At night with the boys tucked in bed, she ached with
loneliness, reliving all those endless evenings she'd
spent waiting for Sam, dreading his shuffling steps,
his hands fumbling at the door, his blurry eyes resting
on, yet not seeing, her. Even with him in the house lying
beside her, he was lost to her. Alcohol took her place
as his companion, as the love of his life. She couldn't

compete with a mistress that enabled him to forget the suffering of his childhood.

What had she become? A woman focused on regrets, instead of counting her blessings—her father and her sons. They were the only men she needed in her life.

What if she lost Ben? A shiver snaked down her spine. She met her father's gaze. "I'm afraid of what Luke Jacobs could do to all of our lives."

"I'm sorry. I know that peddler has you upset, but I suspect you're overreacting." He gave her a smile. "The Good Lord will work it out. Give Him time."

Obviously, her father didn't grasp the enormity of the situation. "Given enough time, Ben could be riding on the seat of that peddler's wagon—on his way out of town."

Her father frowned. "Guess I'll have another talk with that fellow. See what I make of him."

Henry Lawrence wouldn't let anyone harm her or the boys. A load of worry shifted from her shoulders to his. With a lighter step, she scrubbed the surgery and then headed to her father's quarters to prepare lunch.

After they'd eaten, Mary set about cleaning her father's rooms. Michael and Philip had joined their grandfather out back, once again raking leaves but this time burning them in a barrel. Mary kept Ben inside, away from smoke, a trigger for his asthma. Nearby her new son stacked the wooden blocks she'd loved as a child. Her parents saved everything she'd ever touched, no matter how insignificant. She soaked up that realization like a thirsty sponge. She owed them everything, God even more. She hadn't come close to paying the debt.

When she became a doctor, she'd keep her father's

legacy alive in this town, long after he couldn't care
for his patients.

True, going to school and studying, taking care of her
sons wouldn't be easy, but she could and would manage
it all, as soon as her father had help in the practice. She'd
prayed for God to send a doctor. Surely one of the two
remaining applicants would be His answer.

Finished with the cleaning, she strolled into the office and peered out the back window. The boys and her
father had made progress but still had work to do. She
might as well catch up with the accounts. Her work at
home could wait another day.

She sat at her desk and delved into the sorry state of
her father's books. He rarely collected cash. Now Luke
Jacobs picked her father's pockets. As she recorded the
payment of a bushel of apples, her hand shook and ink
splotched the page. If only that man would leave town.

Right then, outside the window, Luke Jacobs strode
past. Slowly, trying not to alert Ben, she rose and inched
closer. At the sign alongside the path leading to her father's office, he paused, reading Henry Lawrence, M.D.
Then he glanced toward the entrance. Mary caught her
breath, held it, her body unbending as steel, ready to
spring into action to shield Ben. A second later, he
moved on.

Mary sagged against the frame. Could he be looking
for her home? Hoping to find Ben? Or merely searching for another place to sell his remedy?

Either way, Mary had a sinking feeling that he'd be
back.

Chapter Six

Luke left the Whitehall Café, his stomach full and his mind grappling with a sense of responsibility toward Ben. As he strolled along the sidewalk, lost in thought, he wondered if he could find a way to see his boy without giving away his fatherhood. Would Miss Graves allow him within a mile of Ben?

Not likely. The woman had it in for him. She might be attractive, but she appeared tauter than an overwound clock. Luke suspected more than his interest in Ben had her in an uproar. His medicine would probably do her good. But he didn't want to get involved with her problems, whatever they might be. He had enough of his own.

This morning at the livery, John Lemming had turned down his request for a job. Mr. Hudson had done the same at the general store. His housekeeper had wired back that she had no place to go and wanted to remain in the house without pay. That didn't sit well with Luke. He planned to take the train back to New York. No point in hanging on to his rig. He'd sell it and send his housekeeper the money. Once the local doctor recommended his remedy—

A whinny, then a blood-curdling scream sliced through the air. Luke whirled toward the sound. A child, half lying in the street, half cradled in a woman's lap. Screaming, she waved her hands over the child's head. A dark stain spread across her skirt. Off to the side, a horse stomped. Bystanders stopped, frozen in place.

Luke broke into a run, dodging wagons and buggies, mentally preparing the next steps before he reached the child. He crouched at the mother's side. "What happened?"

Wide-eyed with shock, she didn't appear to see him. "The horse," the woman said, tears running down her face. "Something spooked the horse. He kicked." She rocked back and forth, holding her son in her arms. "Oh, Lord, my boy! My sweet boy!"

"Ma'am, let me." His gaze met hers, firm enough for her to release the grasp she had on her son. A circle of people crowded around them. "Get the doctor. And get me some rags."

"I'll git Doc Lawrence!" A passerby sped off.

Luke guessed the injured boy to be seven or eight. He checked his pulse. Steady and strong. Good. He lifted one eyelid. The pupil dilated. He checked the other. A concussion.

"Oh, God, save my son!" the mother cried.

Luke eased the boy's head to the side. The horse's hoof had laid open a section of scalp, and a lump formed on his skull. Thankfully, the horse caught the child from the back, not at the temple.

A woman thrust material in his hand. "I bought it to make diapers."

"Thanks." Luke folded one cloth into a pad and laid it over the wound, then wrapped the other around the boy's head and added pressure to stop the bleeding.

The mother wept over her son's frame, her tears disappearing into his sandy hair. "My baby! My baby! Don't let him die."

Another woman dropped to her knees and hugged her close. "I'm praying, Martha."

"We're all praying, Mrs. Cummings," a man from behind said with conviction and an affirming pat on her shoulder.

Hearing the whispers of prayers, Luke tried to imagine such support in a big city like New York and failed. He touched the mother's hand. "Mrs. Cummings, your son is breathing. He's got a concussion and he's going to need some stitches, but skulls are tough. Except for a headache, he'll be fine."

"Thank you, God," someone murmured.

Evidently, the boy's mother heard Luke. She quieted and wiped her eyes with the back of her hand. "Are you sure?"

Suddenly an older man, breathing heavily, his face ruddy with exertion, bent over them. "Let's get Homer to my office and stitch him up."

The boy groaned. "He's coming around," Luke said.

Dr. Lawrence patted Mrs. Cummings's back. "It'll take more than a kick in the head to keep young Homer down."

Mrs. Cummings gave a weak laugh and let Luke take her son from her arms—yet kept a grip on his hand.

The boy opened his eyes. "Oh, my head hurts. Wh-What happened?"

Color returned to the boy's cheeks. "You and a horse

got in a kicking match, and the horse won," Luke said. "You'll be fine."

Dr. Lawrence stepped alongside Luke. "My office is just down the street."

Luke remembered seeing the cozy clapboard house with Dr. Lawrence's shingle out front.

Inside the waiting room, Luke's steps slowed. Mary Graves rose from behind the desk, alarm plain on her face, her gaze fixed on the small, quiet form in his arms.

At the sight of her, Luke's heart hammered in his chest—the same rush of energy he'd experienced helping the boy. The realization sunk to the depths of his stomach with a thud. Careful, Jacobs. Don't get involved.

Mary Graves lifted her gaze to him and her mouth thinned. Obviously the woman could barely stomach him. Perhaps the fact she worked for a doctor explained her intense mistrust of his medicine. Giving Ben that ball had only increased her hostility.

She followed the procession into the surgery, where Luke eased Homer onto the table, being careful of his head.

Taking one look at the matted blood on the makeshift dressing, Miss Graves hurried out. Within minutes, she returned, carrying a basin of water, a bar of soap and towels, the epitome of efficiency and calm.

His gaze collided with hers and held. A flush crept up her neck, and she quickly turned to the boy. In the moment before she'd looked away, something flared in her eyes. She might hate him, but she wasn't unmoved by him. To his dismay, he found the insight appealing.

Miss Graves smiled at the boy and covered him to

his chin with a blanket. "Trying to get out of school, Homer?"

The boy gave a lopsided grin. "No, ma'am, I like school."

Then she looped an arm around Mrs. Cummings's middle and pulled her close. "He looks good, Martha," she said softly, easing the worry lines on the mother's face.

Petite, with wavy chestnut hair and vibrant jade eyes, Mary Graves was more than equal to the task. She knew her way around a surgery, knew how to comfort a patient and his family. Nothing about her demeanor spoke of the woman who'd battled with him on the square. He shouldn't be surprised. At their first meeting, this woman possessed an almost passionate concern for others, though she hadn't shared it with him. Odd how he'd called her Miss Nightingale, as if he'd sensed her medical training.

Dr. Lawrence smiled. "He'll look even better with the new haircut I'm about to give him." Easing Homer onto his side, he snipped a hank of brown hair, then cleaned the wound with soap and water, eliciting soft moans from the patient.

Luke couldn't keep his eyes off Miss Graves, pleased by her calm demeanor at the sight of blood. Of course, he'd expect that of a doctor's assistant. She glanced at him and caught him watching her, then lowered her gaze.

Dr. Lawrence finished cleaning the wound. "Mary, take Martha to the waiting room." Before the mother could protest, Miss Graves led Martha Cummings away.

The older man met Luke's gaze. "Mrs. Cummings is a wonderful woman but prone to fainting. If I let her stay, she'd be on the floor, and we'd have two patients on our hands." He smiled, raising a questioning brow. "So, Doctor, would you like to stitch up that gash, or shall I?"

Luke had wondered how long it'd take Dr. Lawrence to uncover his profession. "I'll hold him," he mouthed, not wanting to alarm Homer.

Doc nodded just as Miss Graves returned to the surgery. She appeared surprised to still see him there. By the tension around her mouth as she prepared the needle, he half expected her to toss him out.

Before she could, Doc came around to meet the boy's gaze. "This is going to hurt and I'm mighty sorry. But once we're done, I've got a candy stick for you."

Tears filled Homer's eyes, but he managed a shaky nod.

Miss Graves handed Doc a bottle of antiseptic. He dabbed the wound. At the sting, Homer shrieked. Luke trapped his arms and legs so he couldn't thrash, while Dr. Lawrence talked a blue streak about fishing, dogs, anything to take the lad's mind off what came next.

While Doc stitched, Mary Graves kept her eyes on the boy, laid a gentle hand on his forehead, crooning that it would soon be over. She stood mere inches away. He couldn't help noticing her scent, clean and starchy, with the faintest touch of something he'd smelled before. Where? Ah, in his grandmother's garden on his parent's estate. What was it? Honeysuckle?

Doc tied off the last stitch, and Luke eased his hold on the boy.

Miss Graves straightened and patted the lad's hand. "You were very brave, Homer. The only thing left to do is bandage you up, and that won't hurt at all." She crossed the room, opened a drawer, brought out gauze and a fine-tipped pair of scissors and in minutes finished the task while he and Doc washed up.

Miss Graves gave the boy his promised treat and his mother a bottle of antiseptic along with instructions to keep Homer quiet but awake. Then she cleared away the mess with the competency of a trained nurse. His esteem for her raised another notch. Whatever needed doing, she did and did well. She and Doc's motions meshed like they'd been orchestrated to music.

Dr. Lawrence tossed aside the towel and patted Mary's hand. "Thanks for your help, daughter."

Luke's head jerked up. "*This* is your daughter?"

"Yes," he said, his tone laced with pride. "I don't know what I'd do without her." He eyed Luke. "So, out with it, Doctor. Why aren't you practicing medicine?"

Miss Graves whirled to face Luke. "*You* are a doctor?"

She didn't look happy about the news.

Mary sagged against the table. This scoundrel, the man whose remedy she'd fought, was a physician? She'd supposed her father's reason for allowing Luke Jacobs to remain in the surgery had been to remove her burden of holding Homer. Never dreaming Luke Jacobs had earned the right.

Her stomach clenched. Worse, this meant his remedy probably had value. If so, he possessed skills of a pharmacist, and he'd attended medical school. Achievements she admired.

But why had he kept his identity a secret? What more did he hide?

"Where did you go to school, Doctor?" her father asked.

"Harvard."

"Ah, Boston. Your accent told me you're from out East. Harvard is a fine school, one of the best. Did you graduate at the top of your class?"

"Yes, not that it matters. I didn't find practicing medicine gratifying. About a year ago, I turned my practice over to my partner and holed up in my lab, searching for cures."

"I tried your medicine. Got the best night's sleep I've had in ages."

A smile crossed Luke's face, lighting up his eyes and softening the edges of his chiseled features. "Glad to hear it, sir."

The man was serious about his work. But that didn't mean he didn't pose a threat to Ben. Still, she breathed easier, knowing he wasn't a drifter.

Dr. Lawrence put his mug on the table. "I liked what I saw today. The gentle way you talked to the boy and his mother, the way you soothed Homer's fear. All signs of a good doctor." He glanced at Mary. "My daughter's nagging me to get help with my practice so I'm sure she'll have no objections. If you're willing, the job is yours."

Mary stifled the gasp rising to her throat. Just like that? Her father would take this man's word, without seeing his credentials?

"I suppose I could remain in town awhile. As long as you understand it won't be permanent."

Her father smiled. "God may have another plan for your life, young man. But for now, that's good enough for me. The pay isn't much, but you're welcome to use the apartment above my carriage house cost-free. And I have an empty stall for your horse."

"Thanks. I'll take you up on that. If it's all right, I'd like to give your address to my housekeeper back home so she'll know where I can be reached."

A housekeeper implied wealth. Why was a doctor peddling medicine, staying in a cheap room instead of a fancy hotel? Why would he take this job? Too much about Luke Jacobs didn't make sense.

"Mary, will you write down the address?"

She hesitated, unwilling to comply, but what could she do? Luke's gaze turned on her. Doubtless her eyes conveyed her feelings. He gave an almost imperceptive nod. She scribbled on a slip of paper and thrust the address at Luke.

His eyes bore into her like augers. "Thanks."

"I have a motive for my generosity," her father said. "You'll be close at hand for late-night house calls."

Luke chuckled, but Mary saw nothing funny about her father's offer.

The two men shook hands. "Come to church on Sunday. Ten o'clock. It's a good way to get acquainted, let the town see the new doc—at least those patients who attend First Christian."

Luke smiled, flashing that dimple. "Sounds good. I'm afraid my church attendance has been sporadic since I left New York."

Luke Jacobs had been thrust into her world. The prospect flooded through her, filling her with foreboding and…worse, oh, far worse, with anticipation. Her gaze darted to Luke. She found him looking at her, his eyes dark, penetrating as if he'd read her mind. He shot her a grin. Inside her chest, her heart tripped then tumbled. Mary sped out of the surgery, barely able to take it in.

Luke Jacobs would be working with her father.

With her.

In this office.

Every day.

She wanted to scream no, yet how could she protest when she'd badgered her father to slow down?

Mary's stomach lurched. Luke Jacobs couldn't be God's answer to her prayer.

He was exactly the wrong man.

Josiah Kelly scuttled in, bent over, grimacing in pain. Mary took one look at his face and ushered him toward the surgery. As she passed the backroom, she glimpsed her father and Luke deep in conversation. The muscles in her neck stiffened. Even three days after entering the practice Luke's presence in the office shook her. Her father looked up. "Be right there."

Bent and gnarled, Mr. Kelly took a seat, cradling his dishrag-wrapped right hand like a newborn babe. "Burnt it trying to make myself some lunch," he said, nodding and sending his wispy gray hair flapping. "Never cooked a day in my life until Betsy up and died on me. Now look what happened. She could've been more considerate."

Knowing the pain of a burn and the risk of it festering, Mary's heart went out to Mr. Kelly. Still, she pitied Betsy, who'd endured over forty years with this cantankerous man who now blamed her for dying, like she'd done it out of spite.

Maybe Betsy had. Marriage didn't guarantee anyone's happiness. "My father will be right with you, Mr. Kelly."

"He'd better be." The old gentleman let out a hiss.

"This thing stings worse'n a nest of hornets. How am I going to cook? My daughter lives miles away. Ain't nobody in this town who cares about an old man."

"Once the ladies at church hear about your injury," Mary said, "you'll have more casseroles than you can eat."

Mr. Kelly eased back in the chair, now looking more content to wait. "Reckon so."

Preparing for Mr. Kelly's treatment, Mary filled a pan with water, added bicarbonate of soda and laid out scissors, gauze and a jar of ointment. Grouchy patients aside, Mary loved working in this office. In between appointments, she tried to make sense of her father's accounts, an impossible task. Her mother had handled that part of the practice, taking pleasure in entering precise figures in long columns.

But for Mary, the human body and its ability to heal both fascinated and challenged her. Perhaps someday, one or all three of her sons would aspire to become doctors. But if that didn't appeal to them, then she hoped they'd find another way to contribute to this world.

Luke entered the surgery. Alone. The room appeared to shrink, barely holding enough air for her to breathe. Where was her father?

"I'm Dr. Jacobs, sir. Dr. Lawrence asked me to take a look at you while he's having lunch."

Mr. Kelly reared back, hugging his hand to his thin chest. "I ain't letting no stranger near this here burn."

"I assure you that I'll be gentle."

Luke's promise cut no ice with Mr. Kelly, who glared up at him. Luke looked to Mary, probably hoping for her support, but she couldn't give it. Mr. Kelly might be a crabby old codger, but he was in pain and deserved coddling.

"Let me," Mary said, stepping between Mr. Kelly and Luke. She removed the dishrag from the patient's hand, revealing crimson, swollen skin, but thankfully no blistering or oozing.

Mary gently cleaned the burn with soap and cool water; then she soaked a gauze pad in the solution and laid it over his hand. With Luke watching her every move, Mary's stomach churned. If her belly had been filled with milk, it would be butter by now.

Satisfied she'd done all she could, Mary applied ointment. Keeping the burn away from the air would ease his pain. Mary laid a pad over the area and then wrapped the hand several times with strips of gauze and tied the ends. Luke reached to help, but Mr. Kelly shot him a warning glare.

Finished, Mary washed her hands then placed an unopened jar of salve, a roll of gauze and a list of instructions in a bag. "Change the dressing once a day. Come back next Tuesday at one o'clock. Come sooner if the area shows any sign of infection, like pus."

The lines of pain on Mr. Kelly's face had eased, but from the scowl he wore, his mood hadn't improved. "How do you expect me to do this by myself—and with one hand, to boot?"

She should've realized Mr. Kelly couldn't change the dressing alone. Luke's presence had her tied up in as many knots as she'd tied in the bandage. "I'll stop on my way home from the office," she said, handing the patient the bag of supplies.

"What I need is a wife." Mr. Kelly laid the sack in his lap and settled back in his chair, like he planned to stay a while. "Every man needs someone to look after him, make his meals and clean his house. Even the Good Book says so."

Mary searched the scriptures in her mind but couldn't come up with that chapter and verse.

"Says so right there in Genesis," Mr. Kelly said. "Adam needed a helpmate so God made him Eve." He harrumphed. "You'd think Widow Martin would be glad for the job, but she turned me down flat. Can you imagine—her with a piddling thirty-five acres to her name?"

Perhaps like Mary, Dolly Martin preferred living with fewer material possessions than being tethered to a man. Mary would put her future in medicine. Treatments could be measured, weighed and relied upon. Unlike a man.

Mr. Kelly pointed his bandaged hand at Luke. "Are you married, young man?"

Luke's brows rose to his hairline. "No."

"Well then, grab Mary here. She's easy on the eyes, a good cook and knows her way around this office. Married to her, you'll fit right in, have a good place to live and a fine nurse if'n you get sick. She comes with kids, but a couple of wads of cotton in your ears should take care of the noise. Works wonders when my old dog gets to snoring."

Mary wished the floor would open up and swallow her, drop her all the way to China. Farther if that were possible.

Luke's eyes twinkled. "Ah, I'm not planning on staying in town long, Mr. Kelly."

"What's the sense of moving on? God plants your feet somewheres, better keep 'em right there. I've kept mine here for nigh on fifty-eight years and been as content as a pig in mud till Betsy died. I've got to get me a wife." He leaned toward Luke. "If you're smart, you'll do the same. A wife is a comfort, like a wool coat on a blustery day."

"I'm not looking for a wife, sir. Or, staying long enough to need a winter coat."

"I don't know why I waste my counsel on the young." With his good hand, Mr. Kelly plucked money from his pocket and shoved the bills at Mary. "Don't give him a dime of this. You did all the work." Shaking his head, he pulled himself to his feet with his good hand, and then shuffled out of the room.

Luke grinned. "I can imagine Mr. Kelly's proposal to the Widow Martin. Can't see what she'd get out of the deal."

Laughter bubbled inside Mary and she giggled. "Ah, let's see. She'd get years of cooking, cleaning and—"

"Being compared to a coat." Luke chuckled and soon they both howled with mirth.

They stood mere inches apart. Close enough to—

As Luke's gaze lowered to Mary's mouth, the laughter died in her throat. Her heart stuttered in her chest. "I can't imagine why Mr. Kelly said all that," she said, gazing into the dark, smoldering pools of Luke's eyes.

"He appreciates a good thing when he sees it." He lifted a hand toward Mary's face but then let it drop to his side. "You're a special woman, Mary Graves, and not for the reasons Mr. Kelly cited."

"What then?" The question left her lips before she could stop them.

His dimple winked. "Where to begin? You're intelligent, capable, hardworking, loyal…"

They were alone in the small room, the only sound

the ticking of the wall clock and the beating of her heart, pumping so hard he must surely hear it. She looked into the warmth of his cocoa eyes. They tugged her closer, forging a connection that coiled between them.

Then she remembered this man couldn't be trusted. Might even be a member of Ben's family. If so, he had the power to remove that little boy from those who loved him. That would be cruel to Ben and break all of their hearts.

She shoved past Luke, heading to the front. A few minutes at the books ought to wipe out those dark, mesmerizing eyes.

But a half hour scrutinizing her father's accounts didn't remove Luke Jacobs from her mind. The man had taken root in her brain. She slapped the pages of the book closed and resolved to never let the man near Ben…nor into her heart.

Luke slapped the reins on the horse's rump. The buggy traveled in the wrong direction—New York at Luke's back, Noblesville up ahead. He and Doc had finished the third house call of the day. Weariness settled over him but also a strong sense of satisfaction.

Early this morning, they'd delivered a dark-haired baby girl, used oil of eucalyptus for a tot's croup and set a broken leg, ensuring the farmer would regain full use of his limb. Out here in farm country, Luke had quickly grasped the importance of the seasons. If all went well, the injured man could return to work in time for spring planting.

Luke had worked in the practice five days. Yesterday afternoon Carrie Foley had brought Ben to the office. His asthma had flared following a game of tag.

Luke saw no sign of epilepsy. But asthma was serious enough. They'd given him a dose of an herbal concoction, easing his symptoms, and then Mary had taken Ben home to rest. Her absence in the office left him relieved and oddly disappointed too.

Watch it, Jacobs. You're getting too close.

"I can't tell you what it means to me to have your help, Luke," Doc said. "I'm starting to lick this awful fatigue."

Pleased the weariness had disappeared from Henry's eyes, Luke smiled over at him. "I'm glad." He didn't want to belabor the point, but he had to. "You realize I'm leaving."

"I'd hate to see you go."

"Well, I'll stay another week or two." Long enough to get to know Ben and ensure his asthma got under control. Even if his daughter wanted him gone, he'd stay until Doc could find his replacement. Then Luke could go on his way, free of ties. The way he'd always done.

So why did the prospect of leaving make him feel as if he'd been doused in a bucket of icy water?

Surprisingly, working in this small town gave him gratification that practicing in New York didn't. These people relied on a strong body to eke out a living from the land. Their ailments weren't fragments of overactive imaginations, boredom with luxury-filled lives or tension from filling each day with frenzied, meaningless activities.

He bit back a sigh. That wasn't true. He'd seen a few folks here suffering from those very things. The difference lay with him. A difference he couldn't understand and didn't want to examine. Even so, the truth came to him. He was getting close to people. Had found the satisfaction he'd only had working in his lab until now.

He could almost envision a life he'd never had, a life with a wife, a family. But the one woman he found interesting made no secret of her hostility toward him.

Though, when he and Mary found themselves alone, the air fairly sparked with tension. Why not admit it, with attraction. If anything, the pull between them had increased Mary's determination to keep her distance. He gave a glance at Doc. Maybe her father understood the burr under his daughter's saddle.

Before he could find the words, Doc turned to him. "However long you're staying, I'm lucky to have you. You're a skilled doctor." He cleared his throat. "Though, I've had, ah, a few complaints about your bedside manner."

"Why? Because I don't hold their hands when I give them a diagnosis? Or don't take time to learn the names of the family pets?"

"All you have to do is drop that distant manner of yours, and show our patients you care."

"If I get too involved with these people, I'll lose my objectivity."

"Are you saying I have?"

Luke shook his head. "No, you're an excellent doctor. You never make emotional judgments. The problem's with me." Luke knew his tone and attitude needed an adjustment, but he couldn't apologize for who he was—a man who didn't warm up to people easily.

"I'm here, if you want a listening ear," Doc said.

Luke nodded but remained silent.

"You have the mind of a doctor, the hands of a doctor. Once you connect with our patients, you'll have the heart of a doctor. Then I'll be able to turn the practice over to you."

"That's generous of you, but my life is back East." Luke clucked to the horse.

"So you've said."

Luke ignored the underlying message Doc's words conveyed. That he, Luke Jacobs, didn't make the decisions about his life. That God did. He hoped Doc was right and God controlled this world. But from the pain and suffering he'd seen, Satan had his way far more than he should.

Turning the buggy onto Tenth Street, he drove south. As they passed homes, then stores along the way, people waved to them. Everyone in town held Doc in high esteem and now they included him in that too. A few called Luke by name. He fought the sense of belonging.

"If you gave yourself half a chance, you might find something here to keep you." Doc chuckled. "I have eyes, you know. You might be the man to make my daughter happy."

Luke bit back a laugh. He and Mary might be drawn to one another. But Mary Graves didn't want a husband any more than he wanted a wife. Still, if he did, this woman was, as Mr. Kelly said, easy on the eyes. She cared intensely about those she loved—

He put away the thought. Mary Graves couldn't abide him. "From where I stand, making your daughter happy is a mighty tall order."

"Contrary to your opinion, Mary's a loving, caring woman."

Luke had seen that side of her. "I didn't get off to a good start with her, and I can't say her attitude toward me has improved."

Doc glanced over at him. "Mary doesn't cotton to peddlers."

"I've seen that reaction before but none as vehement as hers."

"It's not entirely about your remedy. Not even about you." Dr. Lawrence shifted his gaze to the road ahead. "Five years ago, Mary's mother befriended an indigent traveling the country selling his wares. The man got sick. Scarlet fever. Susannah put him up in the same rooms you're living in and nursed him back to health… only to catch the disease herself." Doc paused, ran a hand across his mouth like he didn't want to speak. "He survived and traipsed off without so much as a thank-you, but Susannah didn't make it."

The news sliced through Luke with icy clarity. "I'm sorry."

"Susannah was a remarkable woman. Mary knows as well as I that caring for the sick poses a risk. A risk we take every day. Her distaste for peddlers isn't logical, but she's been through a lot."

The reins hung limp in Luke's hands. "I'm the last man she'd want in town."

Doc heaved a sigh. "Might as well tell you the rest. Two years ago, a gun went off in a tavern brawl, killing her husband. She's not had an easy time." Doc turned to him. In his eyes, Luke read a fierce protectiveness like a lion guarding his cub. "I hope you're smart enough to heed this warning, young man—don't hurt my daughter."

Tugging gently on the left rein, Luke turned the buggy into the alley behind Doc's office. The shadow of the carriage house engulfed them, shrouding the buggy in darkness. "I won't."

He hadn't realized how much she'd endured. He'd never do anything to give her one moment of heartache.

Nor would anyone else hurt her. Not as long as he breathed. He stiffened as a weight heavy as a boulder thudded in his gut. To ensure her protection, he'd have to stay, get involved. Something he could not do.

Saturday morning, the sound of footsteps raised Mary's head from her father's bookkeeping. She looked into sober hazel eyes under creased brows, like the man carried the weight of the world on his shoulders. He removed his hat, revealing an unruly shock of dark brown hair. "I'm Dr. Rodney Brooks, Miss. Dr. Lawrence is expecting me. I'm early for our appointment."

"Oh, yes, Dr. Brooks. He's busy at the moment, but I'll tell him you're here."

He gave a gentle smile. "While I wait, if you don't mind, I'd like to look at his accounts. Get a sense of the size of the practice."

Mary hesitated. Her father wouldn't want anyone looking at his books. Still, Dr. Brooks had a right to know what he could expect if he joined the practice. "The information you're seeking is in this ledger."

She traded places with him and headed for the backroom, leaving Dr. Brooks at her desk with his nose buried in the tome like a terrier in a mole run.

Her father and Luke sat at the table, poring over a book of herbal concoctions while Luke crushed a mixture with a pestle and mortar.

"It's amazing how plants aid in our healing. Makes a man appreciate God knew what He was doing when He created them," her father said.

Luke smiled. "The human body's ability to heal is more evidence of God's wisdom."

Warmth spread through Mary. Luke loved God. She smiled at him and then turned to her father. "Dr. Brooks is here."

Glancing at his watch, Henry's brow furrowed. "He's early."

"No rush. He doesn't appear to be in a hurry." Mary couldn't have spoken more truthful words.

"Take a look at this, daughter." Her father pushed the book across the table. Luke had instilled in him a renewed interest in herbal medicine. Fascinated by the potential that could grow right outside his door, Henry spent long hours reading and experimenting with remedies his older patients touted. By the time Mary read the list of ingredients for the medicine they worked on, and their hopes for it, fifteen minutes had passed.

She hurried back to the outer office, relieved to see Dr. Brooks sat across the room, glancing through a magazine. "I'm sorry for the delay. Right this way," she said, and led him to the backroom.

Henry shook hands with the applicant. "Dr. Brooks, this is Dr. Jacobs."

"I didn't realize the practice supported two doctors."

Luke shook his hand. "I'm only helping out until Dr. Lawrence finds a colleague."

As the applicant's grades and behavior met her father's stiff requirements, Mary watched his face go from mild interest to full attention.

Please, God. Let this be the one.

Then Luke Jacobs could leave.

The prospect of never seeing Luke again twisted in

her belly. Well, his leaving might hurt, but if he stayed, he'd cause her more pain.

Her father settled back in his chair. "Do you have any questions for me?"

"Your daughter allowed me to look at your accounts, Dr. Lawrence. I believe I can get the practice on solid financial footing by instituting a policy requiring cash at the time of service."

Mary stiffened. Many people in this town didn't have the money to pay. Her gaze darted across the table to her father.

His jaw jutted like an anvil. "How do you propose to do that, young man?"

"It won't be pleasant at first, but once your patients understand they have to pay up front or be turned away, they'll—"

"Turned away?" Her father straightened in his chair. "As in refusing treatment?" He met Mary's gaze, and his censor for her latest attempt to ease his workload banged against her heart.

Luke rose and came around the table toward the applicant. "This town isn't inhabited by a bunch of freeloaders, as you seem to think. Good, hardworking people live here."

Her father slapped the table. "And when those people need treatment, I don't ask to see their bank account. I'm not about to turn over my patients to a doctor who puts money ahead of people."

"I'm sorry, but I can't practice medicine out of the goodness of my heart. I have debts of my own. How do you handle so many unpaid bills?"

"I don't do this for the money, Dr. Brooks. I see it as a calling from God."

"As do I, but it's also a business. If people knew they had to pay their bills in a timely fashion, they'd find a way. I'm sure of it."

"I'm too old to change my ways, young man. Too bad medical school don't teach compassion."

Dr. Brooks rose. "I won't waste your time any longer."

Once the outer door thumped shut after him, her father turned to Mary, his face full of disapproval.

How long would it take to find a decent doctor?

How long could she postpone her dream?

How long could she abide Luke Jacobs's disturbing presence?

Chapter Seven

Mary rose early Sunday morning to fry chicken and prepare coleslaw and green beans with ham for the church potluck. Outside her window, the sun peaked over the horizon, streaking the cloudless sky with pink. She thanked God for Ben's return to health and for a perfect day for the church fellowship picnic after the service. The elders had canceled Sunday school classes for the occasion. She'd give this week's lesson next week. One less thing to do.

Humming "Amazing Grace" under her breath, Mary packed the food in her woven picnic basket, setting the cake she'd made last night on top. The song died on her lips. Her father had invited Luke to church. Could he bring heartache to all of them? If so, why did she see those dark eyes and that dimple in her dreams?

She must not forget a handsome face and glib tongue could bring a passel of heartache.

The man's presence in the office had disturbed her serenity, and she couldn't restore it no matter how hard she tried. The struggle left her weary.

On edge.

And feeling more alive than she had in years.

A knot formed in her belly. She'd keep her distance, not easy to do working side by side. Surely if Luke came to church today, he wouldn't share in the meal. But if he did, with everyone milling around, she'd find it difficult to limit his contact with Ben. She sighed. Was she overreacting as Charles had said? Since buying Ben the ball, Luke hadn't paid unusual attention to her son, but she couldn't shake the feeling—call it woman's intuition—that Luke Jacobs had more than a passing interest in Ben.

The clock chimed. Mary gasped then rushed in to wake the boys. Last night, knowing they didn't have to rise early for Sunday school, Mary had let them stay up past their bedtime playing checkers and eating popcorn. Now they'd overslept. Normally as punctual as her father's timepiece, they'd be late today.

She hustled all three boys through breakfast and into their go-to-meeting clothes. By the time she led them out the door, her heart thumped in her chest.

Could her reaction be more from the prospect of seeing Luke in services than from her efforts to hurry the children along? Nonsense. He might be a doctor and his remedy might be real medicine, but Luke Jacobs remained a mystery. She'd best remember that.

Alone, the short trek to church wouldn't take long, but Ben liked to loiter over every bird and insect. Considering the lateness of the hour, she asked Michael to fetch the wagon from the shed. He pulled it up to the front stoop, and Mary tucked Ben and her basket inside.

Philip made a grab for the handle. "I wanna pull the wagon, Mom."

Michael held it tight. "I'm the oldest. It's my job."

"You both can. Now hurry up. We're late." Mary waved a hand, then knowing her energetic sons, she added, "Hold on tight, Ben."

The wagon clattered over the brick, and Ben bounced along, squealing in delight. But inside Mary, tension mounted. She dreaded seeing Luke. Not that the man didn't have the right to attend church, but was his desire to worship genuine?

Oh, my. She'd just judged someone's faith. The realization thudded to the bottom of her stomach. Why would she do such a thing? The answer: Luke Jacobs unnerved her in a way she didn't understand. At the core of her concern lay her inability to trust another man. She'd had confidence in Sam and paid for her naïveté.

Yet in the past few days, working alongside Luke in the office, she'd found herself slipping into a pattern of camaraderie…almost. For a few moments, she forgot her concern about Ben. How easily she could be duped. By compelling charm. A fine-looking face. A stunning smile.

No, never again.

Through the open windows of First Christian Church, voices rose in song. Glancing at the watch on her lapel, Mary released a breath. Only the first song. Near the steps, the boys stopped and Ben crawled out, taking Michael's hand while Philip parked the wagon.

Leaning close, Mary lifted a silencing finger to her lips, and all three boys, eyes solemn, nodded. Her heart overflowed with love for their innocent faces and sweet natures. She prayed God would take care of her precious children all the days of their lives.

Inside, sunlight streamed through the stained glass windows, bathing the worshippers and walls in a soft, ethereal light. Mary steered the little group toward the back pew. A few rows up, her father turned around and motioned them forward.

When they reached his pew, Luke Jacobs sat on the other side of her father. Her pulse quickened. Even expecting to see him this morning hadn't prepared her for his welcoming smile.

Her father stepped into the aisle to let them pass, and Luke slid down the pew. Ben scooted in beside Luke, the grin broad on his young face. Philip and Michael plopped down, one on each side of where their grandfather would sit, forcing Mary to take a seat next to Ben, inches away from the height and breadth of Luke's shoulders, looming above Ben's head.

"Good morning," he whispered.

Nodding a greeting, Mary's eyes met Luke's. His dark regard rippled through her. The scent of his shaving cream and soap permeated the space between them. Her breath stuttered in her chest. She lowered her eyes, taking in Luke's boots planted firmly on the floorboards, and then traveled to his knees, jutting within inches of the pew in front of him. With trembling hands, she plucked the songbook from the rack and tried to join in, but the words lodged in her throat.

The power this man had over her evoked the attraction she'd felt for Sam. Tears stung the back of her eyes. Attraction meant nothing.

The song service ended, and Elder Atkins rose to read scripture. "Open your Bibles to the seventh verse of 1 Corinthians 13." The shuffling of pages and the soft babbling of a baby filled the silence. "Love always protects, always trusts, always hopes, always perseveres."

Mary's heart plunged, weighed down by shame.

When she'd married Sam, she had loved him with every part of her being, but that love had not persevered. If it had, she wouldn't have lost hope the last years of their marriage. Her trust in her husband shriveled and then died. In truth, the last of her ability to trust died with him. Inside her gloves, Mary's hands went cold. She'd read these scriptures countless times, but today the pain of how much she'd failed Sam tore at her, condemned her.

As if possessing a will of its own, her gaze sought Luke's and held. He appeared to see inside her, to know her love for her husband had been tested and failed. She had the strongest feeling he understood, perhaps even shared a similar struggle.

No, she must be mistaken. This rogue might, at this very moment, be plotting to rip Ben out of her arms.

With every ounce of resolve she possessed, Mary looked away, turning her attention to Pastor Foley, who made his way to the pulpit. Mary's thoughts drifted in and out of the sermon.

She struggled to concentrate on what the preacher said. "As Christians, God calls us to service. We're not to shirk our responsibilities to our church, to our employers, to our spouses, to our children."

Beside her, Luke shifted in his seat. She glanced furtively at him, her eyes meeting his. In their chocolate depths, she saw profound sadness and something else. Shame? Her breath caught in her throat. Gone was the confident, take-charge peddler. In his place, a man filled with regret.

"It's only when we do our duty, living in obedience, that we please God. And find peace," Pastor Foley continued, then removed his spectacles and smiled, his gaze resting on Luke. "Before services, I had the privilege of meeting Luke Jacobs, the new doctor in town. He says he's not staying long, but I hope we'll change his mind. For however long he's here, he'll be worshipping with us."

The news churned in Mary's stomach. He'd join in. Become a bigger part of the town's life, her life and Ben's. Parishioners swiveled in Luke's direction, smiling and eager, as if they couldn't wait for the privilege of greeting him.

The moment the congregation sang the last note of the closing hymn Mary sprang to her feet. She'd come to church to worship God, to find peace and strength for the week ahead. Instead Luke had destroyed her concentration and composure. His strange reaction earlier only added to her suspicions. Who was this man?

Mary took her son's hand, but he refused to budge from Luke's side. Mary had never seen a wider grin on Luke's face. Did he have a tie to Ben?

Why didn't she gather her courage and ask him?

What if the answer was one she couldn't bear to hear?

She shivered. Before she could gather her young charge, members of the congregation swamped their pew, forcing Mary to look on while her father introduced Luke. Her neighbors greeted him warmly. Some praised his medicine. Charles, Laura and all her friends appeared taken by the man.

The feathers on Addie's hat bobbed back into Mary's view. "This is fellowship Sunday, Dr. Jacobs. We're having a carry-in dinner." Mary shot her a warning, but evidently her sister-in-law didn't receive the message. "I hope you'll stay. There's always plenty of food."

Luke grinned. "Thank you. Sounds good."

Geraldine Whitehall rushed over. Her husband trailed behind. "Can't say we like Doc snatching you away from us," Geraldine said to Luke. "At least you still take your meals at the café."

"I wouldn't miss your cooking, Mrs. Whitehall," Luke said, then shook her husband's hand. "Pleasure to meet you, sir."

Judge and Viola Willowby stopped to give Ben a hug, then greeted Luke. "Sorry we won't be at the picnic. My wife insists such a long day would tucker me out," Judge Willowby said. "Glad to have you worshipping with us, Doctor."

Viola turned to Ben and gave him a kiss. "See you Monday morning, sweetheart." She took her husband's arm, and they joined those flowing out of the church.

The aisle cleared enough for Mary to slip out, leaving Ben with Luke. For now. Ahead of her, the boys held their grandfather's hands, tugging him down the aisle toward the door, eager to get into the sunshine.

"Mary, what's your hurry?"

She whirled toward Addie's voice.

"Charles told me he'd had a talk with the new doctor." Addie's gaze slid to Luke and Ben still talking near the pew. "But he failed to mention how handsome Dr. Jacobs is."

"Handsome is as handsome does."

Adelaide sobered. "You're suspicious of him just because he gave Ben a ball?"

Mary's belly twisted. "Yes."

"Charles is a good judge of character. He takes Luke at his word, though the news the man is a doctor surprised him."

"Why would he hide that, especially when he's selling a remedy?"

"Once people get wind someone's a doctor, they start listing their symptoms and never give the poor man a moment's peace."

"I'm afraid there's more to it than that."

She and Addie reached the door. Once again, Addie glanced behind her. "Looks like the young ladies of the church are giving Dr. Jacobs a warm welcome."

Mary turned back. A gaggle of single young women surrounded Luke with Ben still plastered to his side. The girls giggled and batted their lashes like they had kindling stuck in their eyes. Luke's dimple twinkled. Obviously, he'd charmed them all. Well, they could have him.

"Good," she said.

Addie laughed. "Your face says otherwise, Mary Lynn Graves."

While she watched, Luke disentangled Ben and himself from the group of admirers and strolled toward the back of the church. His gaze locked with hers. Something passed between them, something warm and personal, connecting them, almost as if they were alone. Mary looked away.

At the door, Luke shook Pastor Foley's hand.

"Hope you're staying for the picnic," the minister said.

Luke smiled. "I can't pass up home cooking."

"You don't want to miss my daughter's chocolate sheet cake," her father said, coming up behind Luke and thumping him on the back. "She's one of the best cooks in these parts."

Heat climbed Mary's neck and flooded into her

cheeks. Mercy, she felt like she and her basket were up for auction and her father wheedled to raise the bid.

Taking Ben and the boys along, her father headed toward the men setting up tables on the lawn. Mary strode to the wagon, eager to put distance between her and Luke. But even without looking back, she sensed he followed her.

"Here, let me get that." He reached around her and lifted the heavy basket with ease.

For a moment his thoughtful gesture softened the wall around her heart, and she smiled but then steeled herself. Luke Jacobs might behave like a gentleman, but he was nothing of the sort. He was overbearing, brash and secretive. A gentleman didn't hide his profession. What else did he hide?

"First Christian makes an outsider feel right at home," Luke said.

"Especially the young ladies." Why had she said that? As if she cared what the man did.

A smile spread across his face. "Jealous?"

"Hardly. This church is made up of decent people, too gullible if you ask me," she rushed on, determined to cover her mistake.

Luke raised a brow. "Are you saying I'm not to be trusted?"

Trust him? A man with rugged features, a wide stance, power exuding from every pore, the kind that sent her pulse skittering. Why, he was the image of a man her better sense told her to shun. "That's exactly what I'm saying."

He stepped closer until she could see the length of his dark lashes, catch the scent of him, watch his chest rise and fall with each breath. Everything within her reacted, going from flustered to something more.

Her breath caught. What would it be like to be courted by Luke Jacobs? Would he cherish a woman? Make her feel special? Share his thoughts with her?

"Is it this congregation who shouldn't trust me, or is it you?" he asked, his gaze locking with hers.

Refusing to get lost in the man's mesmerizing eyes, Mary stepped back. "Well, I… I don't trust you, either," she stammered, her heart racing at his audacity and her own unwelcome feelings.

A shadow passed over his features and he turned away. Thinking about Luke Jacobs in the same breath as courting made about as much sense as dumping a cup of salt into a batch of sugar cookies. Both were recipes for disaster.

Luke set Mary's basket on the long table where she'd be sure to find it, then ambled across the lawn, trying to look composed but fighting an urge to run. What just happened between him and Mary? Whatever had changed, Luke wanted no part of it. He had no intention of caring for that spitfire no matter how much she drew him.

Across the way, Charles Graves headed toward Luke, wearing the tranquil smile of a happy family man. After meeting his wife and children this morning, Luke understood the man's contentment.

Hadn't Luke gotten lost in Mary's green eyes and basked in her dazzling smile? For a moment, he hungered for what Charles had. But a woman like Mary expected a man to stay, to put down roots. He wanted that for his son, but he had other plans.

The editor shook Luke's hand. "I'd like you to meet some of the men."

Evidently, Charles trusted Luke more than his sister-in-law did. Or had the editor decided to keep an eye on what he saw as an adversary?

They strolled toward a group lounging in the shade of an enormous elm. Within minutes, more names floated in Luke's head than autumn leaves on the local river.

The talk turned from him to the harvest, then to the local news. One fellow with sandy hair and clear blue eyes discussed the upcoming election with the fervor and earnestness of the young. As he reached a fevered pitch on the race for Congress, a redheaded, gangly, yet attractive gal plucked him away, bringing a chuckle from the group and a flush to the lad's cheeks.

Luke felt sorry for him yet oddly envious too. Someone cared about this youth enough to brave a wall of men to steal him away.

Charles's gaze followed the couple. "James is a photographer and budding reporter at *The Ledger*. Fannie can't tolerate James being out of her sight." He gave Luke a wry grin. "Not sure he thanks her for it."

Experience taught Luke to avoid smothering women who'd steal a man's energy faster than a hard day's work. His gaze sought Mary, picking her out easily among the line of women standing guard at the tables, chatting while they swatted at flies. This independent woman didn't know the meaning of the word *smother*. She appeared delicate, even dainty. But her fragile appearance disguised a strong will and take-charge nature, in sharp contrast to her easygoing father.

True, she might hover over her sons more than she ought, but she stood on her own two feet. Even if upon occasion, those feet appeared set in concrete…and stomping on his toes.

Luke's breath caught. He suspected Mary Graves could love a man and love him well.

A call went up. Pastor Foley waved his hands, motioning for people to gather in. Except for the chirping of birds in the trees, quiet settled over the gathering.

"Father God, we thank You for this beautiful Lord's day, for the food we're about to partake, for the hands that raised it and the hands that prepared it. Bless our fellowship and each person here. Amen."

A chorus of amens followed, including Luke's. He soaked up the love and harmony he felt now and during worship. The parishioners treated him like one of them. He couldn't explain the feeling, but it warmed him like the sun overhead.

Yet he didn't belong. Not here. Not in New York. Not anywhere.

Off to the side, Luke watched families loading up their plates, filing together like ducks in a row, sitting on folding chairs and gathering on blankets to eat.

Later, he stood, a drumstick in his hand, the spring breeze lifting at his hair, watching Mary do the same with her father and the boys. One of whom was his son.

Luke's stomach clenched, the fried chicken suddenly lost its flavor. All he craved sat on the patchwork quilt across the way. The joy in Mary's eyes, the smiles on Doc, Philip and Michael's faces, the giggles pouring from Ben in a steady stream—they were a family.

Ben might be his child, but he had no right to him. No sense of what it meant to be part of a loving family.

Sure, he had a family of sorts, but he and his parents lived separate lives. Even when he and Joseph were children, they hadn't spent time on a blanket with their parents eating plates of fried chicken, sharing a laugh, a story. Like strangers on a ship, the Jacobses shared nothing of consequence. Well, except secrets. Secrets they dared not discuss.

Swallowing, he turned away. He didn't need any of that. Soon he'd leave, return to New York. He'd get his medicine into production and then return to his lab and salt away money for the hospital he wanted to build, a place where caretakers loved and tended children like Joseph. He'd keep busy and forget this town and these people. But the thought of his old life latched onto his shoulder muscles and tightened.

He felt a tug on his sleeve. "You wanna sit with us?" Ben's big brown eyes looked up at him, wide and happy. "We got cookies."

Luke raised his gaze to meet Mary's across the way. He had no doubt she'd rather see him in another state than on the same blanket, but he found he had a sudden appetite for sweets. "Sure, Ben, cookies sound good."

When Luke approached, Mary drew in a breath. "Dr. Jacobs," she said, then avoided looking at him, acting like a high-strung filly about to be broke.

The image brought a smile to his lips. Breaking Mary Graves appeared unlikely, even if he wanted to, which he didn't. Much. Though the attempt could be mighty interesting.

"Luke wants a cookie," Ben announced, then plopped down, dragging Luke along. He handed him a cookie the size of a saucer, sprinkled with sugar.

Luke gave Mary a what-can-I-do grin. "Ben thought I looked in need of dessert."

"He does like to share," Mary said, plucking at her skirt, ignoring him—or trying to.

"I'm supposed to," Ben said. "The Bible says so."

Doc ruffled his hair. "That's right, son."

Son. This sweet child was Luke's son, yet he couldn't admit the relationship and ruin this boy's life as that admission surely would.

Mary introduced Michael and Philip. While Luke munched on the treat, they watched his every move. Michael's green eyes exuded suspicion, looking at him much like his mother often did. Had some kind of sixth sense warned her that Ben was his?

Philip's gaze lit with curiosity. "Did you help Grandpa fix Homer's head?"

"Yes. How's he doing?"

Philip pointed toward the elm. "See him? His head itches, but he's okay."

"Glad to hear it." Strange to be tucked into this circle of family. Yet, nice.

Using the tree trunk to hoist himself up, Doc stood. "Mary, you're too good a cook." He patted his stomach. "I ate too much and need a walk. Boys, you want to go along? See if we can catch some frogs down by the river?"

Mary opened her mouth, but the youngsters scrambled to their feet before she had time to formulate an objection. Doc shot them a grin and then headed off, three energetic pairs of legs scampering ahead of him.

Leaving Luke and Mary alone. Doc's obvious attempt at matchmaking wasn't lost on Luke. And from the rosy hue now staining Mary's cheeks, she'd noticed and didn't approve. They both held people at arm's length. The insight drew him to her more.

The lonely set of her shoulders got him thinking. "Church gatherings like this must be difficult without your husband."

A shuttered look passed over her face. "Sam didn't socialize much," she said, appearing to pick her words with care.

A deep certainty lodged in Luke's mind. He wasn't the only one hiding something. Had Mary carried the weight of her family long before her husband's untimely death?

Under her wide-brimmed hat, Mary cupped a hand over her eyes to shield them from the bright sun and scanned the lawn. "The boys left without the second cookie I promised them."

"Your father appeared to be in a hurry for that walk. I suspect he wanted to give us some time alone."

"I have no idea why." Mary cleaned the plates, stuffed the last utensil in the basket. "We've said all we need to say to each other," she whispered so softly he strained to hear.

He caught her hand, and his heart went still. Her gaze lifted to his, and he lost himself in the emerald depths. "Did we?" he murmured. "Say it all?" He leaned closer, and she tried to hold back her reaction, to limit it to a flare in her nostrils, a hitch in her breath. Oh, he got to Mary Graves. His pulse quickened. But she also got to him.

"What difference does it make? You say you're leaving." Her eyes issued a challenge. "What I don't understand is why you stay. What's holding you here?"

Luke leaned back, the words striking him hard in the chest. Why did he stay? He rested his arms on his bent knee, thinking. Ben was a precious child, always smiling and brown as a biscuit from hours playing with Philip and Michael in their big fenced yard. He showed no sign of epilepsy. His asthma appeared under control now. Luke could leave with a clear conscience.

He'd told himself he stayed for Doc, to help him in the practice. What he wouldn't say to Mary, what he could barely admit to himself, held him in its claws and squeezed. He wasn't ready to leave his son. But if he stayed, if he cared about Ben…or Mary and her boys, if he got close, he'd regret it. Better to focus on his life's work, his lab. That's all he needed. Ben would be all right. And so would he.

"Nothing," he said, "Nothing more than helping your father until he can get another doctor in the practice."

But as the words left his mouth, Luke had a strong feeling he'd uttered a lie.

Chapter Eight

That evening, Mary put her hand on Philip's forehead. Not hot. Her son complained of stomachaches with some regularity. Usually a day at home with toast and tea set him right. But this time, he curled into a tight ball, whimpering with pain. Could it be something serious, maybe his appendix?

Another groan.

A wave of apprehension crashed through Mary. She put it aside and struggled for the tone she used to calm anxious patients. "Grandpa will be here soon," she said, then kissed her son's cheek.

She'd sent Michael to fetch her father a half hour ago, close to nine-thirty. Where were they?

The front door slammed. Her breathing slowed. Michael had returned with her father. He'd know what to do to ease her son's pain.

But instead of Henry, Luke Jacobs stood in the doorway of the boys' room, carrying his black bag, the dark shadow of a day's growth of beard contouring the planes of his face. A face Mary admired too much. A man she thought of often, too often. Under the scrutiny of those perceptive eyes, Mary's heart thudded in her chest.

Luke's gaze darted to Philip lying on the bed, then returned to her. She leapt to her feet, acutely aware that except for the children, the two of them were alone in the house. Other than the male members of her family, no man had stepped foot in this house since Sam's wake, exactly as Mary wanted it. She swallowed, trying not to show how much his presence overwhelmed her, even as her concern for Philip grew stronger. "Where's my father?"

The sharpness of her tone, laden with suspicion, didn't appear to faze Luke. "Doc must be out on a call. When Michael couldn't find him, he came to the carriage house looking for me," he said, his voice neutral, calm, almost soothing.

With desperation bordering on panic, Mary wanted her father, not Luke Jacobs. But she laid a palm on her older son's shoulder and gave it a squeeze. "Thank you, sweetheart, for thinking of Dr. Jacobs." *Even if he's the last man on earth I trust with your brother.* She nudged Michael toward the door. "You need your sleep. I've made a bed for you on the floor in Ben's room."

Michael's expression turned stony, obviously unhappy with her dismissal, but one glance from Luke and her son obeyed.

Luke set his medical bag on a nearby chair, then peeled off his coat and tossed it on the back. "What are his symptoms?"

She fully intended to ask him to leave, but then Philip moaned again. If the possibility existed that Luke could help, she couldn't allow her son to suffer. "His stomach hurts. He doesn't have a fever and hasn't vomited,"

Mary said, struggling to keep her voice steady, like she would in the office. But this time the patient was her son.

Luke sat on the edge of the bed and rolled Philip to his back. Mary turned up the lamp and then took the position on the opposite side of her son's bed where she could scrutinize Luke's every move.

Leaning closer to Philip, Luke ran a hand over her son's abdomen. "Show me where it hurts."

Philip grimaced. "In there," he said in a barely audible voice.

Mary laid a calming hand on her son's narrow shoulder.

With gentle fingers, Luke pressed on the right side of his stomach, released, then pressed again. "Here?"

Philip shook his head. Mary exhaled a breath she hadn't realized she'd been holding. The pain must not be his appendix. *Thank You, God. And thank You for Luke's tenderness with my son.*

Luke moved his hand lower and to the middle. "Here?"

"A little."

"Here?"

Philip frowned, his eyes filling with tears. "It hurts all over."

A lump formed in Mary's throat. Even with Luke Jacobs's gentle examination, her poor boy must feel like a pincushion. She came around the bed, scooting past Luke, who took up every inch of space in the small room. She retrieved a cloth from the basin on the nightstand, returned to her side of the bed and draped the cool, damp rag on her son's forehead.

"Has he eaten anything tonight?"

"He ate a good supper."

"Did you all eat the same food today? Or could Philip have eaten something at the church social that made him sick?"

"The boys ate the same thing I did, and I'm fine."

Luke nodded. "So, Philip, do you feel well enough to go to school tomorrow?"

"I feel bad. I want to stay home."

Mary started to assure him he could, when Ben wandered into the room, tears glistening on his cheeks. "I hadda bad dream."

Eyes filled with compassion, Luke rose, almost as if he planned to comfort Ben. Mary hustled around the bed and knelt on the floor, tugging her son close. "I'm sorry."

"I was lost and couldn't find you."

"It was just a dream. I'm right here." She massaged his back, waiting for him to quiet and looked up at Luke. His eyes held a kind, even sorrowful, expression. Why did he seem to connect with Ben more than any of their young patients, more than her other boys?

Sniffling, Ben pulled away, rubbing his eyes with fisted hands. Then he spotted Luke. "Did you come to play ball with me?"

Luke chuckled. "Not at this late hour."

"Dr. Jacobs is here to help Philip." Mary kissed Ben's cheek. "It's almost ten o'clock. You should be asleep."

"Why is Michael in my room?"

"Philip isn't feeling well so I asked him to sleep in your room."

Ben scampered onto the bed before Mary could stop him. He patted Philip's cheek. "Do you have an ouchy?"

Philip nodded.

"Show it to me."

Over the boys' heads, Mary and Luke's gazes met. Luke grinned, obviously taken with Ben's innocence.

Mary reached for Ben. "Philip's stomach hurts, Ben. Inside. He can't show you. Now let's get out of Dr. Jacobs's way."

Luke ran a palm over Philip's forehead, then opened his bag and removed his stethoscope. Ben slid away from Mary and dashed to the open bag, peering inside. She caught him and sat at the foot of the bed, holding her squirming son firmly in her lap.

Luke listened to Philip's chest and then checked his eyes, nose, ears and throat. Did he see or hear anything to explain Philip's pain?

"I wanna hear." Ben strained against Mary's hands, reaching for the stethoscope around Luke's neck.

"I'm sorry," Mary said. "I'll take him back to bed."

"It's okay." Luke motioned Ben over and placed the earpieces of the instrument in Ben's ears, then positioned the bell-shaped chest piece over the young boy's heart. Ben's eyes grew wide, his gaze filling with awe.

"That's the sound of your heart beating. It's pumping blood all through your body."

"I hear it!" Ben leaned against Luke's knee, his face aglow with admiration. "Boom, boom! Boom, boom!" Again, his gaze dropped to the medical bag. He reached inside. Mary snatched back his hand. Ben might get hurt investigating the contents of that little black bag filled with pills, potions and syringes, all sorts of dangerous things for children.

"I wanna see what's inside."

"Another time, Ben. Dr. Jacobs can't take time to answer your questions while he's examining Philip. Now off to bed."

Ben's lips formed a stubborn line. He didn't budge. Mary stood with her hands on her hips, ready to haul him out if necessary.

Luke rubbed a hand over Ben's head. "I'll show you my bag the next time you're in the office."

Ben threw his arms around Luke's waist and gazed up at him adoringly. "I like you."

A flash of wonder traveled across his Luke's face. "I like you too, Ben."

Mary wrapped gentle hands around Ben's shoulders and pulled him off Luke.

"Will ya come back in the morning?"

Hopefully, by then Philip wouldn't require a doctor.

"If I'm needed, I will. But right now, you should mind Mary, and go to bed."

"Okay." Ben reached for her hand, and she led him to his room.

When she'd told him to go to bed, Ben ignored her, but he had immediately obeyed Luke. She'd noticed the patient yet firm way Luke handled the boys. No longer ill at ease with children, he'd be a better doctor.

Mary tucked Ben into bed and rubbed his back between the shoulder blades. He yawned. The even breathing coming from the pallet on the floor indicated Michael slept. She hustled back to Philip and Luke, who still hadn't given any hint of his diagnosis.

Luke sat at her son's bedside, his profile stark in the light from the lamp. Hearing her footsteps on the floorboards, he swung his head toward her and smiled, raising goose bumps on her arms. His gaze locked with hers, and everything fell away, leaving just the two of them. Alone, yet linked in some unexplainable way. Luke's pupils dilated, his eyes became black pools. A surge of connection shot through Mary, lodging in her heart.

For a moment, time stood still.

But then with a twinge of guilt she remembered her suffering son. Her gaze flew to Philip. His eyelids drooped with sleepiness. A heavy weight fell away. "He looks better," she said in an unsteady voice.

"He is." Luke gave her son's shoulder a pat. "Get some sleep."

Philip turned on his side. But this time, he didn't curl into a ball. His limbs looked relaxed. The pain had ebbed. A rush of gratitude to God, who'd answered her prayers, flooded Mary.

She kissed Philip's forehead, then lowered the lamp, throwing the room in shadow. And wrapping her and Luke in an intimacy that set Mary's feet hurrying out of the room.

Taking one last look at Philip, Luke retrieved his bag and coat, wishing he'd known how to comfort Ben. Instead he'd stood by helplessly and watched Mary tug Ben onto her lap, holding him close until he forgot the nightmare. Naturally his son had turned to the woman who met his needs every day. She'd earned the right to carry the name *mother*. Father or not, he didn't deserve the title.

By staying out of his life, he'd do right by Ben.

Following Mary out of the room, Luke caught the faint scent of honeysuckle. Tendrils of her chestnut hair had pulled loose from their moorings and curled around her neck. Even with the no-nonsense set of her shoulders, the hollow at her nape gave her a vulnerable air.

Tonight he'd discovered Mary Graves wasn't as tough as she wanted him to believe.

He followed her down the narrow hall to the kitchen. She glanced back at him, appearing startled by his nearness. What happened to the plain-speaking woman who confronted him at every turn?

She paused near the back door, obviously intending to see him out. "It's late. If it's all right, I'll pay you tomorrow."

"No payment necessary," he said.

No "thank-you" for helping her son. No "I'm sorry" for her cold reception earlier. No "where do we go from here?" No answers to the dozens of questions running through Luke's mind whenever she was near.

"You look tired." He pulled out a chair from the four around the table and held it for her. "Have a seat."

A look of annoyance traveled across her face, and she propped a hand on her hip, once again all sass and vinegar. "I hardly need an invitation to sit in my own house."

Couldn't he be a gentleman without irritating her?

A sudden, unexplainable urge to kiss her rose inside of him. But kissing her now would be as risky as kissing a peeved porcupine.

She plopped down across from him, almost as if her legs had made the decision and collapsed beneath her. Luke did the wise thing and pulled out a second chair, placing his medical bag on the floor. Sit. Deal with safe subjects like medicine, ignore that looking at Mary Graves softened his stone heart.

"I can't believe Philip dropped off to sleep. You must have a special touch."

Bracing himself for her reaction to his next words,

he cleared his throat. "While you put Ben to bed, I gave Philip a dose of my medicine."

Mary's mouth gaped open, and she leapt to her feet. "Without my permission? Knowing how I feel about that remedy?"

"Would you have granted your consent?" When she didn't answer, he gave a wry smile. "Ah, Mary, what'll it take to get you to trust me as a doctor?"

She looked away. "I don't trust easily. Especially not…" Her gaze swiveled back to his. "What does it matter? You don't have anything in that little black bag to cure a lack of trust, do you?"

No, he didn't. If he did, he'd have taken it himself. Maybe then he'd have stayed in one place long enough to grow some moss beneath his feet.

To have a life.

To love a woman like Mary Graves.

Luke shook off the thought. He wasn't that kind of man and had no intention of staying. He dug inside his bag, took out the remedy and nudged the bottle to Mary. "Give him one half-teaspoon at the first sign of discomfort."

A desire to refuse paraded across Mary's face, but then the mother in her relented. She reached for what he offered and sagged back into the chair. "Thank you."

Two simple words, and yet, knowing the truth he kept from her, they hit Luke with a tidal wave of guilt. He nodded and then looked away, letting his gaze travel the kitchen's pale apple-green walls and white starched curtains, moving on to a stack of dinner dishes, to the pile of silverware, to a pan soaking on the stove.

Glad this unexpected disarray in tidy Mary's life served as a distraction from her sweet lips and the endless, empty evening ahead of him, Luke stood, rolling up his sleeves. "Looks like you could use some help."

Mary stiffened, obviously misconstruing his comment as a criticism of her housekeeping. "I didn't want to leave Philip's side long enough to clean up after supper."

"You're a good mother. Your children come first, as they should."

"Flattery will get you nowhere." Still she smiled, and the beauty of it zinged through him.

"Hmm, too bad," he said, enjoying her snit. "But maybe lending a hand will. I'm not the helpless bachelor you probably expect. I've learned a few things traveling around this great country alone. One of them is to wash my own dishes, and in far less convenient places than this cozy kitchen."

She arched a brow. "You want to wash dishes?"

"Yes." Actually, he wanted to kiss her badly right now, but that wasn't a good idea. Luke crossed to the stove. He picked up the teakettle of hot water, partially filled the first blue washbasin and then filled the rinse basin. "You act surprised. Didn't your husband—"

"I couldn't rely on Sam…to help." She laughed, the sound forced, without a trace of humor. "Most men avoid household chores," she said, then got busy finding an apron.

True enough, but something about the hard set of Mary's jaw told him there was more to it than that. Hadn't her husband valued the treasure of the wife and family under his roof?

Mary took a dipper of cool water and added enough to the dishpan to keep him from burning his hands, then pulled out a cake of soap, swishing it around until suds formed. Retrieving a washcloth from the drawer, she handed it to him, then found a towel for herself. "Well, if you're determined to help, you can wash. I'll dry."

Taking his place at the sink, his long legs brushed against her skirt, the soft rustling the only sound except for the ticking of the clock in the quiet kitchen.

"Excuse me." Mary took a quick step back, then gathered glasses and silverware, giving him wide berth as she brought them to the sink.

"Thanks," he said, dipping his hands into the water, swiping at a plate.

She glanced at him. "This is a side of you I never expected to see."

"And this is a different side of you." An amiable side, but he kept that to himself. "I'll never forget the first time I laid eyes on you. The day you tried to run me out of town." He grinned. "You were hopping mad."

She laughed. "You reminded me of a gypsy."

Surprised by her mirth and loving the sound, he chuckled. "Dark and dangerous. I like that image."

"A dark and dangerous doctor—are you sure that's good for your reputation?"

"No, but it sounds..." His eyes wandered her face, settling on her mouth. "...kind of...exciting."

Those rosy lips parted. "Yes, it does."

Their eyes met, her smile slipped away and in its place, he saw a lonely woman, a human being as lonely as he. He drank her in with his eyes, forgetting the task at hand. Heart pounding in his chest, he remained at the sink, dishes slipping into the depths of the soapy water.

Turning away, she scraped bits of food off the plates, and then stacked them within his reach, alongside the sink. "Seems like I recall someone promising to do my dishes," she said, her tone a tease.

Smiling, he gave a jaunty salute. "Yes, ma'am." He washed a dish, scrambling for a topic that would return them to safe ground. Something to stop him from contemplating things he couldn't have—with a woman who deserved more than he could give. "It's getting dark earlier," he said. Fascinating tidbit, Jacobs.

"Winter will be here before I'm ready."

A picture popped into his mind—he and Mary cuddled in front of a cozy fire, watching the flames. He tamped down the image. With his desire to get his medicine into production, he'd be gone before the first log crackled to life.

"You don't like the cold?" he said, forcing his thoughts away from such sentimental drivel.

"It's not the cold as much as the overcast skies, the gloom." She smiled. "But the boys love snow. They celebrate the first flakes, while I long for spring, for the warmth and the flowers and the sunshine."

He chuckled. "I love snow too. When I can, I go upstate and ski."

"I've heard of skiing. I can't imagine speeding downhill on thin strips of wood." Her hand stilled from drying a dish. "Is it scary?"

"No, it's exhilarating, especially with a warm fire to come back to."

"Where do you stay? Are there hotels in the mountains?"

He hesitated. "My family owns a lodge."

"Imagine," she said, shaking her head, "two houses."

Luke's breath caught. He came from wealth, while this woman and her children lived with far less. Yet he suspected of the two of them that he was the disadvantaged one.

Mary sighed. "Ohio is the farthest from home I've ever been. When I was twelve, my parents took me to Cincinnati for a family reunion. I wish we could have traveled more, but my father never felt he could leave the practice. Where else have you been?"

"We spent our winters in St. Augustine, Florida."

"A warm, sunny spot sounds lovely." She cocked her head. "Does your family own a house there too?"

Luke scrubbed at food on the plate he held. "Ah, yes."

She gasped. "Three? I can barely manage one."

"The staff does all the work."

"Still, owning three houses amazes me. Your family must be…rich."

His jaw clenched. "Houses don't make a home, and money doesn't buy happiness."

"With all that wealth, why do you live so…frugally?"

Luke set a glass to drain. "I don't want my family's money."

"Why?"

"I'd rather not go into that." He rinsed another glass, and she took it from his hand.

"I'm sorry. I'm not usually so nosy."

"Don't apologize. It's only natural to wonder about my life. I know so much more about yours."

"So tell me more." She grinned. "But only if you want to, of course."

"I'm not close to my parents like you are with Doc. Once I was old enough, my parents sent me to boarding school so I missed most winters in St. Augustine. But even when we resided in the same house, my parents didn't spend time with me or my brother." Luke forced a chuckle, an obvious lack of humor in his effort. "They found ways to ensure their children didn't interfere with their lives."

"But surely your parents loved you."

"I rarely see my parents. Maybe they did—do—in their own way, love me. But not the total, unreserved love you have for your boys. To my parents, my brother and I were…" He paused, searching for the right words. "…like ornamental roses—great for showing off to their friends, but they left our tending to others." Once Joseph's imperfection surfaced, they preferred hiding them away.

"I'm sorry," she said, laying a hand on his arm, her touch delicate, warm and healing. "How sad your parents didn't realize children are a gift from God."

In her eyes, he found acceptance, a woman he'd known for mere weeks, yet a woman like none other. "You were a gift to your father and mother. I've seen the love on Doc's face when he looks at you. I've seen that same love in your eyes for your boys."

Sighing, Mary picked up a plate. "Which explains why it's been hard to watch Philip suffer."

He turned to her, looked into her troubled eyes. "How frequent are his stomachaches?"

Wiping the dish, Mary's hand stilled. "Umm, he complains once or twice a month. Lately, more often." She hesitated, biting her lip. "As often as once or twice a week."

At the admission, her brow furrowed. Luke had a crazy urge to kiss away the lines of worry. Instead, he scooped a plate through the rinse water, then put it on the towel to drain. "Any particular days?"

"What kind of a question is that?"

A good doctor asked questions and listened until he got his answers. Luke washed the glasses, waiting.

She grabbed a tumbler, drying the glass until it squeaked. "I hadn't thought about it before, but I can see a pattern, of sorts." From her expression, the admission pained her. "His stomachaches occur most often on Sunday…and Thursday nights."

"And the next day you let him stay home from school?"

Wiping a glass with infinite care, she nodded.

"And you stay home with him?"

Mary shifted on her feet. "Well, yes. He's only eight. I can't very well leave him alone."

Turning from the sink, he studied her profile, choosing his words with care. "Anything different about Mondays or Fridays?"

She tossed the towel on the counter and whipped toward him, hands on hips. "What are you suggesting? That my son is making up his stomachaches?"

"I couldn't find anything wrong with Philip. He has no exact spot that's tender. Neither is he vomiting, having diarrhea, nor running a fever. You've indicated his appetite is good. He looks like a healthy boy."

"Philip isn't a liar." Her expression dared him to disagree.

Dipping the roasting pan, the last of the dishes, into the rinse water, he set it to drain. "So there's nothing special about Mondays and Fridays?"

Mary's shoulders drooped, and she turned away.

"It's a nice night," he said. "Want to finish our talk outside?"

She nodded, and then removed a sweater from the hook. In case Ben would awaken and find it, Luke grabbed his medical bag, then shrugged into his jacket and opened the door for Mary. High above them, a myriad of stars twinkled in the crisp night sky.

She tilted her head to study the heavens. "God's diamonds," she said, her tone awed.

The beauty of the evening and sharing it with Mary sent a thrill through Luke. "God created all this beauty, such a complex, fascinating, beautiful universe. Makes you wonder what Heaven will be like."

"I like to think God is up there talking with my loved ones."

His brother. Mary's mother and husband. All had passed on to greater things.

Tugging the sweater about her shoulders, Mary kept her gaze riveted on the stars and away from him. "Judge and Viola Willowby are grandparents to Ben. He visits them on Monday and Friday mornings."

Her statement brought him back to the issue, Philip's stomachaches. "So, if Philip stayed home from school, he'd have his mother to himself."

She nodded.

"When did the stomachaches start?"

"Not long after…"

He turned her toward him, bent near, pinning her with his gaze. "After what?"

"After Sam died."

"I'm sorry about the loss of your husband." But the words, offered countless times in his years as a doctor, never rung so hollow. When life turned upside down, words wouldn't right it.

She shivered. "I lost Sam long before that stray bullet took his life."

Holding her arms tight around herself, waves of sorrow swept across her face, slugging him in the gut. He reached for her hand and pulled her close. "I'm not sure I understand."

"It's hard to talk about." Unshed tears glistened in her eyes and ripped at his composure. She crossed the porch and hugged a post, her face turned to the crescent moon, a slice of silver falling over her delicate features. "My husband was a good man, but he was also a…drunk."

The last word hung in the air between them.

A good man? Luke thought of all the drunks he'd treated, the giddy ones, the mean ones, the ones who swore they'd never tip that bottle again, yet within the hour, returned to the tavern. He'd bandaged their scrapes, set their broken bones, watched them die, but he'd never thought of the wreckage they left behind.

The wives. The children.

With sudden insight, he now perceived Mary's sass as strength, her stubbornness, fortitude. All of it born from the necessity. To keep her family together, while the head of that family fell into a well of whiskey.

"I'm sorry you had to go through that."

"Don't feel sorry for me." Her voice was soft, barely audible. "I'm fine. But my boys…"

No matter what she said, Luke knew she'd paid a price. Perhaps was still paying it. His throat clogged, keeping him from offering a word of comfort if he'd known what to say, but he didn't. So he said nothing, just waited, feeling helpless, ineffectual, his stomach churning in anger at the man who'd given Mary and her sons such pain.

She leaned her forehead against the pillar. "I tried to

shield them as much as I could, but sometimes I wonder…how much they knew. How much they saw."

Luke slipped an arm around Mary, the moon's sliver of light now on them both. It all fit. "When your husband died, the boys' world tumbled. Philip is probably worried about it spinning out of control again."

Luke knew about a childhood like that. Knew about having parents you couldn't depend on. Knew far too well about lying awake, dreaming of a fairytale existence that would never materialize. "That anxiety might be affecting Philip's health."

Fighting tears, Mary blinked hard. "I didn't realize…"

Her struggle to control her emotions burned at the back of Luke's eyes. He felt the heavy weight of disappointment she carried. Luke tilted her chin, the words out of his mouth before he could stop them. "Let me help."

She crooked a smile at him. "Are you planning on doing my dishes every day?"

He chuckled. "No, but you're carrying a heavy load, both mother and…father to your sons, assisting in the practice. On top of all that, you run a household alone."

She nodded slowly. "And your point?"

Mary needed to take some time off. Enjoy Ben instead of taking him to a babysitter, not that he didn't trust Carrie Foley to care for his son. But Mary did too much. "Accept me in the practice, just on a temporary basis. Then you'll feel comfortable spending less time at the office and more time with the children. Once your father finds another doctor, you can devote yourself to your sons."

She pulled away from him. "I love my boys with all

my being, but I…have dreams of my own." She took a deep breath. Even in the moonlight, her eyes shone with a glow he hadn't seen. "I'm not looking for a permanent replacement for my father."

"I don't understand."

She took a deep breath. "I… I want to be a doctor."

With three sons to rear—the most important purpose a woman could have—Mary wanted to embark on a new career. How could she manage more? "Why?"

"Why does anyone want to be a doctor? To help people."

"But you have a family. To go to classes, to study, to spend hours following doctors on their hospital rounds, you'll have even *less* time with the boys."

"What you mean is that I can't handle my life now, so how could I possibly hope to become a doctor without my sons paying the cost?" Her voice rose and her eyes flashed. "Well, you can mind your own business, Luke Jacobs! My sons are happy, healthy, normal children, and I won't let you imply I don't know how to raise them."

One of those sons was his. "I know practically nothing about children, I'll give you that. But sometimes, a person is too close to a situation to see—"

"To see my own flesh and blood is suffering? I don't believe things are as dire as you suggest. The boys are doing well in school. They're smart, full of life—"

"And Philip is exhibiting psychosomatic symptoms."

She inhaled sharply.

He dreaded her reaction to his next words. "On the walk over tonight, Michael said something that indicated he considers himself the man of the family, a heavy load for a ten-year-old boy."

She swiped at her eyes. "If you're trying to hurt me, you can't."

Her words licked at his pride. What kind of a man did she believe him to be? "I'm not trying to hurt you. I'm trying to help."

She laughed—the sound harsh, bitter. "By making me question myself as a mother, question my goal of becoming a doctor? Well, I won't let you or anyone run my life. It's been out of my control far too long. You have no right to question my every move, as if I don't know what's best for my family. The biggest help you can give me is to keep your opinions to yourself."

As Ben's father, he had a right to voice his concerns.

Except he'd never been a father to Ben. He wanted to ensure Ben's life would go smoothly, without pain, but even if he could arrange that, he couldn't do it from afar.

Mary moved to the back door of the house and looked into the kitchen, then turned to him. "You may have cleaned up my dishes, but whenever you're near, all you do is muddy the waters." She opened the door, glaring back at him. "Don't tell me how to tidy my life, when I suspect your own is in shambles."

Chapter Nine

Mary slumped over her desk, swallowing against the nausea creeping up her throat, barely able to hold up her head with the horrid pain throbbing in her left eye and thundering at the top of her skull. She thanked God for the overcast day. Bright sunlight would have made the pain unbearable.

Thankfully, Philip felt well enough to attend school. She hated to admit it, but it was most likely due to Luke's medicine. She'd seen her sons off, dropped Ben at the Foleys' and then stopped at Mr. Kelly's to change his dressing, barely managing to function with the headache she'd had when she awakened. But now, the pain reached the point where she couldn't work, could only hang on.

Last night's quarrel with Luke Jacobs had to be the cause. While they worked together in her kitchen, she'd imagined for a moment what it would be like to have Luke for a husband. To share daily activities, to cuddle with, dream with—

Then he'd blasted her goal of becoming a doctor,

the very profession he practiced, as if her wishes didn't matter.

What would he know about feeling inadequate and unworthy?

Her stomach knotted. Where had that come from? None of God's children were unworthy; nor was she. Hadn't her mother and father demonstrated that truth, giving unreserved love and approval? Years with Sam had chipped away at her confidence. Now Luke made her question her goals.

The outer door opened, and Luke stepped inside the office. He took one look at her and his brow furrowed. With long strides, he swallowed the space between them. "Is it a headache?"

Mary's heart stuttered in her chest. His tone and expression said she mattered, that he cared. No, she must not misread a doctor's bedside manner for more. "Yes."

He dug inside his medical bag and brought out his remedy. Mary wanted to shake her head, but she didn't dare move, not even that much. Luke opened the bottle, filled the cap and held it out to her. "Drink this."

At this point, she'd try anything. She tossed back the medicine. He handed her a refill, and she swallowed the second dose. Then he came around the desk, pulled out her chair and helped her to her feet. She staggered, holding her head steady, doing all she could to keep from vomiting on Luke's boots. Last night he'd deserved such treatment, but now, she wasn't so sure.

He directed her steps to the backroom and eased her onto the cot and her aching head onto the pillow. Then he covered her with a blanket, and laid a cool cloth on her forehead, his touch gentle, gaze laden with concern. Barely able to wrap her mind around his thoughtfulness, Mary accepted his ministrations with tears in her eyes. When had Sam been home enough to notice her headaches? Crawled out of the bottle long enough to tend to her needs?

"Lie still," Luke said. "I'll check on you in a few minutes."

Biting back a moan, she closed her eyes and gave an almost imperceptible nod, then heard the door close. She lay quietly, breathing in, out, trying to relax, praying for the pain to ease. She'd learned from years of suffering that tightening her muscles made the pain worse.

Sometime later, she opened her eyes. Luke peered down at her. A dark wave of hair tumbled over his forehead but didn't completely cover the lines etched on his brow. For a know-it-all doctor who should keep his opinions to himself, he looked good. Far too good.

"How do you feel?" he said, his voice tender, considerate.

"Better." She smiled. "Much better." A heavy weight lifted from her shoulders. Not merely because the pain had ebbed. But for Luke's compassion, the care he'd taken with her.

"Good. Rest until you feel strong enough to get up. Don't rush it," he said, then left the room.

She drifted back to sleep. When she awoke, the pain had mercifully gone. She eased upright, carefully, like she balanced a book on her head, waiting for the throbbing to return. But felt not a twinge.

Washing her face, she thought of the countless times she'd endured these headaches, remembering the suffering, the nausea, the lost days, and praised God for this new medicine.

Then she went in search of Luke to give him her

thanks. After condemning his remedy too many times to count, she hoped the words wouldn't stick in her throat.

Catching sight of Mary, her eyes bright and clear, Luke rocked back on his heels. "Your headache's gone."

"Thanks to you." She drew in a deep breath. "*And* your medicine."

She gave him a stunning smile that danced over his defenses and walloped him in the heart. After last night, Luke understood why Mary Graves battled against anyone or anything she felt threatened those she loved. He'd miss this fireball of a woman. His chest ached with the knowledge that the time had come to leave. He'd accomplished what he came for. Ben was in good hands. Luke needed to go.

Well, maybe he'd stay long enough to make sure Ben's asthma didn't flare. But as soon as he could, he'd return to New York to start mass-producing his remedy. Only when the public could purchase it from pharmacy shelves would his medicine make a difference, like it had for Mary and Philip.

That should get his finances on an even keel. Then he could start saving for the facility he yearned to build, a safe place for children like Joseph.

"After this, I guess I'll have to admit the value of your remedy," she groused. "Even recommend it to our patients."

Mary didn't like eating crow, but like it or not, she'd changed her mind about his remedy. He laughed. "Even if the admission has you gagging on the words."

Merriment danced in her eyes. "This isn't the first

time I've had to eat my words, Doctor, but a gentleman wouldn't delight in my comeuppance."

Luke chuckled again. "I suppose not."

She laid a hand on his arm. "Others need your medicine as much as Philip and I. You need to make it available everywhere."

Her approval latched onto Luke, hauling him to her like a well-aimed lariat. But this beast wasn't ready for branding. Mentally, he dug in his heels. Like Mary said, he had goals, things he had to do. If he didn't accomplish them, he'd always feel he'd failed Joseph. "You understand the importance of getting my medicine into production?"

"Yes, I do."

"If so, then give up the idea of becoming a doctor. Your father needs you here." He took a breath and let it out along with the decision he'd put off too long. "I won't be staying."

Anger sizzling through her veins, Mary stomped to the backroom, fighting to control her temper. If she didn't calm herself, her headache would return. She wouldn't give that…that brute the satisfaction of realizing he'd gotten under her skin.

With quick, jerky motions, she took down and then swept up her hair, poking the hairpins with more force than necessary, seeing Luke Jacobs as their target.

Well, the man wasn't indispensable. Far from it. One of the applicants for the job would please her father. And Luke would be gone. It couldn't happen soon enough.

On her way out, she almost plowed into her father. At the sight of his exhausted face, her stomach tightened.

"Luke told me about your headache. How are you feeling, kitten?"

"The pain is gone."

He smiled. "I'm glad, gladder still my daughter's stubborn streak didn't keep her from trying his medicine."

She wouldn't discuss Luke or his medicine, especially with fatigue lining his face. "Daddy, you look peaked. Please, go inside and rest."

"I asked Luke to run to the druggist for antiseptic. We're out, and the waiting room is full of patients. I can't leave them to fend for themselves."

"Until Luke gets back, I'll handle the patients."

"You know a lot, Mary, but you're not a doctor. You can't treat patients alone."

Not yet. But assuming she got accepted into medical school, she would be, no matter what Luke Jacobs thought. "If they need urgent treatment, I'll come in and get you. If not, I'll do what I can until Luke returns."

Ignoring her suggestion, her father's chin thrust in a stubborn line. "Honey, I'm fine. You're seeing trouble where none exists."

Her father's words squeezed her heart. Why couldn't he credit her with the good sense to detect his need to slow down? "Now who's the stubborn one in the family?"

Luke strode down the hall, carrying a sack. She thrust her balled fists on her hips, waiting for whatever he had to say, prepared to speak her mind. But Luke merely glanced at her. His gaze moved to her father, rested there. Taking Henry by the arm, he led him out of earshot and said something in hushed tones. Her father nodded, and Luke escorted him to his quarters.

Mary's jaw dropped. True, Luke had the credentials of a doctor, but the evidence that her father listened to him, while ignoring her, the one who loved him most, clawed at her.

In minutes, Luke returned. "You can bring in the next patient, Mary."

She shot him a glare. "Since you have such a way with people, do it yourself."

Cocking his head, he frowned. "I thought you'd be pleased I got your father to lie down."

"Why would you think I'm not?"

"Must be that steam pouring out of your ears."

Some force, some attraction held Mary motionless under his gaze, and she resisted it with all her might. This man thwarted her dreams, made her question her mothering, like he knew the first thing about children.

But he did have influence with her father, normally a man not easily swayed. "What did you say to get him to rest?"

"I suggested that in his fatigued condition he could make a mistake." Luke crossed to the door and called in the next patient.

Luke Jacobs had come into their lives and managed to take over this office, replacing her, or so she felt, in her father's affections. Ben was clearly smitten with him. Even Philip had softened toward Luke. Only Michael stood against him, determined to resist any man he saw as usurping his father's role. At least one of her sons showed better sense. Mary followed Luke into the examining room, determined to stay as far away from him as she could.

Later, with the waiting room empty for a moment,

Luke appeared, leaning his palms on the desk. "What's wrong?"

The starch left her spine. God couldn't be happy with her attitude. Luke had said what needed saying, and her father had the wisdom to take his advice. "Nothing. The problem is me."

A patient entered, and Luke ushered him to the examining room, leaving Mary alone with her regrets. She prayed the next applicant for her father's practice would be Luke Jacobs's replacement. He made her question too much. Long for something she couldn't name. Saturday couldn't arrive soon enough to suit her.

Mary hurried to the examining room to clear away the disarray from the last patient.

"Anyone back there?" a familiar voice sounding much like Geraldine Whitehall's called from the waiting area, her tone more panicky than usual.

Mary hurried to the front, almost bumping into the café owner, her hand wrapped in a towel mottled with blood. "Nearly cut my finger off," she said, her voice shaking like a reed in the wind. "Where's Doc? Oh, my!"

Luke appeared and took Geraldine on back. In the surgery, he handed Mary an enameled basin. She quickly filled the pan with water. Within minutes, Luke had cleansed the wound then stopped the bleeding enough so he could scrutinize her finger. "It's not as bad as all that blood made it appear."

Head turned away from the proceedings, Geraldine glanced at Luke. "Nothing missing?"

"Not a thing."

She released a gust of air. "Whew, that's a relief. I

didn't look close. Half scared a piece of my finger might have flown into Mr. Kelly's soup."

"I'm happy for you *and* for Mr. Kelly," Luke said with a chuckle.

"Heavenly days, that would be cannibalism, wouldn't it? Why, a person could go to jail."

"Well, I've checked it over good and it's intact. I'll wrap it up tight. If you can coddle the cut for a few days, you won't need stitches."

"Is that right? Well, good. It's my fault. I should know better than to whack at a side of beef while watching fish fry." She sighed. "Fannie can help. She's not much of a cook, but surely for a couple days she won't run off my customers." She pursed her lips. "I didn't see Doc."

"He's lying down."

"Poor man hasn't caught something from one of his patients, has he? Should you check on him? He could be sick, feverish, too weak—"

Luke held up a hand, silencing Geraldine's run to the grave. "Doc's fine."

"Well, if he's not, I've seen that we can trust God to have a remedy for every ache and every pain. All we have to do is come to this office to find it."

A puzzled expression on his face, Luke looked at Mary with a question in his eyes. She wished Geraldine's words were true, not only for medicine but also for affairs of the heart. But in this office, no such remedy existed.

Geraldine paid her bill and left. The afternoon passed quickly. Before Mary left for the day, she wanted to re-assure herself of her father's well-being. She found him sitting on the couch putting on his shoes. Above his head hung the Currier and Ives winter scene, her favorite picture in the house. A stack of books sat at his feet, the crocheted afghan her mother made had fallen to the floor. Mary picked it up and laid it over the sofa's arm.

Her father patted the cushion beside him. "Have you got a minute? We need to talk." Mary sat, and he took her hand, his eyes soft and caring. "I can see how worried you've been about me. While I rested, I realized what needed saying."

Mary's heart tumbled. "You're scaring me, Daddy."

"Nothing is wrong. I'm getting older, that's all. I can't do what I once did." He chuckled. "I'm none too happy about admitting it either." He sobered and gave her hand a squeeze. "But fact is, one day I'm going to die."

Tears sprang into her eyes. "Is it your heart?"

"Kitten, I feel fine." He touched her cheek. "It might not be for years and years, but you're going to lose me, hopefully as a very old man."

Tears filled her eyes. "I don't know what I'll do without you, Daddy."

"You'll be fine. Because you'll know that though my life here is over, I'll have a better existence. I don't want you to fear that. I want you to celebrate it." He lifted her chin. "Promise me."

Tears clogged Mary's throat. "I'll try."

"You remember how much your mother loved the Lord, wanted to be His hands on earth. I know you worried about Sam, about his salvation. He had his problems and wasn't a churchgoing man, but he claimed Jesus as his Savior. I believe Sam's in Heaven with your mother, but that decision is God's, not mine."

Sam had believed, but his faith hadn't kept him out

of the saloons. Still, he'd regretted his failing and the pain he caused her. Nor had her own faith kept her from fearing what the future held. She sighed. No such thing as a perfect faith existed, but if it did, her father and mother possessed it.

"You and I must accept their loss and find our own peace about their deaths. And when we do, we'll sleep better, be happier and ready to love the way God created us to love."

For once Mary didn't see her mother's disease-ravaged body. Instead she thought of the happy times they'd shared. But, wait, her father had spoken of love. "Are you like Mr. Kelly...looking for a wife?"

"No one could take your mother's place. Besides, it wouldn't be fair to ask another woman to live around my schedule. But you're young, Mary girl. I want you to find happiness so when I'm gone you'll have a husband to love, someone to love you."

"I have the boys."

"Yes, but time moves quickly. Before you know it, they'll have their own lives."

"You tell me not to worry, well, don't worry about me, Daddy. I'm happy. Really. I don't want another husband." Perhaps the time had come to share her dream with her father. A shiver of excitement mounted her spine. "I want to do things. Accomplish things. Make you proud. Make me proud of myself."

"I couldn't be prouder of the woman you are." She started to speak, to share her goal to become a doctor when her father held up a hand. "Just know all men aren't like Sam. Look at his brother. Charles grew up in the same house, suffered the same abuse at his father's hand and he's a wonderful husband. He traveled a rough road to get there, but I'm sure he'd tell you every step was worth what he gained. Don't run from life. Follow his lead. Love isn't without pain and disappointments, but love is always worth the risk."

Mary kissed her father's cheek. "I'll remember."

Why had her father given her this talk now? Did he believe Luke cared about her? Hardly. Well, she had a dream of her own and that didn't include a husband.

"I've got to pick up Ben." She squeezed his hand. "All I need is my children and you."

Heading to the parsonage, Mary relived her day, a draining day full of pain and emotion, and looked forward to spending time with her sons. She retrieved Ben at the Foleys', and they cuddled on the sofa, waiting for Philip and Michael.

"Mary," Ben said, peering up at her. "Are you my mother?"

She kissed his forehead. "Yes, I am."

"So…can I call you mom?"

"Nothing would make me happier." Mary cupped his cheeks with her palms. "And I will call you son."

He giggled, his eyes shining.

Michael and Philip tromped in. She fed them all a snack of cookies and milk, then followed them out into the afternoon sunshine. Ben carried his new ball, his favorite possession.

In the distance, a figure loped toward them down Sixth Street. He waved, and Mary's breath caught. Luke Jacobs. What did he want?

As he neared their yard, the boys raced to greet him. Luke laid a gentle hand on Ben's shoulder. The boy beamed with delight. "Mind if I toss a few balls with them?" he said, his gaze resting on her.

He appeared to enjoy all three boys. She no longer believed Luke had a special interest in Ben. If he did, he'd have made that apparent by now. His thoughtfulness toward her sons touched her, softening the sharp edges of her resolve, and leaving her open-mouthed, standing on shifting ground. Sam never supported her parenting. He'd never shouldered the responsibilities of a father. Every time she thought she knew Luke, she saw another facet of his character.

Mary opened the gate. Luke tickled Ben's tummy then scooped him up, dangling the boy's legs over his head before settling him on his shoulders, then trotting into the yard. "How's the view from up there, Ben?"

"Great!" the little boy crowed, holding on to Luke's thick hair like a saddle horn. "I can see the church's tower!"

Michael and Philip, their eyes full of longing to do the same, giggled. Obviously a man could give her sons something that didn't come naturally to her. Boys loved to roughhouse, to be tossed in the air, to ride on a man's broad shoulders and get a bird's-eye look at their world.

She remembered at the cemetery Philip had asked her for a dad. The boys needed a man in their lives. Not a grandfather, but a father, young and strong, full of adventure. No matter what she did, no matter how hard she tried, she'd never fill that void in the boys' lives.

Her throat clogged. And neither had Sam.

For a second Mary envisioned a future with Luke. A future she'd never shared with Sam. Realization leapt through her, scaling the walls she'd erected around her heart, weakening her resolve to spend the rest of her life alone. She could get used to this, could care about this man. She envisioned having him to lean on, to share not only the burdens but also the high spirits of her sons. To be a family.

The image evaporated in the clarity of reason. Luke Jacobs would leave. He had goals that didn't include her or her sons. Why wouldn't he be done with it and go, instead of bringing something into their lives that wouldn't last? Something out of reach they couldn't seize. Something they'd all miss when he left.

At the thought, Mary's breath caught in her lungs. Had her life already become so entangled with Luke's that she couldn't imagine life without him?

Chapter Ten

Fishing poles, some worms and Grandpa would fill the void in her sons' lives. At least that's what Mary prayed when her father had suggested the idea of some fishing after work this afternoon.

Mary hefted the basket of wet clothes and climbed to the bright patch of clear sky at the top of the cellar steps. She and the boys could indeed make do with the family they had. Hitching the basket on one hip, she tugged her bonnet onto her head, shading her eyes from the glare of the sun. If only she could protect her heart from Luke Jacobs as easily.

Across the way, Ben kicked his ball, waiting for Philip and Michael to get home from school. She smiled, happy to see him having fun. Ben was hers and always would be. Philip and Michael trotted into the backyard, calling to her. Arms stretched wide and shouting with joy, Ben raced to meet them.

Mary tugged Philip and Michael close, listening as they chatted about their day.

"Guess what?" she said, unable to resist sharing the news.

"What?" three voices asked in unison.

"Later this afternoon, if Grandpa doesn't have any emergencies, he's taking you fishing." The boys danced with excitement at the prospect.

Philip tugged at her sleeve. "We need to find worms. Lots of worms!"

She tousled Philip's hair. "You know where the trowel is."

Philip sped to the shed, and in a few moments, all three of them had a muddy clump of squirming worms in a can.

With the laundry blowing in the breeze, Mary returned the basket to the cellar. Overhead she heard the clamor of excited young voices. When she reached the yard, her father carried poles and a tackle box, as surrounded as three boys could make him.

Luke stood off to the side of the little group. Sunlight glinted off his hair, kissing his features. Mary's heart stopped, started again, her pulse skittering as crazily as the laundry flapping in the breeze. "Luke. What a surprise."

He grinned. "I'm playing hooky—with the boss's permission."

Her father put a hand on Luke's shoulder. "I told Luke we all deserved an afternoon off. I left a sign on the door, in case of an emergency."

"Or in case Mrs. Whitehall suddenly catches something highly contagious," Luke added, straight-faced, with eyes twinkling.

Her father chuckled. "We're here to take you and the boys fishing."

"Me? Oh, I can't. I have signs to make for the pie social and a stack of mending to do. And I promised Lizzie Augsburger I'd—"

Luke took a step forward, and in an instant, she lost her words.

"Take the afternoon off, and come have fun with us." He grinned. "Doctor's orders."

"If you need a second opinion, daughter," her father added, "I have the same prescription."

Ben beamed. "We've got worms! I helped put them in the can."

"Show me," her father said.

The boys raced off with their grandfather trailing after them, leaving Luke and Mary alone. The prospect of spending time with Luke, of getting to know him even more, made Mary's stomach lurch. He was becoming too real, too much of a man she could care about.

"I shouldn't go," she said, trying her best to resist. "Once these clothes finish drying, I'll have a pile of ironing to do."

He leaned close, trapping the oxygen in her lungs. "You need to have some fun. The work will wait."

"Easy for you to say. The work won't get done if I don't do it."

He gave her an impish grin. "I'll help."

"With ironing?" She laughed. "That I'd have to see."

"Maybe not ironing, but I could cut your grass, rake the leaves." His gaze traveled to the back of her house. "Paint the eaves before winter hits."

She could barely comprehend the idea of this man taking on some of the load. He was behaving like a husband. The husband she'd never really had. As much as she wanted to trust in the image, she knew better. Knew it was as fleeting as a cloudless sky on a summer day.

"There's more to life than work, Mary." He lifted a hand to her face, touching her jaw. "Much more. Time passes in a blink. Don't miss these little moments with your sons."

She looked toward her boys to escape the mesmerizing warmth of Luke's eyes. He was right. She should spend more time having fun with them. If Luke joined in for now, so be it. "How can I resist when I have five handsome males asking me to spend the afternoon with slimy worms and stinking fish?"

Luke laughed. "If I'd known a few fish would win you over, I'd have thrown you a bass that very first day."

All too aware of the pull between them, even at that first meeting, her pulse quickened. She had to put some distance between them. "Fishing makes people hungry. I'll fix sandwiches."

Inside her kitchen, she whipped up egg salad from the dozen eggs she'd boiled that morning, and then spread the mixture between thick slices of bread. She added pears, cookies and a jug of white grape juice, the only kind that didn't stain her boys' clothes.

As she worked, she thought about Luke. He'd allowed her a brief glimpse into his past. His parents had rejected him as a child. Could she really blame Luke for having grown up with his defenses in place? Could he let those defenses down? That remained the unanswerable question.

Tucking the food in the basket, a small flutter of pleasure traveled through her. To take care of a man, a man who wasn't a member of her family, a man with no one to look after him, filled her with contentment. At the prospect of spending an afternoon with this vital, thoughtful man, her stomach tumbled.

She shook her daydreams loose. She'd been down this path before, and the man had let her down. Best not make much of a simple outing. She grabbed her shawl, her wide-brimmed hat, one of Addie's creations, then the basket, and hustled outside. The men loaded the blanket, fishing equipment and picnic basket into the wagon and they headed off. Ben sat on the blanket surrounded by all the gear, holding onto the poles with all his might, his chest puffing with pride at the importance of his job. Allowing Luke to pull it, Michael and Philip led the way, skipping ahead then running back to their grandfather, urging them all to hurry. Mary walked alongside, keeping a watchful eye on Ben and purposely lagging a step behind Luke.

Mary waved at the neighbors on the porches they passed, most giving the group second glances. A prickle of uneasiness traveled through her. This town loved to imagine romance where none existed. Even with her father along, people probably were speculating about her and the new doctor.

She glanced at Luke, took in his long stride, firm grip on the handle, his take-charge demeanor. He looked over his shoulder at her and grinned. Her breath caught, and she ducked her head like a schoolgirl, instead of the matron she was.

They reached White River and then unloaded the wagon. The children wanted to wet a line, but Mary insisted they eat first.

"Luke claims to be one of the best fishermen in the country. I told him we'd have ourselves a little contest. See who the best really is," her father said, helping lay out the blanket.

More and more Luke Jacobs was becoming part of their lives. Tears stung the backs of her eyes. When he left, he'd break Ben's heart. Or hers.

She'd enjoy today and remind herself it meant absolutely nothing. "My father is known as the top fisherman in these parts."

The boys devoured their sandwiches. Between mouthfuls, they boasted about how many fish they'd catch. After they'd eaten, her father took them to the bank.

Finishing the last bite of his sandwich, Luke licked his lips, and the sight of his tongue capturing a crumb coiled in her stomach. "I've never had egg salad before."

All too aware of Luke's every move, she barely ate a bite of food. "Egg salad isn't on the menu in New York?"

He chuckled. "Well, probably, but not in my family. It was delicious. Thank you, Mary." Their gazes met, held for a moment, then he got to his feet. "I'd better give Doc a hand."

Even with Luke only a short distance away, Mary missed his presence; she felt aimless, as if she didn't know what to do. She chided herself. As always, she had a mess to clean up. When she'd finished stowing the litter, Mary strolled to where Luke showed Ben how to hold his pole. Nearby her father helped Michael and Philip bait their hooks.

Soon the men settled on their haunches waiting for a strike. Mary couldn't help but smile at the earnest expressions on their faces. They saw catching a fish as important, even crucial.

Philip's red-and-white bobber dipped. "A fish!" The bobber moved across the water. "He's getting away!"

"He doesn't have a chance with you managing the line," Luke said, helping Philip pull up on the pole, setting the hook, then cranking in the catch, a wiggling bass six inches long.

Dropping his pole, Ben leapt from his spot on the bank and trotted over to watch, her father following close behind. "Wow!" Ben said, lifting a tentative finger toward the flopping fish, gathering the courage to touch its scales.

Luke removed the hook from its mouth just as Michael's bobber disappeared beneath the surface of the water. "I got one!" Michael shouted.

Mary hurried to her older son's side, watched him handle the pole like an expert and bring in his catch, crowing with delight at the size of the bluegill dangling from the hook.

Luke laid a hand on Michael's shoulder. "Great work."

Michael looked at Luke, his face glowing. "Thanks!"

Like he'd gotten too close to a flame, Luke took a step back, but Philip tugged on his sleeve. "Grandpa says bluegills are good eating."

Across the way, Ben's lower lip quivered. "I didn't catch nothin'."

Luke knelt in front of her son. "Fishing takes patience." Then he pointed to Ben's pole snaking across the bank. "Better hurry before whatever's on the end of your line takes your pole under."

Ben's short legs wouldn't get him there in time.

Luke made a lunge for the pole. Amid shrieks of excitement and encouragement, Ben caught his first fish. The little boy's face lit with satisfaction while Luke removed the hook and helped tuck the bass into the wire basket tethered at the water's edge. Soon her father and Philip added another fish. Within minutes, her sons caught five more.

Watching Luke interact with the boys, Mary's resistance to the man crumbled. He treated her sons like a father would. They, in turn, soaked up Luke's attention like parched ground after a long drought. Even Michael appeared to warm up to Luke. For once, her father could take the role of grandfather.

Eyes glistening at the sight of the boys' joy-filled faces, Mary crossed to the blanket. If only Sam had gone fishing with the boys, but on Saturdays, he'd barely managed the heaviest chores before heading to the saloon. Sundays, he slept it off, often still in bed when she and the boys returned from church. He'd had no interest in fishing or baseball or any of the activities his children enjoyed. Sam had failed her, but more importantly, he'd failed his sons.

But here on the bank of White River, they'd found a man who cared, if only for an afternoon, about what lay on the end of their lines.

What if her sons relied on this? How could she protect them without denying them a few hours of fun?

Luke rose and said something to her father, then dipped his hands in the water. Wiping his palms on his jeans, he joined her on the blanket, grabbing an apple from her basket. Then he leaned against the tree, his face relaxed, contented. "I haven't had this much fun in ages."

For a man who didn't know children and occasionally looked out of his depth, Luke had a great way with the boys. But she must remember all this was temporary.

Good with children or not, she didn't know much about Luke, not really.

In too many ways, Luke Jacobs remained a mystery.

For a practical woman like Mary, that made him a risk, a risk she could not take.

Settling against the rough bark of the hickory tree, Luke stretched out his legs, his bones like butter softening in the sun. He took a bite of the shiny red apple, releasing sweet juice that ran down the side of his hand. When had he felt this relaxed?

Even Mary looked at ease. She had removed her straw hat, revealing her glossy thick hair, pulled back at the nape. One luxurious strand curled at her jaw. He had an urge to wind the tendril around his finger, to lean close and pull her to him. But her father and sons sat on the bank, a few feet away. Still, they weren't paying attention. Maybe…

She raised her gaze to his. As if she read his thoughts—or dare he hope, shared them—color dusted her cheeks.

He smiled. "You're lovely, Mary."

Brows arching in surprise, she smiled, and the pure joy in it knocked against his heart. Hadn't her husband told her she was pretty? After that reaction, he'd make a point of complimenting her more.

"Thank you." She glanced at the group on the bank. "And thank you for making time for the boys. You're good with them."

"Yes, well, fishing on a warm fall evening—doesn't get much better than this."

"I think you enjoy more than the fishing." She appeared to look inside him, to see into the innermost part of his being. "I think you enjoy the boys, too, even if they chatter like magpies."

He glanced away. He treasured time with all of them,

but especially with his son, more than he wanted to admit, but he merely shrugged. "They're nice boys."

The spark in her eyes dimmed. His attempt to look indifferent hurt her. But he didn't want to mislead Mary about his intentions toward her and the children. Didn't want to make her suspicious if he appeared to care too much. Why didn't he just tell her he was Ben's father?

After keeping silent for weeks, Mary would never forgive him for not telling her. Her anger would either force him into leaving town or into demanding his son. He couldn't bear to wound her or the boys. He'd not done right by Lucy. He wasn't worthy to rear a child. But even if he were, he had no idea how to be a parent.

A thick silence fell between them. With his free hand, Luke fiddled with a blade of grass growing alongside the tree, while Mary kept her back to him, tucking the remains of their picnic in her basket. The sun lowered in the sky. Soon they'd have to head back. Something he didn't want to do. Not yet. "Do you want to take a walk before it gets dark?"

Mary wrapped her shawl around her. "Yes, that sounds nice."

Luke gave her a hand up, calling to Doc to make sure he could handle the boys' lines.

Doc waved them on their way. "You two run along. We'll be fine."

Strolling along the bank, Luke watched fallen leaves tumble along in the water, splashing against an occasional rock—small sailboats plucked from the trees, now heading to an unknown destination. Much like him.

He must regain control of his life, not continue to let circumstances chart his course. Instead, he'd focus on getting a sanatorium built. Make amends for Joseph's suffering. Even for Lucy's. The responsibility for her death weighed him down, as if he'd killed her himself.

His gaze settled on Mary strolling beside him, a woman with the ability to alter his plans.

But, if she somehow did, he'd disappoint her. Insight slugged him in the gut. Mary wouldn't want him. Their relationship didn't have a chance. So why did he yearn to spend every minute with her? With her and the boys?

He snagged a flat, gray rock lying in their path. With every ounce of frustration inside him, he flung it toward the creek. The stone skipped three times, then disappeared beneath the surface.

Mary searched the ground, found a rock and lobbed it through the air. It danced across the river—skipping four times—before it sank. She turned to him with a triumphant smile.

He chuckled, terribly pleased for some odd reason. "You're a woman of many talents, Mary."

She smiled, giving a saucy toss of her head. She was a beautiful woman, all goodness and light, a total departure from what he'd known growing up.

Without thinking, he tugged her to him, tipping her chin with his hand until she looked into his eyes. Hers went wide. "May I kiss you?" he said, his voice gruff.

She didn't answer, and he held his breath, waiting. Then, she rose on her toes and encircled his neck with her arms, offering her lips to his. He lowered his head and kissed her tenderly with all the pent-up loneliness of his life. A sigh escaped her, and he hugged her closer, every cold crevice inside him filling with warmth.

He cared about this woman so much it scared him. Gently, he set her from him and ran his fingertips over her lips, giving her a crooked grin. "After that, I'll be sure to always ask."

She cocked her head at him. "I may not always give the same answer." But her smile belied her statement. Or so he hoped.

Arm in arm, they walked on, stopping near a gnarled old tree, its limbs reaching toward the river. Sunlight threw the tree's shadow onto a large rock projecting from the bank. Mary skittered down the slope and took a seat, scooting to the side to make room for Luke.

He sat beside her. "You're a wonderful woman, Mary. A gift to all who know you, exactly as your father sees you."

Averting her eyes, Mary studied her hands. Overhead, birds congregated, gathering in the trees, preparing to migrate, their rowdy calls breaking the stillness. "My parents saw me as a gift because... I *was* one—literally." She smoothed the fringe on her shawl, taking her time, and then met his gaze. "As a newborn baby, someone left me in a basket on their doorstep."

The news thudded into Luke's stomach. Joseph, Mary, Ben—all throwaway children. In some ways he was too. And he'd done that very thing to his own child. The weight of his past hung on him like a millstone.

Moving closer, he reached for her hand and took it in his, pleased she didn't pull away. Enjoying its smallness, the calluses on her palms, evidence of how hard she worked. He wanted to ease the burdens she carried, to ease the pain of her admission, which was easy to read on her face.

"I'll always be grateful to my parents for taking me in when my biological mother didn't want me," she went on. "I'm thankful for their love, for everything they gave me. But…" Her bottle green eyes filled, glistening with unshed tears, ripping at Luke's reserve. "It's late. We'd better get back."

Luke couldn't let her leave, not like this. "Don't go. Not yet. Talk to me."

She hesitated, clearly torn about revealing her thoughts. He kept holding her hand, kept holding her gaze. Finally, she released a long, shuddering breath. "Deep down inside, in a place I'm not proud of, can barely admit exists, it hurts I was a throwaway baby." Mary turned toward the river. Near its edge a bottle floated on the current. Just ahead, trapped by a submerged log, an old boot and rusty can bobbed in the water lapping against the bank. She gestured toward the litter. "Someone's trash."

A lump clogged Luke's throat, closing off his air. *Trash.* Joseph. Memories still haunted his dreams. That this amazing woman saw herself as rubbish wrenched his heart. "Ah, Mary." He squeezed her hand. "You're not trash."

Emotions paraded across her face, and Luke understood something she might not. No matter what she'd said, Mary Graves did not see herself as a gift.

Using her free hand, she swiped at her eyes. "It's easy to hear those words but not so easy to believe them when those who are supposed to love you the most don't want you."

Swallowing hard, Luke thought of his parents. Of how they'd shuffled him off to one boarding school after another. How they'd rid themselves of the embarrassment of Joseph. And now he'd done the same to Ben, even before his birth. Would Ben think of himself as garbage one day? Because of him? The prospect hit him like an uppercut to the gut.

"Some people weren't meant to have children," he said quietly.

"Of course you understand. I'm sorry any child has to feel that way. All children deserve love." Mary gave him a wobbly smile. "But you and I have God, and that's enough to tell us we're accepted and loved, no matter what."

Mary wouldn't think much of his faith if he admitted he was Ben's father. What kind of a Christian lived a lie? Yet he couldn't bear to dim that light in her eyes, to see her attitude toward him change. Ben had a good life with Mary. He wouldn't do anything to destroy that.

"I've never told that to anyone," Mary said with a whoosh of breath. "I've never admitted aloud that my wonderful parents, who gave me all their love and everything they had, couldn't remove my feelings of rejection. When a person aches to confront someone, not to try to fit together the pieces of the puzzle, but to lash out, to shout that no reason on earth justifies tossing away their daughter—" Her voice broke. "That desire is ugly, unworthy of a child of God. I'm grateful He forgives me even for that."

Tears spilled down Mary's cheeks. Leaning forward, he brushed them away with both thumbs. "Whether you believe it or not, Mary, you're as beautiful inside as you are out."

"If so, it's only because I'm forgiven." Through her tears, Mary brightened. "I believe God had His hand on my life from the beginning." She gave a wobbly smile. "God has a plan for us all, even babies in baskets."

Tears stung the backs of Luke's eyes. What of Joseph? Luke shook his head and tossed a rock into the water. It pinged off the bottle and disappeared into the murky depths. "In my family, God forgot someone."

"Oh, Luke, God doesn't forget anyone."

A memory slammed into Luke with a tidal force. His six-year-old brother weeping, screaming, arms and legs thrashing, scrambling for footing, while a stranger wrestled him into a carriage. Luke trying to stop him, slamming his fists into the man. His father pulling Luke off. Standing helplessly, watching Joseph reach an arm out of the carriage window, screaming for his mother. Luke hadn't been able to stop it, to do anything but weep. "Tell that to my brother, Joseph. My parents abandoned him."

"Abandoned him. Why?" Mary's voice was soft with concern, with understanding.

Luke's heart raced. Admitting the family secret made him feel exposed, yet Mary had opened her heart to him. And he wanted to do the same, badly. To unburden himself to Mary, to the one person he trusted with something this raw, this personal.

Yet he hid so much from her. He couldn't tell her about Ben and see the anger, the disappointment, even the fear of what his paternity might mean for Ben. He couldn't do that.

"Joseph's transgression? He failed to meet my parents' expectations of what a child should be. He wasn't healthy, wasn't perfect." His throat clogged, and he could barely speak. In his mind, he saw his brother again, grown into an adolescent, lying on a bed, thin, weak, sick and neglected. Even now, Luke could smell the foul bed linens, his unwashed body and the stench of death. "That asylum treated him more like an animal than a human being. He…died, too young."

Mary put her hand to her mouth. "Oh, Luke, I can't understand how your parents could do that, how any parent could."

He lifted a hand to her cheek, silky under his fingers. He sucked in a breath, wishing he could stay forever in her world of purity and goodness. "Nothing about you and your father is anything like my family. My parents were experts at covering up, hiding behind pretty pretense."

Luke was no different.

A bird chattered in the treetop. Mary reached for his hand, holding it in both of hers. Her touch soothed like ointment on a burn.

"After Joseph's death, I wanted to do something that would help others like my brother. I became a doctor, created medicine, to honor his life."

"And you have."

He forced up the corners of his mouth. "My brother had epilepsy. I've worked at finding a cure. I've tried mistletoe, nightshade…but I haven't gotten it yet."

"With God's help, I'm sure you'll succeed."

Why hadn't God helped an innocent boy like Joseph? Why would He help a man like him? Luke had no answers. He rose and grabbed a nearby stick, then scuttled down the bank and shoved the boot and can free of the rock and into the current, watching as they floated downriver. "My brother suffered in that institution while my parents danced at parties and traipsed through Europe." He turned toward her. "Do you wonder why God allowed that?"

"God doesn't control people like they're puppets.

There's a reason for what Joseph went through. Remember, God can bring good from bad."

Luke climbed the bank. "How could anything good come from Joseph's life?" he said, his tone cold, harsh.

She hesitated, her brow knit in thought. "Perhaps only that your brother's life gave you a strong desire to help others. Not that God approved of what your parents did but that He didn't let Joseph's suffering go to waste. God has a plan, Luke. You're part of that plan and so am I."

Luke swallowed hard against the lump in his throat. Did God save some, let others suffer? Based on what? Some heinous sin of an epileptic boy? He sighed. He couldn't blame God. The blame for Joseph's end lay at his parents' door. The blame for Lucy's lay at his.

"From what you've said, I wonder if your parents are believers," Mary said. "Have you tried to talk to them about their faith?"

Luke cleared his throat. He'd been dancing around the issue. No longer. "After Joseph died, I turned to something I thought I could depend on—science. I've studied theories that argued against the existence of God. I lost my faith for a while, Mary. Did things I'm not proud of." And still am not. He shook his head. "I'm not the man to talk to them."

She touched his hand. "What better man than one who walked that path and came out the other side?"

A deep yearning filled him. He wanted to be rid of his resentment, the grudge he held against his parents, a constant burning in his gut that not even his remedy could cure. Luke's heart tripped. He needed to forgive his parents. Worse, he needed to forgive himself for Lucy's death. But he couldn't seem to manage either.

Mary made things sound easy. Yet, he'd observed her struggles to trust God with the future. "If you believe God has a plan for your life, why do you worry?"

"You can evaluate my faith all you want, Luke, even say I fall short—I'd agree in a heartbeat—but don't confuse the strength of my faith with the strength of the One I have faith in. He never fails."

"Yet look at Sam, your birth parents. They all failed you."

"They're human, not God."

"But you suffered because of them."

"If you feel an easy life proves God's love and a hard one denies it, then you don't know scripture." Her eyes widened. "I hadn't thought of this before. Perhaps giving up their baby was the greatest act of love my biological parents could have given me."

Luke stiffened. Mary was right. If he loved his son, he'd leave things alone. Forget Ben existed…if he could. He'd send money through the Children's Aid Society. Mary need never discover he was Ben's father. "I'm sure you're right."

"You look upset. Is something wrong?"

A wall of lies separated him from Mary. Better to move on. "I've got to go. Thanks for a lovely afternoon."

Luke trudged off, striding along the bank, putting distance between him and Mary. A gentle breeze stirred in the scanty collection of leaves still clinging to the trees, fighting their fate. A fate no one could evade.

Along the water's edge, a fat bullfrog croaked at his approach, then leapt below the surface with a splash as if unable to abide Luke's presence. Well, he could hardly abide it either.

Ahead, Doc and the boys gathered their gear. Luke

hollered an excuse about getting home, not stopping to look at their catch, all too aware of the crestfallen faces watching him go.

Dusk had fallen, shrouding him in twilight. He walked on, alone, the burden of his mistakes pressing against his lungs until he could barely breathe.

Chapter Eleven

Saturday turned overcast. By afternoon, the skies ripped open under the weight of unshed rain, drenching the earth, stripping colorful leaves from the trees and sending all of God's creatures for cover—including Mary and the boys. Holding an umbrella against the deluge, they dashed into her father's office. Mary shook out the umbrella, collapsed it near the door and then plunked the Sunday school materials for tomorrow's lesson on her desk, hoping she'd find a few minutes to study them. Time permitting, she would read the article on asthma in the latest American Medical Association Journal.

Her list of chores was long but not long enough to keep Luke Jacobs from coming to mind. Each thought was uninvited, unwelcome and unsettling.

Beside her, the boys shook their heads like drowned dogs, flinging water and bringing her back to the task at hand. Mary rushed into her father's quarters and returned with a towel just as Luke entered the waiting room.

Even with his hair plastered to his head, he looked

ready to handle whatever came his way. Yet now she knew what lurked beneath the surface, what shaped his life. He shrugged out of his jacket, soaked from his trek between the carriage house and the office. Mary intended to sop up the mess on the floor and to wipe down the children, but Luke's gaze locked with hers. She forgot the rain, forgot the dampness of her clothing and the puddle spreading beneath their shoes.

Moments slid through her memory—of Luke in her kitchen, up to his wrists in suds, scrubbing at her dishes. The touch of those hands, this time healing hands, on Philip and on her. And the strength of those hands, his strong, steady grip.

How she wanted to rely on that grip—but with Luke's plans to leave, she must lean, as always, on herself. Yet how could she close her mind to the haunted expression she'd seen in his eyes yesterday, to the pain etching his face even now? Luke wasn't telling her everything. What was he hiding? Too much stood between them. Still, he needed a friend. That much she could be.

She broke the contact between them and bent to the boys, wiping their hair and whisking water from their backs.

"Hi, Luke," Michael said. "We had fish for dinner last night."

"Sounds good."

Philip nodded. "Momma fried it in a pan, but we had to watch for bones."

"I didn't eat it," Ben said. "Fishies are too cute to eat. 'Sides, I might choke."

Grateful for the boys' chatter, Mary tidied the floor, avoiding Luke's gaze.

Michael peeled out of his wet coat, then dug into his

pockets and retrieved a paper. "I brought my arithmetic test to show Grandpa. I got a hundred," he said, trotting off toward the backroom with Ben trailing behind.

Philip's shoulders slumped. "I don't have any good papers to show Grandpa."

Luke ruffled Philip's unruly locks—the result of his cowlick. "Having trouble with your schoolwork? I'll be happy to help."

"My dad was too busy to help," Philip said quietly. "Now he can't. He's dead."

Mary's heart clutched. Her sons had experienced far too many dark days. Oh how she wished to take these moments away from them, to paint them a world filled with sunshine and happiness.

"I know," Luke said, bending down to Philip's level and touching the boy's arm. "I'm sorry about your dad."

In that moment, Mary forgave Luke for every moment of disagreement, every misspoken word. In that expression of concern to her son, a caring man emerged, a man she liked.

Liked immensely.

Yet didn't trust. Had her past destroyed her ability to trust? Or was it something else?

Having Luke in her life posed more of a threat to her well-being than any contagious disease.

"Dr. Jacobs?"

"Yes, Philip?"

Her son looked up at him, his brows knitted in concentration. "You, uh, you don't have any little boys and we don't have a dad, and if you married us, we'd have a family and you would too."

Silence as thick as quilt batting descended on the room. Mary stared at her son. Did she just hear him ask Luke Jacobs to marry her? Her heart tripped in her chest. She'd pictured that very thing yet knew what Philip did not. A chasm the width of the Rio Grande stood between her and Luke. Marriage was out of the question.

Luke's complexion had paled to the color of paste. Evidently he was even more mortified than she.

"Umm, that'd be a really good idea, Philip, and your mother is a very nice lady, but…"

"You don't want us?"

Her son's face fell, dropping as abruptly as a deflated balloon. Mary rushed to Philip's side, unsure what to do, what to say. If only she hadn't brought the boys with her today.

Michael had reappeared and stationed himself on Philip's other side, his expression fierce.

Luke still had his hand on Philip's arm. "Who wouldn't want you? You're a wonderful boy, you and your brothers. Your mom too."

"Then why won't you marry us?" Philip's eyes, big as saucers with the innocent question of a child, brimmed with tears.

"Because…" Luke cleared his throat, searching for the words to explain the complicated issues of an adult. "My work is in New York, and someday soon I have to go back there."

"Oh." Philip considered that and his eyes brightened. "Maybe somebody else will marry us, and we can have a dad."

Far more perceptive than his eight years, he stepped away from Luke's touch. Mary gathered Philip into her arms, only two arms—yet enough to hold and love her son.

Or so she told herself.

Luke rose and turned away, an unreadable expression in his gaze. Was she merely fooling herself? Philip wanted his world restored, to have a life with a mom and a dad.

No matter how hard she tried, she wasn't enough.

Michael, wearing a scowl on his face, obviously wanted no part of such an idea. Tears gathered in her eyes, uncertain which son she worried about more.

Mary hurried to the surgery. She found Ben hanging over his grandfather's every move. She led her son to her father's quarters, settling the boys in the living room with a pile of metal soldiers to do battle with, then walked to her desk, trying in vain to concentrate on tomorrow's Sunday school lesson.

But she kept seeing Philip's sweet face brimming with hope, hope for a dad. A lump rose in Mary's throat. No matter how much she loved him, she couldn't fill the need her son had for a father.

The door opened, cutting off Mary's thoughts. Geraldine Whitehall entered, her eyes wild with dread. Mary bit back a moan.

"Oh, thank goodness, you're here!" Geraldine raised trembling fingers to her lips. "Is Doc in?"

Obviously Mrs. Whitehall had gotten herself into quite a state. Mary grabbed a pad from her desk. "Come on back."

Down the hall, Luke and her father stood talking. At the sound of their footsteps, Luke turned guarded eyes on Mary. Her pulse skittered. Philip's proposal, no matter how much they might try to skirt it, lay between them—forming a connection of sorts, but also an uncomfortable wariness.

The two men entered the examining room ahead of

them. Her father sat across from his patient. "What's wrong, Mrs. Whitehall?"

Clutching her hands in her lap, Geraldine swallowed. "I have lockjaw."

"What makes you say that?"

"I can't open my mouth."

A muscle twitched in her father's cheek. Writing Geraldine's complaint on the pad, Mary clamped her teeth together to hold back sudden laughter.

"Appears to be in good working order to me," her father said.

"I mean wide. I can't open my mouth wide. It kinda locks." She moved her jaw up and down. "Did you hear that click?"

Her father motioned to the patient to take a seat on the examining table and then held the stethoscope to her jaw. "Do that again for Dr. Jacobs."

Luke complied, listening while Mrs. Whitehall opened and closed her mouth like a fish out of water. "Your jaw works normally," Luke said in a gentle tone. "No need to worry. Can you explain why you thought you had lockjaw?"

Whether he intended to or not, Luke was connecting to the townspeople and they to him. All signs of a good doctor. Good doctor or not, he was leaving.

Tears sprang to Geraldine's eyes. "Two days ago, I got a cut. I read in—"

"You read that someone got lockjaw from a cut," her father interrupted.

Her brows rose. "How did you know?"

"Just a guess. Let me see it."

She stuck out a finger. Her father leaned in for a

closer look, turned the finger over, then glanced up, a quizzical expression on his face.

"Right there," she said pointing at the side.

"This little scratch?"

She nodded, blinking against tears. "The article said it didn't need to be a bad cut, like the one on this finger," she added, holding up the still bandaged finger on her other hand.

"Now, Mrs. Whitehall, I see no sign of infection, no red streaks up your hand or arm, no reason to think you've got lockjaw or will get lockjaw."

Hope shimmered in her eyes. "Are you sure?"

"One hundred percent positive. But let's get a second opinion." He turned to Luke. "What do you say, Dr. Jacobs?"

Silent communication passed between the two. Luke and her father worked well together. Once she'd been the only one to assist in the practice. But with Luke here, her father didn't need her. The insight stung.

Luke turned to the patient. "You and your finger are the picture of health, Mrs. Whitehall. Your jaw works admirably."

The café owner sagged with relief. "Honestly, this morning I could barely open my mouth, but I couldn't get here until after the breakfast crowd. I've been so scared."

Her father wrote something on a pad, then tore off the page, handing it to his patient. "I have a prescription I want you to follow to the letter."

Geraldine studied the words written in her father's hurried scrawl. "For four weeks," she said, then hesitated, trying to decipher the letters, "stop reading about illness." She looked up, her mouth gaping, the jaw indeed working fine. "*That's* your prescription?"

"You're a healthy woman, yet you're in here two, maybe three times a month. Usually after you've read or heard about some illness. I want you to set your mind on what the Good Book says in the fourth chapter of Philippians. 'Whatsoever things are true, whatsoever things are honest, whatsoever things are just, whatsoever things are pure, whatsoever things are lovely, whatsoever things of good report—if there be any virtue and if there be any praise—think on these things.'" Henry patted her hand. "Our God is a God of peace. Praise Him for giving you a healthy body, and ask Him to give you a healthy mind."

"You sound like my husband."

"A wise man, Mr. Whitehall."

A contrite look came over Geraldine's face. "I feel so silly. I know how busy you are."

"If you follow that prescription, this office visit will be the best use of my time all day."

"I'll try. Customers are always telling me about their cousin's tumor or their sister's blindness. Within minutes, I see a suspicious puffiness above my collarbone or my vision blurs." She grimaced. "It's a curse."

Luke gave her a kind yet firm look. "A curse you can defeat, Mrs. Whitehall. The decision is yours."

She nodded slowly but didn't look convinced. Then, meeting Luke's gaze, her eyes flared. "You don't believe I make myself miserable on purpose, do you?"

"Not intentionally," Luke said, his tone kind. "But perhaps these imaginary illnesses are your way of avoiding what's really bothering you, something below the surface you don't want to examine."

Luke turned troubled eyes on Mary. Her breath caught in her throat. Was he implying the two of them might have something between them, something they needed to explore?

She turned away. Hadn't she lived with enough heartache without drudging up the past? Luke Jacobs had all the answers, answers pointing blame, but what about his own life? Just when she thought they were getting closer, she sensed he hid something, kept something from her.

But what?

Doc patted Geraldine's arm. "Now, don't forget. No medical articles. If someone starts describing symptoms, run for the hills." He grinned. "Well, at least as far as the café's kitchen."

"I promise. My, I'm relieved!" She rose and headed for the door and then turned back. "Oh, Mary, don't forget the pies you said you'd bake for the school supper next week."

Day after day, endless responsibilities lay heavy on Mary's shoulders. "I haven't forgotten."

Luke looked from Geraldine to her. "Jesus said to rest in Him. I wonder if you ladies know the meaning of the word."

He had no right to chastise her. How could she rest when so much needed doing? Wasn't she to serve others? Why did this man feel compelled to make her question her existence?

Her father waved a hand. "Now go and enjoy life, Mrs. Whitehall. Stop looking for problems."

Again, Mary's gaze connected with Luke's. Her stomach dipped crazily with the sudden urge to walk into his arms, to rest her chin on his chest and be held.

She couldn't fathom her response to him. The man had disrupted her life, made her question her priorities, her dreams. Philip had latched on to him and now hungered for a father. Ben, even her father, held him in high esteem. She could imagine the pain he'd bring to all of them when he left town. Luke had complicated everything. Solved nothing.

So why couldn't she stop thinking about him? Why couldn't she stop comparing him favorably to Sam?

The answer terrified her. Luke Jacobs had become important not only to her family but also to her. Yet his plans didn't mesh with her life. How could she be so foolish?

With Luke Jacobs around, unlike Geraldine Whitehall, Mary didn't have to look for problems. Problems smacked her in the face.

Why had God brought him into her life?

Luke stood in front of Mary's desk. She bent over reading material, unaware of his presence, absently coiling a tendril of hair around her finger. His fingers itched to remove the pins from her glorious tresses. Not smart, Jacobs, not smart at all.

Only a foolish man would hanker after this woman who had one son craving a dad and another erecting walls. And the third, not her son, but his, a secret that would destroy any shred of feeling she might have for him. He should leave—and soon. Yet even as he formed the thought, he knew Mary Graves had crept into his heart, her sons too—boys who reminded Luke of himself. And Ben made him long for a relationship he hadn't expected to crave.

Instead of avoiding her like any sane man would've,

he sat on the corner of her desk. The words poured out of his mouth, "Care to have a cup of coffee?"

Her head snapped up. "Oh, Luke. You startled me." A bewildered expression came over her face. "What did you say?"

"I asked if you'd like to get some coffee."

"Coffee?"

"Surely you've heard of that dark, warm liquid sure to perk you up?"

Her smile hauled him closer. "Yes, I have, and I could use some perking up but—"

Raising a hand, he stopped the flow of excuses trying to push past her lips. "Before you tell me about the coffee in Doc's kitchen and your sons playing in his quarters, your father said to tell you to go. He wants time alone with his grandsons."

She studied her clasped hands, digesting her father's claim, a claim sounding weak even to Luke's ears.

"He also said you work too hard and need to remember even the Lord rested."

She gazed up at him. "All right. Where?"

"The Whitehall Café. I want to give Mrs. Whitehall a chance to forgive me by complimenting her pie."

"You *were* tough on her." She cocked her head. "Who said anything about pie?"

"What's coffee without pie?" He grinned. "And what's pie without lunch?" he said, lost in her fascinating green eyes.

She put a hand on her hip. "Are you asking me to lunch?"

"Yes, ma'am. I thought I'd start out nice and easy. Get you used to the idea of sharing a table with me before I got to my true objective—a meal."

A meal. Nothing more. He didn't want to mislead Mary, yet he couldn't stop wanting to spend time with her.

"But the boys—"

"Your father will feed them."

"What if a patient comes in with an emergency?"

"Doc can send Michael to get us."

Laughing, Mary rose to her feet. "I shouldn't. I have too much to do, but the prospect of being waited on sounds delightful."

"I'll remember that." He held out his arm. She slid a hand in the crook, barely brushing his arm, yet sending his thoughts careening into risky territory.

Whoa, Jacobs.

They sauntered toward the café, clouds scuttling across the noonday sky, but at least for now, the rain had stopped. He was crazy for doing this. Two hours ago, her son had proposed marriage—the institution he steered clear of. He should be avoiding her and all the expectations wrapped up with her, like her family—a family clearly needing a male leader. And he was anything but. Yet Luke found himself drawn again and again to Mary Graves, a stethoscope to her heartbeat. In her presence, he felt whole. As if he was more than a man who created medicine in a lab, more than his profession. With her, he felt linked to another human being, which both alarmed and thrilled him. Mary had appeared in his life, taken his well-thought-out plans and, without meaning to, had tossed them aside. The reasons he'd given himself for staying—Ben's asthma, Doc's need for help—were pathetic excuses.

In truth, Mary Graves kept him here. She and his son.

They were also the reasons he would leave. Not that

she'd have him, but he couldn't tie himself to anyone. Not even two people as special as Ben and Mary.

Inside the café, they spied an empty table in the far corner, greeting diners along the way. Luke held Mary's chair and then sat across from her.

Mrs. Whitehall sped over with menus. Luke shot her his best smile, a smile he hoped would thaw this hypochondriac's heart. "Hello, Mrs. Whitehall. We're here for some of your delicious cooking."

The café owner's cheeks turned rosy. "That's mighty nice to hear." Her gaze moved from Luke to Mary. "You two make a fine-looking couple. Why, Mary, I don't like to lose one of my best customers, but you ought to invite Dr. Jacobs over for a meal."

Now Mary's cheeks dotted with color, and she opened her mouth, probably to contradict Mrs. Whitehall.

Before she could, Luke said, "Hmm, meatloaf is on the menu today." He turned to Mary. "It's excellent."

"Yes, but filling. I want to leave room for that pie you mentioned." Mary glanced at her menu. "I'll have a bowl of the vegetable soup." Then she gave him a playful grin. "Oh, and coffee."

Mrs. Whitehall wrote the order on her pad and then looked at Luke. "Doctor, I want to apologize for getting huffy with you this morning. You're right. The choice is mine. Mark my words. I'm going to be a new woman."

"No need to apologize. It's not easy to change." He could use some changing himself. "I'm proud of you." And he was. Since he'd arrived in Noblesville, a long list of people had touched his life, become important to him—more than he cared to admit. The sense of connection felt peculiar yet comfortable too, like an over-sized threadbare shirt.

Mrs. Whitehall stuck the pencil behind her ear. "Mary, you're lucky to have Dr. Jacobs in the practice. Lots of folks are singing his praises, saying how kind he is." Then she hustled to the kitchen with their order.

Warmth spread through Luke. Evidently Doc had rubbed off on him. Or maybe he'd learned the importance of showing others how he felt—never easy for him.

The clang of silverware and soft hum of conversation in the room filled the silence between him and Mary. Her troubled gaze told him she had something to say but was struggling to work up the courage. Strange, he'd never known Mary to have trouble speaking her mind.

"About that proposal from Philip…" She gave a weak smile. "I'm sorry. That was…awkward."

Ah, now he understood her hesitancy. He'd prefer to avoid the topic himself. "Don't give it a thought," he said, pretending the whole incident hadn't disturbed him, hadn't stuck in his mind, no matter how hard he tried to dislodge it. "I know very little about children, except they can't be muzzled like the family dog."

Mary laughed and laid her hands in her lap. "After this morning, I'm tempted."

Though a part of Luke wondered how he would've responded if Mary had been the one proposing earlier. Not that she would. But for a second, he imagined greeting her at the end of an aisle, lifting a veil to kiss her, knowing she'd always be his. He'd help with chores. Sit at her table. Share the events of their day—be part of a cozy family. The one thing in his privileged life he'd never had.

He'd love her as she deserved to be loved.

Careful, Jacobs. That forever territory is hazardous. The kind you don't walk into without a map. Nothing in his life had prepared him for domesticity.

Removing his handkerchief, he swiped his brow. "Philip is a lot like his mom."

"How so?"

"He's not afraid to speak up."

She grinned. "I suspect you've been tempted to tie a gag on me a time or two."

"And cover that pretty mouth of yours?" He shook his head. "Never."

A blush crept into her cheeks and her lips parted. She never looked more kissable. Not that he'd kiss her. At least, not here, not now.

"You're quite the flatterer, Dr. Jacobs. I'm guessing you've had more than your share of lady friends."

Immediately, he thought of Lucy. Their short-lived involvement had brought about her death. That knowledge made him hold other women at arm's length. "A few." But none like Mary, a mix of fire and purity, homespun goodness and fierce determination.

"So were you ever married?"

He toyed with the salt cellar, avoiding her gaze. "No."

"That surprises me."

"Guess I never met the right woman. Not that I've given any woman much of a chance. My focus is on medicine."

"Leaving you no time for marriage and children."

He left her assumption on the table. Better that than the truth. His misspent years and Lucy's death had destroyed a desire for home and hearth. Besides, he wasn't a man who'd learned how to create a family, and rather than make the mess of it his parents had, he'd move on, give his life meaning creating medicine.

"Blame my grandmother. Everyone assumed I'd enter the family business, but when I decided I wanted to be a doctor, my grandmother stood with me against my parents. She even paid for my education. I can see her yet, leaning on her cane, wagging a finger at them." He grinned. "That's the only time in my life I remember someone defying my parents."

"She sounds like a wonderful woman."

Luke's throat clogged. Even his outspoken grandmother hadn't been able to sway his parents from their solution to the problem they saw as their son Joseph. "She was. When I was eight, my parents sent me to boarding school. My grandmother wrote almost every week, each letter packed with news. Twice a month she sent a package of cookies she made. Snickerdoodles, macaroons, oatmeal raisin, brownies and in December, gingerbread. You could smell those cookies a mile off. All the boys would gather around, and we'd clean out the tin in minutes." He laughed. "I was very popular." Until her death five years ago, his grandmother had been the single most important person in his life. He inhaled sharply. She died the same year as Mary's mother. "Guess I never met a woman who measured up to my grandmother."

Until now.

"Surely your mother wrote too."

He kept his eyes on his folded hands lying on the table. "My mother had a social secretary. Writing me wasn't one of her duties."

Mary's hand reached across the table, and her fingers curled around his. "I'm sorry."

He struggled to keep his tone even. "No need. I had the best schools, the best of everything. Not every child was as privileged as I." Especially one child in particular—Joseph.

She squeezed his hand. "Your parents were the ones who missed out."

Like a cool salve, her declaration slid into the festering wound of his childhood, easing the pain of parents who'd never loved unreservedly and never would.

He was glad Ben lived with Mary. What a gift a woman like Mary was. He returned her smile. "I wish my grandmother could've met you. You two are very much alike. Excellent bakers and   " he took a breath " women who know exactly the right thing to say."

Her gaze softened. "I would've liked her." She shot him a grin. "I'd love to have met any woman who could keep you in line."

He chuckled, grateful to Mary for lightening the moment. He opened his mouth to ask her a question about the practice when across the way, the door opened and a pimply faced youth scanned the room, his shirtsleeves stopping above the wrists of his gawky arms.

With an irregular gait, he hurried to their table. "You Luke Jacobs?"

"Yes."

"Boss saw you come here. He said to look for the man I don't know." He rocked back on his heels and beamed. "That's you."

From the boy's mannerisms, Luke suspected he was damaged at birth. Evidently, his parents had kept him home with them. People in this town appeared to know what mattered.

Mrs. Whitehall arrived at their table, a pot of coffee

in her hands. She greeted the lad and then bent toward Mary. "If you have a second, I meant to talk about the church pie supper."

The two women chatted, and Luke returned his attention to the boy. "Why are you looking for me?"

"Oh, I forgot." Grinning, he handed over an envelope.

A telegram. Who'd send him a telegram? Luke dug in his pocket for a tip.

"Thanks!" the lad said, then hustled out the door.

Luke glanced at the ladies. They still had their heads together. He had time to read the wire. As he slid open the flap of the Western Union envelope, a weird sense of foreboding whooshed through him.

WE NEED TO SPEAK WITH YOU STOP ARRIVAL DATE PENDING STOP FATHER

A chill traveled Luke's spine. He clutched the cryptic telegram. Luke and his parents lived mere miles apart yet rarely saw each other. Something was afoot, but what? And how had his parents discovered his location?

No doubt from his housekeeper. The woman had a heart of gold but never knew when to keep a closed mouth.

Luke read the words again. Then a third time.

What would bring his father out to what he'd consider the sticks? Luke's jaw tightened. Could it be Ben? No, his father had shown no interest in his grandson— even when he'd learned of Luke's plan to find the boy.

No point in speculating. As soon as he and Mary finished here, he'd send a wire, asking the purpose of his visit.

Mrs. Whitehall promised to bring out their food and then bustled toward the kitchen.

Mary motioned to the telegram. "I hope it's not bad news."

Pocketing the envelope into his breast pocket, Luke met her gaze. The tenderness in her eyes socked him in the gut. "No, no, not bad news." At least he hoped not. Until he knew otherwise, he'd focus on Mary, a most attractive distraction.

To think he'd once considered this intriguing woman a thorn in his side. Whatever his father wanted, Luke suspected the biggest risk to his plans came from Mary Graves, a woman who affected him in ways he didn't understand.

Mary returned to her desk. She couldn't help wondering about Luke's telegram. Telegrams usually meant big news, good…or bad. News Luke had not shared with her. Not that he owed her an explanation. Far from it. Still—

Her father interrupted the thought. An unfamiliar young man stood at his side, hat in hand, undoubtedly the third applicant. Mary glanced at the clock, pleased by his punctuality. This might be the doctor to fill Luke's shoes.

At the prospect of life without Luke, a pang of disappointment rammed her heart. A childish reaction, especially since this morning when Luke had reminded Philip that he'd be returning to New York.

"Mary, this is Dr. Sloan. Frank, this is my daughter, Mary Graves."

The bluest eyes Mary had ever seen turned her way. A boyish grin took over the young doctor's face. "It's a pleasure to meet you."

"Why don't you show Dr. Sloan the surgery and examining room while I round up Luke," her father said. "I'd like him to sit in on the interview."

Mary gave the applicant a smile. "Follow me, Doctor." She opened the door to the surgery, proud of the clean, orderly room. "This is where Dr. Lawrence performs minor surgery, sets bones and treats burns. The next room is primarily used for routine office visits."

Dr. Sloan scanned the surgery. "An admirable facility." Then his gaze returned to her. "Do you assist with patients?"

"Yes, whenever I can." But once she finished medical school, she'd be handling patients herself.

"Excellent. I suspect you're good with patients."

Smiling at his assessment, Mary gave a tour of the office ending in the backroom where Luke and her father waited. After examining his grades and credentials, the smile on her father's face proved this man met all of Henry's requirements and then some. "I must tell you that the practice isn't lucrative." Doc turned shrewd eyes on the applicant. "Knowing the pay is dismal, are you still interested in the position?"

"Yes, sir. Working under the guidance of a veteran doctor is invaluable experience."

Her father rose, shaking Dr. Sloan's hand. "In that case, I'd like to offer you the position. If you feel you can work with Dr. Jacobs and me."

Mary frowned. Had her father learned something she didn't know? Was Luke staying?

Chapter Twelve

Luke leaned against the doorframe, his stomach churning with frustration. Down the hall, Sloan leaned closer to Mary, his face animated in conversation. Mary tilted her head, all smiles at whatever the good doctor said.

That very first Sunday, Sloan had attended First Christian Church, squiring Mary like she belonged to him. In the three days since he'd joined the practice, Sloan had complimented Mary's efficiency, her work ethic and kindness to the patients.

If that wasn't enough to make it perfectly clear he had an interest in Mary, Sloan found countless ways to confer with her, asking her opinion on the best grocer and restaurants in town. Even which barber she'd recommend, though the man didn't need as much as a nose hair trimmed. Luke had taken about as much as he could and suggested Frank might want to check with Doc for the name of a barber. Eyes on Mary, Frank had countered—if you want to please a lady, you're wise to ask her opinion. Mary had blushed and suggested Bill's Barber Shop across the square. Then she'd glanced at

Luke's nape and the hair brushing his collar, making him all too aware his cut was long overdue.

Sloan was as transparent as glass. And just as slick. Luke itched to toss his well-groomed hide out the door as far as he could throw him.

The worst of it, since Sloan joined the practice, Mary had a new bounce in her step.

Admit it, Jacobs. You're jealous.

Doc stepped out of the examining room, his gaze following Luke's. "Are you going to just step aside and leave Mary to Frank?"

"She's not mine to hand over."

"I've seen something in her eyes when she looks at you. The exact same look I've seen in yours. So don't pretend with me, young man."

"I won't deny Mary's a wonderful person." The problem—he wasn't alone in that opinion. Nor could he deny that Frank Sloan had a great deal to offer a woman like Mary. "Sloan's perfect for her."

Doc shoved a hand in the pocket of his coat. "I thought maybe you'd be the man for my daughter."

Eyes downcast, Luke shook his head.

"What makes you the wrong man, Luke?" Henry laid a hand on Luke's arm. "Can you tell me that?"

Luke swallowed past the lump in his throat. He couldn't tell him he was Ben's father. He couldn't tell him about Lucy. He couldn't tell him about every ugly part of his life. Since he'd returned to God, he knew the Bible promised God had forgiven him, but that didn't undo his past. A past Mary and her father could never understand.

Luke pulled his gaze away from the lovebirds. "I... I'm not good enough for Mary," he said, and then retreated toward the backroom. Doc called after him, but Luke kept going.

Sitting at the table, Luke leafed through a book of herbal remedies, normally a fascinating subject, but the words on the page swam before his eyes, blending with the image of Mary's face. Only a selfish man wouldn't want Mary to find happiness.

In truth, Sloan was kind. Gentle. He made Mary laugh. He'd mentioned his large churchgoing family overflowing with nieces and nephews. No matter how much Luke searched for evidence to the contrary, he couldn't find one shred of unsuitability about the man. What Luke saw as Sloan's self-absorption, assuming he could fairly assess the guy, might get on Mary's nerves, but in the things that mattered, he'd make a good husband. A good father too.

The possibility this man might rear his son sank to his belly with the weight of an iron anchor. Not that he doubted Sloan would treat Ben well. Yet the prospect stabbed at him.

But as much as he cared about Mary, as much as he wanted to spend every waking minute with her and the boys, he wasn't fit to even contemplate making them his.

So why did he ache to gather them close and promise them forever?

That just proved how little he'd changed. He thought of himself, not of Mary and of her sons. They deserved a man like Sloan, a man who knew how to nurture, how to share his heart. Besides, if Luke told Mary the truth about Ben, she'd never forgive him. Never understand how a man could shirk his responsibilities to the woman who'd carried his child.

He had to get out of town. And soon.

Sloan ambled into the room and sat across from Luke. "Henry said you're looking for a cure for epilepsy."

"Yes."

For a moment, he considered that, then shrugged. "I admire what you're trying to do, but creating medicine is solitary and doesn't appeal to me."

"What does appeal to you?" Luke's jaw tightened. Besides Mary.

"I enjoy working with patients. Once I've gotten experience here, I want to join the staff of an excellent hospital like Johns Hopkins." He smiled. "To practice with the highest skilled surgeons and doctors in the country, to have access to the finest equipment is a dream I've had for a long time."

The news thudded into Luke's stomach with the power of a fisted hand. Did Mary fit into that dream? Or did Sloan see her as a temporary diversion?

Or expect her to share his dream and leave with him?

If so, Sloan was dead wrong.

Mary loved this town, loved the people. Luke couldn't imagine she'd leave all this behind.

And what about Ben? Surely Sloan didn't expect to go from small-town practice to the best hospital in the country. How would Ben handle being moved from pillar to post while Sloan pursued his goal?

Perhaps Frank Sloan wasn't ideal after all.

Mary entered her house, greeted by a pile of dirty laundry, dresses to iron and jars of cherries she had to turn into pies before Friday's school supper. Along with a book she'd borrowed from Addie and had yet to read. A half crocheted baby blanket lay on the arm of the sofa, her gift to Lily, still incomplete. But today, the unfinished work didn't pull at her.

Her thoughts traveled to Luke. She carried the pleasure of the fishing trip with the boys. To watch her sons having fun, to see Luke's gentleness with them, to share the innermost part of her being with a man who listened and appeared to understand, to share that extraordinary kiss, had been wonderful—that is until Luke made it crystal clear he wasn't staying.

Since Frank joined the practice, Luke had backed away from her and the boys. Sometimes he even appeared to encourage her budding friendship with Frank, though upon occasion she caught Luke glowering at Sloan like an angry bull.

She liked Frank. Liked how he dove feet first into the practice, into the town. He didn't have a reticent bone in his body. Unlike Luke, he was an open book with no missing chapters. She'd known Frank less than a week, but she knew the names of his friends and family. Where he'd grown up and gone to church. He was a hard worker, eager to please, and the patients had warmed to him quickly.

Now that Frank shouldered his share of the load, Luke had no reason to remain. They had no future. Not that she'd thought otherwise, yet deep down she realized a smidgen of hope had lived, was now dead.

Well, she had more important things to focus on— like what she carried in her handbag. Her pulse tripped in her chest. This letter would reveal if her dreams would be realized or dashed. She closed the door to her room and then dropped onto the bed and eased the packet out of her purse. The unnatural silence of the house did nothing to quiet her pounding heart. With trembling hands, she slid a fingernail under the flap, then hesitated, afraid of its contents.

Breathing a prayer for strength to live with the decision, whatever it was, she unfolded the paper, scanning the page, unable to absorb the exact words, searching for what she had to know.

Congratulations.... Pleased to inform you that you have been accepted.... Classes begin January fourth, 1899.

Tears flooded her eyes, and praises to God bubbled from her lips.

She'd been accepted. She'd been accepted. She'd been accepted.

Oh, Daddy, I'll make you proud of me. I'll make you so proud.

And her mother too, if from Heaven, Susannah Lawrence knew of her daughter's accomplishment.

Not everyone would react well to the news, but she wouldn't let Luke Jacobs dampen her joy. How could she value the opinion of a man who wanted a say in her life but had no intention of sharing it?

Leaving every one of the unfinished tasks behind, Mary rushed from the house. Something she wouldn't ordinarily do, but today she couldn't wait a minute longer to talk to her father. As she cut through the string of yards separating their houses, the crisp, sunny day never appeared brighter, more dazzling.

She found him at the kitchen table eating a sandwich before the start of afternoon office hours. The counters were piled high with unwashed dishes, but Mary didn't care. "Daddy, I have some wonderful news."

Henry Lawrence turned to her, already smiling at her excited tone. "What?"

"Central College of Physicians and Surgeons has accepted me. I'll start classes in January."

Her father's expression turned puzzled. "Medical school?" Then as her words sank in, a wide smile took over his face, lit up his eyes. "Oh, that's wonderful, kitten! If anyone should be a doctor, it's you."

His words soothed any qualms she held. Years before, Sam had scoffed at the idea. She suspected he'd felt threatened by her plan, like she'd leave him once she had M.D. after her name.

But her father—his approval bubbled up within her until she felt she could burst with joy. "Once I'm a doctor, I can take over the practice and keep your legacy alive in this town."

He chuckled. "Knowing you, I'm sure you have a plan."

"I do." She grinned back at him. "Michael and Philip don't need me as much as when they were small, and Carrie Foley will still look after Ben. I can take the train to the city and be back each evening in time to fix supper." The words rattled out of her like a freight train picking up speed. "With the inheritance from Sam's father and my savings, I have money for tuition."

"My daughter the doctor." Her father beamed. "It's got a nice ring to it. I'll help any way I can." He rose and hugged her. "How did you manage to keep this a secret until now?"

"I filled out the application using Dr. Roberts's recommendation."

Henry's jaw dropped. "That old codger kept it from me."

"He knew I wanted to surprise you." She grimaced.

"To be honest, if I'd told you and didn't get accepted, I couldn't bear the idea of disappointing you."

"You could never disappoint me. Besides, any medical school that didn't accept you would be foolish. God gave you a talent for medicine." His gaze softened, and he raised a palm to her cheek. "I'll miss you around here, but you must seize this opportunity."

"I'll miss the practice too, Daddy, but once I graduate, I'll be right back here."

"Where you belong. Why, you practically grew up in this office. You've heard my concerns for the seriously ill, joined hands with your mother and me as we prayed for the sick and dying, and in the last several years you've assisted in the office. I wouldn't be surprised if you taught the teaching staff a thing or two." Grinning, he slipped an arm around her. "Let's celebrate with dessert at the café."

"What about your patients?"

"No one is scheduled this afternoon. Luke will be back from lunch soon. If someone comes in, he and Frank can easily handle it."

Together they left her father's quarters and ambled into the waiting room where Frank leaned over her desk, checking the appointment book. He looked up and smiled. "You two look mighty cheerful."

"Mary's been accepted into medical school. The same school you graduated from."

"Imagine! Two doctors in the family." Frank rounded the desk, enfolding her in his arms. "Congratulations, Mary."

Frank's embrace didn't elicit one spark, one flutter. "Thank you," Mary said, as the outer door opened.

Luke entered. His lips thinned. "Am I interrupting something?"

Meeting that stony, reproving gaze, Mary jerked away guiltily then scowled. Luke had no right to behave as if she'd done something wrong.

She wouldn't tell him about her acceptance into medical school. She looked at Frank, hoping he'd get the message. "Not a thing. Daddy and I just need a break."

Frank gave an imperceptible nod, his lips curling with pleasure at sharing a confidence.

Exactly as Mary hoped, so why did his smugness rub against her peace? Perhaps because Luke looked dejected, like a lost little boy. She hurried for her coat.

"Can you two manage without us this afternoon?" her father asked.

A question formed in Luke's eyes as his gaze roamed their faces. "Sure."

"Take your time." Frank slapped Luke on the back. "We can handle whatever arises, right, Doctor?"

Luke's features hardened into granite, but he nodded, his gaze sweeping over Mary. "Have fun."

Outside her father turned to her. "I'm surprised you didn't tell Luke your news."

"He'll disapprove."

"Why?"

Unwilling to talk about Luke's assertion that her sons would suffer if she pursued medicine, she shrugged. "Let's not talk about Luke."

Her father appeared to want to ask more but then gave her a smile. In the crisp fall air, they strolled toward the café, shuffling through the leaves, sharing the peace and quiet of the beautiful fall day.

"I remember when you were about five," her father

said, "I found you with my stethoscope hooked in your ears, listening to your dolly's chest."

Mary smiled.

"You said the doll had pleurisy. Guess you overheard that diagnosis at the supper table. But I knew you wanted to be a doctor when you tried to inoculate our cat." He laughed. "Remember?"

"Oh, yes. It's a wonder you didn't regret taking me in."

"Never." Her father squeezed her hand. "You gave your mother and me everything. Everything we ever dreamed of."

In her father's shining eyes, filled with pride and love, she saw the reflection of God's love for her. For all His children. No matter their failings. The exact same way she felt about her sons. Her life was part of God's plan. She smiled, barely able to contain her joy at the sudden certainty she'd never again feel like discarded trash.

They entered the restaurant, all but empty now that the rush of diners had passed. At the table near the window, Henry took her hands. "Darling daughter, you're a very capable woman and will make a valuable contribution as a doctor. You already possess qualities that can't be learned from a textbook." He touched her cheek. "I'm very proud of you."

"Oh, Daddy, thank you."

"Your mother would be popping buttons."

Elation surged through Mary, making her feel almost buoyant. "Do you really think so?"

"I know so. A few weeks before she died, your mom told me that no matter what happened with Sam, she knew you'd be all right because, and I'm quoting her,

'Our girl is heaven-sent. The Good Lord will see her through.'"

And He had. God had walked with her through her mother's death, through the difficult years with Sam and his passing. And He would help her now.

Fannie Whitehall, her curly auburn hair tucked into a scarf, arrived with menus. "You two playing hooky?"

"Indeed we are. We're celebrating." Henry nodded toward Mary. "Mary's been accepted into medical school. She's going to follow in her old man's footsteps."

"Congratulations!" Fannie sighed. "Wish I had something to celebrate…like James's proposal."

Her father chuckled. "Give it time. You and James are still wet behind the ears."

They ordered coffee and cherry cobbler with ice cream. Fannie left to fetch it. From the crestfallen look on her face, her father hadn't said what Fannie wanted to hear.

Mary leaned toward her father. "What if I don't make it? Luke said the work is grueling."

"I don't doubt for a minute that you'll graduate. Once you decide to do something, you're unstoppable."

Her father announced her news to everyone who entered. The congratulations and encouragement Mary received filled her heart to overflowing. Odd her father hadn't told Luke. Maybe he sensed her reluctance. Not that Luke's opinion mattered.

The afternoon flew by as they savored the pie and the camaraderie of having time together, just the two of them, with no patients or children requiring their attention.

"I've never tasted anything more delicious," Mary said, finishing off her slice. She glanced at the clock on the wall. "Oh, my. Michael and Philip will be home soon."

"Best get a move on." Her father opened his wallet. "Since you're running late, I'll pick up Ben at the Foleys'. I could use the exercise."

Outside the café, Mary and her father parted. She'd gotten as far as the kitchen and laid her handbag on the table when the door opened and banged close. Her sons plodded into the room, heads drooping, mouths turned down, looking like they'd lost their best friend.

"Hi," Philip said.

Mary caught a glimpse of Michael's face. She gasped at the cut above her son's left eye, fast turning purple underneath, and the red bruise on his cheek. "What happened?"

His gaze shifted away. "I'm okay. I tripped playing Red Rover."

"Come over to the sink." Mary soaped a dishcloth and gently cleaned then rinsed the cut. On her tiptoes, she retrieved the iodine she kept on the top shelf of the cabinet, then dabbed it on Michael's injury. He sucked in his breath but didn't whimper.

Philip tugged at her skirt. "He didn't cry, Mom."

"You saw what happened?"

Philip shook his head. "Michael told me he didn't cry. I would've."

"It's okay to cry," Mary said, studying her older son.

Michael's eyes flooded. "Men don't cry."

"You're a boy, not a man." Recalling holding her weeping husband in her arms the night he told her about his childhood of abuse, Mary's throat tightened. "And men do cry."

Something about Michael's injuries didn't add up to a simple fall in the school yard.

"Grandpa should be bringing Ben home soon. Philip, why don't you go outside to play? Wear a coat. The temperature is dropping."

Glad for the opportunity to talk to Michael alone, Mary waited until the door closed, and then put an arm around her son's shoulders. "I'm surprised your teacher didn't clean this."

"I guess she didn't notice."

"Didn't notice?" Mary returned the iodine to its place then knelt in front of her son, taking his hands in hers. "Something tells me this cut didn't come from a fall. Maybe didn't even occur at school." She peered into his green eyes, so like her own. "What really happened?"

A sob tore from his throat. "I got into a fight."

The news thudded to Mary's stomach. "With who?"

"Jimmy Augsburger."

"Jimmy's one of your best friends."

Michael's eyes sparked. "Not anymore."

"What did you fight about?"

Pulling his hands away, Michael focused on a spot on the floor. "Nothing."

"You're telling me you and your best friend got into a fight *for no reason*. That doesn't make sense."

He shrugged.

"I want an answer."

"He made me mad."

"*You* started the fight?"

Nodding, his gaze once again sought the floorboards. What was he hiding?

"Oh, Michael, you're not a fighter. Tell me what

made you angry enough to pick a fight with your best friend."

"I can't."

"Well, you'd better, young man, because if you don't, you'll be spending the rest of the day in your room."

"That's fair." Her firstborn shuffled away, his slender shoulders drooping as if he carried the weight of their entire family on his back.

Michael always argued about punishments, and now he took this one without a quarrel? Something was terribly wrong. Should she talk to Mrs. Augsburger? Would she be so angry with Michael that a discussion might escalate the trouble between their sons?

Mary found fighting repulsive. Perhaps she made too much of this. Michael wasn't violent, not even rough-and-tumble like Philip, who loved to run and romp like an overgrown puppy. Her older, studious son enjoyed reading, playing checkers, and fishing. Quiet pastimes.

Why would he attack his best friend?

Oh, if only Sam were here. Her shoulders sagged. If he were, Sam would either be working at the factory or drunk. No help at all.

God, give me wisdom. Help me know what to do.

Luke's words ricocheted through her mind: Michael is trying to be the man of the house, too big a job for a ten-year-old boy. Did this fight have something to do with protecting his family? Had Jimmy said something to wound Michael, something about his family, compelling him to uphold their reputation? Or his father's good name? Her stomach clenched.

Sam died when Michael was eight. She'd taken every precaution to ensure the boys saw their father sober. Not all that hard to do. By the time Sam came home from the saloon, his sons had been asleep for hours. Amazingly, most mornings Sam dressed and headed to work with no sign of a hangover.

She'd hidden Sam's drinking, making excuses for his absences from the boys' activities at school or church. Except for her parents, no one caught on—or so she believed.

The door opened, and Ben and Philip raced in ahead of her father. "Philip said Michael was in a fight," Henry said.

"Yes, he's in his room. I tried talking to him. He's not telling me everything."

"Why don't I take the boys to the café for a snack and drop them back here afterward?"

"Oh, Daddy, that would be a big help."

Mary gave Ben and Philip a kiss, then stood in the doorway, watching them turn the corner and head uptown. The sun lowered in the west, matching the sinking in her heart. Whatever had happened this afternoon, she couldn't ignore the situation.

Please, God, give me the words so I can help Michael handle whatever transpired between him and Jimmy.

She rapped on the boys' bedroom door and then opened it. Michael lay curled on the bed with his back to her. She sat on the edge of the mattress and ran her fingers through his thick, wavy hair, but her son didn't acknowledge her presence.

"I'm sorry, Michael. I shouldn't have sent you to your room. I know you'd never pick a fight unless you felt you had a very good reason."

Her son didn't move a muscle, didn't indicate he'd heard her. The scent of the outdoors clung to his rumpled clothes. The rigid set of his shoulders kept her from pulling him to her, encircling him in the comfort of her arms.

"We need to talk. Please, sit up and look at me."

Michael hesitated but did as she'd asked, sitting cross-legged on the bed. The bruises on his face tore at her. She had to get to the bottom of this, but the look on his face told her Michael wouldn't confide in her.

"I think you're protecting me from something." She glimpsed the tiniest crack of affirmation in her son's stony face. "We're a family, Michael. Families discuss their problems."

Her throat closed at her self-deceit. As the years passed, she and Sam stopped talking about his drinking, about the distance it put between them, as if they feared where that conversation might lead...to the dissolution of the sham of their marriage.

Michael looked away. "You can't do anything."

Years ago, on the school playground, kids had dubbed her "Mary, the basket baby," teasing her for being a throwaway child. She hadn't told her parents. Not because they couldn't have done anything but because they would've tried, and somehow she'd reasoned in the way of a child they'd have made the situation worse.

"Perhaps not, but I'll feel better once I understand why you'd pick a fight. That worries me."

"I had a reason, Mom, a good reason." He folded his arms across his belly.

"The Bible teaches us to turn the other cheek." Mary tilted his face to hers. "Unless you share what happened, it'll eat away at you, Michael. I know. When I was a little girl, children called me a hurtful name, but I didn't tell my parents. Keeping that secret kept me from their comfort. Comfort I want to give you." Then she bent and kissed his forehead.

His face contorted. "Jimmy told a lie. A big fat lie!"

Bracing herself, Mary asked, "About what?"

His lips trembled. "He wouldn't take it back."

Her heart breaking for her son, Mary tugged him close, wrapping his narrow frame in the circle of her arms.

But Michael pulled away, his gaze troubled. Tears welled in his eyes. "Sometimes… Daddy smelled…bad. His eyes were…fuzzy." Michael took hold of her arm. "Was Daddy a…a drunk like Jimmy said?" he asked softly, his voice laced with sorrow.

Mary gazed into her precious son's eyes. Innocence and trust in her rested there. Remembering the pain of learning her real parents hadn't wanted her, had left her on the Lawrence doorstep like a basket of discarded kittens, she couldn't tell Michael the truth.

Confirming Sam was a drunk would voice the reality Mary had tried to hide from the children all those years—Sam had not wanted them. Not as much as a bottle. She never ever wanted her boys to feel that anguish.

"Your father didn't always feel well. He had problems that had nothing to do with you or me or Philip." She took in a sharp breath. *Forgive me, Lord, for this lie.* "Drunk is such an ugly word. It doesn't describe your father. He loved you and Philip. Never forget that."

A knot tightened in her stomach. Once again she hid behind the facade of her fictional perfect life. She should've faced the question head-on, but how could she hurt her son that way? How could she tell him that his family's love and their need for him hadn't been able to stop Sam from derailing like a runaway train?

The knot in her stomach swelled, creeping up her throat, choking her. She'd asked God for the words, the wisdom to help her son, but then she'd lied. No matter what she did these days, she failed to live up to her expectations, but now to fail God…

Unable to look her son in the eyes, she smoothed his collar. "You need to apologize to Jimmy. But I know one thing for sure, Michael. You're a kind boy, a good boy."

Tears ran down her son's cheeks and he sniffed. "I bloodied Jimmy's nose."

Mary wiped away his tears and then kissed the top of his head, holding him tight. "We all make mistakes. When we do, we need to say we're sorry. God understands, and He'll forgive." *Please forgive me, Lord.* "So will Jimmy. It'll be all right, Michael. Everything will be all right."

Wasn't that what she'd said a hundred times over the years of her marriage? Everything would be all right tomorrow, or the next day, or next week.

But it never had been.

Just when she thought she had control over her life, a strong plan for the future, something happened to dredge up the past. Her breath caught. Would covering the truth of that past with a lie make more trouble for her son?

Chapter Thirteen

Luke left the carriage house, heading around the block toward Mary's place. Doc had told him about Michael's fight. Luke couldn't get it out of his mind. For whatever reason, this childhood scuffle gnawed at him. Luke had to see the boy. To see if he could help in some way.

The youngster hadn't had a good day. Luke's hadn't been much better. Sloan was a good doctor, carried his share of the load and got along well with the patients. Mary had to notice his blond good looks and boyish charm. Not that she'd said as much, but Luke had eyes.

And so did Sloan. He lit up like a firecracker when Mary entered the room. Other than his dream of working at Johns Hopkins, Sloan was perfect. Not only as his replacement in the practice but as a husband for Mary, a woman who deserved the best. And as a father for her sons. One in particular. His.

So why did he want to punch the good doctor in the nose?

If only he were free to court Mary. But a secret the size of Gibraltar stood between them. A secret he couldn't confess. How had he gotten himself into this mess? Hadn't he learned anything from the lengths his parents had gone to to hide their treachery?

They'd put on the appearance of a perfect, well-dressed, well-mannered family, complete with drawn-on smiles. Those smiles hid their wretchedness—his parents' rejection of Joseph, whose seizures embarrassed them, and of Luke who'd dared to question their actions.

The result—he'd grown up with a perpetual knot of distaste in his stomach for deceit. And now he kept his fatherhood from Mary. Caught in a deception he had no idea how to extricate himself from. If he told her, he'd lose her good opinion.

He grimaced. Talk about deceiving himself. The fact was he'd never had Mary's approval. Not since the day they'd met. But for some unexplainable reason, he wanted her respect—and wanted it badly. Badly enough he couldn't move on. Something undone lay between them, drawing him to her again and again.

But more than his duplicity plagued him. He hadn't received a response to the wire he'd sent his parents. How like his father to ignore him. Thomas Jacobs loved to be in charge. And keep Luke off balance. They had nothing in common, and whatever meager affection they'd once felt for each other had shriveled and died.

He rounded the corner and approached Mary's house. The boys played in the backyard. Perhaps he could have a private word with her, try to ease the conflict between them.

Mary opened the door to his knock. His lungs caught on a breath and held. "Hello."

One glimpse of Mary, this petite woman who'd built a fortress around her heart as high as his, made him yearn to pull her into his arms. If only he could scale those walls…but he made no move toward her, would say none of what filled his mind. "Doc told me about Michael's fight. I thought I'd check on him…if that's okay."

Mary moved to close the door. "We're fine."

"Have we gone back to acting like strangers?"

"Isn't that what we are? Why put on a charade, Luke? Pretending our relationship might go somewhere."

Had she caught on to his pretense? The thought shook him, but as much as he wanted to deny her claim, he couldn't. They both played that game. He took a step closer, preventing her from shutting him out. "Might it? Go somewhere?"

Mary heaved a sigh. "Why bother? You've made it clear you're leaving. What's the point?"

This woman believed in everything he did not— home, hearth. He *should* turn around. Return to his apartment over the carriage house. Pack his belongings and head for New York.

But his feet stayed planted on her doorstep, every-thing attuned to her, a lure he couldn't resist. She in-trigued him, partly because of her commitment to the things he ran from. All things that, underneath his hard shell, he craved but didn't have. Logic took flight, and he found himself lost in her emerald eyes, inhaling the scent of her, thinking about staying—

"What are you doing to me?" he said, voice husky, even frenzied.

"Nothing," she said on a whisper.

"You have no idea how you affect me." He wanted to kiss her, to pull her into his arms and push everything between them aside. "Let me in."

He didn't mean into the house. By the look in her eyes, she grasped that as much as he did. Everything within Luke coiled tight. A heartbeat passed between them. She opened the door and Luke stepped inside, hoping somehow to find middle ground, a way to combine this blend of vinegar and bicarbonate, without an explosion that hurt them both.

Mary disappeared into her kitchen. Luke followed her to the doorway, taking in the table set for four and the aroma of a chicken. Her comfy kitchen filled him with longing for a real home.

"May I get you something to drink? Coffee?" she said, darting about like a robin in search of a worm.

"No, thanks."

Obviously, his presence made her nervous. Instead of pushing them under her table, he forced his feet back to the living room and sat on the sofa, a cozy spot, even with Mary pacing in the next room like a caged lioness.

She returned with a cup of coffee and sat across from him, on the edge of her seat, ignoring him by making a production of smoothing her skirt. A vision in blue and white, starched and proper, she was the epitome of a lady. His pulse galloped in his chest. Maybe if he got the focus off them, she'd stop being jittery and he'd stop reacting like a schoolboy at his first party. "Is Michael all right?"

"Yes. The fight was merely a school yard dispute. One boy saying something mean."

"I remember those days." Luke chuckled. "Boys get into scrapes now and again."

But Mary dipped her head, studying the dark brew between her palms. "I suppose."

Don't get involved, Jacobs. Don't wrap yourself in

this family any more than you already have. A doctor didn't care about what led to the punch, merely the result. But something about the way Mary avoided his gaze triggered an instinct in Luke. "This fight wasn't merely a childish scuffle, was it?"

Her head snapped up. "I can handle it."

"Letting me help shoulder the burden isn't a crime."

Shifting in her seat, she avoided his gaze. "I don't need your—"

"I know you don't," he interrupted. "But I'm here, so let me help."

She worried her lip, clearly debating the wisdom of telling him anything. And he couldn't blame her. He hadn't earned the right to be her confidante. But in those boys, he'd seen part of himself. Michael and Philip had lived without much of a father, tried hard to be brave, keeping their feelings tucked inside. Luke suspected that led to Philip's stomachaches and Michael's attempt to play the role of an adult. He understood these boys because he'd shared the same wobbly foundation. For as long as he stayed, he wanted to help, if he could.

At the same time, a voice inside him marveled at the irony of a man who never got involved sitting on Mary's sofa pressing to get drawn in. "Tell me," he said, gentler this time.

She put the cup and saucer on a nearby table and glanced through the kitchen to the backyard, checking on her sons. "One of Michael's friends accused his father of…" She swallowed. "…being a drunk."

What a painful thing for a boy to hear, especially from someone he trusted. No wonder Michael had lashed out. "I'm sorry. That had to upset him. Is he all right?"

"Physically, yes, but…" She rose, wrapping her arms around herself. "What his friend did to Michael isn't the worst," she said, her gaze filling with misery.

Luke crossed to her side, not touching her, simply offering his presence. "What do you mean?"

"When Michael asked for the truth, I lied." She looked away. "I couldn't tell him. I couldn't destroy that boy's feelings for his father."

Mary? *Lied?* The idea of her lying churned through him. She'd done it to protect her son. Would she perhaps understand why he'd kept silent about his relationship to Ben? No, he couldn't risk it. He couldn't budge the lie, a barrier of stone. "If one boy knows, the subject may not be dead."

Her gaze flew to him. "It's a chance I'll have to take."

"You're not doing Michael a favor by covering up the truth." How did he dare to give such advice when he did the same?

"This is my life, not yours. My life and my sons. I can't, I *won't,* tell them about Sam's drinking." She planted her hands on her hips. "Right or wrong, the decision is mine. I expect you to honor it."

"Your secrets are safe with me."

"I expect they will be," she shot back, "all the way to New York."

Her words stung, but then the truth often did. As she'd said, he would leave. And she'd be the one to remain, the one who'd raise her sons, the one who'd deal with the consequences of her choices. Not him.

"I'll go." He rose, turning on his heel, and strode toward the door. A sheet of paper fluttered from the tabletop to the floor. Luke reached for it, and noticed the words, Central College of Physicians and Surgeons and below that, Mary's name. And the first word in the letter. *Congratulations.*

Mixed emotions warred inside him. A surge of pride at her accomplishment crashed against a wave of concern for her sons, who'd soon have less of their mother's time. One of those sons was his.

Mary snatched the paper from his hands.

"They accepted you," he said.

Her mouth thinned, the mouth he'd kissed and wanted to kiss again, but he knew he never would. In a year, maybe two, Mary would join the practice and carry on the legacy her father began. Frank Sloan would remain while Mary attended school. Luke wasn't needed in the practice. He wasn't needed here. "That's quite an achievement."

She blinked, and her gaze softened. "Thank you. I, ah, expected disapproval."

How could he explain how proud he was? He hardly understood his reaction himself. "You'll be a wonderful doctor. I've seen how closely you watch procedures at the office, how often I find you reading a medical journal."

A blush rose to her cheeks. "I have a lot to learn."

"And a lot to experience. I'll never forget my first glimpse of a cadaver." He gave a lopsided grin. "I lost my lunch."

She laughed, not a robust laugh, but one telling Luke she'd handle whatever came. "I dread that."

"You'll get used to it and learn so much from examining the human body."

She leaned toward him, her eyes shining, sharing his love of medicine, bridging the gap between them.

"I've been studying the vascular system. The muscles, learning everything I can."

"The work is exciting."

"And challenging."

"In the beginning, I found classes overwhelming. Your life is busy now but nothing compared to the pressure of medical school. Why not wait until the boys are older? When they're more independent, less apt to feel abandoned?"

"Abandoned?" She took a step back. "You're not a parent."

His heart skipped a beat, hoping his face didn't reveal the truth.

She pointed a finger at him. "How do you know what my sons will feel?"

Luke wanted to shout that he'd felt abandoned as a child—that's how he knew, but then it occurred to him that his classmates hadn't reacted the same. The difference between them and him—their parents showed an interest in their sons' lives. They wrote, came to visit. His had not.

Perhaps Mary could handle medical school and parenting. She'd never hurt her sons on purpose, as his parents surely had.

She paced in front of him, clearly gathering up steam. "I love my sons. I'd never neglect them. You think I haven't thought this out and planned every step? While you, Luke Jacobs, don't stick to anything. So don't lecture me."

Even from two feet away, Luke could feel her tension. She was right. He hadn't stuck to one thing, to one place, to one person. For years he'd had no ties, no one in his life who truly mattered. Until now. "I know you wouldn't harm them. I keep putting the feelings I had as a child onto your sons. I'm the one with the problem. Not you."

The people he cared most about lived in this house, in this town. No matter how hard he'd tried to stay detached, he'd failed. The admission shook him. But caring didn't fix the brokenness separating him and Mary.

The back door opened, and Michael and Philip raced inside with Ben tagging along behind.

"Did you come to play with us?" Ben asked, giving Luke a hug around his legs and beaming up at him.

At Ben's sweet, innocent face, Luke's breath caught in his throat. If only he could lay claim to his son. He trailed a hand through the boy's hair. He wanted to say yes but didn't have the right. "I'm not staying."

Philip touched Luke's sleeve. "Hi."

Overcome by strong feelings of tenderness and protectiveness toward all three of these children, Luke could barely speak. "Hi, guys," he said, including Michael in his gaze.

Michael smiled. Luke took in the bruises on his face, nothing to be concerned about medically. Had the need to defend his father's reputation driven this gentle boy to fight? "You've got yourself the king of all shiners, there, Michael."

The boy nodded and then looked away, evidently unwilling to discuss the fight.

"Are you here for supper?" Philip asked.

At her outspoken son's hospitality, Mary's jaw dropped.

Luke thrust out a hand. "Oh, no. Your mother wasn't expecting me. The table's set for four."

"Can I put one more plate on the table? Please, Mom?" Philip said, pleading.

Mary looked trapped, caught between her son's eager invitation and him—a man she wanted gone. Sighing, she nodded toward Luke, then turned and walked into the kitchen.

Face shining, the boy bounced along after his mother. Luke heard the sound of a plate and glass being laid out. Michael joined his brother, and from the clang of metal, Mary's elder son added flatware.

Mary's nod hadn't been much of a summons, yet spending another evening alone held the appeal of Chinese torture. He couldn't resist the chance to be near Mary, near her sons.

Except the family wasn't his and never would be.

While Mary mashed the potatoes, he and the boys tromped outside. He tossed the baseball, and the boys took turns at bat, the four of them having a great time.

Mary called them in for dinner, prompting them to wash their hands. Odd, how such a simple request touched Luke, made him feel like he belonged.

That is, until Mary and her sons bowed their heads in prayer, reminding Luke that God must not condone the secret he kept.

Everyone dug into the food. But he didn't eat. Instead he looked at Mary, watched her lift the fork to her mouth, to her enticing lips, soft, pink. He remembered the moment he'd held her in his arms and kissed her. Nothing on this table, any table, compared to the taste of Mary's lips.

She met his gaze. Silent communication streaked between them, a message of man and woman, alone and lonely. A blush crept into her cheeks, and she dropped her eyes to her plate.

Obviously, a message she regretted.

Forcing himself to stop looking at her mouth, he tasted the creamy potatoes, tender roasted chicken, sweet corn and tangy home-canned applesauce, a feast. "Everything is delicious. Better than Mrs. Whitehall's cooking, and I ought to know. I have breakfast at her café every morning." On those evenings he couldn't abide the silence in his quarters, he ate dinner there too, but he didn't say that. He looked around him. "A restaurant isn't like this kitchen—homey."

"You can eat Mom's cooking every day, if—"

"Philip Earl Graves." His full name and one stern look silenced her son.

Pretending he hadn't understood Philip's intent, Luke cleared his throat and glanced to his left. "Your grandfather told me about the fight, Michael. I'm sure you and Jimmy will work it out."

Michael shrugged. "He's still mad. So am I."

"When the bruises fade, maybe the anger will too."

Michael toyed with his food.

A memory tugged at Luke. Maybe if he told the boy something Michael could relate to, he'd feel better. "I hit someone once." More than once, but he wouldn't say that.

His green eyes widened. "You got into a fight with a friend?"

"Worse than that. At about your age, I punched my nanny. Not very hard, but still I did, even though I knew better."

Philip took a swig of milk and then wiped his mouth with his sleeve. "What's a nanny?"

"A nanny lives in your house and takes care of you."

"Why? Did your mother die?"

A lump lodged in Luke's throat, and he shook his head, avoiding Mary's gaze. Why had he gotten into this?

Michael looked baffled. "Then why did a nanny live in your house?"

Luke had never been questioned by children before. These two would make dandy prosecutors. "Well, my mother had a busy life. You know, doing things. Anyway, the nanny wouldn't let me tell my parents good night."

Ben planted his chin on his folded hands. "How come?"

"They probably had company." He could still picture the elegant partygoers parading through the house. "Whatever reason I had for being upset, when we don't like what someone says, we should talk about it. You know, work it out."

"Instead of hitting." Michael sighed.

"I learned that the hard way." Luke grimaced.

Ben gasped. "Did you get a whippin'?"

"No, but besides apologizing to the nanny, I had to muck out the horses' stalls every day for a week."

Philip scrunched up his face. "Whew!"

Luke and Mary shared a smile.

"Our mom's never too busy to tell us good night," Philip said.

Without realizing it, Philip had gotten to the crux of the matter. Mary and Luke's parents were worlds apart. Not because of money, or status. His mother and father didn't understand love. Mary did. She was a wonderful mother and would never let anything make her sons feel abandoned.

Michael's eyes lit up. "Yeah, and our dad rode us to bed on his back."

Philip giggled. "I'd shout, 'Giddy up, horsey!'"

"Your father must have loved you very much."

Philip sighed. "We miss him."

The expressions of yearning on their faces told Luke they hungered to talk about Sam. The boys had one loving parent, but the one who'd died clearly left a large void, a void Luke related to.

Mary leapt to her feet, clearing the dishes.

Ben's lower lip protruded. "I wanna dad to talk about."

Luke's heart stopped, then started again. Sudden tears blurred his vision. Head down, he made a big production of smoothing the napkin on his lap. He wanted to take his son into his arms and tell him he not only had a dad but his father loved him with everything he possessed. His shoulders hunched against the compulsion to scoop up Ben, all three of these boys, but mind-numbing uncertainty kept him in his chair.

What could he do to give Ben happy memories of his own? "How about a walk?" Such a small thing hardly atoned for his inability to be a father, but wasn't it the small things he'd missed in his childhood?

"Can we, Mom? Please!" Philip pleaded.

Mary glanced out the window. "It'll be dark really soon."

Ben rose and tugged on Mary's skirt. "If you hold my hand, I won't be scared."

"Let's hurry." Michael almost knocked over his chair in his eagerness to go.

Waving a hand at the pile of dishes, the leftover food, Mary remained at the sink. "Go ahead. I'll stay and clean up the kitchen."

If only Mary could see this walk as a spontaneous, fun moment for the boys. He laid a hand on the stack of dirty dishes. "When we get back, I'll help. You know I'm experienced in that area."

A fleeting smile crossed Mary's lips. "All right."

The boys donned jackets and raced to the door. Soon he, Mary and the boys tramped outside, breathing in the cool night air. Beside them, the youngsters chattered about one thing or another. Mary held Ben's hand but remained largely silent. Nothing as simple as a stroll could dispel the obstacles between them, but he could enjoy the moment. Luke took Ben's other hand, cradling the soft palm with his own.

The lingering scent of burning leaves and the sounds of night whispered around them. Overhead, the hoot of an owl, the flapping of wings, and underfoot, the crunch of withered foliage. October ebbed. November loomed. The boys talked of bobbing for apples, drinking cider, eating pumpkin pie.

An unexpected ache spread through Luke. He'd never taken strolls with his family. Never found a woman he wanted to share these things with...until he met Mary. A lifetime ago, he and Joseph had shared the same camaraderie that existed between Mary's boys. These boys took their family for granted. Yet, missing their father, they had a gaping hole in their lives too.

If only Luke had the skills to be a father, but he had the same void in his life. He'd tried to fill it with work, with worthy goals. But nothing compared to feeling cherished.

No matter how much he fought the conclusion with logic, in the deepest part of him, Luke believed his parents' aloofness stemmed from an unknown lack in him. Perhaps if he'd been more lovable…

They looped back to Mary's house, cutting off Luke's dark thoughts. Whatever the cause, the past couldn't be undone.

Nor could the present. He wouldn't risk destroying Ben's wonderful life.

"There's the Big Dipper," Michael said, pointing at the sky, "and the Little Dipper. What is that?"

"That's Orion's Belt," Mary said directing Ben's gaze.

The next thing Luke knew, he lay on his back in the grass, a boy nestled on each side of him, with Mary leaning on her elbows next to Ben, drinking in the constellations. Sharing this moment, Luke's throat clogged with gratitude and with something more…something new…an overwhelming feeling he could only describe as tenderness. He cared for these people, for Mary, Michael, Philip and Ben. He'd never again delude himself that he could return to New York without leaving part of himself—the good part—behind.

"God hung all the stars in the sky. The sun and moon too," Mary said softly. "He made a beautiful world for us."

"The moon has a face. See, Mom!" Ben said, sitting up and stretching his arms as if trying to embrace it.

"Is it God's face?" Philip said.

"No, but we can pretend it is," Mary said. Luke heard the smile in her voice. "Because we know God loves us, and we're never out of His care." She kissed Ben on his upturned forehead.

Tears blurred Luke's vision. If only he could look after this family. *God, watch over these precious children. Take care of Mary.*

Mary rose and pulled Ben up behind her, insisting they needed to go back, breaking the spell. Once they reached the house, she oversaw getting the boys into bed while Luke tackled the dishes. After a while, she joined him at the sink, humming a tune. Before he knew it they sang several songs, ditties they'd known all their lives. Their voices meshed, and the gaiety eased the friction between them.

Mary dried the last dish. "Thanks for giving my sons peace about their father," she said. "And reminding them fighting isn't a solution."

"Maybe you and I need to remember that too."

Her hands stilled, the dish forgotten. "We aren't fighting, Luke. We're just on different paths. You're leaving, remember?"

The lie he lived put a chasm as deep as the Grand Canyon between them. Unlike these dishes, it was an issue that all the scrubbing in the world couldn't remove.

Chapter Fourteen

In the hour before Addie's shop opened, Mary sat across from her sister-in-law, enjoying a moment of peace.

Working with coarse thread, Addie attached a feather to the crown of a black velvet hat. "You look as miserable as Fannie when James won't do her bidding. What's wrong?"

Looking at Lily's sleeping face, Mary forced a smile, hoping the turned up corners of her mouth would pacify her sister-in-law. She loved Addie, enjoyed watching her create the beautiful hats sported by most ladies in town. But at the moment, Addie's probing gaze made her want to dash for the door. "What could be wrong when I'm holding my precious little niece?"

Addie laid down her needle and leaned toward Mary. "Are you falling in love with Luke?"

"Don't be silly!" Lily stirred and Mary lowered her voice. "We're…friends." Though of late, even their friendship was on shaky ground.

"Friends don't make a person look miserable. Or they shouldn't." Addie's eyes grew dreamy. "But oh, I remember the ups and downs of falling in love. Many a time the face reflected in my mirror appeared downright wretched, well, except when I looked like a daisy in the sun." Addie laughed. "So don't be so quick to deny the possibility. Have you seen him outside of the office?"

"He came by the house last night to check on Michael's eye and stayed for supper. Afterward we took the boys on a walk."

"Aha, you enjoy his company. I can see it in your eyes."

"Yes, when we aren't in opposition."

"It's good to share opinions."

Mary laughed. "You paint a pretty picture, Addie, but Luke's and my likeness aren't in your portraits."

Luke Jacobs kept her off-kilter. For a moment last night when they'd worked side by side in her kitchen singing softly, she'd again imagined what it would be like to have him for her husband. She gulped. How could she consider marriage to a man who was a mystery? For reasons she didn't understand, she couldn't share her suspicion with Addie that Luke hid something. Besides, she hadn't come here to talk about him.

"If I look unsettled, it's because I'm unsure of what to do." She laid a hand on Addie's wrist. "I got accepted."

"Accepted?"

"I told you I'd applied—"

"Oh! Accepted into medical school?"

Smiling at the joy on her sister-in-law's face, Mary nodded. "I start classes in January."

"Congratulations!" Addie dropped the hat and hurried over to give Mary a hug. "I knew you'd get in. You're bright. Why, you're practically a doctor already."

Careful not to disturb Lily, Mary gave her a one-armed hug in return. "I hope attending medical school won't harm the boys."

A baffled expression on her face, Addie returned to her chair. "That's nonsense. It's not like you'll leave them for weeks at a time. You'll be home every night."

A niggling of doubt slid through Mary. "Well, I will have lots of studying to do and occasionally I may have to stay overnight."

Addie picked up the hat she'd been working on. "Even so, you're not abandoning your children. Charles and I will help all we can."

"You have three children and work two jobs. I can't let you do that."

"Mary Graves, it's high time you allowed someone to assist *you* for a change."

"At least my father has Frank Sloan to help in the practice once classes start."

Addie's eyes lit. "Maybe two, if Luke is staying. Perhaps he's planning on settling down with a certain someone."

Mary rolled her eyes heavenward. Why couldn't Addie believe nothing of consequence existed between Mary and Luke? They clashed over too much. Luke Jacobs was opinionated and kept people at arm's length. Not the man for her.

So why did she feel so miserable? "Addie, my life is a mess. I've lost control of it."

"None of us have power over life's circumstances."

Yet Mary struggled daily to have that very thing. "I know, but so much has happened that concerns me. I feel like I have my fist stuffed into a hole torn in a dam. I can't stop the leak, can't fix whatever is wrong, and have no time to decipher what the problem is."

"Is Michael worrying you?" Addie said. "William told me about the fight he had with Jimmy Augsburger."

"Yes." Mary sighed. "And Philip still complains of stomachaches."

No matter what, Mary would make herself available to her sons. Help them deal with what troubled them. Another lump lodged in her stomach. With the rigors of school, would she be able to put them first? She'd prayed for guidance but didn't have insight. Yet. Or did she just not want to accept it? "With all the boys are going through, maybe going to medical school is selfish."

Addie waved off Mary's doubts. "Tell me why you want to be a doctor. Besides helping people—you're already doing that."

"Lots of reasons. For one, I want to continue my father's legacy."

"You've got plenty of time to do that."

"And I want to have something in my own right." She ran a finger along the silky edge of Lily's blanket. "Something I earned."

"That makes sense," Addie agreed. "I like the feeling of accomplishment I get from my business."

"Yes, and to never again be dependent on anyone—"

"Don't you mean dependent on a man?"

Mary shrugged. Sometimes she didn't understand herself. How could she explain all these conflicting emotions to Addie?

But Addie's question nagged at her. Perhaps fear of depending on others was at the root of her desire to attend medical school. Sam had let her down a hundred times. If she became a doctor, did she believe she could be, with God's help, her own pillar of strength?

Lily stirred, blinked and yawned, such a sweet, innocent little thing, totally dependent on her parents to meet her every need. Mary's sons might be years older, but they, too, depended on her and had problems she hadn't unraveled.

"Don't use becoming a doctor as an excuse to go through life alone," Addie said, tying off and then cutting the thread. "Marriage isn't losing your independence. Marriage is a partnership."

Mary's union had not been a partnership. Maybe with someone else…

A wave of loneliness crashed over her, taking her by surprise. God's plan for creation to go through life two by two gnawed at her midsection. If only she could find a trustworthy man, a man to share burdens, decisions and emergencies. A man who, by word and example, would train up a child in the way he should go. In many ways, a man like Luke, but Luke ran from commitment. He had no more interest in marrying than she did. He certainly hadn't jumped at Philip's proposal.

Frank was interested in her. From what Mary had seen, he was an uncomplicated man free of the issues plaguing Luke. Yes, and also without Luke's charm.

"I have my sons," she said softly, tucking a wisp of silken hair behind Lily's tiny shell-like ear.

"Children grow up. Faster than I want to admit." Addie's eyes glistened. "You're a passionate woman, Mary. Don't be afraid to fall in love, to marry again one day."

She couldn't take that chance, not with her sons' lives at stake. They were old enough now to see through an attempt to conceal trouble. She could no longer pretend all was well if their world crumpled. "I've learned the hard way that marriage isn't the panacea for happiness. I'm delighted for you and Charles. But I can't risk that kind of misery with another man."

"And you think if you're a doctor, you'll have the financial independence and the sense of accomplishment, of worth, to fulfill you?" Addie shook her head. "Nothing compares to a good marriage, Mary. I run this shop and write editorials for *The Ledger,* but none of that comes close to the joy and satisfaction of my husband and children." She smiled. "You've never known what it means to have a man love you above everything and everyone, except his God. I have that with Charles." Her face glowed with contentment. "I want you to have it too."

Mary looked away. Addie's happiness rubbed against her like coarse sandpaper. "The main reason I want to attend medical school has nothing to do with independence. I'll discover the latest advancements in medicine." She met Addie's gaze. "Maybe learn something to explain why a man drank, when he clearly wanted to stop."

Addie's eyes clouded. "Sam."

Tears pricked her eyes. "Sam hated himself for all of the times he let us down." Her lack of clemency squeezed against her lungs. "Oh, Addie, even after his death, instead of forgiving Sam, I kept on blaming him, keeping the wound of our marriage open and festering." She sighed. "I blame myself more for not seeing what lay ahead—before I married him, before it was too late."

"Don't censure yourself. In the beginning, Sam hid his compulsion to drink."

By concocting excuses to take patent medicine. Mary

swiped at her eyes. "But without Sam, I wouldn't have Michael and Philip, our two wonderful sons. I don't know what I'd do without them."

How often had Mary criticized Sam for drinking, for needing a crutch to handle his past, instead of turning to God for healing? Yet, she hadn't handled her birth parents' rejection. How could she blame Sam for not handling the beatings at the hand of the man who gave him life?

Lord, help me forgive. The anger and pain she'd carried all these years fell away. The time for blame had ended. A backbreaking heaviness lifted from her shoulders and a blessed sense of peace slid through her. "It's taken me far too long, but I finally see Sam did the best he could."

Addie rose and wrapped her arms around Mary's shoulders. "I admire you, more than I can say."

Tears filled her eyes. "Don't. I've been a bitter, unforgiving woman."

"That's not true. To forgive you have to heal first, and healing takes time. I know that from my own life, and I've seen it with Charles."

Thank You, Lord, for helping me to heal, to forgive. Thank You for forgiving me, for dying for me, for never letting me go through one single day alone.

"Now, about your boys," Addie said, as if sensing the need for a change in subject. "Try talking to them. Get their reaction to medical school." Addie met her gaze. "Maybe you should let your sons see what's going on behind that brave front of yours. Show your feelings."

Mary couldn't expose her sons to all she held inside. She needed to protect them, as a mother should, as she'd always done. Maybe one day…

Right now, other things concerned her. Like how her sons faired. "Luke claims Michael sees himself as the head of the house, trying to shoulder the responsibilities of a man."

Addie's face softened. "William behaved like a little old man when he first came to live with us. Chances are, Mary, your sons were aware of the tension in your house. My mother's unhappiness hurt me, not physically like Sam and Charles' father's beatings, but I still paid a price. If only Momma could have explained how the men in her life hurt her. I'd have understood her behavior, and maybe the admission would've brought us closer."

"Oh, Addie, are you saying my sons saw the trouble between Sam and me?"

"I don't know. But I'm certain of one thing. They're fortunate to have you for their mother. They feel loved, while I didn't. Talk with your boys. See if they'll speak frankly. Pray *with* them. Pray *for* them. Charles and I'll pray for all of you."

Mary nodded, determined to talk to Philip about his stomachaches and to Michael about taking on a role too big for him. But she couldn't risk revealing Sam's drinking, a subject better left closed. They were too young to understand. Besides, she couldn't bear for them to think ill of their father.

Mary kissed Lily's forehead and then handed the sleeping baby to her mother. "I'll talk to them. Thanks for listening."

On the way home, Mary realized that even with Addie's support, after talking with her, Mary felt adrift in a world where people walked two by two.

She thought back to yesterday with Luke…and wondered…was it possible to have what Addie spoke of? To have a marriage based on an alliance between a man and a woman, instead of living behind the facade of a happy family?

But then she reminded herself dreams could easily vanish, as hers had with Sam. This time, she'd be like Daniel with King Belshazzar and read the handwriting on the wall. In the case of Luke Jacobs, the writing was crystal clear.

Luke might hold an attraction for her, but he didn't hold any of the answers.

Mary entered the office, hung her coat on the hall tree by the front door and then went in search of her father. She found him in the surgery going through cabinets. "I'm here."

Henry smiled. "Did you have a good visit with Addie?"

"Yes. Lily's beautiful *and* sleeping through the night."

"In all my years of doctoring, I've never seen a more contented baby." Her father chuckled. "Well, except for a lusty protest upon her arrival."

"Where is everyone?"

"Luke's out on a house call. I think Frank's in the backroom. It's been a quiet morning."

"Glad you weren't swamped while I was socializing."

Her father put an arm around her. "With three doctors in the practice, there's no reason you can't take a break."

"You do know Luke is leaving, right, Daddy?"

"Well, he hasn't, now has he?"

Now that Frank had entered the practice, why *did*

Luke stay? Something unnamed inside her tightened, filling her with unease. "I don't understand that either."

Her father winked. "I think I do."

"What are you saying?"

"I have eyes. Luke's are on you, if you're within his line of vision."

Mary glanced into the hall to make sure she had privacy, then turned to her father. "I won't deny there's an attraction between us, but something else is there too." She bit her lip, trying to voice a vague, yet real sense of disquiet about Luke. "I think he's hiding something."

Her father's untamed brows rose. "Like what?"

"I don't know. I just feel it."

"Hmm. From what he said, he found the Lord fairly recently. If he doesn't fully comprehend the forgiveness of God, something in his past may be troubling him."

Could that explain why Luke talked about his difficult childhood, about his career, but glossed over years in between? "Maybe that's it." But guilt didn't explain why he stayed.

"I'll have a talk with him. Make it clear a believer's forgiven, no matter how troubled his past. When a man can't accept forgiveness, he usually hasn't forgiven himself."

That Luke might struggle with regrets as she did pressed against her heart. She might not want to care about this man, but she did. "If that's true, I hope you can help him." She gave him a kiss on the cheek. "I'll be at my desk."

Outside the backroom, she stopped. Frank sat at the table, sipping a cup of coffee and reading a medical journal. "Good morning."

The young doctor rose, beaming at her like the noonday sun. "Mary, join me for a cup of coffee during this lull."

She took in his smiling face, his eager posture. Frank was a good man, open, easy on the eyes, and he was clearly interested in her. He was everything any woman would want. So why didn't she feel a thing when he was near? Perhaps her lack of response was the most compelling reason for giving him a chance. Her attraction to Sam had clouded her judgment and made her rush into a marriage that had gone wrong. Perhaps if she spent more time with Frank... "Thanks, I will."

He grabbed the pot off the stove and filled a mug and then placed it on the table. He pulled out her chair and sat beside her, always the perfect gentleman. "I missed seeing your smiling face when I came in this morning."

"I stopped to see my sister-in-law."

"Oh, yes, Mrs. Graves. I met her at church. A lovely woman."

"Yes, she's more like a sister to me."

"I know the importance of family. I ought to, with four older siblings, all married, and fifteen nieces and nephews." He chuckled. "I'm a late-in-life baby. Sometimes I think my parents are still recovering from the shock."

Mary laughed. "I doubt that. I'm sure they're proud of you."

He grinned. "The whole bunch is busting buttons at having a doctor in the family. I come from hard-working, God-fearing farm folk. I worked on the farm for several years before deciding to enter medicine."

If Frank hadn't gone directly to college, he was probably about her age. Yet somehow he acted years younger, perhaps because he couldn't pass a mirror without combing his handsome head of hair. Well, he might be vain, but a man could have worse faults.

"That life made me who I am today. I'm not afraid of long hours, of doing without while I build my career." He smiled at her. "And I love kids."

Mary's stomach tightened. Frank spoke like a lawyer building his case. What was behind such eagerness?

He took a sip of coffee, studying her. "Tell me about you."

"I'm an only child who grew up under this very roof. As you already know, I'm a widow with three sons."

"And soon to be a doctor."

Her fingers tightened on the handle of the mug. "I hope I make it."

"You will. Any woman who can raise three children, work here and stay involved in the community like you do can handle medical school."

She smiled. "Thank you."

He tipped an imaginary hat. "Just stating the facts."

Sipping her coffee, Mary gazed into Frank's guileless blue eyes. Nothing about him suggested he had anything to conceal.

What a contrast to Luke.

"How about having dinner with me tonight?"

Her breath caught in her throat. Frank moved fast. But she really should give him a chance. Her sons wanted a father. He'd made it clear he loved children and family. Maybe in time, he'd grow on her. "After being away from the boys all day, I don't like to leave them at night. Would you care to join us for dinner instead?"

"Yes, I would. Very much."

"I live a stone's throw from here." She scribbled her

address on a pad of paper, tore it off and handed it to him. "We eat at six."

He took her hand and squeezed it. "Thank you, Mary. I look forward to it."

Luke appeared in the doorway. His gaze dropped to their entwined hands. Mary pulled hers away then chided herself for her reaction. If she wished, she could hold the hand of every man in town. "If you gentlemen will excuse me, I'd better get to work."

Luke frowned as Mary dashed by. He'd obviously interrupted a cozy moment between her and Frank. Isn't that what he wanted? So why did the sight of Sloan holding her hand bang against every nerve? He turned to go.

"May I speak to you a second?" Sloan asked.

Luke nodded, though at the moment he'd prefer conversing with a rattlesnake.

"I feel like I should ask. Is there anything between you and Mary?"

A connection Luke couldn't admit. A child they both loved. Luke shoved his response past clenched teeth. "No."

Sloan smiled. "Good. From the scowl on your face, I was afraid you'd staked a claim."

"Mary's not a piece of land up for grabs." Sloan chuckled, like Luke had made a joke, but he'd never been more serious. "You've mentioned a desire to be on staff at the best hospital in the country. You should know Mary loves this town. She wants to take over the practice one day, continuing her father's legacy."

Sloan's self-satisfied smile set Luke's teeth on edge. "A noble goal, but once Mary discovers a whole world's out there to explore, she may broaden her sights."

Remembering Mary's desire to travel, Luke cringed inwardly. Could she be persuaded to leave? To leave the people she cared about in this town, her father and the legacy she said she wanted to continue?

He hauled in a shaky breath. Perhaps with this dashing fellow she could leave it all behind and never look back.

"I'll have a chance to discuss it with her tonight. She's invited me to her house for dinner."

A muscle worked in Luke's jaw. He pried open his mouth and said, "If you're intending to court Mary, I hope you have permanence in mind."

"Permanence?"

He laid his palms on the table and leaned toward Sloan until they were nose to nose. "Yeah, like a ring on her left hand."

Frank slid his chair back. "It's a bit early for that discussion, but I will tell you this much, Doctor, I don't play games."

"Glad to hear it." With that lie fresh on his lips Luke left the room.

The Children's Aid Society had given him until the end of the month to claim Ben. He couldn't tear that child out of Mary's arms nor could he let Ben go. He cared about his son more than he'd ever imagined possible.

Yet he couldn't stomach the idea of staying and watching Sloan woo Mary.

But to stay, to fight for Mary, he'd have to tell her the truth about Ben. About his past. Once Mary learned he was Ben's father, and the circumstances surrounding his birth, she'd never forgive him. He'd made his bed.

No one had told him lying in it would be this painful.

Chapter Fifteen

In his room over the carriage house, Luke dropped onto his bed. Since the minute he'd arrived in this town, he'd lived a lie. Not in so many words but a lie nevertheless.

He'd done it to protect Ben.

How could he disrupt the boy's life when he had a good mother like Mary and two brothers who plainly adored him? Why rip him from the safe haven he knew? If Luke accepted his paternity, the Children's Aid Society had made it clear he'd be expected to raise him.

But he couldn't be a good father. He didn't even know what a good father was.

If only he knew that Mary could forgive him for his treatment of Lucy, for keeping his fatherhood secret, then perhaps he could stay, could share his feelings for her. Unlikely as it was, if she could find a way to return those feelings, perhaps they could marry and make a real home.

But that meant settling down. He didn't know how to forge a family.

What example did he have? Years at boarding schools

without one shred of interest from his parents, as a small
boy trying over and over again to please them, desper-
ate for one smidgen of approval and failing. Recurring
nightmares of Joseph, the brother Luke had loved un-
abashedly, being ripped from his arms. One scene after
another paraded through his mind, each incident filled
with rejection or pain. His fists knotted at his sides as
anger, guilt and loss galloped through him, eating at
his wounds.

Look where loving had gotten him.

Worse, if Mary could find it in her heart to forgive
and love him, he'd inevitably let her down. The only
thing he excelled at was his work. He thrived in the solitary existence of his lab. There he could make amends
for his failure to help his brother, for his failure to do
right by Lucy.

At some point, what if he got that itch to leave? Or
worse, turned out to be like his father? Harsh, disap-
proving, distant?

But whether he was prepared to be part of a family
or not, once Mary knew the truth, she'd never forgive
him. His heart panged in his chest. The best thing to
do was to leave town, leave Ben in Mary's care, a safe,
comfortable pocket of happiness.

At the prospect of never seeing Mary and the boys,
his throat tightened. It might kill him to go, but by leaving he'd be ensuring Ben had a good life.

Mary opened the door, welcoming Frank into her
home. He swept a black bowler from his head. Dressed
in a suit and tie, he made a handsome figure. "Let me
take your hat," she said, pleased he had the good sense

and decorum to wear one. She doubted Luke even owned a hat.

Her sons stood apart, watching with uncertain eyes. Frank ambled over to them, talking about the latest Cincinnati Reds game. The boys followed baseball, and their eyes shone with excitement. She left the room to finish preparations for dinner, certain her sons hadn't realized she'd gone. Obviously Frank's experience with his nieces and nephews stood him in good stead with her sons. Normally reticent with strangers, especially men, Michael and Philip took to Frank like fleas to a long-haired dog.

Or perhaps Luke's coming around had prepared them for Frank.

Too bad he'd ruined her for any other man.

Where had that come from? She didn't love Luke Jacobs. Barely trusted him, in fact. She'd do well to concentrate on Frank Sloan, exactly what she'd do for the rest of the evening.

Dinner went well. No spilled milk, no squabbles, no whining about the food. When they finished, Mary cleared the table, and the three boys and Frank played dominoes while Mary cleaned up in the kitchen. Frank didn't offer to help with the dishes but then she hadn't expected him to. Her father hadn't done domestic chores and neither had Sam.

Still, a whisper of disappointment ran through her. She couldn't help but compare Frank to Luke. To compare the entire night to one much like this a week ago. Water up to her wrists, she remembered Luke standing exactly in this spot, doing the same. Her heart twisted for a moment. She wished he was here with her now, with that grin of his and that twinkle in his eye.

Yet Luke held things back, didn't want permanence. Too much about Luke Jacobs warned her away.

So why couldn't she put him out of her mind?

Luke opened the door to the waiting room, ready to call back the next patient. Normally Mary took care of ushering people into the examining room, but when appointments ran late as they had today, she had to gather Ben and get home before Michael and Philip came in from school. Whenever Mary left the office, he had the weirdest sense of loss. He missed her. Badly.

A woman sat near the outer door holding a baby. According to the schedule, written in Mary's neat script, that had to be little Quincy Shriver and his mother. Across the way, a man stood in front of the window, his back to the room. The set of his shoulders, the way he held himself all pointed to one man. *Thomas Jacobs.* Everything within Luke froze.

His father turned to face him. "Hello, Luke."

"What are you doing here?"

"Not a very warm greeting for your flesh and blood."

The baby hiccupped, and his mother patted the infant's back, watching the exchange with unabashed interest.

"Dr. Lawrence is in the examining room, Mrs. Shriver," Luke said. "Why don't you and Quincy go on back?"

Once they were alone, Luke strode to where his father stood. Thomas's gaze roamed the room lined with battered Windsor chairs. The bouquet of asters and pictures of the boys on Mary's desk didn't disguise the simplicity of Doc's waiting room. "I can't understand how you could leave a prosperous practice—" his hand swept the space "—for this."

"Small-town practice may not be lucrative, but I find the work satisfying."

His father smirked. "Ah, you've always been the family philanthropist."

"I'll ask you again. Why are you here?"

"Your mother and I have come to meet our grandson."

His parents wanted to see Ben? The punch of his father's words whacked Luke low in his gut, stealing his breath. That his parents had come all this way to see their grandson was so improbable Luke couldn't have prepared for it in his wildest imaginings. What motive did they have?

"Your mother's resting at the Becker House," his father went on. "She found the trip fatiguing."

For a well-traveled woman, that hardly made sense. Was she leery of facing Luke after all the bitter words between them, afraid of his reaction? Whatever her reasons were for not accompanying his father didn't matter. What mattered was protecting his son. "Why do you want to see Ben?"

"I'd think that's obvious. We're his grandparents. We should be involved in his life." The uncomfortable expression on his father's face gave him away. Thomas knew how ludicrous the claim would sound to Luke.

"You didn't show the least interest when I told you about Ben's plight and my intention to track him down."

"Suffice it to say, we've had a tweak of conscience."

All the pain of the past, the images of Joseph, reared

up inside of him. Luke scowled. "That's kind of new for you, isn't it?"

Thomas didn't meet Luke's gaze. "I prefer seeing it as doing our duty."

Luke saw no reason to expose his son to his parents, people who didn't know the meaning of love, who'd carted off their younger son because of his imperfections.

His heart stuttered in his chest. If his parents saw Ben, they'd reveal Luke's identity and ruin Ben's life. He had to convince them to leave. "What if I told you Ben had epilepsy? How would you react to your grandson then?"

Dark, wounded eyes lifted to Luke's. "I'm very sorry to hear that, but that's all the more reason for us to help. We have the resources—"

"What? To put him in an institution? To do to my son what you did to Joseph?"

His father reached for Luke, but he stood too far away and grasped only air. "No!"

"Keep your voice down." Luke glanced toward the examining room. "I don't believe you."

Thomas waved toward the window. "How can you keep him in this podunk town, when in New York, he can have every advantage?"

Hot waves of fury rushed through Luke's veins. "The people Ben loves are here. I won't move him."

Thomas scowled. "As a doctor I'd think you'd want your son to receive the best care for his disease."

Luke sighed. "Ben doesn't have epilepsy."

His father's face crumpled. "So that statement was a test? Do you think so little of me?"

Luke didn't answer. Anything he said would only add fuel to the fire. "I won't let you see Ben." He walked to the window, gazing out at the street. "No one knows Ben's my son, and I insist on keeping it that way."

"You've been in this town for weeks and haven't claimed the boy?"

Luke whirled to face his father. "I won't uproot him like…"

They stared at one another for what felt like forever.

"Like we uprooted Joseph? Isn't that what you mean?" His father pointed a finger at Luke. "Aren't you the hypocrite? You hammer at us for sending Joseph away. Perhaps *you* need to take a long, hard look at what you're doing—denying your own child."

"By not claiming him, I'm saving him."

"That's not how I see it." His father's eyes glinted like flint. "I'll give you twenty-four hours to bring Ben to us. If you don't, in a town this size, it shouldn't be difficult to track him down." With that threat, his father strode out the door.

Luke's thoughts flitted to an image of Mary hugging the child close. A staggering weight the size of Texas dropped onto his shoulders. He hadn't spent much time talking to God since he'd arrived in town. If only God was listening.

Lord, I've made a mess of things. I've kept my identity secret, thinking it was best for everyone, but now, I see my actions are a sin of omission that could ruin Ben's life.

He had to tell Mary the truth before she got wind of it.

God, help her understand.

That would take a miracle.

* * *

Luke took in Mary's rosy cheeks, her green eyes brimming with joy, as she talked about her plan for medical school. This woman, beautiful inside and out, was a rare creature.

He turned to the window, watching the boys cavort in the backyard like puppies, happy and full of life. A normal family lived in this house. A family he'd never had but wanted with a desperation that left him shaken.

Mary saw Ben as a throwaway child, a child like herself. She'd never understand how he could turn his back on his unborn baby. What he must say would destroy the fragile threads of connection between him and Mary. If so, he deserved it, but his son didn't.

Please, God, don't let this harm Ben or Mary's boys.

Luke's eyes stung. His best intentions—all meant to ensure Ben was well cared for—had led his parents to Ben. He'd ruined everything.

"I told the boys about medical school."

"How did they react?"

"Michael and Philip thought it was funny that I'll be going to school like they do. None of the boys exhibited the least bit of concern." She smiled. "I've talked to Carrie Foley. She'll watch Ben while I go to classes, but come January, she won't be available on Wednesdays. I feel sure the Willowbys will love having Ben one day a week. It's all going to work out."

"I'm glad."

"You'll be happy to know I even said no to a request to   " She stopped and shot him an odd look. "What's wrong?"

Apprehension knotted at his throat, skittered down his spine. Would he be able to get the words out? He swallowed hard, fighting for composure, and then took Mary's hand in both of his, meeting her perplexed gaze. "I know you're expecting to receive Ben's guardianship papers." He shoved out the words. "They aren't going to arrive."

"What are you saying?"

He knew no other way to explain it but to tell her the hard truth. "I'm Ben's biological father."

The room stilled as if all the life had been sucked from it. Luke took a step closer, but Mary stumbled away from him.

"What?" Her face paled, oddly devoid of expression. "*You're* Ben's father? How is that possible?" She swayed on her feet. He reached for her, but she slapped at his hand, fending him off. "We've worked side by side, I've had you in my home, we've shared our thoughts and you've kept such a secret from me. *I trusted you*," she said, her voice rising. "Why didn't you tell me?"

"I wanted to protect Ben." He hadn't just been protecting Ben. He'd wanted to keep Mary's good opinion, but by waiting, by living this lie, he'd ensured she'd never forgive him.

"Don't you mean, protect your secrets? Isn't that what's happened since you came to town, Luke? You've kept one secret after another." She shoved out a hand. "You've lied to me!"

"Can't you see? Once I saw how happy Ben was, what a good mother you are, how much he loved Michael and Philip, I couldn't tell you. Couldn't risk ruining what Ben has here." He reached for her hand. "You of all people should understand why. He's happy, Mary. I couldn't tear him from that."

Her eyes misted. "If that's true, why are you telling me now?"

He sucked in a breath. "My parents are in town. They're insisting on seeing Ben."

"See him?" She lurched to the sofa and sank into it as if her legs gave way. "Or take him?" Tears filled her eyes. "If they're determined, with their money, you can't stop them."

"I won't let that happen. I promise."

"Why should I believe you?" she asked. Behind her the fire hissed, as if deriding him too.

He knew, before Mary opened her mouth, what question was coming. The one he hoped not to answer. The one that would reveal him to be a man without a heart, without the guts to do the job God had given him.

"After what you went through, how could you abandon your own child in an orphanage?"

The words hung in the air, caught in the ticking clock, the heavy silence between them. Luke examined his heart, searched his mind for an answer Mary would understand, but came up empty. What words could he offer to a woman who'd been abandoned as an infant that would ever justify his sin?

"I didn't know Ben was in an orphanage." Mistrust pooled in Mary's eyes. It was true—you reaped what you sowed, and he had sown a bad path in those years. "I barely knew Lucy, Ben's mother. When she told me she was pregnant, I didn't want to marry her, to hitch my life to someone who clearly was the wrong woman. And to raise a child when I..." His voice trailed off. "Lucy didn't want me either, but she did want money, so I took the easy way out. I paid her off, shutting that door to my past, or so I thought."

Mary's silence became his judge and jury. She stood as if seeing him for the first time, as if she again saw him as nothing but a peddler, here to steal the townspeople's money and their misguided trust.

He had to get the ugly truth out, all of it. "Ben's mother died from complications a few days after his birth. Without family to help her, she did the only thing she could do and placed the baby in an orphanage. I had no idea until—"

"Ben is your child, Luke! Your flesh and blood." Her gaze went to the portrait of Philip and Michael on the mantel. Her features softened with love. "How could anyone give away their child? Pay for him to go away?"

Tears stung his eyes. "I was a different man then, Mary. That's before I'd found God."

She turned away from the portrait, the warm fire blazing in the hearth, her face cold, erecting an icy wall between them. Luke shivered.

"Are you a different man, Luke? You lied to me. You lied to your own son. All to protect the life you have." Her eyes flared, and she pointed an accusing finger at him. "You wouldn't want to inconvenience yourself with a family, now would you?" she said, her words laced with scorn.

"You don't understand. I'm not the kind of man who should have a family."

"I'd begun to trust you." Her voice broke. "To care about you. You've broken that trust."

He reached for her, tried to take her hand. "I'm sorry."

Her eyes hardened like jade. "Sorry doesn't change what you've done."

"I promise I won't uproot Ben."

"I don't believe anything you say. Please leave."

With Mary's words slashing at him, Luke walked out. In many ways, having the truth out in the open was a relief. He no longer had to watch every word he said. He'd grown up keeping secrets, but could Mary be right? Did he possess the same cruelty as his parents, who'd shuffled off a son who was an inconvenience?

A sob escaped his throat. He didn't know himself at all.

But the bleak, aloof look in Mary's eyes left no doubt in his mind. Any feelings Mary had for him had died, along with her trust.

Luke left Mary's and strode to Doc's office, closed at this hour. Days ago he'd told Henry about Joseph, shared the years of regret over his brother's suffering. Henry had understood and joined Luke's quest for a medicine to control epilepsy. He'd taught Luke how to relate to patients. He'd pushed him to fight Sloan in his blatant campaign for Mary's affections. Doc had been Luke's champion.

And now he had to expose who he was to this man, who'd been like a father to him but who would surely despise him now. Still, he couldn't regret the existence of his precious son whose arrival on this earth should've been cause for celebration and wasn't.

Inside the office, he saw no sign of Sloan and heaved a sigh of relief. He found Doc in the surgery, cleaning instruments.

One look at Luke's face and Doc ushered him to a seat, then pulled a chair up beside him. "What's wrong?"

The words flowed out of Luke. He didn't gloss over

one horrid truth. When he'd finished, Doc sat unmoving. Luke waited for his censure.

At last Henry met Luke's gaze. "I thought something was bothering you but never imagined this. I'll admit it's thrown me." His normally mellow eyes bored into him. "How's Mary?"

"She's furious and frightened that my parents will take Ben. I'll never let that happen."

Doc's lips flattened. "You've hurt my daughter. I warned you about doing that."

Luke's gaze found the floor. "I'm sorry. I never meant to. But it's too late to mend things between us."

"Perhaps things aren't as dire as you believe."

Luke's throat clogged. "She ordered me out of her house."

"Mary's disillusioned with you for not taking responsibility for your son. And rightly so." Doc leaned toward him. "Your mistakes have impacted Ben. All of us."

Luke nodded, sucking in air filled with the scent of antiseptic and soap. If only he could be cleansed as easily as the instruments now drying across the way. Inside he felt dirty. Unworthy. Rotten to the core. "I wish I'd been a better man."

"So you found God after this?"

"Yes. But that cuts no ice with Mary. If I'd claimed Ben immediately, she might've found it in her heart to forgive me. But I didn't feel fit to be a father to Ben." He rubbed a hand over his eyes. "I still don't."

"Do you believe any man feels qualified for such a role? The day Susannah found Mary on our doorstep we were suddenly thrust into parenthood. Mary doesn't know this, but the timing wasn't good. I'd just opened my practice. We didn't have two nickels to rub together. God chose that uncertain time to give us our daughter." He leaned back in his chair and smiled. "It was exactly the right time. Still, I remember the sense of inadequacy."

"But even so, you took on the responsibility. I shirked it. Perhaps Mary is right. I see Ben as an inconvenience."

"Isn't it possible you're just scared? You've had no example of fatherhood. If you're looking for guidance, look at Jesus's life, at His relationship with His Heavenly Father and with His earthly parents. Everything you need is in the Bible." He rubbed his chin. "Give my daughter some time to think about this."

"You have wisdom, Doc, but no concept of Mary's anger. I've not only lost her trust, but I've lost her respect. I should've told her immediately."

Doc's brow furrowed. "I'm not sure about that." He spoke slowly like waiting for his mind to send each word. "What would that have done? Forced you to take Ben right then and there? You were a stranger. Ripping him from his family would've been horrible. Or perhaps you'd have told her but then left without getting to know your son. That would've been a loss for both of you."

Luke hadn't thought through the consequences of claiming Ben right off.

"Not that I'm making excuses for deceit, Luke. But knowing what I do about your brother, about your childhood, about your concern for Ben's health and welfare, I can see you were in a tough spot." He laid a hand on Luke's arm. "You and God need to have a long talk."

"I've asked God to forgive me for what I did to Lucy and my son, for not telling Mary the truth, but that won't fix this mess."

"No, but it fixes things between you and God. Never doubt He forgives a contrite heart. We humans find it difficult to forgive, not God." Doc tightened his grip on Luke's arm. "Right now things look bleak, but God has a way of bringing good out of bad. I'm praying for you, praying for my daughter and grandsons. Sometimes that's all we can do." Doc released his hold and gave a gentle smile. "God has a plan for our lives, even yours."

"What plan are you speaking of?"

"Why, the plan that brought you to Noblesville. You've told me about Joseph, how his death caused you to pursue medicine."

Luke frowned. "What does that have to do with my coming here?"

"Plenty. Joseph's suffering lit a fire in you. I suspect what happened to your brother made you look for Ben. You had to ensure Ben didn't wind up like Joseph. Am I right?"

Luke nodded.

"So, you came looking for Ben, peddling your remedy." Doc rose and plucked a bottle of Luke's remedy from the cabinet. "This has improved the quality of people's lives. You've become important to people in this town. To me. To Mary and the boys. All this happened because of Joseph."

Luke's gut knotted. "If that's God's plan, I've botched it. And I still haven't found a remedy for epilepsy."

"All in God's time."

The past couple of weeks Luke had pulled out the Bible in his nightstand drawer. He's read a great deal about God, learned more about His patience. His justice. His power. His love. Hope roiled through him. Could God work this out?

Doc placed the bottle on the table in front of him. "Your quest is honorable, Luke, but finding medicines isn't enough. Not for a man who loves God. Fight for what matters. Fight for your son. Fight for Mary. In doing so, you'll find your heart—and God's plan." He rested a hand for a moment on Luke's shoulder and then slipped out of the room.

Alone, Luke closed his eyes and leaned against the back of his chair. His throat knotted.

Could God bring good out of bad?

His gaze moved to the bottle. In his mind, he saw Mary opposing him that first day. As if she'd instinctively known he meant nothing but trouble in her life. In Ben's. Doubt coiled through him, weighed down his limbs until he couldn't move.

No matter what Doc had said, his medicine reminded Luke of failure. He'd found no cure for epilepsy. He didn't have the money to build a refuge for those afflicted with the disorder. And he'd let Mary down. He'd let down his son. Worst of all, he'd opened the door to his parents who were capable of anything.

He gave the bottle a shove, harder than he meant to. It toppled, sliding across the table and disappearing off the edge, hitting the floor, splattering liquid and shattered glass in every direction.

A mess. Exactly what he'd made of his life.

Mary sat in the back of Addie's shop while her sister-in-law brewed tea. Tears stung the back of her eyes, but she forced them away. Luke was leaving. She was sure of it. How right she'd been when she'd accused him of not being able to get involved. He didn't deserve her tears. He'd let her down, as Sam had.

The feelings she'd tamped down all her life, the pain of abandonment, throbbed anew in her. Something must exist in her, something ugly, detestable, that made the men she cared about discard her, either in the flesh, or inside a bottle. What difference did it make?

She'd learned her lesson, or so she'd thought, but apparently some lessons didn't stick.

No more.

She'd never, ever trust a man again.

How could she? Under her skirt Mary's foot jiggled up and down, resisting the urge to grab her sons and run as far from Luke Jacobs and his parents as she could get.

She'd prayed, trying with every particle of her being to release Ben's life to God, but fear kept its solid hold on her. Perhaps her sister-in-law could give her hope to cling to.

Addie set a steaming cup of tea in front of Mary. "William and Emma are upstairs. They'll be disappointed you didn't bring their cousins."

"I took the boys to the Foleys'. I can't stay long."

"I can tell you're upset. Has something happened between you and Luke?"

Tears filled Mary's eyes. "More than you can imagine."

"And none of it good."

A rubber band tightened around Mary's throat, tensing her neck muscles, shooting pain into her head. "Luke is… Ben's father."

Addie gasped then dropped into her chair, watching her intently. "How? Who?"

Mary clasped her hands tightly in her lap as she related the details. When she finished, Mary took a deep breath. An innocent little boy faced a horrifying prospect she'd never experienced and couldn't imagine, being ripped from the arms of those he knew and loved. Again. "Oh, Addie, Luke claims he won't take my precious boy." Her words ended on a sob. "But how can I trust him?"

"But the Children's Aid Society awarded you guardianship—"

Mary bit her lip to quell its trembling. "That was before Luke showed up, looking for his son."

"I can't imagine he'd take Ben from you."

"He says he won't, but he has a legal right to Ben. Worse, even if he doesn't claim Ben, his parents are in town and may fight for custody."

Addie's eyes filled with tears. "I'm so sorry."

"I haven't told the boys that Luke is Ben's father." She rubbed her temples. "At some point we'll have to tell him."

She took her sister-in-law's hand. Asking for help hadn't been her way, but when it came to her children... "Pray, Addie. Pray for my boy."

"I will. So will Charles."

"Ben will probably be thrilled Luke is his father until he realizes Luke plans to leave him behind. Or worse, take him to New York. Either way, it will break Ben's heart."

Please God, if it's Your will, let me keep my son. Her breath caught and tears flooded her eyes. She had to put Ben first. *Help me to want whatever is best for Ben.*

"If Luke says he won't take him, believe him. He wouldn't lie about something that important."

Mary jumped to her feet and paced the room. "His entire life has been a lie since the moment he drove into town."

"I'd hoped…" Addie choked back a sob. "I thought he loved you."

Mary laughed, the sound hollow and sad. "I've been such a fool, Addie. I fell for him. Fell hard."

Fell for another charmer.

Chapter Sixteen

Luke stood in Mary's living room, the tension so thick he could cut it with a scalpel, no, more like an ax. The sense of belonging he'd felt here had vanished. He'd probably never find it again, like dropping a rare coin into a churning sea.

The faint aroma of the evening meal lingered in the air, a meal he'd not been invited to share. In the hall, the ticking of the grandfather clock drummed at him, a relentless reminder that his parents cooled their heels at the Becker House. That in less than a week he had to make his decision about Ben.

If only he knew what would be best for his son.

He glanced at Mary. The glint in her eyes, her rigid posture and icy demeanor proved she merely tolerated his presence for Ben's sake. His gaze moved to his son. Ben looked innocent, happy and full of life, but in a matter of minutes, he and Mary would reveal Luke's fatherhood. How would his son react to hearing the truth? Would the admission of yet another secret add to Michael and Philip's problems? Dread settled in his limbs.

Lord, help us do this.

Mary sat on the couch, all three boys crowded in beside her, leaving not one inch of room between them. If the situation wasn't so serious, Luke would have enjoyed the boys' adoration of their mother. Steeling himself for what he must do, Luke forced his body into motion, pulling up a chair in front of them.

"We need to…talk," Mary began.

Michael sighed. "We've forgotten to do our chores. Right?"

"No, ah…what we have to tell you…" Luke swallowed hard, turning to Mary, seeking her help with words that would not come.

The troubled look in her eyes reflected his disquiet. With trembling hands, Mary cupped Ben's chin, meeting the boy's gaze. "Ben, I have something to tell you that's going to surprise you at first. Something about your father."

Ben's big brown eyes widened. "I don't have a dad."

Reaching across the space between them, Luke took Ben's smaller hand in his. "Actually, you do." All three boys stared at Luke as if he'd grown two heads. "I'm… your dad."

The words had been hard to say, had torn at him, reminding him of how much he'd failed this boy. But now that Luke had said them, he wanted to keep saying them. *I'm Ben's dad. Ben's dad.*

"But dads live with kids."

Mary cringed, her eyes bleak. She probably worried Luke would do that very thing. Why must this put him and Mary at odds? They both loved Ben.

The backs of Luke's eyes stung. "Most of the time they do, but not always."

Ben screwed up his face in thought, struggling to understand Luke's claim. "You're my dad?"

Luke nodded.

A smile took over Ben's face, and he leapt from the sofa onto Luke's lap, throwing his arms around Luke's neck. "You're my dad!" He turned to Michael and Philip, who watched with wide, startled eyes. "Luke's my dad!"

Michael frowned, his dumbfounded expression twisting into one of resentment. Philip stared at Luke with accusing eyes. Was he remembering the time he'd asked Luke to marry his mother?

Ben leaned back, gazing up at Luke, eyes shining with adoration. Then his brow furrowed and he cupped his hands around Luke's jaw. "You didn't tell me. How come?"

Mary's gaze drilled into him, striking every nerve. A lump rose in his throat. How could he explain his past to a child? "I should've told you sooner. I didn't mean to hurt you, any of you," he said, more to Mary than to Ben. "I heard you were in an orphanage and had been sent out here on the train." Luke stroked Ben's hair. "I came to find you, but when I saw you were happy, I didn't want to ruin the family you have with Mary and Philip and Michael."

Pulling away from Luke, Ben raced to Mary and buried his face in her lap. "I don't want to leave my mom," he said, his words muffled in the folds of her skirt, but plain enough to stab at Luke's heart.

Michael jerked to his feet and pivoted to his mother. "You said Ben would always live with us. You lied!"

"I didn't tell a lie, Michael. Ben will always be—"

"I won't take Ben from you." Luke met Mary's eyes

now brimming with tears. "In a few days, I'll be going back to New York."

Ben whirled toward him, his face crumpling. "You don't want to live with me?"

Tears slid down Michael's cheeks. "Everybody lies in this family." He swatted a hand at Mary. "You lied about Ben, and you said my father was a good man and he wasn't."

Before Mary could react, Michael darted out the back door, slamming it behind him.

Mary started to rise when beside her Philip groaned, clutching his belly. "My stomach hurts." She reached for him, but he shrugged away and trudged down the hall toward his bedroom.

Ben wheezed and huddled beside Mary, her face ashen, his head buried in her lap. She met Luke's gaze, her eyes hard and cold. What had he done to this family?

"I'll get his medicine." Mary handed Ben to Luke and hurried to the kitchen.

Hugging Ben close, Luke moved to the sofa, then sat the boy on his lap, cradling the wheezing child in his arms. "Don't be frightened, Ben. I'd never take you away from your mother and brothers." Luke sought words to comfort his son, to calm his fears and ease his breathing. "Everything will be all right. I'll visit you. And when you're older maybe you can come to New York to see me."

The hollowness of his assurances stung at the back of Luke's eyes.

Mary returned. "I've put a kettle of eucalyptus water on the stove. It's already starting to boil."

"The steam will ease your breathing, Ben." Luke glanced at Mary. "Do you need me to help?"

"Don't you think you've done enough?"

Her meaning was clear. Luke handed Ben to Mary, took one last look at the two of them and then strode out the door. Inside he felt dry, hollow, a shell of a man. He'd thought nothing would ever hurt him as much as watching Joseph die. But to watch a family disintegrate in front of his eyes hurt far worse.

Because this time the fault of the demise lay at his feet. And his alone.

He wasn't a man who could be trusted with such a monumental job as parenting. Luke knew, oh, he surely knew how easily that job could go awry. How a child could pay the price for a father's mistakes.

He refused to let that happen to Ben. Even as walking away tore a hole in his heart so large and so jagged, he knew it would never heal.

He loved the boy, loved him more than life itself. Fierce longing for Ben, for Mary and her sons knifed through him. But he couldn't be their father or Mary's husband. He'd leave that job to Sloan.

With Frank, they'd have a safe, comfortable life. He must do all he could to see that Mary had happiness, the life she deserved.

Ben's breathing had stabilized, and he slept peacefully. With her older boys preparing for bed, Mary slid off the sofa to her knees, propping her elbows on the cushion, gripping her hands in supplication. "God, I entrust all those I love, my very life to You." She took a deep, cleansing breath. "Give me the words to talk to my hurting sons."

Philip's most recent stomachache undoubtedly stemmed from his world once again shifting beneath his feet. If only she knew what other worries beset her son.

Luke had been right. Anxiety caused her son's stomachaches. She couldn't continue to coddle Philip and ignore what made him sick. Nor could she deny Sam's compulsive drinking and allow Michael to face accusations on his own. If she hoped to help her sons, she must talk to them.

She'd learned her lesson in the last two days. Keeping secrets only meant they'd leap out at the worst possible moment and hurt the people you loved most. The days of avoiding tough problems had ended.

The boys tramped into the room wearing their pajamas. Perhaps under the night sky, they would feel God's presence more clearly. Mary suggested they don jackets and head to the back porch. Outside, the wind had kicked up, and dark clouds scuttled across the sky. In the distance, a storm was brewing. Odd for October but somehow fitting with the turmoil inside her.

Mary plopped onto the steps. Philip cuddled beside her, but Michael scooted as far away as the support post allowed.

She kissed Philip's forehead, close to his cowlick, inhaling the soapy fresh scent of his skin. She'd given him a dose of Luke's medicine earlier. "How are you feeling, sweetheart?"

"I wish Luke was my dad too." Philip's sorrowful tone banged against Mary's heart.

"What difference does it make? He's going to leave," Michael said, his eyes accusing.

"Luke cares about you and Michael. It'll all be fine. Just wait and see." If only she believed what she'd said.

Maybe she should put off this discussion until her sons had time to adjust to Luke being Ben's father.

Coward. No, she had to act.

"You know, Philip, you've had stomachaches a long time…ever since your father died." She gave him a squeeze. "I want to help."

Philip's gaze found the wooden planks of the porch floor. His hands twisted in his lap. Mary ran her fingers through her son's silky hair. "You don't have an illness, but something is making your stomach hurt. Maybe if we talk, we'll understand what's bothering you." Philip leaned into her, avoiding her suggestion. Mary bit back a sigh and looked at her other hurting son.

Elbows on his drawn-up knees, chin resting in his hands, Michael stared into the darkness beyond. Even in the soft light from the kitchen window, he looked glum.

"How are things with you and Jimmy, Michael?" Mary asked softly.

"Jimmy still says Daddy was a…" He stopped, most likely unwilling to speak the word in front of his brother.

"It's okay. You can say the word here with your family." She tilted Michael's chin with her fingertips. "How are you handling what Jimmy says?"

Michael sighed. "I can't keep hitting him."

"No, hitting doesn't solve a thing." Did the boys remember Sam's drinking? Had she deceived herself about their innocence? Her heart squeezed. Children were perceptive, even small children.

Mary reached out and gathered her elder son close, wrapping his narrow frame in the circle of an arm. This time he didn't resist. "It's true. Your father…" She took a deep breath. "…drank…a lot."

Turning to her with condemning eyes, Michael jerked away. "I knew you lied."

Mary's hands turned icy. "I thought you weren't old enough to understand, but I was wrong and I'm sorry." She looked first at Michael, then at Philip. "Do you think you're both old enough to talk about this?"

They nodded—their expressions solemn, looking at her, hanging on to her words.

"You're right. I haven't been honest with you. I'm very sorry about that." She took a deep breath. "God wants me to tell the truth, and I want that too. But honesty isn't always easy, especially when the truth is hard to hear."

Mary's own words stabbed at her self-righteous condemnation of Luke. She'd railed at him for living a lie when she'd done the same for most of her adult life. But her boys needed her now. Thoughts about what to do about Luke would have to wait.

Michael's face twisted, struggling not to cry. "Why was Daddy a drunk?"

Not wanting to speak the words, she bit her lip, but say them she must. "Daddy was trying to forget," she said, barely able to push them past her clogged throat.

A puzzled look came over Philip's face. "Forget what?"

"His childhood."

Philip's mouth gaped. Mary knew her son had no idea a home could be a scary place. How much should she tell them?

Lord, give me wisdom. Give me the words.

No need to tell these sweet boys their grandfather, Adam Graves, hit and kicked and threw his wife and two sons against walls, breaking their bones, leaving them with gashes and bruises, evidence of abuse no one questioned. "Daddy's father wasn't a nice man." *Please, Lord, don't let this knowledge damage my sons.* "He hurt Daddy, not only on the outside but on the inside too, deep in his heart and soul."

She pushed back the hair dipping over her son's forehead. Michael's bruises from his fight with Jimmy had faded. She mustn't say anything to justify Sam's drinking. To do so might lead her sons to find answers for tough situations in the bottom of a glass.

Nor had her attempt to do it all, to give her all, hiding behind a facade of perfection, solved anything in her life. She'd buried herself alive in good works, in causes, covering up the root of her problem—a sense of failure.

She'd failed Sam.

Yet her sons had not. She must make them see they'd had no part in their father's behavior. She looked into Michael's eyes. "The important thing you and Philip need to know is none of Daddy's drinking was your fault. You didn't cause it. You couldn't have stopped it. You are wonderful sons, and I'm proud of who you are, so very proud. Your dad had problems, but he was proud of you too." She kissed their furrowed brows. "And he loved you both very, very much."

A sob escaped Michael's throat. "I loved him."

"Me too," Philip said.

Mary smiled. "Never stop loving your father's memory, precious boys."

Philip sighed. "Why can't Luke be our dad?"

The sky lit with a bolt of lightning. A few moments later, thunder answered. How should she respond to Philip's question? Why had Luke come into their life?

How could she sort this out for her sons when she didn't understand it herself?

"Ben's scared Luke will take him away from us," Michael said.

What assurance could she give when she feared the same?

"I'm scared...you'll die," a small voice said beside her.

Mary's stomach lurched. Was this the cause of Philip's stomachaches? The fear he'd lose her as he had his father? She'd not allow this to fester. "I'm not going anywhere, sweet boy," she said, running a finger down Philip's nose, tapping the tip playfully.

Giggling, the tension in Philip's shoulders eased, and he tucked himself closer to her side.

"What about Ben?" Michael said.

She kissed the top of Michael's head. "Luke promised he won't take Ben away, and I believe him."

"You do?" Philip said.

A deep certainty filled Mary. Luke would never hurt these children. If only she knew his parents wouldn't claim Ben. "Yes, I do. I'm positive." She took a deep breath. "I want you boys to know there'll be scary times in life. God is with us during those times, even when nothing is truly scary except our thoughts. Talk to me when you're frightened. And talk to God. He'll help you."

Michael touched her hand. "Will God stop bad things from happening?"

"The Bible says we'll all have troubles in this life. But we don't go through those problems alone. God loves us. He's merciful. He will give us strength and a way out."

Though she doubted they fully comprehended what she'd said, they nodded. Their expressions were solemn, tranquil. She gathered them closer, holding them tight, hoping they'd found a way to handle their worries.

Soon her sons chattered about school, leaving Mary to her thoughts. She prayed the floodgates had opened and she and her sons could talk openly and honestly. No hiding. From the calm way they accepted the truth, she sensed God had given them His peace. When the time felt right, she'd share her own adoption. She'd dropped the curtain. What lay underneath hadn't been as hard on her sons as she'd feared.

Tonight was a new beginning. She didn't know where the road ahead would lead. Or who would walk with them on that path. But it was enough to know God did.

A sudden downpour was Luke's only companion as he walked the streets, debating the wisdom of returning to New York. He thrust the collar up, trying to slow the rain coursing down his neck, and replayed his parents' insistence that he take custody of Ben, that the responsibility to rear his son was his, not some stranger's. As if Ben, Mary and her boys weren't knitted together like a well-made afghan.

In his mind, he saw the hurt in the boys' eyes. What had transpired after he'd left Mary's? Had the steam treatments eased Ben's asthma? Had Mary given Philip a dose of his medicine? How had she dealt with Michael's anger?

He knew only one way to find out.

With an occasional streetlamp and flashes of lightning to guide him, Luke marched toward Mary's. A huge gust of wind slammed into him, lifting the hair plastered to his head. He pushed on, fighting for each step, fighting his parents' words warring inside him.

Though he had huge qualms about his ability to be a father, intellectually he agreed the responsibility for Ben rested with him. To do his duty by Ben meant taking his son out of Mary's home.

If he took Ben to New York like his parents wanted, he'd destroy Mary and her sons. Ben, too.

If he left town, leaving his son behind, he'd hurt Ben. And himself.

If he stayed in town to be close to Ben, his presence would be a roadblock to Mary's chance at happiness with Sloan.

Lord, give me wisdom. I don't know what to do.

Without the energy to prepare for bed, Mary sat in her living room, her Bible in her lap. After a story and prayer, her sons had nestled under the covers without complaint. All three boys slept peacefully. Outside, rain beat against the windows and the wind howled, matching the storm raging within her. Tired or not, Mary doubted she'd get a moment's rest with the image of Ben, torn between his allegiance to her and his desire for a father, for Luke, stuck in her mind.

Soon, Luke would walk out of their lives. Tears found their familiar path down her cheeks. Her poor boys. First losing Sam, now Luke.

Well, they'd cope. For her sons' sakes, so would she.

She'd done it before. But this time would be harder. Because foolishly, this time, without realizing it, she'd clung to the hope until the bitter end.

Lord, You know our every need. Give us Your peace and comfort.

God would see them through. Hadn't He already? After everything they'd heard and seen that night, Ben's breathing had eased. Philip hadn't needed another dose of medicine for his stomach. Perhaps he'd put his trust in God, as she had.

In the pages of her Bible, she found verse after verse commanding her to forgive. She'd accused Luke of lying, but hadn't her entire life been a lie? Luke had kept silent to protect Ben as she'd done for Sam. She lifted her face heavenward. *Lord, I've accused Luke of lying when I've done the same. Help me to find the words to ask his forgiveness.*

She had forgiven his omission, but she didn't believe Luke was a man who could settle down. Who could ever put her and the boys ahead of the thing he did best—running.

Luke needed to change, to get over his fear of being a father.

Perhaps if he did—

A knock brought her to her feet. Who could that be at this time of night?

She swiped at her eyes with both hands, then fighting the wind, opened the door.

Luke stood on the other side, his jacket drenched, his face carved with remorse. Seeing him filled her with weak-kneed yearning yet profound wariness. Her conflicting feelings about Luke churned in her stomach. She took a step back. Why had he come?

"Mary," he said, her name half whisper, half groan.

She resisted the urge to take him in her arms. Instead she reached for his coat. He shrugged out of it, then brushed past her, awakening every cell in her body. She wanted his touch, wanted his arms around her. Wanted him.

The knowledge sliced through her. No, she wouldn't love Luke Jacobs, a man she might be able to forgive, but a man she could never trust. Still she knew what he'd endured as a child and couldn't turn her back on him.

"Are the boys all right?"

Mary nodded. "They're asleep." She took a deep breath. "I'm sorry for lashing out at you earlier. For judging you. That was wrong."

"Can you forgive me for what I've done?"

She gave him a weak smile. "I'm working on it."

His gaze roamed her face. "I've been worried about you," he said softly. "I took a walk and saw your light."

A walk in this weather? "As you can see, I'm fine."

"You don't look fine."

Mary didn't want to admit her weariness, but a sudden need to sit down sent her toward the sofa. With gentle hands, Luke turned her around to face him. He had solidness she yearned to lean on, strength she needed, but she held herself erect. "Why are you here?"

He ran a palm along her jaw. "I won't let you push me away like there's nothing between us."

She took a step back. "What exactly is between us, Luke?" she said, her voice quaking. "Except a little boy we both love and a tower of distrust."

His eyes, the gaunt paleness of his face, revealed his anguish. "You think that doesn't haunt me?"

Mary crossed to the living room window, seeing her contorted features in the rain-streaked glass, a weeping face, or so it appeared. But she'd wept bucketsful and had no more tears.

"Don't shut me out."

"I can't risk caring for another whirlwind of a man whose charm knocks me off my feet, only to discover he's running from his past. No, you're not hiding inside a bottle, like Sam, but hiding nevertheless—in a lab, behind a quest, whatever excuse you use, the result is the same."

He laid a hand on her arm. "I care about you. You must believe that."

She shook her head, feeling those stubborn tears brimming to the surface, refusing to shed them. Refusing to let him know how much he affected her. Refusing to admit when he left, she'd lose part of herself. "If you're truly leaving Ben here with me, you can go now. Back to New York." She wheeled on him. "Unencumbered."

As if her words were a slap, his face flashed three shades of red. "Can you tell me that isn't what you want too?" He took a step forward, closing the gap between them, invading the air she breathed. "Isn't it easier this way, for both of us?"

When it came to men, she had held herself apart, tried to stay detached. Since Sam. To get involved meant taking a risk. Leaping into uncharted waters. Mary had experienced the sharp rocks looming beneath that water. She couldn't let down her guard. Especially not with this man. Better to step away.

Sudden insight pressed on her lungs. She and Luke were very much alike—two hurting people unable to give their hearts. Luke had grown up in a cold, pitiless family. She'd lived with a man who'd disappointed her time and again, until she couldn't be hurt anymore. Or so she'd thought until Luke had arrived in town, peddling his remedy and his charm.

He took her hand. "You're afraid, exactly as I am."

Had he read her thoughts? "And why shouldn't I be?

My marriage wasn't happy. Sam couldn't put his family before…" Her voice faltered. "…a bottle. I put up a wall." She gave a weak smile. "Much like yours."

He tried to pull her into his arms, but she pulled away, took a step back. "You need to hear this." She sighed. "You think I'm a saint. Well, I'm not."

He raised a hand, as if to draw her near. She shook her head. "The truth is, it wasn't just Sam's fault," she said, the words escaping one at a time. "He had a horrific childhood. A frightful father. He drank to forget. And when he needed me most, I… I failed him."

"How can you say that? Sam failed you, failed his family."

Mary turned back to the window, watching the river of rain chase a path down the panes. "In the beginning, I tried to stop Sam's drinking. Countless times I begged him. I fought with him. I tried everything. And I prayed. I prayed for God to give Sam wisdom, to give me strength. For some kind of answer that would banish his insatiable thirst for alcohol. Yet nothing changed." She traced the path of the rain, her finger smudging the glass, her heart heavy. The admissions kept inside too long now slipped out one at a time. Like stones dropping into a quarry, they echoed through her. "After a while, I stopped."

"Stopped?"

Behind her, Luke's voice softened. His touch warmed her shoulders. But she couldn't face him. "I stopped trying to get him to wake up and see what a gift he had in his sons—" Her voice caught on a sob. "Don't you see? I wearied of carrying him. And so I stood by and did nothing. And he—" the words now a rushing river, tumbling over themselves to escape "—kept going to the saloon, kept drinking, kept leaving us. Until the night he left us forever." She whipped around to face him. "I failed my husband by letting go, by distancing my heart from him."

Luke tugged her close. "You can't blame yourself for Sam's bad choices. I of all people know a man's accountable for his decisions."

She shook her head, refusing Luke's reasoning, refusing his embrace. "I let Sam go, and it's the biggest regret of my life. If I'd talked to him one more time, just one more time, then he might've stayed home. Put down that bottle and   "

"Most likely he wouldn't have."

"Don't you see, I'll never know." She couldn't go through this with another wounded man.

She took a fortifying breath, determined to say it all. "The worst of it is, after the shock of learning about Sam's death, do you know what I felt?"

He didn't answer, merely looked deep into her eyes, his own gentle, sad and guarded, like he dreaded her next words.

"I felt *relieved*. Relieved my husband, the father of my sons, was dead. Relieved I'd never again have to hide the truth of his drinking. Never again have to make excuses for his whereabouts. Never again hide my disappointment that the charming, witty man I married had become a stumbling drunk." She sobbed and shoved against him. "So, don't tell me I didn't fail my husband."

"Mary, do you think I wasn't relieved when Joseph drew his last ragged breath? To watch someone you love die, either imminently or by the inch, hurts. It's natural to want to feel free of the burden…and natural to feel guilt about that too."

His words settled over her, soothing her spirit, a balm to the wound that had never healed. Yet his comfort didn't change the truth. "Maybe so, but the fact is, I let my husband down when he needed me most. I'll never get over failing Sam."

Sorrow skidded across Luke's face. "We all have regrets."

"You will too, if you go to New York. You need to change, to behave like a father."

Pain stark on his face, he shook his head. "I let that boy down before he was even born," he said softly. "I don't know how."

"Don't know or don't want the inconvenience?"

"I love Ben."

"If you love him, then you'll put his well-being before your own. See he feels wanted, loved. Do all the countless things a parent does—help with homework, supervise baths, see that he eats right, teach him to tie his shoes, give him chores, nurse him through sickness. Play games with him, teach him God's Word, the right way to live in this world. Most of all pray for him. Daily. Even when he's grown, never stop praying, never stop caring. The job never ends."

No matter how much she wanted Ben with her, she owed it to the child to give him a father. She must step away and offer Luke his son. She dreaded his answer, but she had to do what was best for a four-year-old boy who wanted a dad. "Ben is your son. He's your responsibility. You must stay and be his father. He needs you."

Luke's troubled eyes met hers. "Do you believe I can rewrite history, Mary? Be a better father than my own?"

"That you want to try says a great deal."

"Ben deserves a dad."

"And you deserve a son," Mary said.

With one fleeting indecipherable look, Luke grabbed his coat and stepped into the growing storm. The rain formed a wall between them, cutting off the sight of him before the door finished closing.

Chapter Seventeen

Luke dashed around the block. By the time he reached the carriage house, he was soaked to the skin. For some reason, he passed by, heading to Doc's office. He entered through the back door, wiping his feet as best he could, and then meandered through the waiting room. His gaze lingered on Mary's desk, the vase of flowers—a reminder of Mary's capacity to brighten a room and a life.

Inside the surgery, he stumbled to the window, staring at the flashing sky, his composure as jagged as the streaks of lightning brightening the night, lighting up the guilt inside him. The anguish in Mary's eyes when she'd offered him her son twisted in his stomach, knotted in his throat. This remarkable woman had insisted, all but demanded, he take responsibility for Ben.

Luke wanted that too. Badly. He'd try to give Ben everything he'd needed his parents to give him. Without a doubt Mary and Henry would help him if he got in over his head. He hoped no one, not Mary, not her boys would be hurt in the transition.

He turned from the window, letting his gaze roam

the room. Why had he come here to this office? Had he hoped Henry would be up and they could talk? But no sound came from Doc's quarters. Luke wouldn't waken him.

Turning to go, his gaze swept the enormous breakfront filled with medicine. Something stopped him, made him open the glass door. Finding what he sought, Luke clutched his remedy and then walked to the table, dropped into a chair and set the bottle in front of him. Doc had said the contents of this bottle mattered. Had been part of God's plan.

Joseph's suffering had led him to find this medicine, to dedicate his life to healing. God had used this remedy to bring Mary, Doc and the boys into his life. The liquid caught the light from above, glistened with a shimmer of gold. An unbroken bottle, unblemished and shining like a new start. Or so he saw it now.

He turned the bottle around and around and in the blurred glass he saw his image, then a glimpse of Joseph near death, his face at peace, his eyes glowing as if a light had filled him, as if he'd seen God himself. His brother's eyes closed, his last breath slipped from his lips, and his pain ended.

With a certainty he couldn't explain, Luke knew His Heavenly Father had spared Joseph more suffering by taking him home. God had not only been there with Joseph but God was here now. With Luke.

And Luke knew without a doubt that God loved him. *Lord, help me to follow Your plan for my life.*

God and family mattered most. Nothing else would ever usurp their rightful place in his life. Not his dream of finding a cure for epilepsy. Not his desire to build a safe haven for its sufferers. Those might come, but they wouldn't be his priorities.

"Forgive me, Lord, for using my goals as an excuse to avoid loving others," he whispered to the room that no longer felt empty. No matter how many times Luke had disappointed God, God had never stopped loving him, never left him, never told him goodbye.

If God hadn't given up on someone like him, then Luke wouldn't give up on him and Mary. Like Mr. Kelly had said that day, God had planted Luke's feet in this town. This was where he belonged. A deep-seated discernment grew. He'd tried to ignore it, bury it with excuses, to pretend other things mattered more, but he could no longer deny its reality.

He was in love with Mary Graves—totally, irrevocably, with every particle of his being.

If she'd have him, he'd make a family with her and the boys. With God's help he'd be a good father. A good husband.

He couldn't wait to tell her, but the middle of the night was no time to announce his love. The best course was to take his time courting Mary…at least a day. He chuckled, hope filling every part of his being.

But before he talked to Mary, he had another fence to mend.

Saturday dawned bright and sunny, reflecting Luke's optimism. He had strolled to the Whitehall Café, his heart full, planning some activities he'd do with his son. He'd just returned to the carriage house from breakfast when he heard a rap on the door.

His parents stood on the other side, elegantly dressed, as if ready for church. Under her hat, his mother's auburn hair streaked with gray, faint lines crinkled at the corners of her eyes. Thomas removed his hat. His hair had thinned, his neck had thickened. His parents had aged yet remained a handsome couple. Luke detected uncertainty in their eyes, perhaps of their welcome. He stepped back to let them in.

"Your twenty-four hours are up," Thomas said. "We want to see Ben."

"I'm not trying to hurt you, but nothing about the way I was raised gives me a desire to have you know my son."

Thomas flinched. "I suppose we deserve that. But what about you? You've taken your time admitting you're Ben's father."

"I'm not proud of that. I'm not proud of anything surrounding Ben's beginnings, but I'm not the same man I was then."

His father's gaze sought the floor. "I suppose neither of us is," he said softly. "We—"

Luke's mother laid a hand on his father's arm. "Thomas."

"Edna, I should say it. Don't you think it's time? Time we both stopped pretending?"

His mother's face crumbled, her high society facade dropping away like a cloak falling to the floor. "Maybe it is."

Thomas took a step closer. "I came here intending to bring Ben home to New York, to hire a lawyer, if necessary, to obtain legal custody of our grandson." He gave a wry smile. "I'm used to getting what I want."

"Or getting rid of what you don't," Luke said softly, almost on a whisper.

A flash of pain passed over his father's face. "Exactly. While we've cooled our heels at the hotel, your mother and I've had time to think, to face and admit mistakes we've made." Tears filled his father's eyes. "You're not the only one who isn't proud of the way he's treated his son," he said, his words ending in a sob.

The words triggered a parade of memories, none of them happy. But how could Luke hold a grudge when he'd done much the same?

Tears streaming down his face, his father stuck out his hand. "What do you say, Luke? Let's leave the past where it belongs."

Could he? Could he move on and put all that had happened between him and his parents behind him? It struck Luke then that if he truly intended to please God, he had no choice in the matter.

He took his father's hand and shook it. "Ben's a wonderful boy, thanks to Mary. Don't hurt him…"

"…like we hurt you," his mother said softly. "You and Joseph."

Thomas sighed. "We can't live it over. But we can give our grandson what we failed to give our sons—a home he knows with the people he loves."

Thinking of Ben thrust into an orphanage, carried by train to live with strangers, Luke swallowed past the lump wedged in his throat. "You're not the only ones who've run from responsibility. I've made a mess of things."

"You're not the villain you make yourself out to be."

Thomas's words filtered through him, soothing the anguish swirling inside him. That his father had cared enough to do that tore at his composure. "God's for-given me for every mistake and has given me a second chance." His voice broke. "I can't do less." Then Luke put his arms around his father.

Thomas hugged him back. "I'm sorry, son."

His mother joined the circle of forgiveness. Luke couldn't remember the last time they'd even touched each other. Tears—healing tears—streaked down their faces. Perhaps in time, his parents would find God and receive the ultimate healing for their pasts.

Mopping his eyes with a handkerchief, Thomas cleared his throat. "What are you going to do about Ben? Have you made plans?"

Luke walked to the window, looking past Doc's quarters to the town beyond, then turned back. "I've decided to move here permanently. Ben loves his mother and brothers. He needs to be near his family."

His father's brow furrowed. "You mention a mother and brothers—what of a father?"

"Mary's a widow."

A smile stole over Thomas's face. "So marry the woman and make a family for Ben."

"It's not that simple. I love Mary, but I… I've lost her trust." He sank onto a chair, dropping his head in his hands.

A knock at the door jerked Luke to his feet.

On the staircase landing, Doc held Ben's hand. His son smiled up at him, his sweet face tugging at the last remnant of Luke's composure. His parents huddled behind him, eager to get a first glimpse of their grandson.

Henry slapped a hand on Luke's shoulder. "Mary came into the office this morning with the boys. She told Ben you're staying. He wanted to see you."

"Hi, son."

Ben's eyes grew as wide as his grin. "Hi, Dad."

Luke itched to scoop his son into his arms and hold him close, but too much enthusiasm might alarm him. "Come in."

"Another time," Doc said, then mumbled an excuse why Mary hadn't brought Ben herself. Luke introduced his parents, then Doc patted Ben's shoulder. "Have fun with your dad." Henry pivoted, heading down the stairs.

Ben held up paper and pencils. "Can we make pictures?"

Luke tousled his son's hair. "Sure."

His parents stepped closer, their gazes feasting on their grandson, swallowing him up. His mother's eyes brimmed with tears. "What a handsome boy."

"Hello, Ben," Thomas said, his voice cracking with emotion.

His parents' reaction to his son welled up inside of Luke, banging against his heart, crumbling the last trace of his doubt about the change in his parents.

Ben stepped to Luke's side, leaning against his legs. "Ben, these are my parents, your grandfather and grandmother Jacobs." Luke laid a protective hand on his shoulder. "This is my son, Ben."

"Hi," Ben said in a shy tone Luke barely recognized.

Smiling, his mother bent at the waist and cupped Ben's chin, tilting his face to hers. "You look like your father did at your age." Edna glanced at Luke, then back at Ben. "Time goes by too fast. If only…" She bit her lip then forced a tremulous smile. "Look at those beautiful big brown eyes. Don't they melt your heart?"

Yearning filled Thomas's gaze. "Sure do."

His father shook Ben's hand, and the boy grinned, proud to be part of this adult greeting.

A beam of sunlight lit the table as they gathered

around it, drawing houses and people, a dog or two. Laughing at what the adults obviously considered pathetic efforts while Ben praised each drawing, finding the good in it, as he always had in Luke.

Tired of the confines of a chair, Ben scrambled down, leaving his stick figure family behind. "I have three grandpas and two grandmas. *And* two brothers *and* three cousins." He whirled in circles, joy bubbling out of him like an underground stream. "And the most bestest mom and dad in the world!"

Luke's eyes misted, awed at Ben's delight with his growing family and his inclusion of him as his dad. Well, he felt the same about Ben, the bestest son in the universe.

Thomas ruffled Ben's hair. "Who are these people, Ben?"

"You and Grandpa Lawrence and Grandpa and Grandma Willowby are all mine," Ben crowed.

Luke hugged Ben close as he explained that poor health compelled the Willowbys to give up their custody of Ben, that his son had been living with Mary, Michael and Philip for months.

Ben tugged on Thomas's arm. "I didn't have nobody. Now I have…" He held up his hands, dancing his pinkies and thumbs, trying to count his family, then frowned. "I need more fingers."

Everyone chuckled. Ben looked puzzled, then his face lit with a huge grin, obviously happy to be the center of attention.

His parents took a seat on the couch and tucked their grandson between them. "How old are you, Ben?"

Ben folded his thumb into his palm. "Four."

His mother tapped each finger, and Ben counted

along. Had she played this game with him as a very small boy? From the natural way she interacted with Ben, Luke suspected she had. His throat clogged.

"Besides drawing, what do you like to do, Ben?"

Luke blinked. When had his father cared what a child did?

"I like to fish. I like storybooks. I like to play ball." He pointed to Luke. "My dad bought me a big ball with stars."

"I'd like to read some of those books to you, Ben," his mother said.

Thomas smiled. "I've fished from boats but never from the bank. Maybe you could show me a good spot to throw out a line."

Ben bounced on the seat. "I know where! Can I show him, Luke, I mean, Dad?"

"I doubt my parents will be in town long enough to fish."

"Yes, we will. We want to spend time with our grandson. If he's staying, we are too."

Luke's jaw dropped. Nothing could have surprised him more. "Don't you have a business to run? Functions you can't miss?"

His father draped an arm across the back of the sofa. "I have an excellent staff. The business runs like a well-oiled machine whether I'm there or not."

His mother tugged Ben close. "What event could possibly be as important as getting to know our grandson?"

Memories rose in his mind, each one a rebuttal against their claim. "I can think of lots of things that kept you occupied when I was a child. Let's see, the theater, your club, dinner parties, teas, strolls in Central Park, balls—"

"You like balls!" Ben clapped his hands. "We can't throw them inside. Mom says we have to play in the backyard." His face brightened. "You can play with me and my brothers!"

"That's exactly what we'll do, Ben," his father said.

Luke tried to wrap his mind around the change in his parents. Was all this for real?

If this miracle had come about, dare he hope for a miracle in his own life too?

With Mary?

Mary sat at her desk, trying to go over her father's books. Michael and Philip stood across from her, their faces glum. "Why can't we visit Luke?" Philip said, his sad eyes tearing at Mary's heart.

"We need to give Luke and Ben some time alone…to get acquainted. Maybe next visit you all can go." Hoping to change the subject, she said, "I brought some cookies. They're in Grandpa's kitchen."

That was all it took. The boys raced off, leaving Mary with her thoughts. Her father had told her Luke's parents were there when he dropped off Ben. She'd tried to turn the visit over to God, but her nerves twanged as she waited to pick him up and return her son to his family.

But now the Jacobses were his family too.

Until she saw for herself that Luke's parents wouldn't harm Ben as they had Luke, she couldn't have peace about their presence in Ben's life.

"Want to take a walk?"

Frank stood only a step away, looking very handsome, his hair impeccably combed, and his clothes hanging on his lean frame with elegance. The serious expression in his eyes suggested he had something on his mind.

"I'd like that," she said, her pulse skittering. What did Frank want to discuss that he couldn't say right here in the office?

Grabbing her shawl off the back of her chair, she wrapped it around her shoulders. The days were colder now. She stepped down the hall to inform her father they were leaving. He promised to keep an eye on the boys.

Outside, she and Frank strolled south, heading away from the center of town. He took her hand, giving it a squeeze. "I think you know I care about you, Mary. You and your sons."

Her breath caught. "Yes, I do."

Frank stopped, turning her toward him. She looked into his eyes. Frank was kind, a good man. Somewhat pompous perhaps, but his values, his background, his calm manner would make him a good father for the boys. But did she care for him the way she should? The way a wife should feel for a husband?

"I was shocked to learn Luke is Ben's father."

"So was I."

"It complicates things, but we're all adults. If you care for me, we'll find a way to blend our lives together for Ben's sake."

At his words, her heart stuttered in her chest. He'd said *we, blend, our.* That could only mean— "What are you asking?"

"We're a good fit, you and I. We both love medicine. We share a strong faith in God. I admire your intelligence, your giving nature, the mother you are to your sons. We'd make a good team."

Frank's praise settled around her. He liked who she was. That meant a great deal. He didn't have her heart, but with time maybe...

"Don't you agree we're much alike?"

"Yes, in many ways we are."

"I'd be a good husband to you, a good father to your sons and any other children we might have."

"I know you would." Could she marry this man, knowing she didn't love him? But knowing he'd do all he could to make them happy?

"You would understand the long hours, the pressure of building my career. The need to move."

A chill streaked down Mary's spine. She wrapped her shawl more tightly around herself. *"Move?"*

"You've told me you'd like to travel. We'll see the country as I further my goals. It'll be an adventure. With you and the boys at my side, I'll have the support, the family, that'll help me stay grounded...no matter how high I rise in my profession."

A gust of wind swirled and, spinning like a tiny twister, lifted fallen leaves and skipped across the ground, much like her churning thoughts. How could she leave this town? "But... Ben's here."

"Are you sure Luke will stay here forever? Might he end up back East?"

"Luke says he won't uproot Ben." Could she be sure?

"Well, then Ben can come for visits in the summer."

"Have you forgotten my plans to work in my father's practice, to continue his legacy here in Noblesville?"

"I understand that'll be a sacrifice, but I'll give you and your sons a good life, Mary. You'll have the freedom to do whatever you want. To get your education, become a doctor and practice medicine or stay home with the children." He took a deep breath then turned to her with a smile, as if he was giving her the gift she'd waited for all her life. "I'll take good care of all of you. I love you, Mary. Say you'll be my wife."

The door to Luke's apartment swung open. At the sight of Luke's familiar face, Mary's heart thundered beneath her corset. His gaze roamed over her, devouring her, or so she felt. Then behind him, a scene slammed into Mary's gut. Ben and a couple who could only be Luke's parents sat at his table eating slices of apple, the smiles they wore evidence the visit had gone well. She didn't know whether to be happy about that or not.

"Hi, Mom!" Ben scrambled from his seat and plunged into her skirt. "I got new grandparents!"

Luke introduced the Jacobses. Their eyes shone at Ben's declaration. Mary had expected harsh lines and stern eyes, not the soft gentle expressions of people obviously smitten with Ben.

"Ben's a great little boy, Mrs. Graves," Mr. Jacobs said.

Mary smiled. "I think so too." Mary took Ben by the hand. "Michael and Philip are waiting outside to play with you."

"Son, we'll walk out with Mrs. Graves and Ben." His father laid an arm on Luke's shoulder. Surprisingly, the gesture of affection didn't appear to irk Luke like Mary would've expected. Perhaps Luke and his parents had found common ground with Ben.

"We'll sit together at church tomorrow, Ben," Luke said. He turned to his parents. "Services are at ten o'clock, if you'd like to come and spend more time with your grandson."

Luke's father's brows rose, obviously startled by the idea. "Well, I suppose we, ah, could do that."

"I'll be at the Becker House at nine-thirty. We can walk over together."

Mary bit back a smile. Luke had used Ben to get his parents to services. Not a bad tactic.

"Will you be at the office for a while, Mary? I'd like to talk to you."

Something in the depths of Luke's eyes banged against her heart. "Yes," she said. Her voice sounded shaky even to her own ears.

A grin spread across his face. "Good."

Outside the carriage house, Ben ran to play with Michael and Philip, leaving Mary alone with the Jacobses, who weren't nearly as intimidating as she'd expected, both surprising and reassuring her. She needn't worry about their conduct with her son.

"Thank you for taking care of Ben," Mrs. Jacobs said. "He's a delightful little boy."

"You're welcome to visit Ben at my home."

"That's very kind of you. He's quite the boy," Mr. Jacobs said, then paused, meeting his wife's gaze. She gave him a nod. "Mrs. Graves, before you go, I want to tell you something."

"What's that?"

He cleared his throat, as if what he wanted to say lodged there. "We sent Luke's brother away. At first we visited him, but then…well, it was easier… Guess we panicked about a disorder we didn't understand and couldn't face. To avoid Luke's censure, we distanced ourselves from him too." He lifted a hand. "Our negligence killed one child. Our aloofness hurt the other." He scrubbed a hand over his eyes. Were those tears? "We'll spend the rest of our lives regretting what we did."

Thinking of Luke as a little boy, rejected and alone, Mary swallowed hard. Surely if his father told her this, he'd also said the same to Luke. That must explain the harmony she'd sensed between him and his parents. "It can't be easy to admit that."

"I'm not telling you all this to get a pat on the back." Mr. Jacobs gave a humorless smile. "Funny, that here in this small town, I've had time to take a long hard look at myself…and at Luke," he said, his eyes damp. "Be patient with him, Mrs. Graves. We wounded our son, and he's been hiding. Afraid to get close to anyone, but that's changing. Because of Ben and we suspect because of you."

Though she knew the credit wasn't hers, Mr. Jacobs's words clung to her, filling her with hope. "Thank you for that, but the change you've seen is mostly because of his faith."

"If that invitation to church is any indication, I suspect he'll try to convert us," his father said.

"Nothing wrong with that." Mary smiled. "I hope you'll come."

Luke's mother laid a gentle hand on Mary's arm. "We want a second chance, a fresh start with our grandson. We appreciate your willingness to let us see Ben."

"Ben deserves his family, Mrs. Jacobs. That family includes both of you."

Watching Ben and his brothers kick the ball around the yard, Luke's mother smiled. "What is it they say? And a child shall lead them? Well, that's what happened here today. A child led us to our son, to a new beginning with him."

Thomas reached out a hand. "Luke's a good man. A far better man than I. Please, give him a chance, Mrs. Graves. You won't regret it."

The outside door of the waiting room banged open. Four men scrunched through the opening, carrying two injured men on improvised stretchers.

"Accident down at the strawboard plant," one man said.

"George Augsburger here mighta broke his leg. Leroy Hawkins, an arm. Both got nasty gashes," another worker said.

Mary sprang into action, pushing aside her thoughts. But as she directed one patient to the examining room, the other to the surgery where her father waited, disappointment burned in the pit of her stomach. From what he'd said earlier, she'd expected Luke to come in, but he hadn't made an appearance. She could cheerfully wring his neck for keeping her on pins and needles.

She assembled water, soap and antiseptic and then sponged the cut above Mr. Augsburger's brow. "How are you feeling?"

"Been better."

Mary nodded. "Any pain on the inside?"

He shook his head. "No."

"What happened?"

"Sheaves of straw stacked to the ceiling toppled. I lost my footing and skated all the way to the bottom. Landed on the tongue of a wagon. I think my leg's busted."

"Doc will be right in."

He reached a hand toward her. "The Missus and I... are heartsick about our youngun's fight. It's our fault. Our tongues got away from us and Jimmy overheard."

The book of James might warn about wagging tongues, but the Augsburger family had done them all a favor, had brought out into the open the secrets she'd exhausted herself keeping. "Don't worry." Mary met his sober gaze. "It gave me an opportunity to say some things that needed saying."

Mr. Augsburger smiled, his relief at her clemency evident in his eyes.

While she cleaned his scrapes, Mary's mind whirled. Because of Luke she'd found the courage to talk openly to her sons. He'd taken responsibility for Ben. She'd loved him since their talk at the river. But were his parents right? Could she trust him?

Beneath her distracted touch, Mr. Augsburger sucked in a breath.

Mary cringed. She'd been preoccupied, affecting her competency. "I'm sorry."

Her father came in with splints. While he slit the leg of the patient's pants, she mixed plaster of Paris and cut gauze. Mary focused on what needed doing, not the workings of her heart, but the confusion inside her kept its steady beat.

She thought of Luke's gentleness with Ben, with Philip and Michael, of his kindness to her during one of her headaches. Well, he'd become a giant headache for her now, stirring her emotions like a whirlwind, leaving her confused and on edge. Where was he?

Finished treating George Augsburger's wounds, she moved on to Leroy Hawkins, finding comfort as she always had in the practice of medicine. She greeted him, offering soothing words, gently cleaning his abrasions and cuts, staying clear of his arm cradled on his chest.

"When my father finishes with Mr. Augsburger, he'll assess your break, Mr. Hawkins."

"As soon as I wash my hands, I'll take over."

Mary's head snapped up. Luke stood across from her. She looked into his face, a face she'd memorized, touched, kissed.

She wanted to run to him, to run from him. All those emotions battled inside her, welled up until she could barely breathe. Because no matter how hard she tried, she couldn't be indifferent in Luke's presence.

"Will somebody do something?" Mr. Hawkins said, ending on a groan.

The patient needed them. Her questions, an endless list, would have to wait. For now.

Luke dried his hands and then cut away Mr. Hawkins's shirt and examined the arm. He didn't speak, simply assessed the situation. Where had he been? Why hadn't he marched over here and declared his feelings for her like Frank had?

Unable to wait another moment, she asked, "What have you been doing since I saw you?"

"Making plans. I wired the Children's Aid Society. Then I looked at a house that's for sale right around the block. As soon as I heard about the accident, I headed here." He smiled at her. "On the way, I talked to myself for courage."

His smile curled her toes. "Courage for what?"

He glanced at the patient. "I'll explain later."

Even in pain, Mr. Hawkins's ears perked up. Then he hissed when Luke moved his arm, preparing to set the break.

A couple of hectic hours passed with no time to talk but then, finally, quiet reigned. The mess had been cleared away, and the injured had been taken to their homes by their coworkers, who'd waited the entire time. Her father went along to make sure the men got settled in and were comfortable.

Mary sat at the table in the backroom, limp with fatigue from the day, feeling wrung out like an old dishrag. Yet at the same time, she'd never felt more alive. The reason now sat across from her, his dark eyes soft, his dazzling smile tugging at her resolve to hold herself aloof.

"God is good," he said, taking her hand. "To see the change in my parents…" His voice broke. "They'll be good grandparents to Ben." He smiled. "My father's going to build a school for disabled children, and he's promised to name it after Joseph."

Mary's eyes flooded with tears. "Oh, my."

The corners of his mouth turned up into that lopsided grin she loved. "I've accepted my past, Mary. It made me what I am, even led me here to Noblesville. I never expected to stay or to practice medicine again, but I did. I never expected to get attached to Ben and everyone in this town, but I did. I never expected to meet you, a woman I admire more than any other, but I did."

She ran a palm along his jaw, tears streaming down her face. "Oh, Luke."

He scooted his chair back from the table and knelt beside her, taking both her hands in his. "The other night I realized I've spent my life running, afraid to care. Afraid I'd get my heart stomped. That's all I knew."

Mary understood those struggles. Something tightened within. The old fear claiming her.

"But you taught me what love is. You've shown me what a family is." He pulled her to her feet and hugged her to him. "I'm not running anymore. I'm in love with you, Mary."

Her breath caught and held. Oh, how she wanted to return those words. But did she dare? Unable to meet his penetrating gaze, she rose and crossed to the window. "I've heard those words before. I'm scared."

He stepped behind her, laid a gentle palm on her shoulder. "I'm not Sam. I won't let you down."

She believed that. But once he really knew her, would he be disillusioned? Feel cheated? Want out? Or worse, remain yet turn away from her?

"It's me I have no confidence in, not you." She swiveled to him. "All of my life, I've wondered why I wasn't good enough for my mother to keep. She didn't care enough to even verify if I lived. Or if I turned out all right."

"Oh, Mary—"

"No, let me say this." She swallowed hard, barely able to squeeze out the words, "Why wasn't I good enough for Sam to stop drinking?" She held up her hands, begging for an answer. "Tell me, Luke. Why?"

Luke tenderly cradled her chin. "What you're really asking is 'Am I good enough to love?' You taught me the answer to that." A smile crossed his face. "If God can love me, then you, my sweet, amazing Mary, are definitely worthy of His love."

She let his words have time to permeate the shell she'd built around her heart. That shell kept Luke out. But it also locked her in. She'd built that shell because she didn't trust her own judgment, her ability to perceive whether a man would stay. But, at the core of it, she felt unworthy of love.

With God's help, she could tear down that barrier. And she would. "How did you get so wise?"

"I had a great teacher." Luke leaned close. "Whatever you make up your mind to do, you can do, Mary. And that includes loving me."

Loving him wasn't the problem. Loving herself had been. She took his hand, giving it a squeeze. "I love you, Luke Jacobs, with all my being."

He hugged her to him. "I was afraid Sloan might have won your heart." He reared back. "Where is he anyway?"

"I don't love Frank. I told him so this morning. He left town soon after."

Luke gave a triumphant shout and then twirled her about the small room, both laughing with the sheer joy of their love.

"Oh, you're making me dizzy."

He lowered her to her feet, then dipped his head, his chocolate brown eyes gentle and soft with yearning. "Marry me. I want to spend my life with you."

"Marry you?" Her heart fluttered. Imagine spending every day with Luke. But first she had to know with certainty. "What about my plan to attend medical school?"

"Doc and I can handle the practice. I'll be there at night to help the boys with homework and get them tucked into bed. I'll send for my housekeeper. She'll be great with the boys. Can keep an eye on them after school, or when you can't get home and I'm on a house call."

Her jaw dropped. A housekeeper? A husband who'd support her? She felt like she was walking in a dream. "You'd do all that? For me?"

"I'd do anything for you, lovely lady." He toyed with a tendril of hair. "Any more concerns?"

"I can't think of another thing to say."

He grinned. "Say yes."

Her full heart brimmed over, spilling love into every wounded part of her, filling her with hope. "Yes, yes, yes, Luke! I'll marry you."

His lips met hers, and Mary leaned into him, returning his kiss with the fervor of a woman starving for closeness to the man she loved. Beneath her palms, his heart thumped wildly, matching the beat of her own galloping heart. He tightened his arms around her, trapping her hands between them on his chest, deepening the kiss until she could barely stand, could barely breathe.

A noise in the hall made them leap apart. Her father and all three boys stood in the doorway grinning like Cheshire cats. Mary knelt and threw her arms wide. Ben dove into them, almost knocking her off her feet. She buried her nose in his neck, drank in his sweet smell and wept tears of joy.

Luke tugged Mary to her feet. Michael and Philip crowded around the three of them. "Boys, I asked your mother to be my wife, and she said yes. Is that all right with you?"

"Luke's going to be our daddy too!" Philip pumped his thin arms into the air. The grin on Michael's face said it all.

"Will that be okay with you, Ben?" Luke said, ruffling the boy's hair.

"Yep! Can we live in the same house now?"

"Soon, Ben. Our wedding can't happen fast enough to suit me."

Her father clapped Luke on the back then kissed Mary's cheek. "'Bout time you two figured it out."

Laughing with joy, Michael and Philip grabbed their brother, and all three of them danced around the backroom, crowing with delight. Mary didn't need to worry about the boys accepting Luke into the family. He'd captured their hearts, as he had hers.

Recalling Mrs. Whitehall's claim that a remedy for every ache and pain existed in this office, Mary knew she'd found hers. "You know, Doctor, I have a cure of my own for you."

He cupped her jaw, his touch a caress, and raised her gaze to his.

"Oh, you do?"

"Take one Mary Graves, make her your wife. Mix in three little boys, best taken on a full stomach. Then add a cup of faith." She smiled. "A daily dose will fix what ails you, guaranteed. And all for the bargain price of…"

Eyes twinkling, he cocked his head. "Three dollars a bottle?"

"Oh, no, Dr. Jacobs, that's far too cheap. This remedy will cost you a lifetime of love."

"Sold!" His dimple winked at her. "Loving you for a lifetime will be my greatest pleasure, Mary Lynn Graves."

Then he pulled her close, holding her in a tight grip—as if he never wanted to let her go. His lips captured hers. With every fiber of her being and all the love she'd hidden inside, she kissed him back, thankful for this man, the Great Physician's remedy for her life.

* * * * *

Janice Thompson is a Christian freelance author and a native Texan. She resides in Spring, Texas, near her grown children and infant granddaughters. Her family is active in ministry, primarily writing, music, drama and evangelism. Janice started penning books at a young age and was blessed to have a screenplay produced in the early '80s. From there, she went on to write several large-scale musicals. Currently, she has published more than thirty full-length novels and nonfiction books (most lighthearted and/or wedding themed). She's thankful for her calling as an author of Christian fiction and knows the Lord has brought her to this point so that she can present stories that will change people's lives. Romances come naturally to Janice, since she's coordinated nearly a dozen weddings, including recent ceremonies and receptions for all four of her daughters.

SPRING CREEK B[RIDES

Janice Thompson

Who knows whether you have come to the kingdom
for such a time as this?
—*Esther* 4:14

In memory of my father, Billy Hanna—
a small-town man with a big-as-Texas heart.

Acknowledgments

To my agent, Chip MacGregor: You are a godsend.
Thanks for believing in me and special thanks
for finding just the right house for this story.

To Krista Stroever: Thank you so much for the
opportunity to write for Love Inspired. You helped
make a long-term dream come true. I appreciate your
patience with the process. You're a true mentor.

To Louise Rozett, my line editor: Thanks for the
spit-shine. You walked me through my first copyedit
at a new company, and I'm so grateful.

To my wonderful critique partners, Kathleen Y'Barbo,
Martha Rogers, Marcia Gruver and Linda Kozar:
Thanks for falling in love with my hometown of
Spring, Texas, with me! Here's to lunch at Wunsche
Brothers Café! Let's meet there again…soon!

To the people of Spring, Texas (past and present):
You have left your mark on my soul.

Chapter One

Spring Creek, Texas, 1902

Ida Mueller pressed a lock of unruly hair behind her ear and rounded the large dining table with a chipped serving bowl in hand. Chair legs scraped against the wood-planked floor as the rowdy lumber-mill workers rushed to sit down for another one of her home-cooked meals. She couldn't help but smile at their enthusiasm.

"Smells good enough to eat!" one of the younger fellows joked.

Ida plopped a spoonful of crisp fried potatoes onto his plate and kept moving as she responded. "You've eaten at my table every day for nearly a year, Carl Walken, and you haven't found reason to complain yet." She reached up with the back of her hand and wiped a bit of perspiration from her brow.

His eyebrows lifted mischievously. "Ain't just the food keeps me coming back." A playful wink followed.

"Ya reckon?" Another of the men elbowed him.

Several of the fellows let out whistles and Ida felt her cheeks turn warm. She scurried to the opposite side of the room and continued on with the chore of feeding the work crew, trying to ignore their usual flirtatious ways.

"None of that now." Her father's stern voice rang out from the head of the table. He always knew how to keep his men in line, especially when it came to his daughter.

"Aw, Mr. Mueller," one of the fellows groaned. "You never let us have any fun."

"Better mind your p's and q's," Ida quipped. "I've got a platter of Wiener schnitzel in the kitchen, but I've half a mind not to serve it."

The men took to hearty grumbling and she returned to the kitchen for the cumbersome platter of meat. For a moment—just a moment—she leaned against the countertop and drew in a deep breath. The south Texas heat wrapped itself around her like a dressing gown.

On days like this, she missed her mama more than ever. Seven years as the woman of the house had scarcely proven Ida worthy of filling her mother's shoes. Papa offered plenty of encouragement, but she struggled daily to keep up with caring for her home, her father and a crew of ravenous workers. And she fought to overcome the grief of losing the one person a girl depended on above all others—her mother. Oh, how she longed for what she could not have.

"I need you, Mama," she whispered. Indeed, at nineteen, Ida found herself in need of a great many things that only a mother could offer. But she had to rely on Papa's manly advice, and cope with the ever-present teasing from the lumber-mill workers, a daily reminder that she, a lone female, resided in a world of men.

"Mama, I don't know how you did it." She whispered the familiar words as she snatched up the plate full of Wiener schnitzel and headed back into the dining room once again.

As she came around the corner, Ida caught a glimpse of her uncontrollable blond hair in the elegant carved mirror that hung above the buffet. Frustrated, she reminded herself to deal with it after feeding the crew. How any of the men could find her attractive was a mystery, to her way of thinking.

Aunt Dinah would never let her hear the end of it if she didn't start taking better care of herself. Ever the proper lady, Ida's best friend and confidant was of the notion that a woman should be able to handle a full day's work, a brisk walk to town to help tend the family store and an hour's Bible reading in the evenings, with time left over for necessary grooming. All in the hopes of acquiring the one thing Ida wasn't sure she wanted—a husband.

Ida remained convinced she would never find a man who even came close to the one she held in the highest esteem—her papa. He was strong spirited, full of goodness and had a heart like a jewel. No, surely such a fellow did not exist. And if he did, he certainly didn't appear to be seated at this table.

"Thinkin' I'm hungry?" Carl asked. Ida looked down, shocked to see that she had placed five large slabs of veal steak on his plate.

"Oh, dear."

Her father's eyebrows arched as if to ask, *Where is your head today, daughter?*

She lifted three of the pieces of meat from Carl's plate. "I knew you had a taste for my cooking, is all."

With fork in one hand and knife in the other, the young man dove into the food. The others followed suit and the air soon filled with the sounds of chomping and cutting.

Her father cleared his throat quite loudly and Ida anticipated his next words.

"I don't believe we've thanked the Almighty yet." His voice deepened in reverence. "So you'll be putting down those utensils, gentlemen, or there will be no dinner for you today. Or any other day, for that matter."

They complied with sheepish grins, as always.

Ida noticed that her father's German accent became stronger as his prayer began. "Almighty God, Maker of heaven and earth, we thank Thee for this, Thy bounty. For Thy goodness is everlasting, from generation to generation, and Thy blessings overflow. Be with each of these men today as they seek to serve Thee with their labors. Amen."

"Amen," the men echoed, then tore into their food once again.

Ida slipped away into the kitchen, anxious for another moment's peace. Perhaps here she could think clearly. Once the dishes were done, of course.

She worked at a steady pace, allowing her thoughts to drift until a familiar shrill whistle signaled a train's arrival. The afternoon run from Fort Worth came like clockwork at one-thirty, just as she finished the dishes. Some things could be depended on.

Others could not.

Mick Bradley peered out of the grimy train window and took in his first glimpse of Spring Creek, Texas. Not quite what he had pictured and a sure sight hotter. He pulled a handkerchief from his pocket and dragged it across the back of his neck to remove the moisture.

No point arriving in town looking like a vagabond. Not with so much at stake.

As the train crawled into the station, the porter approached, pocket watch in hand. "Just a few more minutes, sir."

Mick nodded in his direction, but said nothing as he took in the sights of his new home. Off in the distance a large hotel with a freshly painted sign greeted him. Sellers Hotel. And to his right, The Harvey House. After locating a barbershop, he'd have to settle on one or the other.

A bustling mercantile appeared to be doing quite a good business. Shoppers scurried to and fro with packages, stirring up dust on the street. A couple of women were about, but for the most part, he only saw men. Hundreds of men.

Yes, the booming little town of Spring Creek must surely need his services.

Mick's brow furrowed as he counted the saloons. He strained to see a bit farther down the street. Three? In such a small area? Their owners would be a source of contention, no doubt. Surely they would seek to complicate his plans to build a new gambling hall.

But he had encountered plenty of trouble when he opened his first place up North. These Texans couldn't be any worse than Chicago's most notorious, whom he'd handled with ease.

At that moment, two men took to brawling in the middle of the street, not twenty feet from the jailhouse. The taller, more muscular man clearly had the upper hand. A crowd gathered round, cheering them on. Before long, the two were on the ground, tussling. They went at it, cheek to fist, until one of them was knocked out. With such a large group about, Mick couldn't tell which one had taken the fall, but it must surely be the smaller of the two. That's how life was, after all. The boisterous crowd thinned as it declared a victor and the short man stood and raised his fist in the air with a triumphant shout.

Maybe these Texans weren't going to be so easy after all.

The passenger in the seat next to him stood and gave a polite nod as the train came to a stop. Mick returned the gesture and rose to his feet. His back ached from sitting so long and his cramped legs begged for a good, long walk. How many trains had he boarded over the past several days? Somewhere between Illinois and Texas he'd simply lost count.

The next few months would give him plenty of opportunity to stay put, however. He had his work cut out for him. And before long, he would be the talk of the town.

Probably sooner rather than later.

Chapter Two

The afternoon journey to town provided Ida with an opportunity to think about the day ahead. She didn't mind the walk, though the late-spring heat continued to fold her in its sticky embrace. Her skirts, dusty and ragged on the ends, twisted about her ankles as she moved along the tiny, jutted road that connected the lumber mill with Midway, the town's main street.

She looked both ways before crossing the tracks, contemplating the barreling locomotives and the havoc they'd brought with them. Somehow it all seemed exaggerated in the heat. She tugged at the neckline of her dress, and a trickle of perspiration rolled down her back.

Surely Aunt Dinah would scold Ida for her appearance. Ah, well. Nothing Ida could do about that. Nor did she care to. If living among men gave her a tomboyish appearance, so be it. There were worse things, to be sure.

As she made her way from the tracks to town, Ida struggled with the usual attentions from the railroad men. Many let out a whoop or a holler as she passed by The Harvey House, and still more as she eased her way past Sellers Hotel, which happened to be known for a bit more than rooms to let.

As was her custom, she ignored the men, keeping her mouth shut to avoid giving them a serious tongue-lashing. She would gladly tromp through mud, splashing dirt upon her gingham skirt if she thought it would cause them to turn their irksome attentions elsewhere. Let her hair remain mussed. Perhaps then they would focus on their work and not on her.

"Come on, Ida," one of the fellows chided. "Just one glimpse into those perty blue eyes. They melt me like fresh-churned butter."

She kept her eyes on the ground and continued walking. The irritating fellow reeked of alcohol and pipe tobacco, and his work clothes were in serious need of washing. His scent, coupled with the overpowering smells coming from the nearby livery stable, almost brought her stomach up into her throat. Add to this the foul odor from the outhouses and the lingering stench of cigar smoke and one could scarcely stand it.

Yet this seemed to be her lot in life. Ida longed for a quieter, more genteel existence that did not include such aromas. If only Spring Creek could return to its former state—a quaint town with good, wholesome neighbors who greeted one another with pleasant hellos.

"C'mon, honey," the man pleaded, oblivious to her thoughts. "Can't ya give me a wink or somethin'? Some sign that I stand a chance with ya? I'll die if you don't." An exaggerated groan followed, one meant to get the attention of others nearby.

She willed herself not to look up. Why encourage him?

"Aw, yer killin' me." He doubled over and fell onto the road, eliciting a roar of laughter from the other men.

Ida managed to maintain her sense of dignity and simply kept walking.

She made the turn onto Midway and peered up long enough to gauge the distance. If she could just make it beyond the Wunsche Brothers saloon, the jailhouse, the barbershop and the bank, she'd be fine. *I can do this*.

A minute later, she reached the overgrown lot next to the mercantile and breathed a sigh of relief. Just twenty more paces and she'd be in the store. Dinah would be waiting, as always. Probably with pursed lips, but waiting, nonetheless.

The clock above the bank sounded two piercing gongs. *Why is it I can never arrive at a place on time?*

Ida picked up the pace and ran head-on into one of the men. With her cheeks flaming, she looked up at the fellow, ready to give him a piece of her mind for not watching where he was going. Why were these railroad men so careless?

Words failed Ida as she took in the handsome stranger with his polished good looks. She'd certainly never seen a man like this before, with such a finely tuned air about him.

Tall and sturdy, the stranger wore a fancy suit and big-city shoes—no cowboy boots like the rest of the fellows. His expression gave the appearance of dignity and confidence, unlike so many of the railroad men. Surely this man didn't work for the Great Northern, though he'd likely traveled in style aboard one of the nicer cars, from the looks of him. Yes, this was a man with money.

Perhaps he was a banker. Or better yet, a preacher, come to convince the wayward menfolk they were in need of repentance. Then again, he could be a socialite, headed toward the Houston area. Many well-mannered men had passed through Spring Creek on their way to other locations. Oh, if only they would stay and put down roots. They would balance out the bad with some good.

"Pardon me, miss." The gentleman spoke with a deep, rich voice. He tipped his hat, all politeness and charm, then gave a gracious bow. "My fault entirely."

Ida stammered in response, mumbling a few twisted-up words that amounted to little more than gibberish. He gave her a curious look and paused, likely to see if she might try again.

Ida managed, "Oh no, please don't apologize. I take the blame solely upon myself." She felt the heat rise to her cheeks as she spoke, noting his remarkable gray eyes. Remembering her manners, she quickly added, "I am sorry. I didn't mean to run you down." His sandy-colored curls drew her eye up. My, but he was a tall fellow. Stately, even.

He flashed a warm smile. "Oh, you can run me down anytime you like."

Stifling a smile, she shifted her gaze to his tailored suit and spiffed-up shoes. In all her years, she'd never seen a man with such a handsome wardrobe. Only in catalogs had she seen such finery. Up close, it was a little intimidating.

"Pleasure to meet you."

"And you," she managed.

"Have a good day." He gave her a nod then began to

move in the direction of the barbershop. Ida watched as he disappeared through the crowd.

One of the railroad men shouted, startling her. "Ida, sweet pea, you're the woman of my dreams."

"More likely the woman of your nightmares, if you don't back away and let me pass," she muttered under her breath.

Shaking her head, she plowed forward. Four paces. Three. Two. One. Ida crossed over the threshold of the mercantile and let out a huge sigh of relief. Now, if she could just keep her mind off handsome strangers and on her work, all would be well.

Mick eased his hat back onto his head and continued across the street, ignoring the magnetic pull of the petite blonde. His heart had quickened at the sight of her, likely the result of her undeniable beauty. He was taken with her simple, small-town appeal, her flushed cheeks and determined expression—all things he loved in a woman.

And spunk. Yes, he could read the spunk in those flashing blue eyes, eyes whose image would linger in his mind for quite some time.

Mick quickly reminded himself of his reason for coming to Spring Creek. Not to find a woman, but to build a gambling hall. They were two very different things. Best to stay focused on the task at hand. After all, he had his investors to answer to.

Then again, he would need the help of the local women, wouldn't he? Yes, he would surely need barmaids and dancers. However, the woman he'd just fixed in his mind looked like the sort who was more at home on a church pew than a bar stool. If all the women of

Spring Creek were like the one he'd just met, he'd have to look elsewhere for employees.

But he suspected that the blue-eyed beauty who'd practically run him down was one of a kind. One of a kind indeed.

Chapter Three

Ida entered the mercantile at exactly five minutes past two. She slipped on her apron and started arranging canned goods.

"Well, it's about time."

Ida's brow wrinkled in concern as she heard Dinah's voice. She looked up, seeing the strong family resemblance in her aunt's stern eyes. Papa and his younger sister bore the same features, without question. And they had similar temperaments, as well, despite their vast difference in age. Dinah was a mere twenty-eight, though her mannerisms often led folks to believe otherwise.

Dinah had suffered much over the past couple of years and the cares of life had aged her somehow. But since the death of Dinah's husband, the family had grown closer than ever and Ida treasured her friendship. Papa had taken his only sister and her son under his wing, caring for their every need. No one could doubt his generous nature or his kind heart. And that very kindness had prompted him to purchase the mercantile and place it into Dinah's capable hands last fall.

"Because I know you will do it right," he had proclaimed. "You will make the Mueller family proud."

And indeed she had. Nestled amid saloons and restaurants, the store remained the town's last sensible place, where folks could come to share a good story, purchase life's necessities and hear Dinah's ardent presentation of God's love. The shop stayed full from morning till night with those hungry for companionship and direction.

And Ida, always ready to lend a hand, came every day at two o'clock to spend time behind the counter so that Dinah could focus on Carter, her five-year-old son.

Only two o'clock never seemed to come at the right time, particularly not on days like today with so many chores to be done.

"I'm sorry I'm late. Really, I am." With a gesture toward the street, Ida added, "But this time I have an excuse. I wasn't watching where I was going and I ran right into this man. He was… It's hard to describe. He wore the most beautiful clothes. He must have just arrived on the train. Funny—I didn't even get his name."

Dinah gave her an inquisitive look. "Why, Ida, I don't think I've ever seen this side of you. You're smitten."

Dinah's comment startled Ida. She tried to busy herself arranging jars of honey. "I would hardly call it that. I'm simply curious." She paused to think about her aunt's words before adding, "It's just that he's so different from all the other fellas. Those railroad men are…they're impossible. This stranger was a true gentleman." She put down the jar and looked out the window at a couple of men who'd taken to scuffling with each other in the street.

"Are they still giving you a hard time on your trip

to town?" Dinah picked up a broom, as if ready to do business with anyone who dared to enter in a flirtatious state of mind.

"Yes." Ida's dander rose as she revisited the trip down Midway. "Our little town is looking more like Houston every day. Railroad men. Taverns. Primitive behavior in the streets. The place is losing its innocence, which is why it's so refreshing to see a man of refinement for a change. I do hope he's here to stay, and not just passing through on his way to Houston."

"Most of the strangers who come to Spring Creek do not come with the best of motives." Dinah crossed her arms at her chest, looking more concerned than ever.

"Oh, I know." A sigh escaped Ida's lips as she reflected on the problem their town now faced. "And you can be sure the afternoon train brought in more riffraff. Every day they come, headed to the land agent's office to buy up their piece of the pie. The town is growing up too fast. It's frightening." She felt a little shiver run up her spine.

"At least business is good." Dinah gestured to the cash register with a smile. "I sold several pounds of coffee this morning. And there's not enough chewing tobacco in the state to keep these men happy." She paused a moment as she gazed around the very busy shop. "Best of all, they pay cash." She lowered her voice to a whisper. "Unlike so many of the locals. I can't tell you how many of them buy on credit and then don't pay their bills on time. It's a problem, Ida."

"I know, but—"

"I've traded some of my best merchandise for butter, eggs, herbs, even chickens," Dinah said with exasperation. "And then there's Mrs. Gertsch! Would you

believe the woman actually wanted to trade in a stack
of her used dime novels for honey?"

Ida couldn't help but chuckle at that news. After all,
she'd sold the elderly woman those dime novels in the
first place—they'd spent hours discussing the adventure stories. But this might not be the best time to share
that information with Dinah.

"I'm not saying I mind so much," her aunt continued, "but cash money is a good thing for a business."

"Still," Ida argued, "I'll take a hardworking local
over a cash-handling railroad man any day to make
the town safe again. It's hardly worth risking life and
limb just to get down Midway. Whatever happened to
our sleepy little town?"

"Woke up, I guess." Dinah took to sweeping the
floor.

"Humph." Ida shook her head in defiance. "I'd give
my eye teeth for a return to the way things used to be."

She continued to look out the window, trying with
all her might to remember the little town that had captivated her heart when she was a child. In her mind's
eye, she saw what Spring Creek would be like now, if
the railroad had never come through. She saw churches,
fields of sugarcane and delightful little shops. Women
and children walked about in safety, packages in their
arms and carefree smiles on their faces. Men gestured
kindly to one another, never shouting obscenities, and
never, ever whistling at women. In that quaint place,
people would feel safe, secure.

Dinah's son, Carter, bounded into the room, breaking into Ida's thoughts. Jam stains covered his face,
from brow to chin.

"Son, what have you done?" Setting the broom aside,

Dinah rushed to his side and pried the jar of homemade strawberry preserves from his tightly clenched fist.

"Mine, Mother." He grinned with mischief in his eyes. Though Ida knew he deserved a good scolding, she had to stifle a laugh.

"At two o'clock in the afternoon?" Dinah asked as she placed the sticky jar on the countertop. "You believe this to be the proper time for sweets?"

"Anytime is the proper time, so long as it tastes good. Right, darlin'?" Ida scooped her young cousin into her arms and spun in circles until they were both dizzy. Carter let out a giggle, which bounced around the room and startled a few of the store's patrons.

Ida didn't mind a bit. In fact, she couldn't help but spoil this precious child, who was the spitting image of his father. Oh, if only Larson had lived to see his son grow up. If only that awful railroad man hadn't—

No, she would not focus on the family's losses today. Surely this blessed little boy was the good Lord's reminder to all who gazed upon his innocent face that life could go on, even after tragedy.

"Oh, fine." Dinah shook her head. "You're a big help."

"I know, I know." Ida carried Carter to the back of the store where she located a rag and some lye soap. "Give us a minute for a Texas spit-shine, and we'll be as good as new!" she hollered.

She gave the youngster a good scrubbing. He fought her attempts, but only in fun. When they finished, she led him by the hand through the carefully organized aisles of dry goods up to the front, where Dinah stood waiting, hands on her hips.

"See?" Ida grinned. "Cleaner'n a whistle."

Carter skipped behind the front counter and eyed the candy jars. "Jelly beans, Mommy?" he begged.

"No, son. I think you've had enough treats for one day."

"Peppermint?" He pointed to a second jar.

"Absolutely not."

Ida stepped in front of the row of glass jars so they would present no further temptation. Surely he would be pleading for licorice whips or gum before long. Or taffy. He loved the colorful, hand-wrapped delicacies from nearby Galveston Island.

Safely distracted, Carter grabbed his bag of brightly colored marbles. As he settled onto the floor to play, the bag spilled open and they rolled around in every direction, making all sorts of racket against the wood-planked floorboards.

"Peawee, Mother!" he hollered, then dashed underneath the counter to capture his favorite marble in his tight little fist. "Peawee!" he said again, holding it up.

Dinah sighed as she reached to pick up the other wayward marbles.

"The only problem I see with boys," Ida said with a wink, "is that they grow into men." She joined Dinah behind the counter in preparation for the usual midafternoon influx of customers.

"You'd best not carry on with that train of thought," Dinah said, "or you will never catch a husband."

Ida rolled her eyes as she responded, "I'm not looking for one, I assure you." Before she could stop it, an image of the handsome stranger floated through her mind. She quickly pushed it away, determined to remain focused. Sensible girls were not swayed by fancy clothes.

She thought of her childhood friend, Sophie Weimer, who had no greater wish than to marry and present her husband with a half-dozen children in steady succession. Ida shuddered at the very thought of such a life. No, she would not marry—at least not unless the Lord presented her with exactly the right man. And she wasn't likely to stumble across the right man in a place like Spring Creek.

At that moment, a couple of rough-looking railroad fellows made an entrance. They jabbed one another in the ribs and let out simultaneous whistles in the direction of the ladies.

"None of that in here." Dinah faced them, brow furrowed, ready for a battle. "Or you'll have me to contend with."

Their gazes shifted to the floor and they wandered off to play dominoes, pulling wooden-slatted chairs around a barrel and settling in for a game. The menfolk often gathered in the store to pass the time this way. No wagering, of course—Dinah would never abide such a thing.

Ida didn't mind their presence in the store so much, as long as they kept their language clean. And they were better off here than in the saloons, after all. There was nothing wrong with an innocent game of dominoes.

"I wish I had your patience." Ida spoke to Dinah in a hoarse whisper. "Truly. I can't seem to look a man in the eye without wanting to slap him."

Dinah gave her a sad smile. "That's because you haven't yet loved a man."

Ida nodded, as if Dinah's words settled the matter, but a feeling of uneasiness settled over her. Love did not carry the same appeal for her that it did for others.

It almost seemed to be more trouble than it was worth. "I could happily live my whole life without knowing what that feels like."

"Oh, my dear," Dinah said, turning to face her. "I predict you will one day look a man directly in the eye and slapping him will be the furthest thing from your mind."

Mick managed to locate the barbershop in short order and entered to the sound of raucous laughter from the patrons inside. The barber, an elderly fellow with smiling eyes, introduced himself as Orin Lemm, a native of Spring Creek. His assistant, a young fellow named Georg, ushered Mick to a chair and promptly took to lathering up his whiskery chin, a minty smell filling the air.

"Work for the railroad?" Orin asked as he finished shaving a man in the chair next to Mick's.

Mick guarded his answers. "I'm from the Chicago area. Just visiting." There would be plenty of time to explain his reason for being here later on.

"Really?" Orin's face lit up. "I have a cousin who lives in Sha-ka-gee. Maybe you know 'im." He dove into a monologue about his cousin's liver condition, scarcely pausing for breath.

Once Mick was lathered and ready, Orin moved over to take Georg's place. As the older man worked the razor this way and that, he continued to talk nonstop. His knowledge of Spring Creek was clear, and his pride in the town surely exceeded that of anyone else. In fact, Mick couldn't remember when he'd ever heard someone brag to such a degree.

"Spring Creek was just a tiny place when I was a

boy," Orin explained with great zeal. "Mostly farm-land."

"Oh?" Mick found that hard to believe, considering the current state of the town. How long had it been since the hotels and stores had been built? Likely they'd come about as a result of the influx of railroad workers.

"Yep. Sugarcane and cotton," Orin continued. "But when the railroad came through, everything changed overnight. Much of the land was acquired by the railroad. We're a major switchyard for the Great Northern now. Fourteen lines of track and a roundhouse."

"Not everyone's happy about that," one of the railroad men interjected. "Folks 'round here've made me feel about as welcome as a skunk at a picnic."

Several of the others made similar comments, though most agreed they'd grown to love the area, in spite of the heat and the poor reception from the locals. Mick wondered how they'd stopped perspiring long enough to fall in love with the place.

"I've got no complaints," Orin was quick to throw in. "Having you men in town has really helped my business. Never seen so many whiskers in all my days. And life's not boring. That's for sure."

His young assistant nodded in agreement. "You won't hear me complaining."

Orin proceeded to fill Mick's ears with all sorts of town gossip, covering everything from who was bickering with whom to where to buy the best liquor. He thought the whiskey at the new Wunsche Brothers Saloon was the best around.

And he discussed, in great detail, the shapely legs of the dancing girls at the town's most notable saloon, The Golden Spike. This certainly got Mick's attention, though not because of the women who worked there or their legs. Any saloon, notable or otherwise, would soon pale in comparison to his gambling hall. If everything went according to plan, anyway.

On and on Orin went, discussing the exceptionally warm weather and the cost of a meal at The Harvey House, a place he heartily recommended, especially on the nights when Myrtle Mae was cooking. Whoever she was.

Orin snipped away, shifting his conversation to the women in the town. "Not many to be had," he commented, "so I hope you haven't come with hopes of finding a wife like the rest of these fellers."

"The thought never crossed my mind." Though appealing women back home had drawn his eye, he'd never spent enough time with any one of them to be tempted. Not that he had any negative feelings regarding marriage in general.

No, Mick had no bias against matrimony. And he had nothing against the women in Texas, either, for that matter. He'd already taken note of at least one lovely female. His thoughts shifted to the beautiful blonde he'd just met. Why hadn't he asked her name?

Well, no matter. In a town this size, surely someone would know her. He would have no trouble giving an accurate description, having memorized every detail, from the wild hair swept up off her neck, to the blue eyes, to the determination in her step.

The barber finished up his work, and Mick stood to leave. His cheeks stung from the brush of the razor strokes and the pungent smell of the lather lingered in the air. He rubbed his palm across his smooth chin and smiled at the older man. "Thanks so much."

"My pleasure."

Mick dropped a couple of coins into Orin's hand and turned to leave. Exhaustion washed over him. He needed to locate a quiet room for the days ahead, a place where he could sleep off the train trip and begin to sort things out.

After a few paces, he found himself in front of The Harvey House. From what he'd been told, it was the nicest place in town. Hopefully, it would turn out to be the quietest, too. He'd check in first, then visit the local mercantile to make a couple of necessary purchases, then get some much-needed sleep.

Holding back an escaping yawn, Mick climbed the steps to the hotel, wishing a rainstorm would come along to wash away the sticky south Texas heat. He stood atop the steps and turned to look out over the little town. He couldn't quite put his finger on it, but Mick actually felt the definite stirrings of a storm ahead. Only this one likely had nothing to do with the weather.

Chapter Four

❧

Ida tended to the shop throughout the afternoon. Seemed no matter how hard she worked, she could scarcely find space enough for all the goods. Every square inch of the mercantile was stacked high with barrels, boxes and bins, from front to back. It always seemed to be this way when the season changed. The goods in the store shifted to accommodate seasonal needs.

With time, Ida managed to make sense of it all, but not without a considerable amount of strategy on her part. Boxes of summer goods were emptied, jars and bins were stacked and spring items that hadn't yet sold were placed on a sale table.

As she worked, the locals came and went—many making purchases, others just passing the time. Ida swept the wood-planked floor, and then began the arduous task of dusting the upper shelves that housed the store's finer merchandise, above the pine showcase. She smiled as she studied the handiwork of the showcases, which held higher-priced glassware. They ran the entire length of the store, from back to front. Papa had worked for weeks on the detailing, and it showed.

After dusting the shelves, Ida opened a showcase and repositioned the china dolls inside. Why in the world Dinah would stock such delicate items in a town like this remained a mystery. Ida had never asked, wondering if perhaps Dinah secretly longed for a daughter, someone who might play with beautiful dolls like these. Regardless, these breakable beauties would likely never sell in a town like Spring Creek.

Ida turned her attention to a hand-painted porcelain washbowl and pitcher. It reminded her of the one her mother had used each morning. Determined not to grow sad, Ida forced the memory from her mind. Only hard work could head off a somber attitude and with the heat hanging so heavily in the air, she could scarcely imagine adding a sour disposition to an already difficult day.

A few minutes before four, the brother of her friend Sophie entered the mercantile, red-faced and clearly upset. Ida didn't intentionally listen to Eugene Weimer's dissertation, but his booming voice rang out across the store, leaving her little choice.

"Just came from the barbershop," he explained in a huff. "A big-city fella in a fancy suit and hat rode in on the afternoon train from Chicago. Really tall fella. Maybe ya seen 'im."

Ida stopped what she was doing. She knew exactly who Eugene was talking about.

"Chicago?" several of the men echoed. One mumbled "Yankee" under his breath.

Ida hadn't considered the fact that the man might be from up North. Still, she couldn't imagine why that would make much of a difference these days.

"What's he doing here?" one of the fellas asked, his eyes flashing with anger.

"That's the problem," Eugene said. "No one seems to know. But be sure he doesn't look like one of us. Mighty suspicious to me."

"Traveling salesman?" another man asked.

Ida secretly hoped the man didn't turn out to be of that particular occupation. Traveling salesmen had poor reputations, at least the ones who'd dared show their faces and their wares around these parts. They were often ushered onboard the next train out of Spring Creek. And Ida was never sad to see them go. They stole business from the mercantile, after all, and their highly touted products usually left much to be desired.

Eugene shook his head and shoved his thumbs into his belt loops. "He was traveling light, from what I could tell, so I doubt he's selling anything. But my gut tells me he's got a story to tell, and it ain't a good one."

"Likely he has family in the area is all," Ida said with a shrug, unable to resist joining the conversation. How dare they judge the man without even knowing him! Didn't they know the Bible spoke against such things?

"Nope," Eugene said. "Orin weaseled that much out of him. He's got no people here. And he don't work for the railroad, neither."

"Hope he ain't come to Spring Creek lookin' fer a wife!" one of the men hollered out. "He'll have to get in line. And if'n he tries to cut in front of me, I'll take him down in a minute!"

Ida held her tongue, though it took every ounce of strength to do so. If he had come looking for a wife, he'd jump to the head of the line simply because of his genteel nature and fashionable attire, no doubt about that.

Eugene folded his arms at his chest and shook his head. "I'm guessing he's here to buy up land, not fetch a wife."

"I heard someone bought the Salyer farm," Ida interjected. "Maybe he's the new owner." Yes, an explanation like that would make perfect sense, wouldn't it? Purchasing a local farm wouldn't make him suspect, by any stretch of the imagination.

"He don't look like any farmer I ever saw," Eugene said. "Dressed all uppity-like. And his shoes—never seen a shine like that on any man's feet. I could almost see myself in 'em."

"Hmm." Ida knew the men would find this the most suspicious evidence of all. Every man in Spring Creek wore boots—nothing but.

"What kind of a fella would show up in a place like this, wearing slick, show-offish shoes?" one of the older men grumbled.

Eugene leaned in to the crowd and spoke in a strained voice. "I'm guessin' he's here to buy up our local businesses and take over the town. It's been happening all over the state—not just in Spring Creek. Yankees movin' in and buyin' up shops and mills on the sly whilst the locals are lookin' the other way. I'd wager he's a sly one, and well trained at that."

"Well, we ain't gonna let him get away with it," one of the fellows hollered out.

"We've had enough of that," another added.

Eugene squared his shoulders and added his final thoughts on the matter. "The whole thing just gripes my gizzard. I've had enough of folks sweeping in and taking over." He began to list all the times such a thing had happened, and Ida sighed. She couldn't argue the point. Spring Creek had been taken over by out-of-town-ers, after all.

"What is this man's name?" she asked when Eugene finished.

"Bradley." Eugene's eyes held a gleam of suspicion. "Mick Bradley."

"Did someone call my name?"

The crowd grew silent and a parting of the waters seemed to take place as Mick made his way through the throng. Ida kept her distance, just in case the men got riled up.

"Someone got something to say to me?" Mick asked as he looked around at the crowd.

No one uttered a word, and the beating of Ida's heart seemed to drown out everything else for a moment. Even though he might have come to town to create trouble, she still found him an inordinately handsome man. With a fresh, clean-shaven face, no less.

Focus, Ida.

Nothing in the fellow's air spoke of ill will for the people of Spring Creek. Surely the others were wrong about him. Likely, he would turn out to be the new owner of the Salyer farm, was all. And, if so, she would take over a pecan pie once he got settled in. Just to be neighborly, of course.

Just then he looked her way and they exchanged a glance. She couldn't help but notice the pleased look in his eye when he saw her. She tried not to react, but the edges of her lips betrayed her. Ida swallowed hard, trying to maintain her composure.

When no one responded to Mick's question, he tipped his hat and went on about his business looking over the items on the shelves. He asked Ida to help him with a toothbrush and tooth powder. A feeling of contentment washed over her. *See there. He's well groomed in every conceivable respect. And he didn't come in to purchase chewing tobacco, like most of the other men. No, this one is certainly different from the others.*

Ida waited on Mick at the register, ignoring the whispers and stares of the others in the room.

When he left the store, another lively conversation erupted. Ida did her best to ignore it, though she was as intrigued by Mick Bradley as they were. But she was hoping for the best, while they were expecting the worst. Would he be good for Spring Creek, or bad? Ida didn't know, but she was sure of one thing—she would take a dozen Mick Bradleys over those foolish railroad men any day.

As Mick made his way across the street to the hotel, he thought about the reception he'd just received in the mercantile. Just the little bit of conversation he'd overheard while entering the store had been enough to convince him of their distrust. But what had he done to prompt such a reaction? What motivated such a hard and swift judgment on their part?

His suit, maybe? Some of the fellas had seemed to give him a once-over, taking in his clothes. Sure, most of the Spring Creek men were dressed in more casual attire. But a man's suit shouldn't make him suspect, should it? A few men had looked at his feet. So what if he opted for shoes over boots? Nothing odd about that, at least where he hailed from. Were Texans always this skittish as far as Northerners were concerned?

Mick tugged at his collar and willed the heat to go away as he entered his room. How in the world would he stand this? Surely in this sort of heat, the pine trees must be whistling for the dogs.

Why had he come to Spring Creek again? From his second-story window at The Harvey House, the town didn't seem terribly impressive, at least not in comparison to Chicago.

Well, that's why I'm here. To make it impressive.

He chuckled as he lay down on the bed, remembering the greeting he'd received at the front desk when he'd checked in earlier.

"You ain't from 'round here, are ya?" the clerk had asked.

"No, sir. I'm from the Windy City."

"Amarillo?"

Mick couldn't help but laugh. The fellow had looked a bit miffed.

He certainly wasn't making a lot of friends here in Spring Creek.

Maybe, as Orin had suggested at the barbershop, the local men feared he'd come to town to find a wife. Mick found himself smiling as he thought about the blonde. What a lucky coincidence to see her again. And luckier still that he'd learned where he could find her on a regular basis. She'd given him an impish smile, one that made him want to visit the mercantile again soon.

Well, no matter, Mick thought as his eyes began to close. He shook off any ill-conceived notions of courting her or any other woman in the near future. No, he'd better keep his head on straight while he was in Spring Creek. Otherwise someone might just come along and knock it off.

Chapter Five

Mick's stomach rumbled for the umpteenth time. Now that he'd had a good rest, he was ready for a meal. The smells coming from the kitchen caused his stomach to leap as he entered the dining room. *Wonderful, blessed food.* How long had it been since he'd had a meal in a room that wasn't rocking back and forth as he ate, the clacking of train wheels reverberating in his aching ears? Too long.

He glanced around the noisy room. Dozens of men, mostly railroad workers, he would guess, filled the place. He couldn't help but notice their inquisitive stares, their eyes filled with distrust. Had the rumors of his presence spread that quickly?

He observed his prospective patrons. He'd seen worse than this scraggly bunch. Before long, these fellas would be his allies.

Mick soon found himself seated across the table from a stern-looking older man with a broad cigar hanging from his lips. Unlike the others in the room, he was dressed well. Surely he didn't work for the Great Northern.

"Cain't say as I've seen you 'round these here parts,"

the fellow quipped, the lit cigar jumping up and down as he spoke.

Mick nodded. "New to the area."

"Come in on the afternoon train?"

"Yes, sir."

The man gave him a pensive look. "Don't look like the other railroad fellas." He paused for closer inspection. "There's something different about you."

I was just thinking the same of you.

"Ah. Well, that's because I don't work for the railroad." Mick hoped the conversation would shift in another direction.

At that moment, the waitress appeared with a menu in hand. Mick quickly ordered the largest steak in the place, along with sliced potatoes and a huge piece of apple pie.

His dining companion made introductions, though the look in his eye did little to make a stranger feel welcome. "Name's Chuck Brewster."

"Mick Bradley." He extended his hand and gave the fellow a hearty handshake, then turned his attention to a glass of sweet tea.

For the better part of the meal, Mick avoided the older man's probing questions. Brewster could be a local businessman sniffing out competition. Or maybe he worked for the law. When Mick asked him a question or two, Brewster was as cagey as Mick had been about answering. For sure, he had something up his sleeve.

Mick left the restaurant at a quarter after six with a very full stomach, surprised to see the sun only just leaning toward the western sky. The slight oranges and reds ran together, casting a colorful haze across the street. For half a minute, the town almost looked presentable. He pulled a map from his pocket and began to walk in the direction of the property where his new facility would go up, passing the land agent's office on the way. He'd have to stop by first thing in the morning to seal the deal. After that, nothing could stop him.

He located the lot in question, and found it to be an overgrown field next door to the mercantile—a ragged piece of property at best.

Mick looked it over with a careful eye. A considerable amount of work would need to be done before any building could begin, but at least the patch of land was strategically nestled between the bank and the mercantile, perched and ready for notoriety. In his mind's eye, Mick saw the place—roulette wheels spinning, cards slapping against tables, glasses filled with alcohol, barmaids laughing, the heady scent of tobacco hovering in the air…

Only one thing seemed poised to get in his way. He turned and looked directly across the street at Spring Creek's largest—and from all rumors most notorious—saloon. The Golden Spike. The name shimmered in lights above the doorway. And standing just beneath the glittering letters was a familiar man with a lit cigar dangling from his lips.

With a silent nod in Chuck Brewster's direction, Mick turned and headed back toward the hotel.

Chapter Six

The late-May sunshine rippled through the trees, causing the pine needles overhead to glisten like an emerald-green parasol. Ida wound her way beyond the gristmill, through the comfort of the familiar forest, and entered the clearing to the west of Spring Creek's tiny schoolhouse. The rustic wood-framed building hadn't changed much over the years. Indeed, it had remained every bit the same since Ida's childhood days.

Standing there brought a rush of warmth to her soul, and memories surfaced. She saw herself as a little girl once more, rolling hoops with a stick across the schoolhouse yard. Pigtails bounced about on her head, and gingham skirts twisted around her ankles, just as they did now. Oh, the joy of those days! What sweet and simple times she had known as a child in this blessed place. What innocence and wonder.

Immediately, a dark cloud hovered over her reminiscing. Would the few children who remained in Spring Creek fare as well? How could they, with the town on such a downward spiral?

Ida's thoughts shifted to a conversation she'd had

with Papa just that morning, a most revealing chat about Mick Bradley, the handsome stranger in the fine suit. Unfortunately, he was not the man of integrity she'd made him out to be in her imagination. No, his intentions were clearly of another nature altogether. According to Papa, who'd heard it from the sheriff, Mick Bradley had come to Spring Creek to build a gambling hall.

Ida trembled with fury at the very idea. Didn't the townspeople have enough trouble with Chuck Brewster and his house of ill repute? And weren't there two other such establishments in town already—places where the railroad men and all those who were just passing through could get liquored up and wreak havoc? Did they really need another?

No indeed. And now that she knew the truth, Ida would do everything she could to stop Mick Bradley in his tracks before he brought more pain and corruption to her town. With determination taking hold, she resolved to do all she could to dissuade him from his task.

Just one small piece of business to take care of first.

Ida made her way across the schoolyard. The pungent scent of gardenias filled the air, the bushes nearly bursting with excitement. She remembered the day they were planted, just six years ago. Her teacher, Miss Marta, had thought it a lovely idea to offer the children a flower garden of their very own.

Of course, Miss Marta was Mrs. Hollander now. She had long since married and moved on to Houston, like so many others. But the flowers remained a testament that things of strength continued to blossom and grow, in spite of adversity.

Was Spring Creek strong enough to keep blooming

with so many villains about? And how could she, a simple girl, accomplish the kinds of changes she sought? Only one way. She must seek out help—and she knew just where to begin.

Ida tiptoed a bit closer and squinted in an attempt to see through the classroom window. The boys and girls squirmed at their desks. With school letting out in less than a week, they were likely to be anxious for a romp in the sunshine.

Sophie Weimer, her dearest childhood friend, stood at the front of the classroom looking quite scholarly as she gave the children their assignments. Her shirtwaist showed off a tiny waist, and her broad skirt swished this way and that as she tended to the needs of her students with great enthusiasm and a broad smile.

"It's a shame you're only filling in until a real teacher can be found," Ida whispered as she watched her friend at work. "You're quite good at this." She tugged at her collar, trying to gain some relief from the heat. "Come on, Sophie. It's time to ring the bell. Let 'em go."

As if she had somehow heard Ida's thoughts, Sophie reached for the bell on her desk and dismissed the students for the day.

Out they flowed, like tumbleweeds rolling across a plain. Little Maggie Jordan shrugged off the attentions of one of the boys—a bully by the name of Everett. Several of the lads raced from tree to tree. Ida watched them all with amazement. How long had it been since she and Sophie had run from that same door, headed out to pick dewberries? And how many years had it been since she'd worn her braids twisted up on her head like so many of these little darlings?

Ida walked up the steps to the schoolroom and peeked inside, taking in the familiar desks and inkwells.

A smiled broadened her friend's face. "What brings you to our schoolhouse this afternoon?" Sophie asked.

Ida pressed a hair behind her ear and gave Sophie a knowing look. "I've come to see what kind of a teacher you make."

"I've heard from the students that I make a fine one," Sophie said with a laugh. "Of course, I also made a fine waitress for The Harvey House, and a fine worker at the gristmill before that. And I can shoe a horse with the best of 'em. Any other questions?"

"I dare say, you excel at everything," Ida said with a nod, "which is exactly why I've come to ask your opinion on something."

"What is it?"

"I've come to speak with you about a matter of utmost importance to our community," Ida stressed. "Something I believe you will find *very* troubling."

"Ah. I see." Sophie closed up the classroom and together she and Ida stepped out onto the playground, where several of the children were still gathered around.

"Run along home now, boys and girls," Sophie instructed. "I'm sure you've afternoon chores to get to. We don't want your parents to worry."

Everett let out a groan. "Aw, Miss Sophie, you're no fun."

"If they had any idea the kind of trouble you stirred up as a child," Ida muttered under her breath, "they might think otherwise."

Within a matter of minutes, the students had all scattered to the winds, their childish ramblings now just a whisper among the pines.

"You look as if you don't feel well," Sophie commented as they started on the path to town. "Has something happened?"

Ida sighed. "I'm afraid so." Pulling out a handkerchief, she swabbed the back of her neck to rid herself of the moisture underneath her hairline. "You know that piece of property next to the mercantile?" She folded the hankie and tucked it into her sleeve.

"Yes, of course."

"Any guesses as to who's bought it?"

Sophie spilled out a long list of names, and Ida shook her head with each one.

"Who, then?" Sophie asked.

They stopped walking and Ida looked Sophie in the eye. "A stranger. From up North." She felt foolish as she realized how easily she'd been taken in by the man's polished exterior. Why, if not for the sheriff's conversation with Papa, she might very well have continued on with her fanciful notions about Mick Bradley. But no more. Now that she knew the truth, justice would surely follow.

Concern filled Sophie's eyes. "I'd been told that piece of property would be ideal for a new feed store. Mr. Skinner was looking into purchasing it, wasn't he?"

"That's not to be. Mrs. Skinner told Dinah that her husband is considering building on the outskirts of town to avoid the chaos on Midway, or perhaps abandoning the idea of a new store altogether."

"Can't say as I blame him."

"Me, either." Ida sighed again. "But there is more to the story."

"Do tell."

"I heard Papa talking to the sheriff, who stopped

by our place just this morning. The new owner of the property next to the mercantile is a gambling-hall fellow from Chicago named Mick Bradley, come to bring more greed and despair to our town. He's going to open a place for the railroad men to load up on liquor and gamble their earnings away."

"No."

"Yes." Her anger intensified as she continued on. "And right next door to our store, no less. Can you imagine? Isn't it enough that we have to contend with the brawls from Chuck Brewster's place? And the Wunsche Brothers' saloon? The last thing we need is another such place."

Sophie paused, her brow furrowed. "This is a matter for prayer, Ida."

"Yes, of course. But don't you think the Lord would ask more of us?" Ida said as they continued to walk.

"More?"

"Someone has to *do* something," Ida implored. "We've watched and waited, prayed and pleaded, but things are only getting worse. It's time to grab the horse by the reins."

Sophie shook her head. "Oh, Ida. Have you talked to your papa about this? I can't imagine he would be happy to hear what you're saying. You know how he feels about your concerns."

"My papa is a strong man," she said. "And he has raised a strong daughter."

Sophie nodded. "To be sure."

They rounded the corner onto Midway, where activity abounded. Ida clamped her handkerchief over her nose as the overwhelming scent of horse manure assaulted her.

"Little good this does," she grumbled. The tiny square of cloth could do nothing to block out the mix of nauseating aromas—the ever-present stench of railroad men in need of a bath, the smell of soot from the nearby trains and the overwhelming scent of burnt grease from the restaurant at The Harvey House.

With great determination, she pulled the handkerchief away from her face and looked Sophie squarely in the eye. "I am on a mission," she stated quite plainly. "One from on high."

Sophie chuckled. "You have such a way of putting things, Ida. Perhaps you should be writing novels, not just reading them."

"I am quite serious, Sophie. Have you not read the book of Esther—in the Old Testament?"

"Of course I have." Sophie gave her a quizzical look. "But what does that have to do with you?"

"Esther was put upon the earth to save her people. The Bible says she was born for such a time as this. Remember?"

"Yes, of course. But—"

"I have no doubt that *I* was born for such a time as this," Ida explained, triumphant. "To save our little town from the evil influence of men like Mr. Bradley."

"Ah." A hint of a smile crossed her friend's face. "If I believed anyone were capable of saving our little town, it would be you."

"Truly?"

Sophie gave Ida a pensive look and arched an eyebrow. "You and the Lord working together, of course."

They stopped in front of The Golden Spike as Nellie DeVries, one of the dancing girls, sprinted past them in full regalia, almost knocking them down.

"Sorry!" the young woman called out with an apologetic giggle. "Chuck needs me inside."

Ida drew in a breath and kept walking. "This is just the sort of thing that concerns me most, now that a new gambling hall might be opening up," she whispered. "Barmaids. Saloon dancers. The few women left in this town will eventually have little choice but to turn to occupations such as these."

"I do hope you're wrong." Sophie fanned herself.

Anger took hold again as Ida said, "What other choices will they have? All the reputable businesses will be gone, if these strangers have their way. And I, for one, won't have it. I will not allow the girls of Spring Creek to grow up into women such as…such as…" She pointed at the door that Nellie DeVries had just vanished behind and sputtered, "Women such as that!"

Sophie looked at Ida carefully. "Ida, perhaps you're judging a bit too—"

Ida never heard the rest. Her attentions shifted to Mick Bradley's property across the street. She gave it a stern once-over. "This is the spot where that good-for-nothing out-of-towner hopes to weave his web. And I plan to stop him in his tracks." Ida turned to look her friend in the eye. "I do need the Lord's help. But I've come to ask for someone else's assistance, as well."

Sophie's eyes lit with understanding. "Ah. You mean me."

"Indeed." Ida nodded, knowing Sophie would understand the depth of her meaning. "I mean you." She leaned in, and added, "Even Esther couldn't manage alone, you know."

Sophie linked arms with Ida. "In that case," she said with a smile, "I am all yours. Someone's got to keep an eye on you, Ida Mueller," she teased. "At this rate, you're likely to set the entire town ablaze with your great passion for propriety."

Irritation set in as Mick gazed at his property. Only three days into his new venture and already his plan was fraught with problems. The land agent—the same one who had assured him by letter that the lot would be his as soon as money changed hands—had suddenly turned up with another offer. The scoundrel was probably just trying to up the ante, but Mick wasn't playing that game.

Still, he had come a long way, and for what? To lose the piece of property he'd been assured would be his? Could he risk that? What would the investors back in Chicago say?

Maybe he should up his offer, just to be safe.

On the other hand, folks weren't exactly warming up to him. The local sheriff, a burly fellow with an overgrown mustache, had paid a visit to his hotel room just last night. What was it he had said, again? Ah, yes. Something about making his visit to Texas brief. Not exactly a threat. More of a warning.

And the ever-present stares from the saloon owners—especially Chuck Brewster—who clearly saw him as a threat to their businesses, did little to calm Mick's troubled mind. How could he keep the peace and still get the job done?

Maybe he could convince the pretty blonde to help people see him as the upstanding businessman he was. She probably knew everyone in town, since she worked at the mercantile. Perhaps he should pay her a visit and see if he could win another one of those lovely smiles. Purely for business reasons, of course.

Chapter Seven

"You're late, Ida."

"I know, Dinah. I know." Ida flashed a sheepish grin as she slipped behind the mercantile counter. She busied herself refilling a jar with black licorice, avoiding her aunt's accusing glare.

"I'm partly to blame," Sophie added as she leaned her elbows on the countertop, a habit Ida knew Dinah disliked. "We got to talking and the time slipped away from us."

"Still," Dinah said, glancing at the clock and then at Ida with a look of frustration, "you are exceptionally late...even for you."

A guilty sigh escaped from Ida's lips. "I am sorry. Truly. But I needed to ask Sophie's opinion about the new gambling hall that's going in next door."

A couple of their regular customers passed by the counter, slowing as they heard mention of the gambling hall. Ida closed her mouth and continued on with her work, an act of penance.

"Ah." Dinah's eyes narrowed. "I see. And what does your friend have to say about this latest dilemma?"

"That it is a matter for prayer," Sophie said, looking at Ida.

"The Lord is calling us to action," Ida explained, "and I'm to lead the way." She contemplated delving into her story about Esther, but decided to keep it to herself for the moment.

"Oh?" Dinah raised an eyebrow.

"I've arranged a meeting with Reverend Langford tomorrow afternoon. He will know best how to advise me. And I am convinced he will agree that we cannot sit idly by with the enemy so clearly at work."

"Reverend Langford is a good man," Dinah agreed, "and a sensible one. He will give you a reasonable answer. He is not prone to violence, so he will respond with caution."

"I am not advocating violence, of course," Ida insisted. "But the Almighty expects his people to take action, to face their enemies with courage. Remember David and Goliath? Remember Shadrach, Meshach and Abednego?"

"Your second example bears little practical application, Ida," Dinah corrected, "but I can certainly see the resemblance between our situation and what young David went through as he faced the mighty giant. Perhaps we've a goliath of our own in this out-of-towner."

"Yes, that's it." Ida's heart quickened at the thought. "And the saloon owners want to see this latest one gone, as well. They're on our side for once."

Dinah crossed her arms. "I dare say the saloon owners make for somewhat strange and uncomfortable allies." She lowered her voice. "And I suspect they have their own reasons for wanting to see him gone."

"True," Sophie responded. "He will surely steal much of their business. That won't go over well."

Dinah drew in a deep breath and the look on her face grew more serious. "I hate to think of what will happen if they become angry. We will find them a force to be reckoned with, to be sure."

Ida could hardly imagine what sort of trouble the saloon owners would stir up, if crossed. She'd never thought about any of this from that angle before. Truly, she only wanted to stop Mick Bradley.

Carter interrupted their conversation as he scurried behind the counter, chattering merrily. He opened his palm and showed them several of his most colorful marbles, gabbing all the while about his favorites.

Ida reached down and lifted the tiniest one from his hand to serve as an illustration. "I might be small like David. But with just one little stone, I could take those giants down. I could take them *all* down!"

She looked up, triumphant. Immediately her heart plummeted. Directly across the counter stood Mick Bradley with an amused look on his face. The little marble slipped between her fingers and hit the floor, *plink-plinking* against the wood-planked floorboards as it rolled out of sight.

As they all stood in stunned silence, Ida wondered just how much the man had heard. Dinah finally came to her senses and gave him a welcoming smile. "Can I help you, sir?"

"Yes, please." He extended his hand, and Dinah gave it a shake. "I need to make a few purchases." He handed Dinah a list to be filled.

Dinah took to gathering the items, but Ida couldn't seem to move. In fact, she could scarcely breathe as she took him in. Funny, standing here in this close proximity, he didn't look like the criminal sort at all.

But you could never tell with wolves, especially those so carefully disguised. This one's smoky gray eyes were a distraction, that's all—like puffs of smoke from one of the passing locomotives. And his broad smile was clearly a well-rehearsed bit he'd learned somewhere up North. A true Texan could sense dishonesty, particularly in a Northerner. His sandy-colored curls caught her eye again, but she forced her attention elsewhere. She was a strong woman. She could overlook them with little trouble.

Couldn't she?

Mick flashed that practiced smile in Ida's direction and approached her.

"I don't believe we've officially met," he said.

"I know who you are, Mr. Bradley," Ida replied, trying to ignore the fact that she couldn't seem to overlook his handsome features after all. *No, I will not be taken in by this heathen from up North, this tool of the enemy come to bring corruption and vice.*

"And you are?" he asked, extending his hand.

Ida didn't want to answer his question, and yet her hand clasped his and her mouth spoke the words, "Ida Mueller."

"It's a real pleasure, Miss Mueller," he said, tipping his hat and holding on to her hand. For a moment, she was lost in his gray eyes, until Sophie cleared her throat, reminding Ida of her manners. She quickly removed her hand from his.

"This is Sophie Weimer, Mr. Bradley."

"Please, call me Mick. I'd appreciate it, ladies," he said, shaking Sophie's hand but keeping his eyes on Ida.

Ida felt a flush rise in her cheeks, and she took Sophie by the arm, pulling her to the storeroom.

"Th-that's him?" her friend whispered, eyes wide. "Why, he's the handsomest thing I ever did see. Better than a picture in a book, to be sure. You forgot to mention that part, Ida!"

"Sophie," Ida whispered, "do not be deceived. This is not a man to be trifled with. He is evil through and through, despite his looks and fancy clothes. Besides, do you not remember what the Bible says? The enemy comes at us like a wolf in sheep's clothing." She turned back and gave Mick Bradley another look through the doorway. "He is on the prowl, even now."

Yes, that wolf of a man was certainly adorned in sheep's clothing. His fine gray suit. His shiny shoes. His stylish felt hat. In fact, she couldn't say when she'd seen a finer-looking sheep.

Sophie gave Mick a second glance. "There's no denying, he is the most handsome man I've ever set eyes on. I can't help but wonder if he's married."

"Sophie!" Ida shook her head in exasperation.

Dinah called out her name, and Ida left the storeroom with Sophie following on her heels. Ida turned and gave Sophie a stern look. "What's come over you?" she whispered. "You're acting like a smitten schoolgirl."

A slow smile spread across Sophie's face. "Why, Ida Mueller. I do believe you're jealous!"

"Jealous? How can you say such a thing?" Ida sputtered.

"I think I'm not the only one who's wondering if Mick Bradley is married."

"Don't be ridiculous," Ida said, reaching to straighten

several bolts of fabric that were already straight. "And please wipe that annoying expression off your face."

Sophie tried to look serious. "Will this do?"

"Now that's the girl I know and love," Ida replied.

Sophie broke into laughter as Ida turned in a huff and joined Dinah to fill Mick's order with haste.

The dirt-streaked hotel room window provided Mick with a near-perfect view of the town. From here, he could almost see the sign on the front of the mercantile. Why he felt drawn to the place, he could not say. If anything, he should steer clear of it at all costs. The women inside that establishment clearly took issue with him, though they were all politeness and smiles during his visit. He sensed their concern and would do his best to put their minds at ease. No point in quarreling with the neighbors, after all, especially one with startling blue eyes, like Ida Mueller.

Mick was perplexed by the change he saw in her. Was it not just a few days ago she'd smiled at him in that particularly fetching way? Now, suddenly, she'd taken on a different attitude, one he didn't much care for. The way she'd said, "I know who you are, Mr. Bradley," was all business, and he'd opted not to ask for her help, as he'd originally planned. Maybe she'd discovered his reason for being here and had taken it as an affront.

Why he cared what she thought remained a mystery. They scarcely knew each other, after all. Still, from the moment of their first encounter, he'd locked those beautiful blue eyes into his memory.

"Stop it, man. Don't be thinking about a woman. You'll be back in Chicago before long and there are plenty of sensible—or not-so-sensible—women there to fill your thoughts."

Indeed, as soon as the gambling hall began to go up—he'd decided to call it The Lucky Penny—Mick would search out the perfect candidate to run the place in his stead, someone from his neck of the woods, most likely. If he selected a local for the job, the community would surely turn on the poor fellow; the whole thing might even end in bloodshed. No, he couldn't risk that. Wouldn't be good for business. It would have to be someone his investors approved of—someone with a head for numbers, a heart for turning a profit and big-city experience.

Shouts rang out and Mick turned his attention to the street below. Several of the railroad men had gathered there, instigating yet another fight. These Texans were certainly boisterous, and a sure sight more complicated than he'd figured. Prideful, to be sure. And standoff-ish. Maybe it had something to do with all the dust they swallowed as the trains barreled by. Clogged up their throats. Regardless, many of them had already voiced an opinion by refusing to do business with him. Pure stubbornness.

And then there was the issue with the property. According to the land agent, the owner—a man from the Houston area—was holding out for more money. Mick would pay it after all, just to get the game under way, though he hated to give in to such tactics.

He sighed as he thought about the situation. Really, what did it matter, when all was said and done? The payoff would be worth it. And he needed to get started on the building as soon as possible.

"Soon, fellas." He watched the brawling men as the

quiet words slipped from his lips. "Soon you will have much more to do than duke it out in the streets. Soon you will be sitting at The Lucky Penny dropping all your hard-earned money into my lap."

If everything went as planned, the new building would be up before summer's end.

Mick used his sleeve to wipe the sweat from his forehead. Troubling thoughts continued to plague him as he climbed into bed. He ached to shut the window, to drown out the whoops and hollers from below. Mick knew that many of the sounds came from The Golden Spike, just a few doors down, and that knowledge only added to his aggravation. Unfortunately, the heat simply wouldn't allow him to reclose the window. He shoved the pillow over his head in an attempt to silence the ever-present shouts and laughter of the men.

Out of the darkness, a shot rang out. Mick sprang out of the bed and raced toward the window, his heart pounding. With great relief, he saw that the sheriff had fired the shot into the air to send the men on their way. They scattered with little trouble, drifting off to the various hotels and boardinghouses.

Mick fell into bed a second time in a more hopeful state. Surely these Texans would eventually thank him for coming. Once The Lucky Penny opened, offering them more gambling opportunities, better liquor and a classier decor with a real stage for entertainment, Mike felt confident he'd be Spring Creek's new hero, if they'd just give him half a chance.

Chapter Eight

The shrill whistle of the morning train from Galveston roused Ida from her groggy state. The grinding of brakes, the piercing squeal of metal against metal, the rhythmic clacking of wheels against lines of track—these familiar sounds at daybreak merged with the shouts of the railroad men as the cars inched their way by. *Why must we live so close to the switchyard?*

Papa had built the lumber mill years before the track was laid. But then the railroad had come through and taken over the town—in a hundred different ways.

Ida stretched for a moment and allowed her eyes to become accustomed to the sunlight peeking through the lace curtains. She propped up her pillows and sat up in the bed. Then Ida reached for the worn Bible on the bedside table, one of her most precious possessions, and ran her finger across her mother's name inside.

"Oh, Mama, I wish you were here." She missed their morning prayers together and her mother's nightly readings from the worn book.

Ida leaned against the pillows and opened the Bible to the book of Esther, where she read, for the hundredth time, the story of the young queen approaching the king's throne with fear and trembling.

Ida closed her eyes, deep in thought. Every time she pictured Esther approaching the throne, she couldn't help but envision herself doing the same thing.

Oh, but what would it be like, to come into the king's chambers uninvited? To approach without invitation? And yet, Esther braved the journey, taking one courageous step after the other, and all because of God's calling—*for such a time as this.*

One step at a time, Ida saw herself inching toward the Savior's outstretched arms.

Come to me, child. Don't be afraid.

At some point along the way, fear gripped her heart and her eyes flew open.

"I am afraid," she whispered as she clutched the Bible to her chest, tears springing to her eyes. "I'm afraid I won't be able to do what You have called me to do. Or that I will somehow do it incorrectly. And I'm afraid—" she paused, startled by her thoughts "—that Papa will die someday, too, and I'll truly be alone."

She began to cry in earnest now. Where did this fear come from? Just because she'd lost her mother didn't mean Papa would soon follow.

She wiped her tears from her face. No, she wouldn't give herself over to mourning and fear—not right now, anyway. Ida needed to be strong for her people. Esther wouldn't have given in to fear, would she? No, Esther was a woman of great strength, and Ida would be, too, regardless of the cost. She would meet with Reverend Langford today, as scheduled, and he would help her take a stand for the people of Spring Creek.

A rap at the door startled Ida back to her senses.

"Ida, are you all right? It's time to wash up and get started on breakfast." Her father's reassuring voice brought comfort. The sun now streamed in the window as reality set in. *I'm late.*

"I'll be there in a moment, Papa." She quickly got up and went to the washbasin to scrub the anxiety from her face. Her father would know. He always seemed to, though he rarely questioned her moods anymore. If anything, he simply left her to her ponderings and watched her out of the corner of his eye.

Ida scrambled into her dress and pulled her hair up into a messy knot on the top of her head. Another quick glance in the mirror gave her an opportunity to rehearse a smile, one she hoped to use on Papa as soon as they met in the kitchen. She knew he would be seated at the small table in the corner of the room, waiting for his coffee, ready to talk about what the day ahead held for them both. Hopeful and happy, as always. If only she had inherited that tendency.

She scurried down the stairs and into the spacious kitchen. True to form, Papa sat, spectacles perched on the tip of his nose, reading his Bible.

She forced the smile. "Morning, Papa."

Ida kissed him on his forehead and he reached to squeeze her hand. "Child, you're troubled this morning."

She tied an apron around her waist. "I'm fine. Truly."

"Humph." His eyes narrowed. "I've never known you to be dishonest, daughter."

Ida focused on the coffee, hoping to avoid his penetrating gaze. For some reason, she couldn't utter a word. Not over the lump in her throat, anyway.

He pushed his spectacles up. "Why not share what's

in your heart? Don't you think it would make you feel better, after all?"

"I will, Papa," she assured him. She brushed tears from her eyes before facing him. "As soon as I'm ready."

With biscuits to knead, eggs to scramble and thick slices of ham to fry, she managed to avoid more conversation with her father. Thankfully.

At six forty-five sharp, a rap on the back door signaled the inevitable. Papa welcomed in ten hungry workmen. Their clothes, dingy and ragged, still carried the odors of a thousand yesterdays. How many times had she asked if she could launder their shirts and underclothes? Their pride appeared to be stronger than their noses, no question about that. And on this morning, she thanked the Lord for the smell of the food, which—at least temporarily—masked the stench of sweat and sawdust.

The men stampeded in, tramping mud all over her once-clean kitchen floor. One by one they pulled off their hats, revealing hair in want of trimming. Why couldn't they take better care of themselves? Bathe once in a while? They could all take a lesson from Mick Bradley.

No. She would not think about him today. Pray for him, yes. Think about him, no.

"You've no manners a'tall," Ida scolded as the men guffawed and slapped one another on the back, paying no attention to her words. Nothing new there.

One of the fellows reached toward the platter of ham steaks on the countertop and snatched a loose piece with his fingertips. Ida slapped his hand. "Enough of that. Now get to the table, all of you. You'll be serving yourselves, today Plates are on the buffet, silverware and napkins in the drawer beneath." After giving instructions, Ida poured steaming cups of coffee for all, then retreated to the far side of the room as they bowed their heads for the morning blessing.

"I'll be in the kitchen if you need me," she explained afterward as they stared at her in confusion. Her father cast a curious glance from across the table and she offered up a weak smile. In truth, she simply needed to be alone with her thoughts. And the heat in this room, especially with so many pressed together, proved more than she could bear.

Ida went to work at once on the pots and pans. Her mind drifted to the man who so often captivated her thoughts of late. He'd surely made his presence known. At the mercantile. In the streets. And everywhere she turned.

The more she learned about Mick Bradley's shameful plans, the more she distrusted him. And the more she distrusted him, the stronger was her resolve to see him gone. Or to make him see the error of his ways.

To Ida's way of thinking, a man like Mick Bradley would be a tough sell to the Almighty. Pressing him through the pearly gates would take a bit more than Southern hospitality. It would truly take a miracle. Of course, the Lord was in the miracle-working business, but Ida still found it difficult to imagine.

She made up her mind to drop in on a few of the shopkeepers and encourage them to refuse his business. Of course, kindhearted Dinah would probably flinch at that idea. She tended to mix her faith with kindness, perhaps too much so.

I'm not unkind—just firm.

For a moment Ida reflected on the stubbornness she'd

seen etched in Mick Bradley's handsome face. Ironically, it mirrored her own.

Regardless, she would teach him a thing or two about how to do business in Texas.

Mick breathed a sigh of relief as he left the land agent's office, the deal squared away once and for all. Now to begin the arduous task of clearing the land and purchasing lumber. He'd heard rumors about a lumber mill nearby. Surely that would be just the place to acquire all the pine he'd need.

Minutes later, as Mick neared the mill, a two-story house came into view. White with green shutters. Well maintained. Must be the lumber-mill owner's home. Should he knock on the door to inquire about purchasing lumber, or head around back to the mill?

Then, just as he drew near, the front door to the house swung open, and Ida Mueller appeared on the front porch with a bonnet in her hands. She scurried to close the door. In a hurry, as always.

He stood just yards away from her, close enough for his heart to nearly stop beating altogether. What was it about this woman? Why did he lose the ability to think clearly at the very sight of her?

"Miss Mueller." He removed his hat and flashed a smile, hoping she would return the gesture. When she did not, he popped the hat back into place and weighed his options. Common sense finally won out. He was here to do business, after all. "I've come to purchase some lumber."

"Oh?" She crossed her arms and gave him a curious look. From up there on the porch, her stern stance gave the illusion of height, though he calculated she couldn't be much more than five feet tall, at best. Still, her presence filled the porch.

"Yes," he replied. "Who would I speak to about that?"

"You would want my father." She nodded toward the mill. "Though I can't imagine he will be selling you lumber today or any other day."

"Oh?" His smile faded. "And why is that?"

"Mr. Bradley, in case you haven't noticed, we're not keen on a gambling hall going up in town—we've got enough trouble with the saloons as it is. It's not likely my papa will lend his support to you or your establishment in any form or fashion."

The truth, at last. The reason for the coldness in her stare, the stiffness in her stance.

"But your father is a businessman. Surely he will see past any bias his daughter might have to sell me the lumber I need."

"I wouldn't count on it." Her blue eyes flashed with determination. "Though you are welcome to ask him yourself, of course. I was just headed into town for the afternoon to work at a reputable place of business."

The corners of his mouth turned up in amusement. "So you've taken on a job as barmaid at one of the saloons?"

Ida's hands went straight to her hips. "How dare you suggest such a thing? You take that back," she said angrily.

Disappointment washed over him—she'd found no humor in his joke. He wished he could indeed take his words back, but there was little he could do to remedy the situation now. "I'm sorry, Miss Mueller. I spoke in jest."

"There was nothing funny in what you said. Nothing at all."

"Again, I apologize." After a brief, awkward pause, he offered, "If you will wait until I'm done, I will escort you back to town."

Ida shook her head, slipping the bonnet over her blond curls and tying it at her chin. "That will not be necessary. I make the walk every day on my own, thank you kindly."

"But I've seen how the men jeer at you." He gave her what he hoped would be a fatherly look. "An escort would prevent that from happening, I assure you. Please wait for me."

Ida shook her head once more. "I would rather risk the jeers of a hundred railroad men than have a gambling-hall owner walk alongside me. And that is my final say on the matter." She marched down the steps with her chin jutted forward.

Mick stepped out of her way, realizing she would not be stopped. He followed her with his gaze until she made it to the street. Did she really consider him to be a bigger threat than the fellows who whooped and hollered as she walked by? Did she not recognize a true gentleman when she saw one?

Mick made his way around the house to the mill. Whether or not Ida's father would sell him the necessary lumber remained to be seen, but Mick wouldn't give up. No, he would proceed with his plans. And no one—not even feisty and determined Ida Mueller—would stop him.

Chapter Nine

After a particularly long day, Ida arrived home to find Papa dressed in his Sunday best. She looked at him with curiosity as he straightened his tie, and asked the obvious question. "Going somewhere?"

"Into town for supper." He turned to her with a mischievous grin.

"But I'm planning to cook bratwurst. That's your favorite," she argued.

"It's pot roast and potatoes night down at The Harvey House," he said. "And Myrtle Mae has invited us to come for dinner."

"Myrtle Mae Jennings?"

Ida saw her father's thick mustache twitch a bit. That always meant a smile hid underneath.

"Papa?"

"What, Ida? Can't a man eat pot roast without a hundred questions from his daughter?" he asked, eyes twinkling.

"You can eat anything you like," she responded, "but I suspect there is more to this story than meets the eye. Am I right?"

After clearing his throat, he offered up a vague answer. "Myrtle Mae is a fine woman." He glanced in the mirror to check his tie. "And a mighty fine cook."

"So am I," Ida said, hands on her hips.

Her father reached over and gave her a light peck on the cheek. "Yes, but we never know what the future holds."

"What are you saying?" She stared at him in disbelief. "Are you telling me I'm being traded in for someone who knows nothing about cooking German fare?" Her papa cut potential arguments short with a shake of his head.

"Daughter, I'm not trading you in or asking you to give up cooking. Trust me when I say I would never do that. I'm just in the mood for pot roast and potatoes, that's all."

"Sure you are."

"Now don't make more of this than need be. Come along and be a good girl now. Let your papa escort you to town for a nice dinner."

Her father headed toward the door, gesturing for her to follow. However, Ida stood with her feet planted firmly. Surely he must be joking. Why had he set his sights on Myrtle Mae Jennings, of all people? Everyone in town knew she was a busybody and, well, a chatterbox. Such a thing could hardly be tolerated in a woman.

On the other hand, perhaps Ida shouldn't judge too harshly. Dinah had flat-out accused *her* of gossiping recently, with regard to Mick Bradley. But that was different, of course.

"Come, Ida. We are to arrive at six-thirty," her father said impatiently.

"But, Papa—"

"Come." He opened the door and extended his hand. She glanced in the mirror. "Can't I even have a minute to freshen up?"

"One minute." He gave her a wink. "I'll be on the porch swing, dreaming about that fine meal we're going to have."

"We could have had a fine meal at home," she muttered after he'd gone. However, after a long day of work, she might actually enjoy an evening of being waited on.

Even if it meant eating someone else's cooking.

Ida took advantage of her time alone to tuck some loose curls into place. And she couldn't very well go into the restaurant at The Harvey House wearing her dull brown gingham dress, could she? No, she might as well put on her Sunday blue with the puff sleeves. It wore well, and brought out the color in her eyes—or so she'd been told by Sophie, who knew more about fashion than anyone else in town.

As she dressed, Ida thought about the meeting she'd had with Reverend Langford earlier. He'd suggested they all do what they could to win Mick Bradley to the Lord. Not exactly the response she'd been hoping for. It seemed that no one was taking this gambling hall as seriously as Ida. She'd work to change that, surely.

Nearly fifteen minutes later, Ida made her appearance on the front porch. Papa started to scold her until he noticed her attire. "Why, Ida Mueller. I dare say you're as pretty as a field of bluebonnets."

"I'll take that as a compliment." She took his arm and together they made their way into town, talking all the way. Though she wished to avoid the subject of Mick Bradley, Ida could not. She found herself telling Papa everything she'd learned at the mercantile—how he planned to begin work on the gambling hall within days, and how he'd already hired men to clear the land.

Papa drew in a deep breath but did not respond, at least not at first. When he finally did speak, his words stopped her cold. "I did business with Mr. Bradley this very afternoon. Found him to be an amiable fellow."

"What do you mean?" She stopped and stared at her father, stunned. "Surely you did not sell the man lumber for that den of iniquity he is building."

"Daughter, I cannot control what people build with the lumber I sell them. Nor did the Lord tell me to avoid selling to him. This is not a matter of my linking arms with the man. I'm simply treating him with the courtesy I extend every customer."

"Papa." Ida shook her head, so upset she could barely speak. In her nineteen years she could not recall questioning any of her father's decisions. And yet, in one short day, he'd managed to arouse suspicions twice. Myrtle Mae and Mick Bradley? Had Papa lost his mind?

Pushing her misgivings aside, Ida entered the restaurant on her father's arm. The most wonderful aroma filled the air. Ida breathed it in, suddenly quite glad she had agreed to come.

She closed her eyes for a second. The noises in the room captivated her. The clinking of silverware and glasses. The sounds of waitresses bustling back and forth with their full skirts swishing this way and that. Boisterous laughter from a couple of men at a nearby table. Voices raised in conversation. The Harvey House was a lively place, no doubt about that.

She opened her eyes, noticing familiar faces in the crowd. To her great surprise, Sophie's entire family sat at a large table near the center of the room. The Weimer

boys—Sophie's three older brothers—ate with gusto.
And her parents looked up with matching smiles, motioning for Ida and her father to join them.

After taking her seat, Ida glanced at the menu, then
turned her attention to the conversation at hand. The
Weimers were talking about the upcoming church picnic on the Fourth of July, and the annual cobbler contest.
She was about to express her desire to enter the contest
this year when she spotted Mick Bradley at the restaurant door. Flustered, Ida tried to hide behind her menu.

"Is everything all right, daughter?" Papa asked, easing the menu down to look into her eyes.

"Oh, yes," she offered. "Everything just looks so
good, I can hardly decide. I need to take a closer look."
She peered up over the menu to look at Mr. Bradley
once more.

"I'm having the pot roast," Papa announced to everyone within hearing distance.

"As you can see, so are we," Mrs. Weimer replied.
"It's truly the best thing on the menu." As she sang
Myrtle Mae Jennings's praises, Ida couldn't resist the
temptation to groan.

"Are you all right?" Sophie gave her a curious look.

Just then Myrtle Mae entered the room with a broad
smile on her face. She eased her ample frame through
the crowd of tables, clapping her hands together when
she saw Ida's father.

"Why, Dirk, I'm so happy to see you." Her cheeks,
already flushed, deepened a shade as their eyes met. Ida
took note, wondering when this attraction had begun.
How had she missed it? And what could she do to keep
it from going any further?

Her papa's mustache began to twitch at once. "After

all I've heard about your pot roast, I wouldn't miss it."
And then he winked at her.

Ida tried not to gasp aloud, but stifling her surprise
proved difficult.

"What about you, Ida? What's your preference?" Sophie asked.

"My preference?" Ida stole another peek at Mick
Bradley, who suddenly took notice of her. He gave her
that smile and she felt her cheeks warm. Embarrassed,
she pulled the menu back up. "I'm not sure what to
order."

Sophie, puzzled by Ida's behavior, looked up and
noticed Mick. "Well, you are certainly studying that
menu," Sophie said with a hint of laughter in her voice.
"You will have it memorized before long."

"Must be mighty hungry," Mr. Weimer added.

"More likely she can't find anything she likes," Papa
interjected. "Ida has a tendency to prefer her own cooking over that of others."

"Oh, you really must try my pot roast, Ida." Myrtle
Mae gave her a pat on the shoulder. "Perhaps I'll make
a believer out of you," she said, smiling as she headed
back to the kitchen.

Ida found it increasingly hard to concentrate, what
with Mick Bradley standing directly across the room.
Who could eat, when a man like that had just made his
presence known?

Mick took a seat at a table well within view. For a
brief moment, Ida actually felt sorry for the man, dining alone in a room full of strangers.

Sophie leaned over and whispered, "Perhaps we
should ask the man to join us."

"Hush! He'll hear you," Ida replied.

Sophie laughed at Ida, and looked back at Mick. He raised his hand in greeting, and Sophie waved back. "He is one good-looking man, Ida. Surely looking at Mick Bradley gives you reason to rethink your position on marriage," she teased.

The only thing she wanted to rethink right now was her decision to join her papa for dinner at The Harvey House in the first place.

Mick took note of Ida the moment he entered the restaurant. He couldn't help but notice her dressed like that. Nearly a dozen times during the meal he glanced her way, just to see if she would look back. He wanted to see how her eyes matched up against that beautiful blue dress. He imagined they'd knock him off his chair if he got a close enough look.

Unfortunately—or perhaps fortunately—that never happened. All too soon, Ida and her father left the restaurant with the group they'd been eating with. Mick had sensed her discomfort at his presence, and yet a wave of disappointment washed over him as she left.

On some level, Mick envied Ida, sitting with people she loved—in a group that size—to share a meal. He wondered if he'd ever know the love of a daughter, one who looked up at him with such awe. Or the admiration of sons, who hung on their father's every word like the trio of older boys sitting with Ida. Would he ever gather together with loved ones, praying over food as he'd heard them do, eating pot roast, and singing the cook's praises loud enough for all to hear?

For the first time in ages, Mick acknowledged that losing his parents twenty years before had left him with an emptiness inside. His brother had taken him in and fathered Mick as best he could, but he couldn't fill the void left by his parents. Watching Ida with her friends and family left him feeling lonelier than he'd ever felt in his life.

Would he ever again have a sense of wholeness—of family—like he'd had as a child before his parents passed away?

No. Likely he never would.

And the realization left a hole in his heart the size of Texas.

Chapter Ten

Mick awoke the following morning with a splitting headache. He wasn't sure which had made it harder to sleep through the night—the ruffians in the street or the sounds of retching coming from the room next door. Regardless, he could scarcely function when the morning light streamed through the window of the hotel room.

He hadn't been able to stop the images of Ida Mueller in that blue dress—maybe that was the real reason he couldn't sleep. He'd wanted to catch a glimpse of her up close, but she'd walked right by him, never even looking his way. Had she done so on purpose, avoiding him deliberately?

He shook her out of his mind and sat up slowly. Plenty of work awaited him, and he needed to get to it.

He dressed quickly, and made his way out of the hotel and onto the street.

Ambling down Midway, he was amazed to find it nearly empty at this time of morning. Except for a few railroad men gathered at the station, the place was quiet. The morning dew left the first hint of a pleasant aroma in days. He paused for a moment, thinking perhaps he'd stumbled into a different world altogether.

At last, Mick came to the property. His patch of land. Within the hour, workers would begin to clear the spot. In his mind's eye, he could see how different the lot would look without the overgrowth of weeds. Come Monday, the foundation would be laid, and then the beams erected. Then the exterior walls would come together in no time at all.

Mick glanced over at the mercantile and saw Ida place the OPEN sign on the door. Their eyes met and he tried to read her expression. The hardness he'd sensed yesterday still remained. Surely there had to be more behind that look than his plans to build a gambling hall.

Mick's thoughts were interrupted by a child, probably four or five, running out the door with a puppy in his arms.

"Carter!" Ida scolded. "Your mama's told you a dozen times to keep that mongrel out back. She doesn't want you dragging him through the store."

"He's hungry, Ida." The pup wriggled loose from the little boy's grasp and ran out into the street.

Mick reached the squirming ball of fur just as it bounded onto his property. He walked to the mercantile and handed the pup to Ida with a smile. "I do believe this belongs to you."

"Thank you so much." He noted her attempt to muster up a stern look, but a hint of a smile took its place as the playful pup settled back into her arms. "We're so grateful."

"Puppy!" Carter took the little fur ball from Ida and headed back into the store.

"He's quite a handful," Ida said, "but the dearest thing in the world to me."

Mick looked away. His heart now rushed with a new emotion, one he'd never felt before. What would it feel like...what would it *be* like to have a woman like Ida to come home to? And a child?

Mick could hardly believe the thoughts that raced through his head. Men like him didn't marry, at least not until they were old or out of money. He had no real need for a wife. And she—whoever she was—would certainly not tolerate his desire to put financial dealings before matters of the heart. No, family was not for him, no matter how lonely he'd been feeling lately.

He tipped his hat then turned back to his property, happy to get away from Ida Mueller and those blue, blue eyes that made him forget himself.

"Ida, I can't thank you enough for coming in on a Saturday morning." Dinah continued to fuss with her hair, then turned to Ida with a shrug. "How do I look?"

"Wonderful, but you're going to be late for the meeting."

With the wave of a hand, Dinah responded, "I doubt Millie and Reverend Jake will care. We're just talking about the Fourth of July picnic is all. But they want to include me. They're always going out of their way to make me feel needed."

"They're not *making* you feel needed," Ida said. "You *are* needed. There is a difference. The reverend and Millie couldn't possibly pull off the annual picnic without your help, and you know it."

"Still," Dinah said, reaching for her bonnet, "I don't want anyone to feel compelled to include me." She gave

Carter a kiss on the cheek. "Now, you be a good boy for Ida, son. Don't give her any trouble."

"No, ma'am."

"No, ma'am, you won't be a good boy, or no, ma'am, you won't give her any trouble?"

Carter giggled. "No, ma'am, I won't give her any trouble."

"That's my boy." Dinah patted him on the head, then turned back to Ida. "Thank you for minding the store. I'll be back before noon, I feel sure. And if you need anything—"

"Go, Dinah. Don't fret."

Her aunt drew in a deep breath, looking around the store, clearly anxious. "I forgot to mention there's a shipment of sugar due in and Mrs. Gertsch said she would be coming by to trade some items. Don't let her get away with too much, Ida. You know how she is."

"Yes." Ida tried to hide the smile.

"If her bartering goes on too long, she'll end up owning the store."

"I'll handle everything." Ida shooed her aunt out the door. "Now go on. How are Carter and I ever going to have any fun if you stay here?" Ida watched Dinah disappear down the street. Her heart secretly ached for Dinah. How such a dear, sweet woman could go on, day after day, after the tragedy she'd faced.

Ida shivered as she remembered that terrible night when Larson had leaped in front of an oncoming train to save the life of one of the railroad men, who was drunk on liquor purchased at Chuck Brewster's saloon.

He should have been the one to die, not Larson.

Ida drew in a deep breath, determined not to allow herself to focus on the past. If Dinah could move ahead, surely she could do the same. Carter needed them both to be strong.

Ida turned back to her cousin with a forced smile. "Would you like to play with your jacks while I'm tending to the cash register?"

"Yes, ma'am."

As she dusted the glass cases, Ida heard noise coming from next door. She looked out the window, stunned to see a crew of men working on the empty lot, clearing the weeds. Some of them were Papa's workers! Likely that scoundrel Bradley had offered them an exorbitant salary. What traitors! And Carl Walken, of all people. After all the food she'd served him, it seemed like a personal betrayal to find his feet planted in the enemy's camp.

Off in the distance, Mick Bradley spoke to one of the men, giving orders. Ida's skin began to crawl. Imagine, putting up the gambling hall next door to a perfectly respectable general store where children played and folks gathered for decent conversation and honorable transactions.

The door opened and Sophie entered the store with her mother. She drew near to the register. "Did you see the goings-on next door?"

"How could I avoid it?"

"What are your thoughts?" Sophie leaned against the counter.

"I think they are making entirely too much racket for a Saturday morning. They are distracting my customers and that will soon affect my business."

Sophie looked around the empty mercantile. "Your business? But I don't see—"

"Exactly." Ida nodded as she yanked off her apron.

"So, if you don't mind watching the register a few minutes, I'd like to go have a word with Mr. Bradley."

"Mind yourself, Ida," Sophie said with a smile. "Don't say anything you might regret later."

Ida gave her a look of warning and turned to catch her reflection in the glass case so she could tidy up her hair. No point in arguing with the neighbors with messy hair. She needed to put her best foot forward.

With nerves kicking in, she made her way to the door. One foot in front of the other. Then out onto the boardwalk. Then onto the street, nearing the spot where Mick stood in his high-falutin' shoes and dress coat, talking to Carl Walken, no less.

"Mr. Bradley!" Ida shouted to be heard above the noise of the workers clearing the lot.

He turned to her with a smile. "Lost that puppy again?"

"No." She shook her head, determined to keep her focus. "I am here with a complaint, one I hope you will take seriously."

"Oh?" His eyes twinkled with mischief. "And what sort of complaint would that be?"

"First of all, I feel compelled to tell you that the Bible strictly forbids gambling. For this one reason alone, I cannot bear to watch this building go up. And next door to a respectable business like the mercantile. Ridiculous!"

He opened his mouth to speak, but she forged ahead. "And one more thing." She pointed to his workers. "It's one thing to hire a man to do a job—it's another altogether to steal your workers from another man. These fellas work for my papa. They've got no business here in town working for you."

"Now hold on there, Miss Mueller. I haven't stolen anyone. These men are working on the weekend for extra cash—"

"Cash that will be spent in a saloon." She pointed to Chuck Brewster's place. "This is ill-gained profit, and you are behind it all."

"But I—"

"And have you not thought about the children of Spring Creek? No, you have not! I dare say, if you'd given one minute's thought to our children, you would realize that their innocence has already been assaulted. How will they ever remain pure and untouched by the vices of this world if a man such as yourself continues to build—" she sputtered the words "—a g-gambling hall!"

"Well, I—"

"And another thing!" She felt her courage rising. "I am accustomed to peace and quiet on Saturday mornings and so are my customers. With all the noise coming from your lot, the customers are staying away. We're losing business because of you."

"I would hardly think—"

"Now, my papa might not have been able to stand up to you, but I can. And will. And I can assure you, the saloon owners will stand up to you, too. There's not a one of them who's happy to see you here. Not a one. So I'd watch out if I were you, Mr. Bradley. I fear you may be taking your life in your hands if you continue building of this gambling hall of yours."

"Are you quite done?" he asked at last.

"I am." Ida was completely exhausted and shaking to the core. Still, she kept her hands firmly planted on her hips, and never let her gaze slip from his.

Mick let out a whistle. "Well, if that doesn't beat all!" After a chuckle, he added, "I do believe you've missed your calling, Miss Mueller."

"Oh?" She brushed a loose hair behind her ear, puzzled. She suddenly realized the men had stopped working so they could listen to her talking to Mick.

"If it's true that preaching is left only to the menfolk, then the church has done you a great disservice," Mick announced. "Why, I can see you up there now, pounding your fist on the pulpit, shouting at the parishioners, pointing out the error of their ways."

A roar of laughter went up from the crowd of workers. A couple even slapped their knees. As a smile lit Bradley's face, she weighed her options. Fighting the temptation to do or say the wrong thing, Ida bit her lip until it nearly bled.

Clearly, the man refused to see the light. But he knew how to get his digs in, didn't he.

His expression softened a bit as he added, "Look. Don't you think I've got enough trouble from the men around here? Why would a pretty girl like you want to add to my grief? What have I ever done to hurt you?"

She began to tremble in anger. Why, if he didn't understand what he'd done to hurt her after all the time she'd just spent explaining, then he must be daft. Ida could hardly control her temper as she spouted, "You're…you're…impossible!"

She stomped her way back into the store, outraged and overwhelmed. No man had ever made her feel so… confused.

Sophie took one look at her and sighed. "Oh my goodness, Ida. Whatever happened out there?"

Ida couldn't answer at first. Speaking over the lump

in her throat proved to be nearly impossible. Finally, she managed a few strained words. "He said I've missed my calling." She reached for her apron and, in her fervor, tied it a bit too tight. As she loosened it, she said, "According to Mick Bradley, I should have been a preacher."

Sophie laughed so hard she couldn't speak for a full minute. Then she said, "You know, he may have a point. You do have passion!"

"Sophie, I'm not looking for you to agree with the man."

"And you have a mighty fine vocabulary to boot! Not to mention the fact that you know the Bible stories inside and out!" Sophie collapsed in laughter again.

"Sophie, I thought you were in agreement with me about the gambling hall!"

"I am, Ida, of course I am. I'm sorry for laughing. I just think that Mick Bradley is impossible, don't you?" she asked.

Instead of replying, Ida reached for a broom and began to sweep—vigorously. Yes, Mick Bradley was impossible, all right. No question about that. So was her friend Sophie. Those two deserved each other.

The thought of Sophie and Mick together suddenly overwhelmed Ida with such jealousy she had to excuse herself and get her bearings. She had no idea what was happening to her, but she didn't like it at all. Not one bit.

Chapter Eleven

Mick watched from a distance as the foundation was laid on his new property. He always loved this part, watching the concrete, soft and pliable, harden into something of great strength. He understood such a hardening—he had lived through it himself.

Some of the workers had questioned his use of concrete. Most of the buildings in the area had the usual pier-and-beam foundation. Still, Mick wanted to work with the latest technology, and a concrete slab was the way to go, from what he'd learned. Especially in a humid climate like this, where termites made regular appearances.

Not that he really minded what the locals thought about his decisions, anyway. They already considered him odd; the concrete had only served to reinforce that fact in their minds.

What mattered—what really mattered—were the opinions of his investors back in Chicago. They were the only ones he had to please. And surely they would agree with his choices. He needed to build a place that would withstand the elements and any other forces that might come along. The stronger, the better. He had a feeling the building would have to withstand some interesting challenges before all was said and done.

Mick allowed his gaze to shift to the mercantile next door. Several times he'd caught Ida peeking through the window, her interest in his business more than a passing fancy, no doubt. Once he'd even waved, just for fun. Naturally, she hadn't waved back.

Mick looked out over the lot once more. Tomorrow morning, the framework of the building would go up. And though he'd hired a perfectly fine contractor, Mick would be right here, watching every move the builders made.

Lost in his thoughts, Mick didn't notice the man who sidled up next to him until he heard, "Young fella, how're you doing?"

Mick sized up the old man, wondering if he was friend or foe.

The stranger removed his hat, revealing a near-balding head that glistened in the sun. "We've howdied, but we ain't shook yet," the fellow said with a smile.

"I beg your pardon?"

"I've seen you about town," the man explained, "and I've heard yer name from plenty of folks, but we ain't been formally introduced." After a short chuckle, he extended his hand. "Jake Langford, local reverend."

This guy sure didn't look—or sound—like any reverend Mick had known. Not that he'd known many.

Langford looked out over the lot with a hint of a smile. "I reckon yer wondering what I'm doin' here."

"I figure I know what you're doing." Mick crossed his arms, ready to do business. "You're here to tell me you'd like to see me out of here, like all the others. And to tell me you'd like to see my place shut down before it even opens."

"Well, if I had my druthers, I'd see 'em all shut down," Langford said. "But that ain't why I'm here. On the contrary. I'm just wonderin' why yer drinkin' downstream from the herd."

"Beg pardon?" For the life of him, Mick couldn't make sense of these Texans.

Langford chuckled. "Seems to me, you'd be drinkin' upstream. Tryin' somethin' different. We've got an overabundance of saloons in town as it is. Why not try yer hand at something more practical? We've a need fer a proper feed store. In fact, this property was going to be used for the new feed store, but Skinner changed his mind. That'd be a good venture, and a profitable one, at that."

"Feed store?" Mick laughed, long and loud. "I don't know the first thing about feed stores—unless the 'feed' happens to be whiskey or gin."

"What about a boardinghouse?" the reverend asked. "Goodness knows we could keep it filled up."

"Don't plan to be keeping any of the fellas through to the morning."

Langford shook his head and looked him square in the eye. "What are you searchin' for, son?" Langford asked.

"Searching for?" Mick wondered if he'd heard right.

"I'd have to say a young fella like yourself must be lookin' fer somethin'. Maybe yer thinkin' you'll find it in this here gamblin' hall you've got yer heart set on buildin'."

"I'm looking to please my investors, Reverend. That's my job."

"A place like this must be very excitin'." Reverend Langford rubbed his chin as he looked out over the property again. "But I have a feelin' a man could walk away feelin' near empty."

"Empty pockets, maybe, but he will have enjoyed himself."

As the older man leaned forward, Mick noticed a jagged scar on his forehead and a dozen questions passed through his mind.

"I understand emptiness," the reverend said. "Been there myself. I could tell you all sorts of stories, if'n you had the time."

Mick looked at his pocket watch, anxious to get back to work. "I'm not sure where this is headed, Reverend."

"You can say what you want about yerself, but that don't change the facts."

"What do you mean?"

"I'm jest sayin', you can put yer boots in the oven, but that don't make 'em biscuits. Yer no more a gambling-hall owner than I am."

Mick laughed again. "I've been a gambling-hall owner for quite some time now. And I'm not sure what you're trying to accomplish, but if you think you can talk me into changing my mind about The Lucky Penny, you may want to reconsider."

The man's expression remained the same. "No man can change the mind of another. But if you'll give me a minute or two, I'll be happy to explain where I'm headed with all this."

Mick gave a curt response. "Talk fast. I'm a busy man."

The reverend's brow wrinkled. "When I was a young feller in Albuquerque, not much more'n a boy, I had an eye for nice things. No money to buy 'em, so I got in the habit of stealin'. Started small. Candy from the mercantile, that sort of thing. Then one thing led to another and before you knew it, I was takin' from folks in a big way—robbin' at gunpoint, even." He shook his head. "Hard to imagine now, ain't it?"

"Well, I certainly never met a preacher who'd spent the better part of his life running from the law, if that's what you mean." A chuckle escaped from Mick's mouth.

"I didn't run fer long. The law caught up with me in Denver. I'd robbed a man who happened to be armed. He shot me three times. Hit me in the belly. I spent several days in the jailhouse with the doctor tending to my wounds. Many was the time I thought I was a goner. But God—"

"God met you in the jailhouse?"

"I guess you could say that." Reverend Langford smiled. "Truth is, He sent a pretty young thing to carry in my meals. She had such a peaceful way about her, always whistling and singing about the love of the Lord. I'll admit, it was her beauty that caught my eye at first. But sooner or later, those stories she told me were naggin' at my conscience."

"What stories?"

"About a God who could forgive, and give me a second chance—if I was willin' to change, to give my heart to Him. She told me that He would forgive me my past, and give me a fresh start. And that's just what happened."

"I see," Mick said politely.

The reverend gave him a pensive look. "God'll do the same for you, if you ask."

Didn't sound quite like Mick would expect a sermon

to sound, no hellfire or brimstone at all. Surely Ida had outdone the reverend in that respect. The man's words were kind but firm. Still, the effect was the same as if he'd heard them hollered down from a pulpit with a finger pointed directly at him.

"Thank you, Reverend Langford, but God and I parted ways a long time ago, and I don't think we have much to say to each other these days. However, I do appreciate your stopping by." Mick shook the man's hand and then saw him off the property.

Mick left the site that evening with a headache, more exhausted than he'd been in months. The sun had barely tucked itself in for the night when Mick decided to turn in. Unfortunately, he couldn't sleep. He tossed and turned, thinking about the reverend's words. For whatever reason, he couldn't seem to shake them.

Whether Mick wanted to admit it or not, the fellow was right on some level. He did feel empty. And alone. Odd, how you could feel that way in the midst of so many people. What was it the old guy had said again? *You can put your boots in the oven, but that don't make 'em biscuits...*

Despite that riddle rattling around in his head, Mick was finally able to drift off to sleep.

Chapter Twelve

On Wednesday afternoon, Ida was pondering the gambling-hall situation in a less volatile state of mind. After several days of thinking through Reverend Langford's Sunday sermon on forgiveness, she decided she'd best keep her temper in check, lest it get the better of her and spoil her whole plan.

It had taken several days, but Ida had indeed come up with a plan. She would arrange a protest, with the help of others in the community, of course. Surely if they linked arms, God would move on their behalf. The shopkeepers would join her, no doubt. A petition was in order, and maybe even a march through the center of town, ending at Mick's site. And if she was very lucky, she might even be able to convince her father's men to stop working for him.

Yes indeed. Together they would end Mick Bradley's dream of building a gambling hall in the town of Spring Creek.

In this excited frame of mind, Ida stopped at the church to speak with Reverend Langford on her way into town. She wanted to ask him if she might use the church for a planning meeting. He met her on the front steps of the tiny building with a smile.

"Howdy, Ida. Pleasure to see you. What brings you here midday?"

She mustered up the courage to speak her mind. "Reverend, I've come to ask a favor."

"What can I do fer ya?"

"I know we have spoken in the past about Mr. Bradley and his gambling hall."

"Sure, sure. And I need to update you. I talked to Mick yesterday afternoon. Seems like a right nice fellow, though a bit off course," the reverend said.

Perhaps this would be harder than she'd thought. If Mick Bradley had won over the reverend with his persuasive speech, Ida had a tough road ahead of her. "Yes, he is a nice man, I'm sure," she responded. "But that doesn't change the facts. His plan to build a gambling hall puts our town—and its residents—at greater risk than ever. With that in mind, I would like to ask your permission to hold a meeting at the church this evening after midweek service to discuss a plan of action."

The reverend gave her a pensive look. "Instead of talkin' about him, why don't you invite him to join us at the meetin'? We'll see if we can't reason things out with him—let the love of Christ shine through. Wouldn't that be the best way to handle things?"

"I just can't help thinking it's a bad idea to involve him without talking things over with church folks first, to get their input. Surely, if we all put our heads together we can come up with a practical solution to this problem—one we can all live with, including Mr. Bradley."

The reverend let his hand rest on her arm. "We must be careful in our approach, Ida. We don't want to get folks riled up. Goodness only knows what they'll do if they get too upset."

"Oh, no. Indeed. I'm looking for a peaceful resolution to this problem, I assure you. Perhaps start a petition, that sort of thing. Maybe hold a prayer meeting in front of Mr. Bradley's lot. I want to see this come to a satisfactory conclusion—for everyone."

"Truly? For everyone?"

She swallowed hard before answering. "Truly, Reverend. I want the best for Mr. Bradley, whether it appears that way or not. I'll admit I haven't exactly shown him the kindness of the Lord. I let my temper get the best of me, and spouted off like a teakettle gone to boil. But I've prayed about that and asked God to forgive me."

"Have you, now?"

"I have. I don't mind admitting that I still have my doubts about whether he'll come around. But I think we stand a far better chance of convincing him if we band together." After a brief pause, she added the words that had been nagging at her conscience all along. "I want him to be won to the Lord. Truly I do. I can think of no happier ending."

"Mmm-hmm."

"Mr. Bradley just needs a bit of convincing, is all." Ida's excitement grew as she spoke. "We'll show him the light—one way or another. And I promise to pray before the meeting. In fact, I've been praying ever since the man came to town." Indeed, she wasn't sure when she'd ever spent so many hours in worship.

"Well, I will add my prayers to yours, then, and we will see what the Lord does." Reverend Langford offered up a comforting smile. "In the meantime, feel free to use the church for your meeting tomorrow night.

But promise me you will talk with your father about this first. I don't want to come between a man and his daughter."

"Thank you, Reverend, I will."

Ida fanned herself as she continued on into town. One meeting with the fine church folks of Spring Creek should suffice. She would present her case, focusing on the safety and well-being of the children. She would remind folks how simple—how safe—their lives were before the saloons came in.

Then, when she had them convinced, Ida would turn her attention to a reasonable plan of action. They would pray, of course. And with everyone in accord, they would pay Mick Bradley a visit at his construction site for a peaceable demonstration—one meant to make their position quite clear. Surely he could be persuaded to listen to a group of folks who approached him in Christian love.

Ida pushed aside images of Mick's handsome face and tried to stay focused on the task at hand. *We're not trying to drive him out of town...necessarily.* No, she would be more than happy to see him stay—once he saw the error of his ways.

Mick watched as the exterior walls of The Lucky Penny started to go up. He could see it all now—this building would be a gem, standing out above every other place in town. It would be an establishment local folks could brag about, and one that would draw railroad men from near and far, bringing revenue into Spring Creek in a number of ways.

Yes, the locals would no doubt eventually link arms with him and offer their support once they realized he wasn't here to hurt them. Of course, he hoped to make a profit from the gambling hall. So did his investors. But their success would mean success for the townspeople, as well.

As Mick pondered these things, Ida Mueller hurried by. Mick gave her a nod, and added, "You're late."

She paused and looked up at him. "Beg your pardon?"

"You always arrive a few minutes after two." He reached for his pocket watch and gave it a glance. "It's nearly two-thirty. You're late. Later than usual, I mean."

"Well, I've had other business to attend to this afternoon. Let's just leave it at that," Ida said.

"I do hope the railroad men haven't been a bother."

"Not this time." Ida's brow furrowed as she looked at the construction going on. "I see you've been busy." Her words sounded strained.

"Yes. Things are going well. Listen, Miss Mueller, I don't want to be at odds with you. Can't we come to some sort of arrangement where we agree to disagree? That sort of thing?"

She used the back of her hand to tuck a loose hair behind her ear. "Mr. Bradley, while I applaud your entrepreneurial efforts, I cannot—and will not—support the gambling industry or another place of business that provides alcohol to the men." Her hands began to tremble, and he watched as she pressed them behind her back. "As long as you insist upon proceeding with your current plans, any hope of finding common ground is out of the question."

"So there's nothing I can do."

"There's plenty you can do," Ida responded passionately. "I'm going to ask you one more time to reconsider. Use this piece of property for something other than what you've planned. Please think of the families, the children."

The pinging sound of hammers against nails continued. Mick looked at the building—could almost see it in its full glory now. He turned back to her.

"I'm sorry," he said. "I'm a businessman, Miss Mueller, and it's my job to build this hall."

She let out a lengthy sigh and turned to enter the mercantile, her skirts nearly getting tangled around her feet.

Mick watched her go, saddened that he was on the opposite side of the fence from the one person whose opinion suddenly meant more to him than almost any other.

Probably best if he didn't think about the implications of that.

Chapter Thirteen

The Wednesday-evening church service drew to a close and Ida shifted in her seat, anxious for the meeting to begin. She looked at her papa for reassurance. They'd spent their dinner hour talking through a plan of action, during which he had done his best to convince her that more flies could be caught with honey than vinegar.

Ida wasn't completely convinced. Continuing to pray for Mick would be the best plan of action, according to Papa. That, and encouraging others to pray for him, as well. Then, if the church folks agreed, they would hold a prayer meeting in town in front of the gambling-hall site, followed by a meeting with Mr. Bradley to discuss other options for his new building. Perhaps the walls of Jericho would come tumbling down if the good Christian people of Spring Creek would unite and pray.

And perhaps, in taking a slightly softer approach, the Lord would somehow reach Mick, cause him to see things in a new light. Papa seemed convinced, and Ida dared hope—in spite of his words earlier this afternoon—that Mick Bradley might be persuaded to reconsider his current plans.

As the service ended, Reverend Langford addressed the congregation. "We'll be takin' a break for about five minutes, then I'll be callin' the meetin' to order."

The congregants stood and stretched their legs. Several of the womenfolk approached Ida to thank her for taking such a strong interest in the town.

Mrs. Oberwetter, a widow, said, "You're a brave girl to take on a goliath like Mick Bradley."

"I hear you're the one behind this meeting, Ida," Mrs. Gertsch offered as her eyes filled with tears. "I believe your mother would be so proud of you. She was a woman of strength, and you're so much like her."

"I... I am?"

"Oh, indeed." The older woman slipped an arm around her shoulder. "She was always one to protect others. I see you've inherited that same spirit." She leaned in close to whisper in her ear. "Just let the Lord lead you, child. Don't get ahead of Him."

"I won't." *I hope.*

Reverend Langford called the meeting to order, than prayed a heartfelt prayer for Mick Bradley. As Ida listened to his words, her heart seemed to flip-flop. Though she wanted to see an end to Mr. Bradley's gambling hall, there was still something about the man that very nearly caused her to lose control of her senses. It was such a confusing sensation, given that he stood for everything she felt was wrong with Spring Creek.

After praying, the reverend turned the meeting over to Ida, who approached the front of the room with her knees knocking. She wondered if this was how Esther had felt. Did her throat feel tight and constricted? Did her hands shake? Did her feet feel like mush?

As Ida turned to face the crowd, she took a moment

to look at the faces of all in attendance. She'd known and loved so many of these folks since birth. Many of the women had swept in when her mother died, looking after her as best they could.

She would do no less for Spring Creek's children. She would follow in her mother's footsteps, caring for those who could not care for themselves.

With courage mounting, she began to speak. "I want to thank you all for staying for the meeting, and special thanks to Reverend Langford for allowing me the privilege of speaking out in the church. I count it an honor.

"As you all know, we're here to discuss the building of the new gambling hall. Now, I know as individuals we've spent many an hour in prayer about this already, but I also know there is power in the prayer of agreement. That's why I've asked for a bit of your time this evening. I've heard some of the scuttlebutt about Mr. Bradley's gambling hall. I've even been a part of it, I must confess. But merely talking about it isn't the right approach. I believe the Lord is calling us to do more."

Ida's thoughts shifted at once to Esther. Her heart stilled a bit and she forged ahead. "We can talk all day and night, but folks are still going to come into our town and build what they like. Truly, the only resolution to this is prayer, followed by carefully thought-out action."

The crowd began to stir, and she stilled them by raising her hand. "Surely the Lord would have us link hands and hearts in prayer and in action. I would like to suggest a civilized meeting with Mr. Bradley on his lot, but not until Saturday. We need time to pray first—to seek the Lord for what He would have us say. When we are all in agreement, we will choose one of the men to represent us as we all stand face-to-face with Mr. Bradley."

She paused a moment as she contemplated the image of the congregation standing in front of Mick Bradley. How would he respond? Could he be persuaded?

"This is my suggestion, anyway," she continued. "With that in mind, perhaps some of you have questions or suggestions."

Hands quickly went up all over the place. Mrs. Gertsch quoted a lengthy passage from the Bible, advocating a prayerful approach. Mrs. Oberwetter interjected, suggesting they run the man out of town on a rail before Spring Creek's children were swept away by the raging tide of sin and corruption. Papa countered with a passage on love, and several of the other men offered their middle-ground thoughts.

"I don't believe it's necessary to insist upon Mr. Bradley's leaving town," Ida explained. "Though I felt so at one time. Papa has convinced me—and Reverend Langford, too—that the Lord must've had a reason for bringing Mick Bradley to Spring Creek. And surely we—" she gestured around the room with a smile "—are part of that reason. Now let's get to work and see if we can win Mick Bradley to the Lord."

No sooner were the words spoken than the back door to the church opened. Ida gasped aloud as Chuck Brewster and the other saloon owners entered. Brewster removed his hat and nodded in her direction, then took a seat in the back pew, the others joining him. Folks turned around and stared.

The reverend went back to welcome the men. As Ida watched him shake hands with Chuck Brewster, a shiver ran down her spine. She couldn't help but think that these rough and rowdy fellows had a plan all their own.

* * *

Late Wednesday evening Mick finished up his dinner at The Harvey House and took a stroll down Midway, curious as to why the street seemed so deserted at eight o'clock in the evening. He noticed a bit of activity coming from Brewster's place, but other than that, very few people came and went—a fact that confused him.

"Ah, yes," he said aloud as he remembered. Wednesday night. The townsfolk were likely in church.

The strangest sensation came over him as he thought about Reverend Langford. Was he standing up in front of the congregation now, preaching? Convincing folks of the error of their ways? Was Ida sitting in the front pew, hanging on every word? Preparing another speech about the sinfulness of his plans?

Mick turned his attention back to the nearly empty street, noticing a couple of men ambling in his direction, likely fresh off the evening train. As he approached the mercantile, he saw an unfamiliar man with dark hair, a bit younger than himself.

"Mercantile closed?" the fellow asked.

"Yes, they close at five," Mick said. "Half the town's in church tonight, anyway."

"I wondered why it was so quiet around here." The man stuck out his hand. "Johnsey Fischer. Just got off the train. I work for the Great Northern."

"Mick Bradley," Mick said, nodding his head. "You staying in town?"

"Harvey House," Johnsey replied. "Seller's is full up. And I don't think it'd be wise to rent a room at Wunsche Brothers. Too much going on over there." His cheeks turned red, and Mick nodded in understanding. So this was a good boy. Well, no problem there. Despite what Ida seemed to think, Mick didn't care much for the houses of ill repute—he'd rather men spend their hard-earned money on liquor and cards, not women.

Johnsey tipped his hat and turned back toward the hotel. Mick continued on with his walk, and then returned to his room to get ready for bed.

Just as he was falling asleep, Mick awoke to a suspicious sound outside his door. He rose from the bed and inched his way across the room, then leaned his ear against the heavy wood to listen. A rustling of paper and rapid footsteps moving away piqued his curiosity. Looking down, he noticed a piece of paper on the floor. He picked it up, startled to find the words, "Stay in Spring Creek at your own risk."

The note must've come from Brewster or one of the other saloon owners. Would they act on this threat, or was this some sort of a bluff? He read the words over several times. Surely they were meant to inflict fear, though anger rose in him instead of intimidation. He'd faced tougher adversaries in the past. These Texans wouldn't get to him.

Mick decided he'd better check on the lot. He dressed quickly, grabbed a lantern and made his way over. A scrap of paper had been tacked to the front exterior wall, one that left nothing to the imagination. "The train north leaves at three. Be on it."

Mick turned on his heel. He knew, of course, that Chuck Brewster would be standing outside The Golden Spike with a cigar dangling from his lips, looking his way.

What he didn't know was that half a dozen of Brewster's henchmen would be standing alongside him.

Chapter Fourteen

Ida rounded the corner onto Midway at the usual time, surprised by the crowd in front of Mick Bradley's lot. The sheriff stood near Mick with his arms folded at his chest, and a concerned look on his face. The workmen appeared to be closing up shop for the day. Strange, at two in the afternoon.

And Mick. She couldn't help but wonder at the look of pain in his eyes.

Ida groaned internally as she saw that the exterior of the structure had gone up. It was a fine-looking building, as buildings went. If only he could be persuaded to reconsider its purpose. On the other hand, it looked as if Mr. Bradley had a lot to contend with this fine day.

Ida hoped to overhear a bit of the conversation but the sheriff turned and walked away just as she passed by. Was it possible their prayers had already been answered? Surely something had happened here.

Ida entered the mercantile and looked around in amazement at the crowd. The stirrings next door had certainly increased their business.

As she untied the ribbons on her bonnet, Ida tried

to catch Dinah's eye. Her aunt tended to a customer at the register, too focused on her work to respond to Ida's inquisitive look. A short time later the crowd thinned and Ida finally had an opportunity to ask, "What has happened next door, Dinah?"

Her aunt spoke in a lowered voice. "Some of the men threatened Mr. Bradley last night. I heard the shots fired myself. It was terrifying."

A shiver ran down Ida's spine, and she found herself wondering if Mrs. Oberwetter's approach might not be best after all. Driving the saloon owners out of town—Mick Bradley included—would put a stop to all this nonsense once and for all.

Dinah let out a sigh, the crease in her brow deepening. "I prayed that the saloon owners would link arms with the church folks and approach Mr. Bradley in a peaceable way. It is certainly not God's plan to drive the man out of town with threats and physical violence." Her aunt shook her head. "I have the strangest feeling, Ida."

"What do you mean?"

"Perhaps he's not the villain we've made him out to be."

"You can say this when your life was in danger because of him last night?"

"Ida, it wasn't Mr. Bradley organizing mobs and brandishing firearms. And the sheriff wouldn't even listen to his story until this afternoon. He's not being treated fairly. Maybe he is just a man—"

"Set on bringing more grief?" Ida crossed her arms. "I will continue to pray. I know you will, too. But this situation seems to be getting worse every day, not better."

She quieted her voice as an unfamiliar customer approached. The man looked to be in his early thirties, with dark curls and a well-trimmed mustache.

"Can I help you?"

Ida noticed that Dinah's cheeks flushed as she spoke.

"Yes." The fellow nodded. "I wonder if you might help me locate the home of a—" he glanced down at a piece of paper in his hand "—Mrs. Gertsch."

"Emma Gertsch?" Dinah asked.

He gave the paper another look. "I suppose. They didn't give me a first name."

"May I ask who 'they' is?" Ida said.

"The folks at The Harvey House," he explained. "That's where I've been staying. But to be honest," he said, lowering his voice and looking around before continuing, "it's too rowdy in town. With all the noise and fighting, I think I'd prefer something a little farther out. I understand there's a Mrs. Gertsch who has rooms to let."

"She does, although I can't be sure of her situation at this time," Dinah said. "She lives just up the road apiece. I would be happy to give you directions."

The fellow flashed a contagious smile. "I'd be in your debt, Miss…"

"Hirsch. Dinah Hirsch."

"Nice to meet you, Miss Hirsch." He folded the paper and put it in his pocket. "Johnsey Fischer from Centerville. I work for the Great Northern," he said, extending his hand.

"N-nice to meet you." Dinah's gaze shifted to the front door as the bell jangled. She quickly withdrew her hand as another customer entered the store.

"I have such fond memories of this place after my

last visit," Johnsey said. "But Spring Creek has changed since I was here last."

Ida wondered if they had discovered a kindred spirit here, someone who might be able to help them save the town. "How long has it been?"

"Three years." He shook his head, a forlorn look in his eyes. "And true, the place has grown. But I'm referring to more than just a physical change. Something I can't quite put my finger on."

"You needn't say more." Dinah sighed. "I see the transformation all too clearly, and it's not for the better. I pray every day the situation will improve."

"Then I will add my prayers to yours." He gave them a sympathetic look.

Carter interrupted their conversation, appearing with marbles in hand. He took one look at Mr. Fischer and promptly began explaining the details of his prized collection. Thankfully, the newcomer appeared to be taken with the child and spent several minutes talking with him.

The fellow finally left, and the color seemed to go out of Dinah's cheeks as he did. Ida took note but did not say a word. Instead, she went on about her business, tending to the needs of shoppers, including Myrtle Mae.

"I heard about what happened next door," the older woman whispered. "And I'm praying for you all, honey. For your protection."

As Myrtle Mae left, Chuck Brewster came in. As was often the case, he was seeking chewing tobacco and coffee, along with crackers and peanuts. He gave Ida a curt nod after she waited on him, and she returned the gesture out of politeness, though a chill went through her. Had this man been responsible for the shots fired at Mick Bradley? If so, had something in their meeting last night stirred him to action?

Ida took a peek out the window and saw Mick standing in front of his new building. A feeling of shame swept over her. Perhaps she'd been too hasty in condemning him. Maybe, with a bit of help from above, he might see the error of his ways—if she left the matter in God's hands and didn't try to handle this on her own.

Another glance out the window at Mick's stooped shoulders and somber expression convinced her once and for all to release both her bitterness and her determination to fix this situation—and to do exactly what she'd told the church folks she would do. Pray.

Perhaps in her haste to become like Esther, she had overstepped her bounds. Surely the time had come to step aside, and just let God…be God.

Mick Bradley had never been one to tuck his tail between his legs and back his way out of town, even in the worst of situations. Still, as this nuisance of a day continued, the temptation to do just that gradually took hold.

A man should be safe, standing on his own plot of land, shouldn't he? He shouldn't have to duck passing bullets, or fend off foul-mouthed ruffians. And yet the last twenty-four hours had brought both, and in just that order.

Last night's bullets, according to the sheriff, must've been an accident—the result of a misfire, perhaps, or a couple of railroad men blowing off some steam. Funny, no railroad men had been nearby at the time. Based on the angle, there was no doubt the shots had been fired from The Golden Spike.

And the drunken visitors who'd paid him a visit moments later, sticks in hand? The ones who'd threatened to take him down if he didn't hightail it out of town? Just railroad fellas, up to no good, according to the sheriff. Mick had to disagree. The threats from Brewster's henchmen had been quite real, and left little to the imagination.

And to top it all off, his workers had abandoned him today. So much for doubling their pay.

Everything about this just had a bad feel to it. Brewster's men would surely continue to harass him, not giving up until he boarded that train headed north.

Maybe he should just save them all the time and trouble and do just that.

Chapter Fifteen

Ida awoke to the sound of shouting and pounding on the door. She followed on Papa's heels down the stairs, fearful of whatever news awaited them.

Carl Walken stood there, gasping for breath, with a lantern in hand. Even with only the tiny flicker of the flame inside, Ida could see that the man was shaking.

"There's trouble in town, Mr. Mueller," Carl said.

"What sort of trouble?" Ida asked.

Carl gestured for them to step out onto the porch. Though the sun had not yet risen, an eerie glow lit the skies, and the smell of smoke filled the air. Ida turned back to her father, eyes wide. "Fire!"

"Where is it?" her father asked, concern etched on his brow.

Carl couldn't respond for a second as he continued to fight for air.

"Mick Bradley's place?" Ida asked.

He nodded. "After all the work we did getting the building up. The whole thing's burned to the ground. Such a waste."

A fierce trembling began in Ida's knees and quickly

moved up to consume her whole body. "Th-the mercantile?"

Carl shook his head. "Doesn't look to be much damage there. The west wall is scorched, but I believe it's external only. And I think a couple of windows have blown, but they're easily replaced."

"My sister and nephew?" her father asked.

"They're safe, Mr. Mueller. That's one of the reasons I came by, to let you know so that you wouldn't worry. But we'll know more about the mercantile after the sun rises."

"I cannot wait until the sun rises." Ida turned back toward the door with tears in her eyes. She managed a frantic prayer, thanking the Lord for Dinah and Carter's safety. From the beginning she'd argued that they shouldn't live in town above the store, but Dinah had her heart set on it. If only Papa hadn't sold that lumber to Mick Bradley, none of this would have happened.

Seconds later she chided herself for such thoughts. Her papa was the finest man she'd ever known, and always had the best of intentions. And likely the men who'd set the fire would have never gotten so riled up in the first place if she hadn't created such a stir. Oh, was she to blame for all of this? What if something had happened to Dinah or Carter—or Mick? She brushed away her tears, suddenly more angry at herself than anyone else.

Papa reached over and patted her arm. "I'll come with you, Ida. We'll take the wagon."

Minutes later, they were making the journey to town. The stench of smoke grew stronger the closer they got. Ida covered her mouth and nose with a handkerchief and tried to hold back the fits of coughing before they erupted. She could scarcely imagine what they might find in town if the smoke was this thick on the outskirts.

As Papa led the team onto Midway, Ida pulled the handkerchief away and gasped. She'd never seen so many people gathered together like this before. Many of the men still wore their nightclothes. Black soot covered the faces and shirts of many of the others.

She looked in the direction of the mercantile. Thankfully, it remained standing, seemingly unharmed, at least from what she could tell from the wagon.

But where were Dinah and Carter?

When the wagon drew to a stop, Ida scrambled down and began to run through the crowd. She couldn't find her aunt anywhere. On she went, through the throng of men, in search of her loved ones. She heard Papa's voice calling out to her but she did not stop.

As she reached the front of the store, another familiar voice rang out above the din. "Ida?"

She looked up to see Mick Bradley. A feeling of faintness swept over Ida and she grabbed his arm at once to keep from falling.

"Are you all right?" he asked.

She shook her head, and her knees began to go out from under her. She felt herself scooped up and carried down the street, away from the crowd. The coughing fits came in force now, and she took the handkerchief he offered.

Embarrassment washed over Ida in waves, along with nausea and dizziness. She struggled against his arms. If only he would put her down, she could find her aunt and cousin.

"Please…please put me down," she managed at last.

"Are you sure?"

When she nodded, he eased her down, though he didn't release his grip around her waist.

"I'm fine. I promise." She waited a moment for the dizziness to pass. "Do you know where Dinah and Carter are?"

"They've been taken nearby to The Harvey House," he explained. "I was taking you in that direction so you could be together."

"I think I can make it the rest of the way on my own." She squinted to see through the thick cloud of smoke.

"I'd feel better if you let me escort you there myself," he said. "Please." He sounded like a completely different man than the one who'd offered to walk her into town all those days ago. How could she turn him down?

She nodded and he extended his arm. She took it, if for no other reason than to keep her knees from buckling. Within minutes, they were climbing the stairs to the hotel. He pulled open the door, and right away she saw Dinah and Carter seated in the lobby on the velvet sofa, still dressed in their nightclothes. Carter clutched the puppy in his arms. To Ida's great surprise, Nellie DeVries sat nearby tending to her aunt and cousin. So did Johnsey Fischer. Ida couldn't help but notice the look of concern in his eyes as he cared for Dinah.

"Dinah!" She ran to her aunt, arms extended. "I was so scared." After a lengthy embrace, she grabbed Carter, wrapping him tightly in her arms. "I don't know what I would have done if something had happened to you—either of you."

Carter's eyes grew wide. "I saw the flames, Ida! They were taller than the store—all the way to the sky."

"You're my big, brave boy." She placed several kisses

on his forehead in haste. "I am so glad you are unharmed."

Just then the hotel manager appeared with a sheet in hand. Dinah wrapped it around herself to cover her dressing gown. "I wish I could say the same for the store," she said with a groan.

"What happened to it?"

"The windows on the west wall were shattered during the explosion, and the outside wall is scorched, I'm sure."

"Explosion?"

"Oh my, yes." Dinah shook her head. "This started with the most awful explosion. And the flames were so close." Her hands began to tremble. "It was terrifying."

"I can't even imagine."

"I heard it myself," Nellie said. "I was in a sound sleep, but the noise woke me up. Took me a minute to figure out where it had come from, but I went running into the mercantile the minute I saw the flames."

"You…you saved Dinah and Carter?" Ida asked, amazed.

"Well, I would hardly say that." Nellie's cheeks flushed. "They were already headed down the stairs. I just offered a bit of assistance to get them out the door."

"She helped me with Carter," Dinah said. "And she went to fetch the puppy from out back. Truly, I don't know what I would have done without her. I could scarcely collect my thoughts, I was so afraid. You know how it is when you're awakened by something frightening—you can hardly think straight."

"Yes, I know," Ida agreed.

Dinah shook her head. "The smell of smoke is bound to have settled into everything porous. There's no telling how many things in the store will have to be disposed of. The bolts of fabric, for instance. And anything else that might have absorbed the odor." She shook her head and tears followed. "And we have a lot of water damage, as well."

"Dinah, I'm so sorry." Ida knelt down at her aunt's side and took her hand. "But Papa and I are here now, and as soon as the sun is up, we will start working. I'm sure others will help."

Mick, quiet till now, said, "I'll see if I can gather my workers, and they will be at your disposal. Anything you need…"

With a tip of his hat, he excused himself to tend to that task.

"And I'll talk to some of the girls," Nellie offered. She bounded from her spot next to Dinah, sprinting toward the door.

Ida looked at Dinah in amazement. "Who would have thought it?" she whispered. "Mick Bradley and Nellie DeVries coming to our aid. Could such a thing really be happening?"

Dinah nodded and a hint of a smile graced her lips. "I have no doubt they are both troubled souls. But clearly they have good in them, Ida. I truly believe they, like others, can be won to the Lord if we simply live the kind of lives before them that exemplify Christlike behavior."

Johnsey chimed in with a quiet, "Amen."

Ida felt the familiar tug of shame on her heart. "I think, in my haste, I might have judged them too harshly. And not just Mick and Nellie, either. The railroad men, as well. All of them." She shifted her gaze downward as she added, "I never really took the time to get to know them as individuals before drawing such stern conclusions."

No, until this morning they had been sinners, plain and simple. Not even sinners in need of saving. Just sinners in need of, well, a swift kick.

Ida's thoughts shifted to Mick Bradley and she realized that today was the day they were supposed to confront him. *The day we were going to try to reason with him about the gambling hall.*

Now there was no more gambling hall.

She couldn't help but wonder what Mick was thinking right now. If his dream had burned to the ground, would he finally succumb to the pressure and board the train north?

Ida found herself hoping against hope that he wouldn't.

The sun rose, revealing the extent of the damage. Mick stood in the center of the street, looking at what had once been his building. Gone. Not a beam left. Not a stick of wood untouched by the flames. Only the charred slab remained.

He'd awakened to the sound of shouts in the street and had known. In his gut he had known. One glance out the window proved that his plans were indeed going up in smoke.

Strange, the first thing he'd thought about was the folks residing inside the mercantile. As he'd run toward the lot, he had even offered up a prayer, of sorts. If that's what you wanted to call it. Thankfully, he'd seen Dinah and her little boy right away and had offered assistance. Taking Ida to join them had given him a small sense of purpose, at least for the moment, though he had to wonder what she might be thinking about him now. Surely her opinion of him had spiraled down even more, if such a thing were possible.

Now, staring at the damage on the west wall of the mercantile, he couldn't help but feel guilty as he contemplated the truth of it. None of this would have happened if he'd just left town when he was threatened.

But Mick wasn't the sort to turn and run. Never had been, never would be.

Only, where did that leave him now? Likely his investors would not take this news lying down, but neither would they send more money for rebuilding if they heard the particulars. No indeed. They were more likely to insist that he return their money or build elsewhere.

Anger gripped Mick's heart as he surveyed the damage. He should have paid attention to the mood of the town. Many people didn't want this hall. Hadn't Ida said as much? And hadn't others in town been all too clear about their feelings? A sense of failure washed over Mick.

He had no doubt where things stood. A few more minutes of staring at the charred rubble clarified that point in his mind. He would never convince his investors to try again in a town like this. The risk was too great.

Still, as Mick thought about Spring Creek, as he contemplated the fact that the town—or at least one of its residents—had somehow lodged in his heart, he could hardly imagine boarding the train.

He'd just have to figure out another way to satisfy his investors. Because he had no intention of leaving Spring Creek as long as Ida was still here.

Chapter Sixteen

The next few days were spent working to clean up the mercantile. Ida watched, humbled, as Johnsey, Mick and several of the other local men labored alongside her family members, emptying shelves, washing everything down with soap and water and replacing the missing windows. Nellie stopped by to bring food and water for the workers. Surely Ida had judged them all too harshly, just as she'd told Dinah the morning of the fire.

She prayed about her hasty judgments, asking God to forgive her. Still, in spite of His gentle nudging, she could hardly forgive herself. Many times Mick looked her way with a pained expression in his eyes. She read the guilt there. He felt responsible for the damage to the mercantile; that much was obvious. But would he give up on the gambling hall now, after all that had happened? That decision was in the Lord's hands. No longer would Ida make suggestions, one way or the other.

By Tuesday afternoon all the men had gone back to their regular jobs—all but Mick. Ida secretly wondered why he lingered in the shop, looking for things to do. She watched him out of the corner of her eye as the store finally reopened for business. He seemed to celebrate with the others, smiling as he welcomed folks at the door.

Ida pushed a few loose hairs out of her face and surveyed the store with a keen eye. Yes, it would be some time before new bolts of fabric arrived, and certainly the smell of smoke lingered in the air, but folks still came, as always. In fact, some arrived in haste, anxious to make their purchases.

"Glad to see you back up and running," Orin Lemm said, as he purchased razor straps.

Ida thanked him, and sent him on his way with a smile, pleased for the business.

"You've done wonders with the place, Ida," Mrs. Gertsch said with a smile as she traded in her homemade candles for sugar. The older woman then leaned in with a smile and whispered, "I missed coming in to see you."

Ida knew the older woman missed their conversations. And Ida had missed them, too. In fact, she'd missed nearly everything related to the running of the store.

"That Johnsey Fischer is a nice fellow." Mrs. Gertsch gave an admiring smile. "I've enjoyed having him at the house. There's nothing like a man's voice in a place to make it feel like a home."

Just then Johnsey let out a laugh and Dinah, who stood nearby, turned to him with flushed cheeks.

"I've seen that look before," Mrs. Gertsch whispered. "Dinah is smitten."

Ida contemplated Dinah and Johnsey as she turned back to her chores. Her aunt did seem to act a bit strange when Johnsey was around, but they scarcely knew each other. Just a few short days, was all. Why, she and Mick had known each other longer than that and they hardly gazed at each other in such a way.

Ida looked up and met Mick's eyes. Her stomach did a strange little flip and she felt her own cheeks flush with color. Perhaps Dinah wasn't the only one who was smitten after all.

Midafternoon, Sophie and her mother stopped by to drop off a pan of corn bread and a pot of pinto beans.

The influx of townspeople with food in hand reminded her of when Mama had died. So many people had swept in around her, trying to heal her broken heart with potatoes, venison and the like. She hadn't been able to consume much of it back then, but this time around she and Dinah delighted in each new dish.

Ida turned to Mrs. Weimer with a smile. "Thank you so much. You will never know how much this means to us."

"Oh, posh." Sophie's mother gave her hand a squeeze. "Just be sure to share with the menfolk," she said, nodding at Mick. "He looks like he's been working hard."

"And I dare say he's more handsome than ever, even with his hair all mussed up like that," Sophie said, grinning at Ida. "Wouldn't you agree?"

Ida looked over at him. "He has many admirable qualities." Ida released a lingering sigh. "In spite of my earlier thoughts on the matter."

"Indeed he does," Sophie said, giving Ida a playful wink and heading off in Mick's direction.

Mick turned to face Sophie with a smile, and Ida's heart lurched. As she watched her friend chatting with Mick, a mix of feelings coursed through her, feelings she had not anticipated—and yet could not seem to control.

* * *

Mick watched Ida as she closed up shop for the day. She looked tired, he thought. Understandable, given the fact that people had been in and out of the store non-stop, all day long, spending generously. It moved him, to see how everyone in Spring Creek pulled together to lend their support.

Ida glanced his way as he swept the floor. "Are you hungry?"

He grinned at her. "Starved. What've you got in mind?"

"Sophie and her mother brought some corn bread and pinto beans earlier," she said. "Dinah's upstairs warming them up, and she wanted me to extend an invitation to supper."

"Really? You want me to stay?" he asked before he could stop himself.

"I'll admit, it won't be as good as Myrtle Mae's cooking," Ida confessed, "but it's a free meal, and one you've rightly earned. We'd be happy to have you."

Mick readily agreed and within minutes they were all seated at Dinah's table in the upstairs kitchen, eating mushy beans and chasing down dry corn bread with large glasses of cold milk. As they ate, Dinah and Ida talked through the events of the day, commenting on the various people who'd come in and out of the shop.

Mick found himself thinking about a comment one of Brewster's men had passed his way while in the store this morning. Another threat. *Be on the afternoon train to Centerville or there will be a price to pay.*

It was as if Brewster and his men knew he wanted to stay in Spring Creek. But even he didn't know yet what to do about The Lucky Penny. He had to send word of the fire to his investors, but he couldn't do it until he had a plan.

The women continued to talk, oblivious to his ponderings. Mick finished up his bowl of beans and leaned back in his seat, giving Dinah a smile. "You do quite a healthy business here. And your customers are loyal, to say the least."

"Oh, yes." She nodded. "I've known many of these folks for years. And the locals—the ones who were born and raised here—will do anything to help out when there's a need. It's always been like that."

"Until the last few years," Ida added. "When the Great Northern came through, I honestly thought our little town would never recover from the shock. But it looks like I was wrong, and I'm happy to admit it. It would appear the fine folks of Spring Creek, Texas, still know how to lend a helping hand to a family in need, and for that I'm so grateful."

Dinah whispered a quiet, "Amen," and Mick almost joined her. Right now, seated here with these two women, watching Carter ladle beans from an oversize spoon into his mouth… Mick almost felt right at home.

"It's going to be dark out soon," he said to Ida, nodding toward the window. "I'd be happy to walk you home."

Her face reddened. "Oh, that's not necessary. I'll be fine." She started to push back her chair and he stood to assist her.

"Let me walk you as far as the tracks," Mick suggested. "I'd feel better if I knew you weren't walking through town with the sun going down. It's just too dangerous."

"He's right, Ida," Dinah agreed. "You've stayed much

later than usual, and there's no telling what sort of trouble you could run into along the way with the men so riled up. I'd feel so much better if you let Mr. Bradley walk you home."

Ida tried to argue, but Mick—to his great pleasure—managed to stop her before she declined his offer. They said their goodbyes and headed down the stairs and out onto Midway. Mick took note of the fact that Chuck Brewster's men were gathered in a cluster in front of The Golden Spike. He pushed aside the uneasy feeling that took hold, though he couldn't seem to shift his gaze.

The men looked his way as he and Ida turned in the opposite direction. Mick focused his attentions on the beautiful woman to his left, determined to protect her from these ruffians.

They made their way to the edge of town and beyond the tracks. He felt sure she would stop him there, telling him she could make it the rest of the way on her own, but she did not. Instead, they talked easily and at length as the sun settled into a heavy sky off in the west. All too soon they arrived at Ida's house.

"I'm so grateful for your time," Ida said. "Thank you."

"My pleasure." He wanted to say so much more—to tell her how sorry he was that he'd been the cause of so much trouble, to say that he'd figure out a way to make it right. And yet…

As he gazed into Ida Mueller's beautiful eyes, as he studied the color of her hair and the sound of her voice, Mick felt torn between two worlds. Part of him longed to link arms with this Southern beauty, walk her to church and join her as she fought to defend her town. Another part of him wanted to rebuild the gambling hall, give it another go, see if he could make things work—for his sake and the sake of his investors.

Oh, if only he could live in both worlds at once.

"Good night, Mr. Bradley." She opened the front door and took a step inside, then turned back to give him a smile that nearly sent his heart into a tailspin.

With a tip of his hat, he turned back toward town.

As Mick made his way along the road, the vibrant colors of the setting sun faded into a haze of gray. Night began to fall around him, shadows hovering overhead. As he reached the roundhouse, a feeling of unrest came over him.

Something felt…wrong.

Off in the distance, just beyond the building, Mick heard what sounded like hushed voices. Then footsteps. Walking. Then running.

As the sound drew near, he inhaled deeply. He was torn between wanting to run and needing to defend himself. Still, as the darkness swallowed him whole, neither seemed like a viable course.

Mick felt the first hit.

And the second.

By the time the third one came, everything had faded to black.

Chapter Seventeen

A deafening fog enveloped Mick and he fought to breathe. Every few seconds a searing pain tore across his jaw and his head and the taste of blood on his lips served as a chilling reminder of what had just happened.

He tried to sit up, but the searing pain in his right leg stopped him cold.

Dear God...

Mick's thoughts, rapid and scattered, were interrupted by a strange tightness in his chest—a crushing feeling that caused him to wonder if his heart might explode.

He couldn't make a bit of sense out of any of it. Nor could he see. A light, white and hot, blinded him and forced him to think he must surely have drifted into a ghoulish nightmare.

"You all right, mister? Answer me if you're all right."

Mick heard the words but couldn't will his head to nod. Or to move at all, for that matter. Instead, he lay quite still, fighting to remember where he was, what had brought him to this agonizing place. He could taste blood on his lips, and pain tore through his jaw. But it was nothing compared to what he felt in his right leg. He began to lose consciousness.

"Ready for bed, son?" His mother's voice brought comfort as she brushed the hair from his brow. "Let's say our prayers before we settle in for the night." Her smile, bright and reassuring as always, made him want to bow his knees in prayer. And her beautiful eyes—caring, compassionate. How they danced with joy.

He tried to respond, but found himself unable to.

"Now I lay me down to sleep... What's next, son? Say the next part."

Mick whispered, "I pray the Lord..."

She joined him for the rest. "...my soul to keep."

A gripping pain crushed Mick's chest, as if in an attempt to squeeze the breath out of him, and he could not continue. His arms broke free from their numbed state and he reached up, hoping for someone—anyone—to ease the pain.

"Mister, don't move. Whatever you do. We'll do our best to help you, but you're going to have to work with us."

If I should die before I wake...

Mick faded into a world of dreams.

As Ida took a long, hot bath, she did everything in her power not to think about Mick Bradley. She tried not to reflect on the color of his eyes. She did her best to push aside the gentle sound of his voice as he'd offered to walk her home.

Oh, if only she could banish all thoughts of him. Then life would return to normal. She would get back to work, saving her town from ruin, and he would...

Her stomach knotted as she thought about the pos-
sibilities.

He would leave.

The idea of Mick Bradley leaving Spring Creek
didn't hold the same appeal it once had. Not in the
slightest.

She dressed for bed and prayed before settling in
for the night. No sooner had she done so than a knock
came at the door. Ida rose at once, knowing somehow
that the news would not be good. She waited at the top
of the stairs as her father answered the door.

"I-I'm so sorry to bother you, sir," said a breathless
Johnsey Fischer.

"Nonsense, son. What's happened?"

"It's…it's Mick Bradley."

A gripping sensation took hold of Ida's heart. "What
about him?" She descended the stairs, clutching her
dressing robe.

Johnsey stepped into the front hall and she read the
concern in his eyes in the flicker of the lamplight. "He's
been attacked. At the roundhouse."

"No!" Ida gasped. "How bad is it?"

"It doesn't look good, I'm afraid. One of the railroad
men found him. He's barely alive."

"Where is he now?" A violent trembling took hold of
her. Oh, how she wanted to be there. To help in whatever way she could.

"Doc Klein is on his way to the roundhouse as we
speak. Dinah feels sure the men will take Mick back
to Doc Klein's place within the hour."

Ida wanted to ask a thousand questions. Why the
roundhouse? How badly was he hurt? Who did this
unspeakable thing?

She knew, of course. Knew that Brewster's men had been behind this. Surely Mick knew it, too. If he was still...

As the word *alive* flitted through her mind, Ida's tears started.

"Dinah wants to be freed up to offer her assistance, if needed. She's hoping you will watch Carter, Ida, if you don't mind," Johnsey continued.

"Of course I don't mind." Ida flew into action, rushing to her room and changing clothes as quickly as she could, a prayer winding its way from her heart to her lips as she raced to and fro.

"Lord, I beg you, please protect Mick. Don't let him die. Oh, God, forgive me for getting the men so stirred up. Lord, I..."

She dissolved into sobs. Mick Bradley was dying... because of her.

Every now and again, Mick shifted into his right mind. He attempted to understand what had happened.

Shouting.

Tugging.

Agony unlike anything he had ever experienced before.

Someone kneeling over him. He heard the tearing of cloth and then felt the person wrapping his leg. But why? As Mick tried to reach down, he found himself restrained and fought against it. He did not want to be led to the bowels of hell bound like a prisoner.

If, in fact, hell was his destination.

Again he fought those who tried to restrain him, but this time their voices attempted to soothe his troubled soul.

"Easy now."

He shook his head, the bitter taste of bile rising up into his mouth. *If I should die*...

Mick groaned in pain as men came from every side—lifting, twisting, pulling...

Through the haze, Mick felt a crowd gathered around, sensed their presence. Surely a band of angels wouldn't have offered any more comfort.

"Let's get him out of here, boys." Within minutes, Mick had been loaded on a wagon and was on his way back to town. Whatever awaited him there was completely beyond his control.

Chapter Eighteen

Ida paced in the kitchen above the mercantile, trying to remain calm.

"Ida, all the worrying in the world won't make things any better," Dinah said.

"I know, I know." Ida twisted a worn dishcloth in her hands, released it and then twisted it again. Her heart felt much like that rag, as if it had been pummeled and then released, only to take a beating once more. First the fire, and now this.

She turned to face her aunt head-on. "What am I to do? I can't help but worry. This is all my fault. If only I hadn't gotten everyone so worked up when he first came—"

Dinah gripped her hand, prying the dishcloth loose. "The Bible instructs us not to worry, only to pray. And you spoke very plainly to the church folks on Wednesday night, encouraging a prayerful approach to Mr. Bradley. This is not your fault, Ida."

"Still—"

"Whenever worries arise, we need to go to God at once. And I can't think of a better time than now."

Dinah took a seat at the breakfast table and motioned
for Ida to do the same.

Ida dropped into a seat, her eyes filling with tears.
She didn't feel like bowing her head or praying. No, she
wanted to join the doctor as he cared for Mick, tending
to his wounds. She wanted to jump in and fix things, as
always. Only now, she could fix nothing. Perhaps Dinah's idea to simply pray made sense after all.

As if reading her thoughts, her aunt reached across
the small table and took hold of Ida's hand once again.
This time, she began to pray aloud. "Lord, we ask You
to watch over Mick. Bring healing and comfort. Be with
Doc Klein as he tends to Mick's wounds. Be with the
sheriff as he pursues the men who did this. Make Your
presence known in the midst of this tragedy, Father.
May every heart turn to You. We place this tragic situation in Your capable hands and acknowledge Your role
as Sovereign King and as One who knows all things.
Amen."

Ida echoed with a quiet "Amen," then gazed up into
Dinah's eyes. "I don't know how you do it."

"Do what?"

"You're so strong, Dinah. You've lost so much, and
yet you always manage to find the good in everything.
And everyone. You turn to God first, when others would
simply panic. And you somehow manage to keep the
rest of us calm whenever there's a calamity."

"I struggle more than you know. Especially on days
like today." She brushed away a tear and Ida knew her
thoughts had shifted to Larson. Dinah's back stiffened
and she dried her eyes. "But every time I reach the
point where I feel I cannot go on, I am reminded of the

Lord's hand at work in my life. And in Carter's. I must trust Him, Ida. And you must, too."

"Yes. I know."

"He will look after Mick, and will shine His searchlight on those who have committed this awful deed. They will be brought to justice."

"But if Mick should die—"

"Ida, you can't think like that."

"Don't you see, Dinah? Papa's right. I try to fix everything. And everyone. I attempted to fix our little town by making Mick miserable enough to leave. Then, suddenly, I felt as if sending him away was the last thing the Lord wanted. Mick Bradley was sent here for a reason, perhaps to come to know the love of the Lord through our good witness. I see that now. But if he's been killed—"

"We have no way of knowing that," Dinah cautioned, "so don't spend time dwelling on it. We will deal with the details as they are revealed. In the meantime, we must busy ourselves in the best possible way. Doc Klein will likely need my help, as always. He was so kind to train me as an assistant for situations like this. Could I leave Carter here with you so that I might offer my services?"

"Of course." Ida worked to press all fears from her mind as she stood. "Just promise me you'll send word. If you're able, I mean. And to be careful, Dinah."

"Of course."

Dinah and Ida looked in on Carter as he slept, and then Dinah planted a kiss on her son's forehead. "He's growing up so fast," she whispered.

"Indeed. And he will be such a wonderful man one

day, Dinah. I'm sure of it." Even as the words were spoken, Mick Bradley's face flashed before Ida's eyes.

With a heavy heart, she said goodbye to Dinah and settled in to wait for news.

"Son, can you hear me?"

Mick awoke to the sound of a strange voice. Through the fog, he looked up into an unfamiliar face. A man with kind eyes. An angel, perhaps? Had he died?

"Son, I'm Doc Klein." The older man's voice sounded soothing, reassuring. "I'm going to take good care of you."

"What happened?"

"Never you mind that now. Just know that I'm going to do the best I can, and lots of folks are praying for you, so you rest easy."

Mick would have laughed if he'd had the strength. Even if the good folks of Spring Creek banded together to offer up prayers on his behalf, why would the Almighty listen?

A violent shaking began and Mick gave himself over to it. How could he possibly be this cold in the middle of summer? Everything swirled around him in a haze. The taste of blood lingered on his tongue and the pain in his chest grew worse with every breath.

Dear God, just take me. Please. Put me out of this pain.

Would death bring an end to the unbearable suffering? Suddenly, he wasn't so sure.

A sound at the door drew his attention. He wanted to turn his head but could not seem to move. He soon heard a familiar voice.

"Mick, it's Dinah. I've come to help Doc Klein as he operates."

"Operates?"

"Yes, son," the doctor said. "We've got some work to do on that leg. And I'll wrap those ribs afterward. See if we can ease your pain."

None of this made any sense. Not a bit.

"I'll be giving you morphine, son," the doctor said, "so you'll be asleep soon. I'll do the best I can to piece you back together."

Mick wondered if he deserved to be pieced back together. Probably not, he concluded. Just as well. The best thing that could happen to him now—and to Spring Creek, and to Ida—was if Doc Klein couldn't put the pieces back together. Save them all a lot of trouble.

Chapter Nineteen

"I'm sorry, Dinah, but I had to come. Carter is with Mrs. Gertsch. I simply couldn't sit still and do nothing. Not when I feel so...responsible."

For once Dinah did not scold her. Instead, she gave Ida a compassionate look, then brought her in the room to see Mick.

Ida gasped at the sight of him—a bloody, mangled mess. "Oh, Dinah!" She knelt at his bedside, her throat in a knot. She finally managed a whisper. "Will he make it?"

Dinah put her finger to her lips and ushered Ida back out of the room. "He just came out of surgery and Doc says it's too early to tell. He's lost a tremendous amount of blood and has several broken bones. His leg is shattered. Even if he does live..." She stopped speaking and simply shook her head.

"What? Please say it."

"Even if he makes it, he might not walk again. And then there's the issue of all the broken ribs. Doc was afraid his lung was punctured, but praise God, that doesn't appear to be the case. Still, it doesn't look good. But we mustn't let him see that."

"Has he come to yet?"

"No. He's on a heavy dose of morphine and will be out most of the night."

Ida's heart twisted. Dinah reached to slip an arm around her waist.

"We need to be strong for him, Ida," Dinah whispered. "If he sees us falling to pieces, imagine what that will do to him. We have to speak words of hope and give him the best possible care."

Ida nodded and did her best to swallow the lump in her throat. "You are right, of course. And I will do whatever you need me to do."

"Go back to my place and get some sleep. You're going to need your strength over the next few days. I have a feeling we're going to have our hands plenty full trying to care for a patient and run the mercantile."

Ida nodded, though she wanted to stay put and sit at Mick's bedside until he awoke. She went into the room again and gently placed her hand on his shoulder, offering up a silent prayer.

Lord, I beg You, spare this man's life. Give him another chance, Father.

Give me another chance.

No sooner had she sent the prayer heavenward than Mick's eyes began to open.

"Doc Klein!" she called out. "I think he's waking up."

If I should die before I wake...

Mick fought the blinding pain in his leg and attempted to cry out, but words wouldn't come. He groped about with his right hand, ignoring the throb in his mid-section as he aimed for his leg. *Dear God, please let it still be there.* He found the answer to his prayer as his hand lit upon a gaping wound.

He worked to open his eyes. *Have I been drugged?* What in the world had happened to cause such pain?

A familiar face appeared in a haze above him. Ida.

Mick tried to sit up, tried to make sense of things, but his rib cage wouldn't allow it. At that moment, the doctor appeared at his side. "Take it easy, young fellow. You're just waking up from surgery, but you're not well enough to sit up just yet."

"Wh-what—"

"Don't talk. Just lie still. I'm going to give you more morphine to ease the pain. Just let me examine you first."

The man leaned down and touched a stethoscope to Mick's chest.

"You had some major injuries, son," the doctor explained as he pulled away a sheet to reveal a bloody array of bandages. "We operated on you a couple of hours ago. Your lungs are both fine, but you came awfully close to losing your right leg. If not for the grace of God…"

The grace of God? What kind of a God would allow something like this to happen?

Mick's head throbbed and he closed his eyes once more. Just as he felt a wave of agony break over him, a small, cool hand grasped his and calmed his racing heart.

"You'll be all right, Mick. You'll be all right," Ida said.

He wished he could open his eyes to see her lovely face, but sleep claimed him once again, the feel of her hand sending him into a deep, dreamless slumber.

Chapter Twenty

Ida raced through her morning chores at the house and fed her father's work crew their hastily prepared breakfast while still in a groggy state. In the three days since Mick was attacked, she'd had scarcely more than a few moments of sleep, and it was starting to show—both in her actions and in her appearance. But some-one had to keep up with the daily routine. And with Dinah so preoccupied now that Mick had been moved to a room above the mercantile, she felt compelled to do all she could.

"These eggs are runny, Ida," one of the lumber-mill workers complained as she slapped them down onto his plate.

"If you want 'em any stiffer, cook 'em yourself."

He shifted his gaze to the plate and took a big bite, not saying another word.

Ida went on dishing out food until all had been served. Perhaps she needed to apologize for her sharp tongue, but with so much festering in her heart and mind she could barely separate one task from another.

Exhaustion now gripped Ida, and she struggled not to give herself over to it.

Still, just about every time she started to feel sorry for herself, Ida thought of poor Mick Bradley. She hadn't been able to get him off her mind. His eyes, filled with pain, lingered in her mind, though she tried to force the image away. What was it about the man that captivated her so?

She headed to the kitchen to respond to the whistling teakettle, whispering a prayer for him, asking for the Lord's intervention. Surely Mick needed intervention. He'd hardly spoken a word since Doc Klein operated. She had never seen a man in such a state of brokenness. Daily, she pleaded with the Almighty not only to spare his life, but to touch his hardened heart, as well.

As she started on the dishes, Papa entered the kitchen, interrupting her thoughts. "Daughter, I'd like to speak with you."

Ida looked into her father's soft blue eyes. "About what, Papa?" She reached up with the inside of her elbow to wipe the perspiration from her brow.

He gestured for her to sit, something he rarely did in the middle of her workday.

"If I stop now, I'll never make it to the shop by two o'clock," she said.

"Dinah will do just fine without you for a few minutes, I feel sure."

Ida wiped her hands on a dish towel and approached the table, wondering what her father might want to say.

"There are so many things I love about this town," he began.

"The way it used to be, you mean?" She sat, intrigued by the direction of the conversation.

He shook his head. "No. I mean the way it is now. I love the pine trees, tall and sturdy, and the creek, loaded with catfish. I love the rumble of the trains in the night as they shake the back wall of my bedroom, and the way you can count on them to come and go at just the right time." He smiled. "And I love the way the boys banter back and forth over every little thing."

Ida bit her tongue so as not to speak her mind. He liked the sound of the trains coming and going? How could he? And the bickering of the men? To her way of thinking, the lumber-mill workers took advantage of her father's good nature by conversing too much as they worked.

"You know, Ida," her father continued, "my parents came to Texas because they wanted to be in a place where they would have an opportunity to purchase land at a fair price, raise a family, start a farm. It wasn't until they settled in Spring Creek and saw these beautiful East Texas pine trees that my father considered lumber-mill work. His craftsmanship with pine drew a lot of praise from the locals."

"Really?" Ida marveled at this new insight.

"Your grandfather, God rest his soul, was a man who genuinely loved people," Papa explained. "And I've always tried to be the same way." He paused and looked at her intently. "It is important to always let the love of God show, even under the hardest of circumstances."

"Of course." She shifted a bit in her chair and wondered at the sudden uneasiness that gripped her heart as he spoke.

Papa's brow wrinkled a bit as he continued. "Just this morning I read one of my favorite scriptures from the book of Timothy. Would you mind if I shared it with you?"

She looked toward the sink full of dishes. "Of course not, Papa."

"Paul wrote this to young Timothy as a reminder," Papa started. "'Christ Jesus came into the world to save sinners; of whom I am chief.'" He gave her an inquisitive stare. "Do you understand why I'm sharing this with you, Ida?" She shook her head.

He reached out to squeeze her hand. "You are, without question, one of the strongest women I have ever known," he said. "But I'm afraid sometimes that your strength works against you." He drew in a deep breath and continued on. "You are so much like your mother, it hurts."

These were new words from her father and they rushed at Ida with a force completely unexpected. "I am?"

"Yes," he responded. "She was always one to fix everything, make everything right again. You have most assuredly inherited that tendency from her. Now me," he said, leaning back in his chair, "I'm more likely to overlook a few of the flaws in a man's life in order to seek out his heart. Give him the benefit of the doubt."

"I've been guilty of judging people harshly, Papa," she admitted. "I know that, and I'm working to change it. Every day I pray about it—now more than ever."

"Of course you do." He continued to hold her hand. "And I'm not saying you're judgmental. More likely, I'd say you so desperately long for all to be well that you feel compelled to make it so."

Tears welled up and she brushed them away.

"I'm not scolding, Ida." Papa patted her hand. "From

what Dinah has told me, you have been harder on your-self than I could ever be. I just want to remind you of one little thing. Jesus cannot abide the sin, but He con-tinues to love the sinner."

Ida's gaze shifted to the floor. "I... I know that."

"Of course you do." He slipped an arm around her shoulder. "But we could all use a reminder now and again. That's all." He stood rather abruptly and reached for his hat. "And speaking of loving sinners, I do believe the Lord would have me spend a little time ministering His love to Carl Walken this afternoon. I understand he ran into a bit of trouble in town last night at one of the saloons, and might require a bit of godly counsel."

Her father headed out the back door, all smiles and good nature. Ida went to the sink to finish the dishes, unable to think of anything but her father's words. She was embarrassed that he'd felt the need to speak with her. But he was right, as always.

Love the sinner. It was so simple and yet she'd been so determined to follow in Esther's footsteps that she'd completely lost her way.

It was time to make amends.

Chapter Twenty-One

As Ida made the walk to the mercantile, no hecklers called out. No jokesters offered marriage proposals. On the contrary, the men in town seemed to avoid her, their eyes shifting away as she walked by. Was it possible that some of these fellows had participated in the attack against Mick Bradley? A shiver ran down her spine at the thought of it.

Ida entered the mercantile, pulled on an apron and took to straightening the shelves. "I have a suspicion you've not rested at all, Dinah. Am I right?" she said by way of greeting.

Dinah sighed, but did not answer.

"Am I right?"

"Nellie DeVries has been by to help on occasion."

Even though Nellie had helped save Dinah and Carter, Ida still could not accept that the young woman carried on every night over at The Golden Spike, doing whatever it was that saloon girls did.

Love the sinner, she reminded herself.

She sighed as conviction settled in. Hadn't she already committed to reserving her harsh judgments?

How many catastrophes did she have to go through before she finally caught on? God loved everyone in the town of Spring Creek. Men, women, children—everyone.

And Ida would do her best to love them, too.

Dinah continued. "I tried to prop my feet up for a while around noontime, but with my new boarder to feed…"

"Just as I suspected."

"When I put Carter down for his nap, I struggled with the temptation to join him." Dinah yawned. "But I knew better."

"And now *I* know better." Ida flashed what she hoped would be perceived as a motherly smile. "And I'm telling you to take a nap. You need it, Dinah. You'll not be able to go on if you don't get some rest."

"Oh, I couldn't."

Ida took the broom from her aunt's hands. "You can, and you will. Now don't argue with me. You know how irritable I can be when I'm crossed." She gave a mock scowl and Dinah smiled.

"Yes, I know all too well."

"Then up to bed with you. If your houseguest needs anything, I'll be here."

But before Dinah made it to the staircase, the door opened and Johnsey Fischer came in, hat in hand. Dinah's smile at the sight of him nearly lit up the room.

"How are you today, Dinah?" he asked.

"Fine," she replied.

"She's worn to a frazzle, actually," Ida added. "I'm trying to send her up for a nap."

"If anyone deserves it, Dinah does. I don't know how

you keep going, to be quite honest," he said to Dinah, causing her cheeks to redden.

"Have you heard any scuttlebutt about who might've done this? Was it Brewster and his men?" Dinah asked, clearly changing the subject.

"I can't rightly say." Johnsey shrugged. "I'm so new in town that most of these folks are unfamiliar to me, though it makes perfect sense that Brewster would have instigated the attack. Still, everyone's pretty tight-lipped, and I hear the sheriff's having a hard time getting anyone to share any information at all."

"No doubt Brewster's got them all tongue-tied," Ida said. There was a slightly awkward pause as Johnsey looked at Dinah, Dinah looked at the floor and Ida struggled to keep from giggling over what she was witnessing.

Ida cleared her throat as a mischievous idea came into her head. Perhaps she could get some information about Johnsey on behalf of her smitten aunt. Was meddling a sin?

"Until recently, I thought all railroad men were wicked to the core," Ida said with a smile.

Johnsey laughed. "Well, I dare say, many of them are—at least, when they're cooped up between runs. That's when you'll find 'em bored and liquored up. Rest assured, I'm not like that. And besides, my visit to Spring Creek has nothing to do with the railroad," Johnsey explained.

"Oh?" Dinah said.

"My father currently lives in Centerville, but he recently purchased a farm in the area. It's on the north end of town."

"The Salyer place?"

"Yes, that's it." Johnsey smiled. "My father has always wanted to move back here. And, of course, I plan to live here with him."

Ida noticed Dinah blushing again. How lovely it was to see her aunt like this—enamored, perhaps falling in love. It changed her. She looked like a teenager, full of hope and possibility. Ida hadn't seen her like this in years.

"How wonderful," Dinah said. "Your father will be so happy."

With a hint of a smile in his eyes, he added, "My father will be happy as long as he settles near the creek and can spend his days with a fishing pole in his hand. You should see the look that comes over him when he talks about this place. His memories of Spring Creek are chiseled deep, to be sure."

Ida marveled as she watched the two of them talking. Dinah was getting a second chance and it couldn't happen to a more deserving person. Finally—some joy in the midst of turmoil.

Ida headed to the staircase quietly, not wishing to disturb the small miracle that was taking place in the mercantile.

"How are you feeling today, Mr. Bradley?"

Mick opened his eyes to see Ida in the doorway. He mumbled a halfhearted response and turned his gaze to the window, not wanting her to see him in such a downhearted state.

"Doc Klein says you're on the mend." Her cheerful demeanor was affected—he could sense it in her voice. Mick knew she blamed herself for his injuries. He'd heard all about the meeting at the church, and how Ida felt she'd riled up Brewster's men.

But he didn't blame her. He had continued building the gambling hall after the trouble started when he should've known better. Now he had absolutely nothing to show for his time here in Spring Creek.

On the other hand, many a townsperson had paid him a visit over the past few days, starting with the good reverend. And Myrtle Mae, with an amazing plate of chicken and dumplings. Her food very nearly rivaled Ida's. He'd certainly been spoiled by these women and their tasty fare.

Maybe these Texans weren't as standoffish, now that he didn't pose a threat. If only his investors would be half as gracious. They'd be looking for their money, plain and simple. And he'd have to figure out a way to get it to them.

"I hate to be a bother," Ida said, "but Doc Klein says I have to tend to your wounds while you're here. I hope you understand." She began to unwrap his dressings.

Mick grunted once again—not an altogether cooperative patient—and leaned back against the pillows as she went to work pouring alcohol in his wounds until they stung.

"You're not much of a talker these days."

For a second, he contemplated opening up and telling her about his life back in Illinois. Losing his parents at a young age. Getting swept up in the world of heavy-handed gambling-hall owners. Giving in to the temptation to join that world.

Could he tell her about the tightness that took hold of his chest every time he thought about his investors? How they'd come looking for him if he didn't produce enough income to pay then back—and then some—within a few months?

Likely not.

Mick clenched his fists to avoid showing the pain on his face as Ida worked. In such close proximity, he could see that her determination matched her beauty. No point in avoiding the fact; the woman was quite lovely to look upon. Hadn't she captured his eye that very first day? Seemed like years ago, not weeks.

Ida explained her actions as she worked on him. "I'm so sorry to have to do this, Mr. Bradley, but we don't want infection to set in."

"I understand. And please call me Mick. If I remember correctly, I asked you to do that some time ago."

She smiled. "And please call me Ida."

Mick nodded, pleased. "I would like the doc to bring me some crutches. I want to get up and start moving. No sense in lying here all day and night."

Ida's eyes widened. "You can't get up on that leg. Not yet. Maybe not…"

She didn't finish. She didn't have to. He understood her well enough, and her words angered him. Deeply.

"Don't talk like that. I'm going to walk again. Doc Klein says I should try to put a little weight on it soon."

"Not this soon. He said in six or eight weeks, and even then you'll have to move slowly."

Mick shook his head in disbelief. This woman was downright impossible at times. "I appreciate the vote of confidence." He regretted the words almost as quickly as they were spoken.

Her eyes filled with tears, and she stood and turned toward the door. "I'm sorry. It's none of my business."

His heart twisted at the pain in her voice. "Ida, please

don't go. I'm the one who's sorry. I didn't mean to spout off. I'm just going out of my mind lying here in this bed."

Her face brightened. "We'll get you out of here soon. And if you'd like, I can have your bed moved to the window so you will be able to see outside."

"That would be nice." He looked up into Ida's eyes, taking them in. Her eyes were truly the loveliest things he had ever seen. And that hair, and that smile.

There were worse things than being cared for by such a woman. He should enjoy it while it lasted.

Chapter Twenty-Two

Ida kept a close eye on Nellie DeVries over the next few days as the young woman came and went from the mercantile.

Nellie had turned out to be a fine helper, and kind-hearted, as well. There was nothing questionable in her demeanor or her attire. She wore a simple calico dress and kept her long, dark curls swept up in a fashionable do. Other than her beauty, there was nothing extraordinary about her. During the daytime hours, anyway.

Perhaps Ida had judged too soon—again. After all, she didn't really know what saloon girls did in the evening. Not really.

"Is there anything else I can do for you before I leave?" Nellie asked late one afternoon.

Ida paused a moment, brushing back her damp hair with the sweep of a hand. "Did you wash out the bandages?"

"I did."

"And you helped Dinah with the laundry?"

"Yes." Nellie nodded. "I've taken everything off the line and folded it. And supper is started, as well." She glanced up at the clock. "If you don't need me for anything else, I really need to get going. It's almost five."

"Of course. Thank you so much for your help."

Ida longed to delve into a very different conversation with Nellie. She wanted to know what happened over there at the saloon and whether Nellie could be persuaded to reconsider the source of her livelihood.

Whatever Nellie did at The Golden Spike remained a mystery, at least to Ida. Perhaps ignorance was bliss, at least in cases like these. Surely, if she knew the particulars, Ida would feel compelled to draw Nellie away from such a place. In short, she would want to fix Nellie. Likely the Lord wanted to take that job on Himself.

Nellie said her goodbyes and headed off. As she reached the door, Sophie entered, nearly running her down.

"Pardon me. Are you all right?"

Nellie laughed. "I'm not one of those china dolls in that case over there. I won't break." She stepped outside and sprinted across the street in the direction of the saloon.

Sophie shook her head as she entered the store. "It's such a shame about that girl. I hate to see her working in a place like that. But what can we do?"

"To quote an old friend of mine, 'This is a matter for prayer.'"

"Indeed," Sophie concurred. "So how's our patient? Is Mick better?"

"I'm very concerned about Mick, Sophie."

"These words can't be coming from the girl who wanted him to leave town so badly." Sophie chuckled. "If memory serves me right, you—"

"Sophie, stop."

"I'm sorry, Ida. I was just teasing."

"Stop. Please. I feel bad enough already."

Sophie gave her a stern gaze. "Ida, you can't do this to yourself. No one bears the blame for what happened except the men who committed the act. And in case you have forgotten, you were *right* to oppose plans for a gambling hall. You're most often right, and I do hope you will keep that in mind."

"Thank you," Ida whispered, attempting a smile. "I can always count on you to cheer me up. You're the dearest person I know."

Indeed. If not for her good friends, Ida didn't know how she would ever forgive herself and begin again.

A man could go crazy lying in bed for days on end. How long could a person lie still? Would he eventually lose his mind?

Lying in bed day after day gave Mick far too much time to think. Thinking was dangerous. Thinking could get a man in trouble, especially when those thoughts were all twisted up around the empty hole in his heart. For whatever reason, he couldn't shake Reverend Langford's story. Perhaps it had something to do with the fact that the man had visited every day since the accident.

And then there were his injuries. The ribs would heal on their own—in time. Doc Klein had done the best job he could to reset Mick's broken leg, but the prognosis was still unclear. With one leg shattered and the other foot sprained, just getting out of the bed proved problematic. If he could get up out of this bed, he would track down Brewster's henchmen and...

And what? They'd already managed to burn down his business and beat him half to death. They'd also managed to elude the sheriff, at least thus far. What other evidence did he need to prove their guilt?

Ida slipped away to the back room, taking a seat atop a closed barrel for a moment's rest after closing up shop. From here, through a tiny window, she could see the burnt piece of land next door and her heart grew heavy. She knew that God had plans for that piece of property, plans that were yet to be evident. Perhaps, after she spent a bit of time in prayer, He would reveal those plans to her.

In the meantime, she had some forgiving to do, and sitting alone gave her the perfect opportunity. Ida poured out her heart to the Almighty, asking Him for the courage to forgive herself not just for treating Mick Bradley in such a manner, but for so quickly judging others, like Nellie.

How long had she been in the business of passing judgment? After a bit of reflection, the truth registered. From the moment the railroad men had laid that first bit of track through her tiny town, she'd become judge and jury. And every step of the way she had used the Bible to spur her on. She'd taken the words of the Great Book and twisted them around to condemn instead of love.

Ida sighed. What a pickle she found herself in. After all, gambling *was* wrong. And dance-hall girls *should* seek more appropriate work. And those whiskey-drinking railroad men *did* need to give up their brawling ways. And yet...

She took a moment to think about Jesus, to ponder the kind of love He had shown tax collectors and prostitutes. He hadn't condemned them, had he? No, surely

He had loved them into the kingdom, just as Dinah had suggested.

Love them into the kingdom.

Where did one begin after harboring nothing but frustration and animosity? *With prayer. Start with prayer. That is the only place to start.*

With renewed strength, Ida climbed the stairs to the rooms above, determined to show the love of God to all she came in contact with.

She gingerly tapped on Mick's door. As soon as her knuckles rapped against the wood, the trembling began.

"Come in."

She entered with a cheerful smile and he returned it, his eyes lighting up.

"I'd almost given up on you." He gave her a woeful look, one she imagined he'd spent some time rehearsing.

"Nonsense. I'm here every day, as you well know." Ida approached his bedside to check his wounds, doing everything in her power to hide the effect he had on her, but her hands continued to shake. "So, how are you feeling?"

"I'm having a hard time keeping this leg still," he explained. "It seems to have a mind all its own. To be quite frank, I want to get out of bed and run around the room."

"No doubt," Ida said sympathetically.

"I'm not one for lying around," Mick explained. "I'm itching to be doing something. If you can think of anything…"

"Do you enjoy reading? I have quite a few books downstairs." Not that the man would be interested in Mrs. Gertsch's used dime novels, but she felt compelled to offer.

"I suppose I could read a bit. Might help to pass the time. Might even keep me still in this bed without feeling that I'm going crazy."

"There's a Bible on the bedside table." Ida gestured. "Perhaps you could—"

"Maybe. One day."

"Well, staying in bed is best for now. You must let your body mend itself." Ida noticed that his gaze never left her as she unwrapped his bandages. This made her even more nervous. "Looks like Dinah did a fine job of fixing you up this afternoon," she said in an attempt to make small talk. "Clean as a whistle."

"Yes. She's the closest thing to an angel I've seen in a while. So is Nellie. You all are."

"I doubt many would agree with that assessment, at least as far as I'm concerned." Ida couldn't help but sigh. "But I do appreciate your kindness. Just remind me to polish my halo before I leave."

He let out a chuckle then grabbed his midsection. "Oh, don't make me laugh. These ribs of mine are so tender, I can hardly stand it."

"Do I need to wrap you a bit tighter then?" She looked into his eyes and found herself captivated by them in much the same way she'd been captivated the first day they'd met on the street below.

When Mick nodded, Ida reached to help him out of his shirt. She then went about the task of tightening the linen strips around his midsection to hold the ribs firmly in place so they could mend properly. As she worked, she began to feel a bit light-headed. Perhaps it could be blamed on the early-evening heat.

Ida did her best to still the fluttering in her heart and turned her attention to aimless chatter. On and on she went, talking about the weather, the lumber-mill workers—anything and everything to avoid the sudden anxiety that gripped her as she worked to ease Mick's pain. An unusual sensation swept over her, one she did not recognize.

What in the world is wrong with me? She rambled on nonstop as she worked, pausing only to look up as a rap on the open door caught her attention. Sophie stood in the doorway.

"I didn't mean to interrupt." Her friend gave her a curious look. "Just wanted to let you know that Dinah needs your assistance in the kitchen."

"I'll be there momentarily." Ida finished wrapping Mick's ribs and helped him back into his shirt. All the while, she felt his gaze on her.

"Is everything all right?" she whispered.

"Mmm-hmm."

As Ida drew close to him one final time to help with his buttons, she very nearly swooned. She quickly stood and said goodbye, scurrying from the room before trembling overtook her entire body.

Chapter Twenty-Three

Several days went by, and Ida settled into a steady routine. After watching the railroad men in action, she had concluded that they weren't all bad—especially if you factored Johnsey Fischer into the mix. The out-of-towner had become a regular at the mercantile, helping Dinah around the shop, giving up much of his personal time to look after Carter so that she could care for Mick.

Nellie had also wriggled her way into Ida's heart. Still, every afternoon, just before closing up shop for the day, when the young woman excused herself to go to the saloon, Ida felt both troubled and confused. Finally, she could take it no longer. She stopped Nellie at the door.

"If you don't mind my asking, what is it, exactly, that you *do* at the saloon?"

Nellie turned, and with the most innocent face, responded, "Well, I fetch drinks fer the men, mostly." She shrugged. "And I dance with 'em, too. Sometimes I have to pinch my nose to kill off their breath, what with the stench of chewin' tobacco and hard liquor. But I don't really mind. I just do what I can to keep 'em happy. That's what Chuck wants."

Ida felt a wave of nausea wash over her at the mention of Chuck's name. She didn't want to think about him sitting over there at The Golden Spike, going on with life as if nothing had happened. He was responsible for the attack on Mick. Everyone in town knew it. Now, if only the sheriff would find the evidence he needed to arrest the man, all would be well.

"I'm just grateful I don't have to sing, like some of the girls do," Nellie continued. "My mama always said my voice could scare away the chickens. I sure don't want to run off any of the men!"

Ida wondered how she could get Nellie to stop elaborating on her job at the saloon, now that she'd got her started. It didn't seem possible.

"Oh, but I'd really love to be a real showgirl, like the ones out west," Nellie proclaimed. "I've seen some mighty fine ones, especially the gals in Houston, where I worked last." She lifted her right leg, pointed her toe and twirled it around, revealing far too much ankle, and began to sing an unfamiliar little ditty, completely off-key.

"None of that in here now," Ida scolded. She glanced around to make sure no one else had witnessed the girl's sudden display.

"I'll behave—leastways 'round you. I know you don't care for girls like me anyhow. Chuck told me to watch my p's and q's while I was here."

Ida drew in a deep breath, as she tried to figure out a way to explain herself. "It's never the sinner I choose to dislike—only the sin." Almost as soon as the words were spoken, Ida wished she could take them back.

Nellie gave her a pensive look. "Are you sayin' what I do for a livin' is sinful?"

"Well, I can't rightly comment on such things," Ida said. "It's not my place."

Nellie's cheeks flashed pink. "Well, it's a good thing the menfolk don't feel that way. Otherwise I'd be poor as a church mouse." After a brief pause, she added, "I sure wish Mr. Bradley would stay on in Spring Creek and open his new gambling hall."

Ida was so shocked she couldn't respond.

"There's some real money to be made, from what he's been telling me." A smile lit up Nellie's face. "I've been trying my best to convince him to make another go of it. He told me all about how they operate up North, and I think it sounds wonderful."

Ida felt the blood rush to her head. Didn't Nellie realize the danger to Mick if he decided to rebuild the gambling hall now, after everything that had happened? Why, Brewster's men wouldn't rest until he was in his grave.

Nellie leaned in and whispered, "In Chicago, the saloon girls make a commission on all the drinks they sell. The more whiskey they ladle down the men, the more money they make. That sounds like a mighty fine deal to me."

Anger took hold of Ida, but she did not say a word.

"He told me that he'd hire me on the spot, if he ever changed his mind and decided to open The Lucky Penny," Nellie added. "I'd go to work for him in a minute, no doubt about it. Though I don't think Chuck would be very happy."

Ida was more than a little troubled by these revelations. Surely the man couldn't be rethinking his original plan. Hadn't he already laid that idea to rest once and for all?

Nellie took hold of Ida's arm. "I know you don't like what I do, Ida. But my mama's awful sick, and I send nearly every penny I make back to Houston to pay for the doctors and medicine and such. When she's well enough to travel, I want to bring her here to live. That's why it's so important for me to make money. And working in the saloon is the best way for me to do it."

Ida did her best to calm down, though she'd decided to speak her mind to Mick, should he ever again bring up the idea of The Lucky Penny.

"Well, thank you for helping out, Nellie," she said with a nod. "We're very grateful indeed."

"I've enjoyed it so much." In an uncharacteristic gesture, Nellie threw her arms around Ida's neck and gave her a tight squeeze. "And I don't care what Chuck says about you and Dinah. I still feel like we're sisters!"

She turned on her heels and headed for the door, looking back just long enough to wave goodbye. Ida tried to make sense of the conversation they'd just had. Good all mixed up with bad. Nellie saw her as a sister and that made Ida happy. And yet, for all her sisterly qualities, Ida couldn't think of a way to counsel Nellie without the risk of bringing more offense. Perhaps in time the Lord would show her how to approach her new friend with truth. Tempered by love.

Still, all that business about how they did things up North. Ooo! Ida could wring Mick Bradley's neck for bringing up such things in Nellie's company. Did he not realize the temptation his stories presented?

Ida climbed the stairs to check on Mick and give him a telegram that had arrived nearly an hour before. And she hoped against hope that she'd be able to resist that urge to give him a piece of her mind, as well.

A knock at the door interrupted Mick's thoughts. Ida popped her head inside.

"I've got something for you." She stepped into the room. "I very nearly forgot to bring it up. It was delivered more than an hour ago."

"More of Myrtle Mae's pot roast, I hope?" He licked his lips in anticipation.

"No, but an admirable guess."

"Your ham and beans, then? Or maybe that amazing Wiener schnitzel you're so famous for?"

"Not even close." She reached into the pocket of her apron and pulled out a piece of paper.

As he read the words *Western Union,* Mick's heart sank. A telegram. Ida handed it to him and he could see it was from Chicago. He opened it, stunned at what he read. Somehow they knew about the fire, the threats, his injuries—everything. But how? Brewster. Brewster had figured out who'd fronted him the money for the gambling hall and contacted them. Mick would bet money on it.

After a few moments of silence, Ida gave him a concerned look. "Is everything all right?" she asked. "You're as pale as a ghost."

"Mmm-hmm." He folded the paper and stuck it under his pillow. His investors were ending their original agreement and demanding repayment by the end of September. How could he possibly pay them back in such a short time if he couldn't even walk?

"Mick," Ida said, hesitating slightly. "I need to ask you about something. Something that Nellie told me.

She made it sound like you're still hoping to open the gambling hall and I—"

Mick held up his hand. "Ida, please. I'd rather not have this conversation. I know exactly how you feel about my plans. But right now, I've got to figure out how I'm going to pay back my investors before they come to Spring Creek looking for me."

"Is that what your telegram was about?"

He nodded, his head aching.

"Well, I'm sorry to hear that, but I don't think the solution is to rebuild the hall. What do you think Brewster's men will do to you next time? They might not leave you alive!" Ida's beautiful cheeks flushed with color.

Mick stared at her for a moment. Slowly, a smile spread across his face.

"What on earth are you grinning about, Mick Bradley?"

"Ida Mueller, I do believe you're worried about me."

Ida opened her mouth to speak, but no words came out. She quickly turned on her heel and left the room before he could say anything else.

"Good evening," he called after her, chuckling.

His laugher was short-lived as the reality of his situation sank in. Even if he started rebuilding the gambling hall now—today—he'd be hard-pressed to raise the necessary funds by summer's end to cover his debt. And Ida was right—once the building started to go back up, Brewster and his men would likely come after him again.

What in the world could he do lying here in bed?

Anger kicked in and Mick fumed over the mess this venture to Texas had become.

Over the next hour or so, Mick watched the sunset through the window. The sky changed from yellow into shimmering shades of orange, and then a fiery, angry red. It seemed to mirror the rage that now filled his heart every time he thought about Chuck Brewster.

Even from the second floor, there was no mistaking the noises coming from The Golden Spike. Strange, when you could hear something but not see it firsthand. He envisioned the dance-hall girls lifting their skirts and exposing slender ankles, drawing the gazes of the men.

All for one purpose, of course. Money. Money spent on drinks, so the fellas could work up the courage to speak to the girls between dances. And money spent on the girls themselves. If Chuck Brewster ran the usual kind of saloon, anyway.

Every now and again, Mick heard the sound of laughter and jealousy gripped his heart. He tried to force it away, but it would not budge. As much as he hated to admit it, Mick envied Brewster tonight. Why should a man like that—ruthless, hardhearted, dangerous—get his piece of the pie and everyone else's, as well?

Mick closed his eyes and images of his gambling hall took over.

He envisioned Nellie at the center of the room, serving drinks.

Heard the laughter of the patrons.

Saw the money changing hands as the railroad men handed over their wages for a bottle of this or a glass of that.

Mick could see it all so clearly. And the more he saw, the more he longed to try—one last time—to make it happen.

Chapter Twenty-Four

Early on Friday afternoon, Ida came up with an idea to lift everyone's spirits, including her own.

"I'd like to have a special dinner tonight with the whole Weimer clan," she explained to Dinah. "I was thinking about doing it here so that Mick could join us."

"A spectacular idea!" Dinah's face lit up at the prospect. "I'm sure your father won't mind having supper in town tonight. And I know how much Mick raves about your cooking. He's probably fit to be tied with my lousy meals."

Ida laughed. "You're a wonderful cook, and your apple strudel is the best in town."

"Then we will have apple strudel for dessert," Dinah said.

"We will give everyone a fabulous meal—one they won't soon forget."

"What's this I hear about a fabulous meal?"

Ida turned to see Johnsey Fischer.

"We are cooking up a feast tonight," Ida said. "Dinah is making the dessert. Would you like to stay for supper?"

"Would I!"

"Wonderful! Dinah, would you mind if I went to Sophie's place to issue the invitation?" Ida asked, pulling off her apron. "I'll be back in just a few minutes."

"Of course. I'll manage without you for a while."

"I'll be here to help her," Johnsey said with a smile.

Ida grinned at Johnsey and practically sprinted out the door. She headed to the Weimer farm just a few blocks from town and found Sophie's mother on the front porch, fanning herself and drinking lemonade.

"Why, Ida, as I live and breathe. You're the last person I expected today." Mrs. Weimer stood and embraced her, then began to fuss with her hair. "I must look a sight, what with this heat and all." She tucked a few loose gray hairs behind her ear.

Sophie appeared on the porch. "Ida! Has something happened? Do you need my help in town?"

"No." Ida laughed. "For once it's good news. I've come to invite your family to dinner tonight. I'll be cooking at Dinah's place. Sausage sauerkraut balls. Dinner will be served promptly at six-thirty. You are all welcome to attend."

"Will Mr. Bradley be sharing the meal with us, by any chance?" Sophie asked.

"He-he will," Ida stammered. It was becoming increasingly clear to Ida that her dear friend had designs on Mick Bradley, and Ida didn't like the way that made her feel. At all.

Sophie gave her a wink. "I still find him the most handsome man in town. What should I wear tonight?"

"Oh, I wouldn't worry about that. It's just friends and family, after all."

As Sophie declared that she would wear her favorite pink dress, Ida's heart plummeted. As much as she hated to admit it, inviting Sophie to dinner might not have been the best course of action. Mick needed to focus on getting well…nothing else.

Unless, of course, that something else had a little something to do with *her*.

Ida quickly chided herself. Did she really want to draw the eye of a man like Mick Bradley, one who clearly didn't yet know the Lord? Definitely not.

"You are so kind to invite us," Sophie said.

Mrs. Weimer's face broadened into a smile. "Yes, thank you for the invitation, Ida. We accept." After a slight chuckle, she added, "With this heat, I wasn't looking forward to cooking, anyway."

"We will see you promptly at six-thirty," Sophie said with a twinkle in her eye.

Oh, if only the invitation could be withdrawn. Then, perhaps, Ida could rid herself of the sinking feeling in the pit of her stomach.

Mick stared at his reflection in the mirror. Not bad for a man who'd spent the better part of the last month in bed. He ran a comb through his hair and contemplated the fact that it needed to be trimmed. Perhaps tomorrow he could call for that younger fellow, Georg, from the barbershop. Right now, he had places to go, people to see—and the idea of getting out of this room lit a fire underneath him.

For once, Mick would share his supper with the others. Dinah had made the suggestion earlier in the day, and he had happily agreed. Though from the smell of things, he would be eating something quite unique, something he wasn't sure he was going to like at all.

Mick reached over to grab hold of the makeshift wooden crutches the doctor had brought by a couple of days ago. Finally! He could get around a bit.

After another glance in the mirror, Mick inched his way toward the door. He'd almost made it when Ida came barreling in, nearly knocking him down.

"Oh, I was coming to fetch you." She gave him a warm smile, though he couldn't help but notice she looked a bit wary. He'd not seen her since their little discussion about his future yesterday.

"I don't need fetching, as you can see for yourself." He took another hobbling step in her direction, trying to stay balanced on the crutches. Turned out it was trickier than it looked. For a second, he very nearly toppled over. She reached out to grab his arm and he steadied immediately.

He felt her hand linger on his arm. They gazed into each other's eyes, and a comforting feeling washed over him. A feeling he could get used to. He refrained from making a comment for fear of embarrassing her and sending her fleeing from the room again.

She pulled her hand away. "The others are waiting in the kitchen."

He made his way along slowly with Ida following behind him. "I've been smelling the food all afternoon," he said, "but I can't place it. What are we eating?"

She laughed. "Likely, it's the sauerkraut you're noticing. It has a smell all its own, to be sure. I've made German sausage sauerkraut balls. They're Papa's favorite. Sophie's, too."

They entered the very full kitchen, and Mick smiled as the others greeted him. Johnsey Fischer had proven to be a likable soul, and Dinah—well, what could be said about a woman who gave her life to help others? Carter bounced up and down in his seat, ready to eat.

Quick introductions were made, though he recognized Sophie's family from that night so long ago at The Harvey House. Funny, he'd spent that evening wondering what it might be like to sit around a dinner table with such a family. Now he would find out firsthand.

No sooner had they taken their places than Ida's father appeared at the door.

"Sorry I'm late." He leaned over and kissed Ida on the head. "Ran into a bit of a problem with a couple of my men."

"It's fine, Papa. We're just glad you're here." Ida gave him a loving smile.

The food was passed, and Mick had just reached for his fork when Mr. Mueller cleared his throat.

"We're going to pray," Ida whispered, reaching for Mick.

Mick allowed her small hand to slip into his own. He remembered her holding his hand once before, when he'd been in so much pain. He'd welcomed the feeling then, and he certainly did now.

They began to pray, and Mick closed his eyes and tried to imagine what it must be like to live like this all the time. How would it feel, to sit around a table every evening with a family of his own?

After the prayer, the noise in the room intensified. Mick bit into one of the sauerkraut balls, more than a little cautious. With relief, he found it to be quite tasty. And so were the accompanying noodles. How could he have doubted Ida? Why, her cooking was by far the best he'd tasted—North or South.

"Do you like it?" she whispered.

He nodded vigorously and took another bite.

A lively conversation ensued, and Mick listened closely, wishing he could join in. Unfortunately, he knew very little about the sugarcane industry, which happened to be the topic at hand. He continued on, eating like a man who might never see food again.

From across the table, Mick caught Carter's eye. The youngster gave him an impish smile, and Mick knew he'd found a friend.

He had to admit—he'd found more than one. Nearly everyone here had proven their friendship to him over the past few weeks.

Especially Ida.

Johnsey piqued Mick's interest when he mentioned the oil strike in Beaumont. "Lots of money to be made in oil," Mick said. "I'd given some thought to moving to Beaumont before I settled on Spring Creek."

"Well, we're glad you chose us instead." Dinah smiled.

"I'm not sure I chose Spring Creek," he replied with a tinge of embarrassment. "It's looking more like Spring Creek chose me."

A resounding laugh went up from everyone at the table.

"It's been that way for many of us," Ida's father admitted. "I dare say most of the residents here had their hearts settled on other places at one time or another. But God seems to draw folks here, like flies to honey."

Mick pondered the man's words. Had God drawn him here? Surely not. The Almighty probably didn't care for gambling halls any more than Ida did.

"Have you given thought to the fact that the Lord has kept you here for a reason?" Dinah asked.

Mick looked across the table, stunned. How could he begin to answer such a ridiculous question?

"I'm not sure I..."

Dinah continued on. "The Lord has spared you and I am convinced it is because He has great plans for you. Texas-size plans."

"For me? I highly doubt that, Dinah."

Johnsey gave him a smile of understanding. "I understand your hesitancy. Been there myself. There was a time when I had made my own plans—laid my own track, if you will. I thought I knew what was best for me."

"What happened?" Mick asked.

"God got hold of me. I was going one way, and the Lord turned me around, sending me off on the track He wanted me on."

"I'm going to be perfectly honest, Johnsey, you don't look like the sort of man who's ever ventured off the straight and narrow."

"Looks can be deceiving, my friend," Johnsey said.

"God has big plans for me, bigger than I've had for myself, is that what you're all saying?"

"Much bigger," Ida said with a nod. "But it means putting your trust in Him."

"Don't know as I've ever figured out how to do that—put my trust in a God I can't see. Whole thing sounds like some kind of a fairy story my mama used to tell me as a child, one I never quite took to."

Thankfully, the conversation shifted as Dinah rose from the table and returned moments later with a plate of beautiful apple strudel in her hand, saying, "I hope everyone saved room for this." She placed it in the center of the table.

Mick sighed as he looked at the tempting dessert. What was it with these people? One minute they were trying to feed his soul; the next, they were heading straight for his belly.

Chapter Twenty-Five

Ida lay back against the pillows with a pounding heart. She tried to make sense of the feelings that had gripped her since holding Mick Bradley's hand at the dinner table, but could not. Surely the Lord would sweep these feelings away. Perhaps then she could think clearly.

Unable to rest, Ida finally rose from her bed and paced the room. When her heart would not be silenced, she slipped on her wrap and tiptoed out into the hallway. With great care, she eased her way along the wall in the dark, then down the stairs, careful not to wake her father. Opening the front door was trickier, since it tended to squeak. But she made her way out to the front porch without making a sound.

Settling into the porch swing, she breathed in the cool night air. Off in the distance she heard the sound of the train cars locking up. Funny. She'd grown so used to the noise that she scarcely noticed it anymore. It was a comforting sound in a way—familiar.

Ida eased the swing back and forth. The steady movement calmed her, and she closed her eyes.

She had reached for Mick's hand instinctively at the

table earlier this evening, never imagining he would take hold of it with such a comforting squeeze. Their hands had fit together perfectly—his soundly grasping hers as if to say, "I am here for you."

Ida opened her eyes, determined to shift her thoughts to something else. She tried to recapture some of the funny stories Sophie had told at the dinner table. But all Ida could remember was the look on her friend's face after Papa's prayer. Jealousy, perhaps? If so, Sophie had no reason to be jealous. None at all.

Or did she?

Mick tossed and turned during his first hour in bed. The elevated temperatures presented a problem, as always, but the type of heat he struggled with tonight had little to do with the weather.

All that talk about God having big plans for him— why did it aggravate him so much? Seemed to Mick his own plans were big enough—building the gambling hall, acquiring the necessary patrons, filling his pockets with cash. Sounded pretty grandiose. Plenty large, even for a state like Texas. Then again, his plans hadn't exactly panned out, had they? And if he didn't come up with the money for the investors by summer's end, he might as well cash it in anyway.

Surely, if the Almighty had big plans for him, as Ida had suggested, if He *really* wanted him here in Spring Creek, then starting over with the building of The Lucky Penny made perfect sense. Why else would Mick have ended up right back where he started, if not to finish what he'd set out to do in the first place? Strange, he'd never thought about it from that angle before. Someone—or something—wanted him to stay put in Spring Creek.

On the other hand, every time he thought about rebuilding the gambling hall, Mick could picture the look of hurt and disappointment in Ida's eyes. She would not approve—this, he already knew.

He tried to imagine how the conversation would go, what he would say to her, if the opportunity should arise. With a few well-chosen words on his part, she might come around, might see the logic in his plans. She was a reasonable woman, after all.

Mick rolled over onto his side and closed his eyes. He remembered the feel of her hand in his as they had prayed, her soft fingers intertwined with his, and the look of pride in her eyes when he complimented her amazing food.

Whether he wanted to admit it or not, the woman was working her way into his heart.

Mick reached for his crutches and attempted to stand. He wanted to get up and pace the floor but soon realized how impractical that desire was. After a few uncomfortable hobbling steps, he sat back down. As he reached over to light the lantern on the bedside table, his hand brushed up against the Bible— the same one that had been sitting there for weeks, untouched.

Sure, he'd seen a Bible or two in his life. Who hadn't? But as for really picking one up and reading it, he'd never bothered. Looked like he wasn't going to get any sleep tonight, anyway; what would it hurt to read a few words? He opened the book up and turned to the first page. *Genesis.*

Suddenly, several shots rang out. Mick jolted, and the Bible flew from his hand onto the floor below. A woman's screams filled the night. He struggled to sit up in the bed, the pain in his leg so intense he cried out.

Mick heard footsteps, then a knock on his door, followed by Dinah's familiar voice. "Mr. Bradley?"

She entered the room with a lamp in her hand. Mick struggled to rise with the aid of his crutches.

"No, please stay where you are." Dinah moved toward the window. "I hate to bother you, but I heard shots from across the street. Your window has the best view of the saloon. Did it sound like Nellie's voice to you?" Dinah turned to face him.

Before he could nod, someone pounded on the downstairs door. Dinah disappeared from view and Mick did his best to stand. He wanted to know what had happened. And how he could be of service.

Somehow he managed to make it from the bed to the hallway. He could hear the goings-on downstairs, homing in on the voice of one of the railroad men, asking for Dinah's help. He heard her frantic footsteps as she raced back up the stairs.

She met him, breathless, with the news. "It was Nellie. They're bringing her here because Doc Klein doesn't have room at his place. We'll put her in my room so I'll be close by."

"Of course. What can I do?"

"I'm not sure what we will need. The doctor will tell us. In the meantime, the only thing I can think to ask you to do is pray."

Pray? He hardly knew where to start, but with a nod of his head agreed to somehow try.

Minutes later, a couple of the men eased their way up the stairs with Nellie, pale and limp, in their arms. Blood oozed from her left shoulder, and he tried to assess where she'd been struck. Hopefully not close enough to the neck to be life-threatening. Still, one could never tell with gunshot wounds.

Mick stood in the doorway of Dinah's room as they laid Nellie in the four-poster bed. Every few seconds she would cry out and reach for her shoulder, then she would drift out of consciousness again. Dinah worked feverishly to clean the wound.

Thankfully, Doc Klein arrived in short order, and put Dinah to work boiling water and preparing bandages. Mick sat at the kitchen table, wishing for something, anything to do. He tried to mutter a prayer, but had little to go by. He managed a choppy sentence or two then turned his attentions back to the fellows who'd brought Nellie in. Had these men been the ones who'd caused his injuries? His blood boiled at the very idea. Still, he had to keep his head on straight if he wanted to be any good to Nellie.

The sheriff arrived, full of questions. "Do you know how this happened?" he asked. "Did either of you see anything firsthand?"

"Carl Walken had one too many," one of the fellows said. "Got all riled up about something or another, and pulled his gun on Eugene Weimer."

Weimer? Sophie's older brother?

"I don't think Carl meant to hurt anyone at first," the other man explained. "He got to bragging about something. Started out as a joke, I think. But the next thing I knew, his gun was pointed straight at Eugene, and shots were fired."

The sheriff pulled off his hat and ran his fingers through thinning hair. "Don't look like he's a very good shot."

The man shook his head. "The bullet flew right past him and hit Nellie. She was up on the stage, dancing her heart out."

Mick felt sick as he listened to the story. Sick for Nellie, and sick for Carl and Eugene, who would sober up soon enough and realize the harm their drunken recklessness had caused.

And in the pit of his stomach, Mick also felt sick about the fact that this whole thing could have just as easily happened at The Lucky Penny if he'd carried through with his plans to rebuild.

As the men went their separate ways and the doctor tended to Nellie, Mick finally found the words to offer up that prayer he'd promised Dinah. He said the only thing that seemed to make sense: "God, please help that poor girl." It was his best attempt at reasoning with the Almighty. Surely, with both his leg and his heart in such a torn-up state, the Lord would understand.

Chapter Twenty-Six

Ida drew near Nellie's bedside with a heavy heart. She knew what Doc Klein had said, of course—that the wounds weren't life-threatening. Still, as she knelt next to Nellie's bed, she prayed for more than just her physical recovery; she prayed for her very soul.

Ida managed to interject a few words on Carl's behalf, as well. And Eugene's. Her mind still reeled at the fact that Eugene Weimer had been in The Golden Spike in the first place. Surely the news must have brought pain to everyone in the Weimer household. Sophie hadn't been by the mercantile this morning, though she usually came to town in the wagon with her mother on Saturday mornings to shop. No, likely today would be spent at home, the whole family coming to terms with what had happened.

Nellie came awake and squinted at the sunlight that peeked in the window.

Ida stood and smoothed back Nellie's hair. "Good morning."

"Ida?" Nellie attempted to sit up, but could not.

"Just rest easy."

Nellie leaned back against the pillows, her face still quite pale from the blood loss. "Wh-what happened?" she whispered. "How did I get here?"

"You don't remember?" When Nellie shook her head, Ida explained. "There was a shooting at the saloon last night, and a stray bullet hit you."

Nellie touched her shoulder and cried out. "Is it bad?" she whispered.

"I truly believe the Lord protected you." Ida took a seat on the edge of the bed and reached for Nellie's hand. "Doc Klein said the bullet came within inches of hitting a major artery in your neck."

Nellie's eyes grew wide.

"The doctor had a doozy of a time getting it out, but you're all patched up now, and he says you should be fine within days. But you have to take it easy. And we have to keep it clean, to guard against infection."

Again, Nellie tried to sit up, a frantic look in her eyes. "I have to get well quick. I need to get back to work. My mama—"

"Don't fret over anything right now," Ida said. "Please. And if your mother needs financial help, I will speak to Reverend Langford. Likely the folks at the church will want to do what they can to assist you."

"Why would the church folks do anything for a girl like me?" Nellie's eyes filled with tears. "Ain't it true what you said before? Don't they think I'm a sinner?"

"I'm sorry I ever said that, Nellie. Sometimes my mouth gets me in trouble. Truth is, the church folks are ready to help anyone in need, whether they know you or not. The purpose of the church is to care for the broken and wounded," Ida explained.

"I do feel broken." Nellie reached for her shoulder

once again. "Chuck won't wait long. He'll put another girl in my place. I know he will. So I hope I heal up right quick."

Ida gave Nellie's hand a tender squeeze. "If I had my druthers, I'd keep you from ever going back to work in that saloon. I'd find you a different job, something with less risk involved."

"Oh, but—"

"We will see what the Lord does. In the meantime, you just rest. Please. And let me know when you're hungry. Myrtle Mae came by with some of that famous pot roast of hers."

"Mmm." Nellie nodded. "Maybe after I've napped a while." Her eyes fluttered closed, and Ida turned to leave the room.

As she entered the hallway, she caught a glimpse of Mick Bradley's felt hat on the stand in the corner. Had it really only been last night they'd all shared a meal together? And had he really, as Dinah said, worked through the night to help out?

Surely he must be exhausted today.

Well, she'd have to stop by for a chat to see for herself.

Mick eased his weight down into a chair at the kitchen table and turned as Ida entered the room.

"There you are." She gave him a broad smile. A good sign. A very good sign.

"Did you need something?"

She pulled up a chair and took a seat across the table from him. "No, not really. I just wanted to thank you for looking after Dinah last night. And Nellie, of course.

From what I hear, they both had a rough time of it, and having you here to help meant the world to my aunt."

Mick didn't even try to hide the grin. "You know," he said, "I still can't get used to the fact that she's your aunt. Dinah can't be more than, what…say, seven or eight years older than you?"

Ida nodded. "Yes. My grandmother gave birth to Dinah in her later years. An unexpected blessing— that's what folks around these parts call a late-in-life baby. Papa was an only child until then. My grand- mother truly thought she would never be able to have more children." A wistful look came into Ida's eyes.

"Have I brought up a tender subject?" he asked.

"I never knew my grandmother. She passed away giving birth to Dinah. Papa was a grown man by then, and he and Grandpa Max raised the baby by themselves, at least for a time." Looking up at him with a smile, she added, "Can you imagine? Two rough-edged German men raising a little girl? Of course, my papa up and married my mama when Dinah was about five or so, and from what I hear Mama fell in love with her. Took the little tomboy under her wing."

"It's hard to imagine Dinah was ever a tomboy." Mick laughed as he thought about the prim and proper Dinah climbing trees and playing with frogs.

"From what I hear, she was quite a handful. But my mama raised her to be a right fine lady."

"If you don't mind my asking—"

"What happened to Mama?" Ida sighed and sadness registered in her countenance. "She passed away about seven years ago. Yellow fever. Not a day goes by that I don't miss her."

"I'm so sorry. I lost both of my parents some years

ago." He reached out and took her hand. Fortunately, she did not pull away. Mick proceeded to tell her his story—how his parents had lost their lives together—and she listened with sympathy. They sat together for a few seconds, hand in hand, until they heard Dinah's footsteps in the stairway. At once, Ida pulled away.

Dinah entered the kitchen, took one look at Ida's flushed cheeks and proceeded to ask if something had happened to Nellie to warrant concern.

"Everything is fine." Ida's gaze shifted out the window. "We were just visiting." She looked at her aunt with a smile. "I was telling Mick what a rough-and-tumble little girl you were."

"You were not."

"I was." Ida grinned and for the first time Mick noticed tiny dimples in her cheeks.

Dinah took to fanning herself as she turned to Mick. "Well, don't believe everything you hear. Besides, there are any number of stories I could tell about Ida as a youngster, if you're of a mind to hear them. Though I must warn you some of them are sure to embarrass her."

Ida rose from the table, her cheeks now crimson. "Well, there's no time for stories now. I'm sure the shop is full of customers."

"Hardly. Looks like most folks are staying home this morning after hearing what happened at Brewster's place. People are more afraid to bring their children into town on the weekends now. I don't know what's going to happen to the mercantile if these saloons stay in business." She looked at Mick and clamped a hand over her mouth. "Oh, I'm sorry."

"No, don't be. If I've learned anything over the past twenty-four hours, it's that Spring Creek has plenty of activity for the railroad men without another gambling hall going up."

"So you've laid the idea to rest altogether?" Ida looked at him, her eyes bright with excitement.

"I don't know what the future holds." He eased his way out of the chair. "But I don't ever want to see another night like the one we just spent."

He had to face the facts. Looking at these two civilized young women—realizing the challenges they now faced in their once-pristine little town—he suddenly wanted nothing more than to offer them his protection. And, as he looked into Ida's blue eyes, still sparkling at his news, he was tempted to sweep her into his arms, to assure her all would end well, as long as she stuck by him.

The words from Dinah's Bible ran through his mind once more: *In the beginning...*

Sitting here with these two women, Mick Bradley felt as if he might just get his first-ever shot at that. A new beginning.

Chapter Twenty-Seven

The following Monday afternoon the postman came through town with the mail delivery. Ida spent much of her time at the mercantile sorting through it all. She bundled up stack after stack, much of it for the locals, but quite a bit for The Harvey House, as well.

She tried to remain focused on the task at hand, but found it difficult. With so little sleep the night before, she could barely keep her eyes open, let alone get her work done. And the feelings that arose every time she thought about Mick didn't help, either.

Lord, I ask you to guide me every step of the way. And, Father, please reveal Yourself to Mick. May he come to know You.

Dinah came down the stairs moments later with a smile on her face. "You will never guess what I did," she whispered.

After waiting on a customer, Ida turned to respond. "What?"

"I invited Mick to the Fourth of July picnic at the church."

"Oh, Dinah, I don't know—"

"Isn't that the most perfect idea?" Dinah said with a grin. "We've been trying to get him through the doors of the church all along, and if he comes with us to the picnic this Sunday, he will have to attend the service first."

"Well, yes. But I'm not sure this is the best timing for that." Ida chose her words carefully. "After all, he can scarcely get up and down the stairs. How will he make it all the way to the church? It's a good half mile from here."

"I need to take the wagon this Sunday anyway," Dinah explained. "Reverend Langford and several of the men are coming by the store early in the morning to load up barrels and food. And I could never make it on foot with the pies I'm baking."

"Still—"

"Can't you see how the Lord has arranged this?" Dinah's eyes flashed with excitement. "The men can help him down the stairs and onto the wagon. Reverend Langford thinks it's a wonderful idea, and I am inclined to agree, even though I did think of it myself. Now, if only I could figure out a way to get Nellie to agree to come, too. Wouldn't that be a miracle!"

"Of biblical proportions," Ida agreed. Somehow, she could scarcely imagine the saloon girl seated in a pew with a hymnal in hand. Then again, imagining Mick there was nearly as difficult.

"Her shoulder is healing nicely, and she should be able to travel by Sunday." Dinah shrugged. "I will pray about it and see what the Lord does."

"And I will add my prayers to yours," Ida said.

"In the meantime, I've come up with another idea. One I think will help Nellie along on her journey."

"Goodness, Dinah, you are full of ideas this afternoon!"

"Her mother lives alone in Houston and suffers with health problems."

"Yes, so I've heard."

"I think it would be a wonderful idea to bring her here, to Spring Creek. That way she and Nellie can be together. And I've spoken with Doc Klein. He will be able to tend to Mrs. DeVries's needs as well as any of the doctors in the big city."

"But how does Nellie feel about this?" Ida asked. "Does she want her mother to know what she does for a living?"

"I don't know. I haven't mentioned any of this to her yet. But I have laid aside a bit of money for Nellie's mother to travel, if she likes the idea. And they can both stay on here with me. Once Mick is fully healed, I will have plenty of room upstairs. And if I have my way…"

"What?"

"Well, if we could afford it, I would hire Nellie to help around the shop. She's quite good with the customers, and a hard worker at that."

Ida pondered her aunt's generosity. Oh, if only she could be as good and kind. How did a person get to be so good?

A noise in the stairway distracted them, and Ida looked up, startled to see Mick hobbling down the steps on his crutches.

"What do you think you're doing?" Ida and Dinah spoke in unison.

Ida took several steps in Mick's direction, then slipped an arm around his waist and helped him maneuver the bottom two steps.

His expression changed when she touched him. His look of pain quickly shifted to a look of contentment. She did her best to focus on helping him, and deliberately avoided his eyes. "I can't believe you actually tried to come down those stairs on crutches. You might've fallen."

"Sorry, but I had to get out of that room," he explained. "I couldn't take it anymore." He looked around the store, smiling when he saw several of the local men playing dominoes. "Thought maybe I'd find a game going down here. Looks like I was right."

She helped him over to a chair where he joined in a friendly game with some of the others. Ida returned to her work, but kept a watchful eye on Mick. She listened as laughter rang out across the room when Mick won his first game. Laughter truly was the better medicine.

Later, when the crowd thinned and Dinah had gone upstairs to tend to Nellie, Ida offered Mick a cup of coffee, which he accepted with a smile.

He gestured to an empty chair. "Sit for a minute."

Ida glanced around the store. "All right, just for a minute."

"Believe it or not, I was reading Exodus last night in that Bible Dinah left me." Mick smiled at the look on Ida's face. "Seemed like one minute Pharaoh wanted Moses to stay put. The next, he was chasing him out of town. The whole thing reminded me of, well, myself. My time in Texas. One minute I want to stay, the next I'm ready to go. I can't help but wonder if Spring Creek is my Egypt." He reached out and took her hand. With a twinkle in his eye, he added, "Or maybe it's the Promised Land."

Ida held back a chuckle. So Mick had given thought

to what he'd read. The Lord appeared to be moving in his life, drawing him in, wooing him.

After a moment of contemplation, Ida realized that Mick still held her hand. He also held her gaze, which only served to fluster her more. She pulled her hand away, embarrassed.

Ida sighed. Why did she always seem to act like a foolish schoolgirl when Mick was around? As she gazed into his twinkling eyes, she had to admit that acting in a sensible fashion might be out of the question altogether.

Mick watched as Ida placed the CLOSED sign in the window. Then he inched his way toward the stairwell, knowing he must somehow make it back up to his room. He did not look forward to the challenge. His broken leg still ached, and the usable one did not appear to be as strong as it once was. Getting down had been difficult enough. How would he manage to get back up?

He tried the first step on his own, using the crutches to lift his weight. Ida approached with a stern look on her face. "Oh, no, you don't. You are not climbing those stairs by yourself."

"Would you mind helping me?"

As she approached, the scent of verbena drew him in. Why did she have to smell like that, anyway? The scent bewitched him almost as much as the tiny bits of blue in her gingham dress that matched her eyes perfectly. Did she have any idea what that could do to a man?

"Careful now," Ida said as she took hold of him at the waist, her hand resting firmly on his back. She gazed up at him with a look that melted his heart.

"I'm always careful." He paused, taking in the color of her hair—the same color as wheat in the summertime. He reached with a fingertip to stroke it and she flinched at his touch, her eyes filling with tears. He gently lifted his hand.

"D-do you still need my help?" she whispered.

"I do." He refused to move. Instead, as he felt her breath against his cheek, he drew her closer still and spoke softly. "I might go on needing it for some time."

"Mick." She shook her head.

"Shh." He put a finger to her lips, then traced it along her cheek. Instead of pulling away, she closed her eyes. "Do you have any idea what you're doing to me?" he asked in a hoarse whisper.

Ida looked at the ground. Mick leaned down to wrap her in his arms. He felt the trembling in her hands and wondered what she might be thinking, but didn't ask. This wasn't the time for talking.

With his free hand he cupped her chin and she looked up into his eyes. Boldness took over, and he leaned down to press his lips against hers. To his great joy, she wrapped her arms tightly around him, and he wondered if he would ever be the same again.

Seconds later, she slipped from his grasp, her face white as a sheet as she pulled away. "I-I'm sorry."

"I'm not." He whispered the words into her ear.

The jangling of the bell at the door snapped him back to reality. Despite the sign, someone had come in unannounced.

"Ida?" Sophie's voice rang out from beyond the shelves.

Mick tried to take a step up, but lost his balance. Ida steadied him.

"Ida, are you here?"

Ida's face reddened. "I-I'm over here, Sophie," she called out.

He couldn't help but notice the look of desperation in her eyes, as she stepped down onto the floor. For whatever reason, the whole thing made him want to laugh. With common sense taking over, he forced himself to stay calm.

Sophie, who now stood directly in front of the stairwell, looked stunned.

"Sophie, I was just..." Ida took a couple of steps in her friend's direction and reached for the broom once again. "Just cleaning up," she said, crossing away from Sophie.

"Mmm-hmm." Sophie watched Ida, and then looked at Mick. She grinned. "I'll come back another time," she said and made for the door.

At this point, Mick began to chuckle. He plopped down onto the stair on his backside and began to ease his way up one step at a time.

Ida, whose cheeks flamed crimson, continued sweeping, apparently unable to look at him.

Not that he minded. No, indeed. She had given him plenty of attention already, and it had changed his life and his heart forever.

Ida ran from the shop and didn't stop until she reached the railroad tracks. The trembling in her hands hadn't ceased since Mick swept her into his arms.

Why hadn't she pulled away? Why had she allowed herself to be so easily pulled into his web? She'd felt safe in his arms, safer than she would have dared dream.

As she stepped over the tracks, ready to run the rest of the way home, the truth came barreling toward her, like a Great Northern out of control. Somehow, some way…she had fallen for Mick Bradley. Little by little, he had inched his way into her arms, and into her heart.

How Ida would get *this* train to stop, she had no idea.

Chapter Twenty-Eight

Ida spent Saturday afternoon doing laundry. Her labors gave her plenty of time to think through the events of the day before. Though she tried to forget about how she'd felt in Mick's arms, she couldn't. Oh, how wonderful she'd felt with her head against his shoulder, how safe. And his kiss…

In all her years, she had never known such sweetness. Why then did she feel so guilty? So frightened?

As she did the wash, she pondered what it would be like to have a husband, someone whose clothes she would wash every Saturday and hang on the line to dry.

Ida's cheeks heated up at the very thought.

She tried to focus instead on tomorrow's picnic, making plans for what she would cook later this afternoon. Pies, naturally. And sausage sauerkraut balls, of course. Folks at the church would never let her hear the end of it if she didn't bring her staple. She would also bake several loaves of bread and a hefty cobbler.

Not that she minded bringing so many items. Ida rather enjoyed the attention that went along with her cooking skills. Though she could barely admit it to herself, Ida now hoped to one day have a husband and children to cook for. She could picture it—little ones gathered around the table, clamoring for more of her home cooking.

Ida swatted away a pesky mosquito as she pondered the idea. She'd never imagined herself married until recently.

Until Mick Bradley.

But she couldn't possibly set her sights on him. He was, in every way, her opposite. And yet...

As she recalled his most recent thoughts on the Bible, as she pondered his interest in her cooking, as she thought of his declining interest in building a gambling hall...she could almost see a glimmer of hope.

Still, if such a miracle were to take place, the Lord would surely have to orchestrate every detail...which meant she had to back away and risk losing the one thing she suddenly realized she wanted more than anything else in the world.

Sunday morning, the Fourth of July, dawned bright and clear. Ida found herself in a cheerful state as she prepared for the picnic. Usually she and Papa walked the half mile to the tiny wood-framed church, but they would take the wagon today, what with so many items to carry.

Ida wore her favorite blue dress. She prayed it would stand up to the heat and the outdoor activities. Surely by day's end the puff sleeves would be a bit deflated. Not that she cared, really. On days like this, when folks gathered together to enjoy one another's company, no one much paid attention to such things.

"Time to leave, Ida," her father called.

She went over a checklist in her mind. "I do hope I haven't forgotten anything. It seems I always leave something behind."

Ida stepped up into the wagon to join her father, and they were soon headed toward the church.

"Daughter, I would like to speak with you about something of a serious nature," her father said as they made their way along the dusty road.

"What is it, Papa?" Ida opened her mother's lovely old white parasol to shield herself from the sun. She noticed that her father's cheeks had turned pink, and wondered if perhaps the heat bothered him, too. "Are you not feeling well?" she asked.

"Oh, I am very well. Indeed." The edges of his mustache began to twitch.

"What is it, then?"

"Well—" he snapped the reins to encourage the horses to pick up speed "—I just wanted to tell you something while it's on my mind. And I must confess, I have a lot on my mind this morning."

"What, Papa?"

"Let me start by asking you a question." He kept his eyes on the road. "How do you feel about the institution of marriage?"

"M-marriage?" Ida's heart quickened. Was he trying to marry her off? "To be honest, in my younger years I never pictured myself married, as most little girls do. I know I'm nearly twenty, but until recently I've never felt…" Instead of completing her sentence, she simply shook her head.

"Never felt you needed a man to sweep in and rescue you?" her father asked. "Like so many other girls?" He laughed. "Don't think I don't know about the plan you made after your mama passed on—never to marry. I've heard bits and pieces of it over the years. Truth is, I feel sure the Lord will one day bring just the right person into your life. If you are open to the idea, that is."

She drew in a deep breath and gave careful thought to her next few words, the sweetness of Mick Bradley's kiss still lingering in her mind. "I am not opposed to the idea of marriage, overall."

"That's good." He turned to give her a smile. "Because I've decided to propose to Myrtle Mae."

"Wh-what?" Ida could hardly believe it. After all, Papa and Myrtle Mae had scarcely had time enough alone to consider the possibility of a romantic union, had they?

Her father's shoulders rose and his chin jutted forward. "I love her, Ida. And she loves me."

"But how do you know?"

Papa laughed. "Oh, trust me, I know. I know what love looks like. What it feels like." He reached to put his hand on his heart. "When you're in love, everything suddenly makes sense. All the confusion fades away and in its place an undeniable peace settles in your heart."

By that definition, Ida would have to conclude she did *not* love Mick Bradley. Whenever she thought of Mick, peace scattered and confusion took hold. Any future she might have with the man was fraught with complications, no matter how she looked at it.

"I plan to give her a ring at today's picnic, one I secretly ordered from a catalog," Papa said, grinning.

"How did you manage that?" Ida asked, stunned.

"Dinah helped me."

"So Dinah knows about this? A fine kettle of fish this is. My aunt knows before I do. Hardly seems fair."

Her father leaned over and gave her a playful peck on the cheek. "I'd like your permission, Ida, to propose to the woman of my dreams."

"Why, Papa, you're a grown man. You certainly don't need my permission to marry the woman you love."

"I might not need it, but it will comfort me to know we have your blessing."

"Myrtle Mae is a good woman. She will make you a fine wife. And you will eat well, what with both of us here to cook for you."

"And you are fine with that?" Her father gave her an inquisitive look.

Ida laughed. "To be quite honest, I will be happy to have someone to share the responsibilities. Cooking for the lumber-mill workers is quite a challenge, I don't mind saying. And with Myrtle Mae there to help, perhaps I can assist Dinah more. There is much work to be done at the store."

Her father slipped an arm around her shoulder. "I love you, Ida. You've grown into a fine woman, one I'm proud to call my daughter." With a much softer voice, he added, "I'm sure your mother would have been so proud of you. You're very much like her."

Ida blinked away the tears and clutched the parasol a bit tighter. "I often wonder what she would have thought of me."

As they approached the church, Ida's father turned to her. "Pray for me today," he whispered. "I surely hope I can do this."

"You can do it." Ida gave him a pat on the back.

"You've achieved so much in your life. No doubt you can handle the likes of one lone woman."

"Oh, I don't know…" Her father gazed out at his bride-to-be. "Some women are enough to make you think you've married three or four."

"At least you'll never be lonely," Ida said with a giggle as the wagon drew to a stop. She looked out over the church property, noticing tables had already been set up outside for the picnic after the service. Several of the local women, Mrs. Weimer included, set food out on the largest one.

Ida looked around, anxious to see if Dinah had arrived yet.

And more anxious still to see if Mick had come with her.

Not until she heard his voice offering to give her a hand did Ida's heart rest. She looked down into his sparkling eyes, and eased her way down from the wagon… landing squarely in his arms.

From the moment Ida Mueller landed in his arms, Mick Bradley committed to attending church every Sunday morning. He would be right here, waiting for her with the same rush of joy that flooded through him now.

Of course, he'd do a better job of assisting the petite beauty if he could throw away the crutches once and for all. As it stood right now, he could barely handle both at once.

Mick released his hold on Ida and reached to grab a flailing crutch. She quickly slipped her arm around his waist.

"Careful now."

He didn't want to be careful. No, Mick wanted to toss caution to the wind, wrap her in his arms and kiss her squarely on the lips, right here in front of her father and all these fine church folks.

On the other hand… He looked up into Mr. Mueller's concerned eyes and stepped back, gripping his crutches a bit tighter. Perhaps waiting would be a better option.

Mick took note of Ida's blue dress and smiled. How would he ever stay focused on the service with her in that dress? "Will you sit with me?" he whispered.

"I don't know." She continued walking, not looking his way. Was she nervous? Worried about what folks were thinking?

Sure enough, he noticed the stares of others nearby and wondered if they could see into his heart. If so, they surely knew he must sit next to this woman or die trying. He continued easing his way along on the crutches, wishing he could be rid of them forever. Would this leg never heal? If not, would she even look twice at him?

"I suppose it would be proper, as long as Papa joins us," Ida whispered back.

He reached over and took her hand, giving it a squeeze. She squeezed back then released it quickly.

As Mick reached the door of the building, Reverend Langford met him with a handshake. "So glad you could join us. Welcome."

Mick offered an abrupt nod. After skimming through that Bible Dinah had left on his bedside table, there were a number of things he'd like to discuss with his reverend friend. Perhaps they could wait until a later date. Likely, Reverend Langford would come by for a visit one day this week, anyway. Then, in the privacy of his room, Mick could ask the primary question that had bothered him all week—or most of his life, depending on how you looked at it. If God loved him as much as the Bible said He did, why did He allow the tragedies of the past few weeks? The fire. The attack. His injuries.

And why had God allowed his parents to be taken from him at such a young age? Surely the Almighty could have prevented their deaths. Instead, He'd left a young boy alone in the world without anyone to tend to his needs except his brother, and strangers. A more merciful God would've kept his parents alive, right?

Pushing aside all such morbid questions, Mick allowed Ida and her father to help him up the stairs. He entered the tiny building with its rough-hewn pews and looked around, surprised at what he saw. "This is nothing like the churches in Chicago."

"Oh?" Ida gave him a curious look.

He shrugged. "I only remember the church my mother took me to as a child, and it was all stained glass and steeples, that sort of thing. The pews were polished to perfection. This place is—" he glanced around, taking note of the small, plain space "—very homey."

Ida smiled. "It's not that we're opposed to fancy buildings. I saw a few in Houston, and they were quite breathtaking." She looked around the room with a smile. "But I grew up in this little church and it suits me just fine."

As they sat in a pew near the front, Mick wondered what his mother would've thought of this place. He somehow felt she would love it here.

Two women came in and looked down their noses at Mick. He heard one of them whisper, "What's he doing here, anyway?" The other one quieted her. "Shush, Cora. Maybe the Lord wants to do business with him."

Had the Lord brought him here to perform some sort of business transaction? A feeling of discomfort slithered over Mick. What was it about churchgoers, anyway—always trying to get folks to change their ways. What made them think their way was best?

Before he could think about this any longer, Myrtle Mae sat at the piano and began to play a hymn, one he vaguely remembered from childhood. He couldn't seem to recall the words, but the melody…

Mick closed his eyes and could almost see himself, a youngster of six or seven, standing with his mother's hand tightly clasped in his own, singing.

Ah, yes. As the residents of Spring Creek rose and began to sing "Tell Me the Old, Old Story," Mick opened his eyes and listened with interest, the words coming back to him in full force.

Tell me the old, old story of unseen things above,
Of Jesus and His glory, of Jesus and His love.
Tell me the story simply, as to a little child,
For I am weak and weary, and helpless and defiled.

He looked over at Ida, watching as she sang the words in a voice as clear as any angel could boast. Like the songwriter, Mick understood feelings of weakness and weariness. The past few weeks had taken their toll. Every inch of his journey had worn him down a bit more. And despite his best attempts to appear strong, he felt completely helpless, just as the song said.

And now, as he attempted to stand, his heart reacted to the haunting melody. It reminded him far too much of his mother—a memory he couldn't bear, the pain of her loss still so deep. The parishioners carried on.

Tell me the story slowly, that I may take it in,
That wonderful redemption, God's remedy for sin.
Tell me the story often, for I forget so soon;
The early dew of morning has passed away at noon.
Tell me the same old story when you have cause
to fear
That this world's empty glory is costing me too dear.
Yes, and when that world's glory is dawning on
my soul,
Tell me the old, old story: "Christ Jesus makes
thee whole."

Empty glory reminded Mick of his now-empty lot.
And that line about Jesus making you whole made him
think of something Reverend Langford had said the first
day they'd met. *You can put yer boots in the oven, but
that don't make 'em biscuits.*

The pain in Mick's leg intensified, to the point where
he ached to sit. He tried to shift his weight, but found
himself more uncomfortable than ever.

As Mick finally gave in and eased his way down
into the pew, he pondered the dilemma he now faced.
At this point, he couldn't be sure which bothered him
more—his leg, or his still-empty heart.

Chapter Twenty-Nine

Out of the corner of her eye, Ida kept a watchful eye on Mick. She could tell the song was affecting him. His entire demeanor changed the moment Myrtle Mae's fingers hit the keys.

Longing took hold of Ida's heart as she realized what surely must be taking place, and she whispered up a silent prayer for the Lord to somehow woo Mick into His arms. While she had once thought his salvation an impossible task, even for the Almighty, Ida now pleaded for that very thing. She approached the Lord in a humble state of mind, asking Him to forgive her for ever having doubted His love for Mick. What an arrogant, narrow-minded girl she had been, to think the Creator wouldn't be bothered with a gambling-hall man.

She sang the final words to the song. *Tell me the old, old story, Christ Jesus makes thee whole.*

The old Ida—the prideful, biased one—spent the next few moments allowing God to do just that. The fears and failings she had struggled with in the past dissipated as the final notes to the song were played. And by the time she took her seat next to Mick, Ida truly felt the words taking root in her heart.

She listened with renewed interest as Reverend Langford delivered his sermon, using the Fourth of July as the foundation for a powerful message on liberty in Christ. Though she had known the Lord from childhood, had given her heart to Him as a youngster, something about today's words stirred her heart anew.

Just a few lines into his text, a rustle at the back of the building caught Ida's attention. She looked back to discover the door flung wide and Nellie DeVries standing there, arm in a cloth sling, a nervous look on her face. Reverend Langford interrupted his message to welcome her at once, and she eased her way in, looking for a familiar face.

Thankfully, Dinah caught Nellie's eye and waved for the frightened young woman to join her. As Dinah scooted over to make room, Ida noticed Johnsey Fischer seated next to her. She caught Dinah's eye and smiled.

Reverend Langford continued on with his message, the words ringing clear across the sanctuary. The resounding theme of the morning—Christ's ability to heal His weary, wounded children from the sins of their past, and the resulting liberty when one placed one's trust in Jesus's work on the cross. A liberty far more precious than any Fourth of July celebration, and one that involved a chorus of angels singing with heavenly gusto.

The weeping started quietly at first. But as the message reached its peak, Nellie's sniffles evolved into full-fledged sobs. Ida wanted to wrap the young woman in her arms. When she looked over her shoulder, she noted that Dinah had already taken care of that.

Myrtle Mae approached the piano for the final hymn,

and the congregation rose to sing. Ida wasn't sure which made the stronger impression on her heart—the undeniable glistening in Mick Bradley's eyes, or the wails coming from the pew behind her.

The service drew to an end, and Mick breathed a sigh of relief. Unlike Nellie, he had resisted the urge to go to the front for prayer as the final song concluded. No, he would rather do business with God—if that was truly what was happening—on his own. One private step at a time. And, no matter how much Reverend Langford turned up the heat, Mick still wasn't sure he was ready to pull his boots out of the oven.

Not that he owned any boots.

The message had served to shift his attention away from his problems for a few minutes, at least. His animosity toward Brewster, his ever-present thoughts about the investors—somehow they'd all taken a back seat to Reverend Langford's powerful words.

Ida excused herself to help set up for the picnic. Mick took the opportunity to visit with Mr. Mueller. However, the older fellow looked a bit off-kilter today. Pale, even.

"Are you not feeling well?" Mick asked.

"Oh, fine." Mr. Mueller pressed his hands into his pockets and looked to the front of the sanctuary. Mick followed his gaze, noting Myrtle Mae rising from the piano bench with sheet music in her hands. Ida's father eased his way through the crowd to offer his assistance.

So that was it. The man had his eye on a woman. And in church, at that.

Well, could any less be said of Mick? Though he'd listened to Reverend Langford's sermon, his mind had wandered a time or two to the gorgeous woman on his left. And who could blame him? His heart felt as if it would leap from his chest every time Ida opened her mouth to sing.

Easing his way around on his crutches, Mick turned and found Johnsey standing behind him. Happy to see a familiar face, Mick smiled and shook his hand.

"What did you think?" Johnsey asked as they made their way toward the door.

"Not quite what I was expecting. I rather imagined more red-faced shouting, that sort of thing."

Johnsey laughed. "It's hard for me to picture God hollering at folks, so it never makes much sense when I see preachers doing it."

Mick pondered his friend's words before adding, "Well, I guess I just figured God was in the shouting business. Never knew the difference."

Johnsey offered his assistance, and before long they had reached the bottom of the front stairs. Colorful quilts dotted the church lawn, the patches of vibrant blues, whites and yellow providing a nice contrast against the green grass and the shade trees overhead. The hot afternoon sun blazed down on them, and he longed for a breeze to blow through.

Mick watched as Ida prepared a spot off in the distance. Dinah was spreading a quilt next to hers, so he and Johnsey headed in that direction.

"Looks like we're both thinking the same thing," Johnsey said with a laugh.

Mick nodded. "I don't mind admitting, she's done something to me."

"You've got it bad, haven't you?" Johnsey slapped him on the back and chuckled. "I know just how you feel. As far as I'm concerned, Dinah is manna from heaven."

Mick watched as Ida interacted with Carter and the other children. Listened to their voices raised in song as she led them on a Pied Piper trail around and through the pine trees.

A woman like that could certainly get under a man's skin.

Johnsey went to sit with Dinah, and Mick made his way through the throng of people to Ida's side, happy when she turned to him with a welcoming smile. Reverend Langford called for everyone's attention and led the group in a prayer before the meal.

Then the real fun began. Folks gathered in long lines to fill their plates. Mick willingly agreed to let Johnsey fetch his plate for him, and stretched out on the blue and white quilt underneath a canopy of pine trees, alongside Ida and her father. And Myrtle Mae, of course.

Mick kept a watchful eye on several things. Ida, who seemed more than a little giddy today. Her father, who acted like a nervous cat. Myrtle Mae, who gabbed with Emma Gertsch about those ridiculous dime novels—the same ones he'd secretly taken to reading. And Nellie, who talked quietly with Dinah about her ailing mother in Houston.

After eating his fill of Emma's homemade pickles, Myrtle Mae's fried chicken, baked beans from the reverend's wife and plenty of Ida's lemon meringue pie, Mick settled back to watch the entertainment. A couple of the men, including Sophie's father, stood with fiddles in their hands and began tuning them. Within minutes, hands were clapping, toes were tapping and several of the children had taken to skipping beneath the pines, their merry voices reverberating against the dense forest behind them. My, but these Texans sure knew how to throw a nice lawn party.

Mick took a sip of his lemonade and looked at the crew of people gathered around him on the quilt, his heart feeling as though it might burst at any moment. They looked for all the world like family...a family he could learn to love.

A startling idea entered Mick's mind, one he could not ignore. The more he chewed on it, the more he realized it made perfect sense. Within a few minutes the idea grew into a workable plan, a perfectly wonderful one. Why hadn't he thought of it before?

Mick leaned back and contemplated the idea rolling around in his head. It had come from somewhere. The Lord, perhaps? Anything was possible.

Maybe, just maybe, Mick could pay his investors back by September after all.

If he could just get the townspeople to join him— and keep a secret.

Ida finished up a plate of ham and baked beans, and offered her remaining piece of chicken to Johnsey, who gladly accepted it. Then she took a sliver of lemon meringue pie, eating it slowly. The sun hung bright and heavy above them, and she felt herself perspiring. Glistening, as Dinah called it. Thankfully, she'd chosen a spot underneath the trees to place their quilt. The shade provided a bit of relief.

She looked over to the Weimers' quilt and saw Sophie watching her. Ida lifted a hand in greeting, but did not get up to say hello. Sophie waved back, a strange look on her face. Ida felt uneasy for reasons she could not explain. There was something between them, something she could not identify. A tension...

Once the fiddlers got to fiddling, Ida leaned back against a tree and closed her eyes. Her mind wandered—until the music came to an abrupt, unexpected halt. She heard a giggle of embarrassment from Myrtle Mae. Ida's eyes flew open at once, and she saw her papa on bended knee in front of the woman he loved, his hand tightly clasping hers. Even from here, Ida could see the trembling.

He reached into his pocket and came out with a slender silver ring, which he held up for all to see. "I want my friends and neighbors to witness this," he said in a resounding voice. "I am a man in love."

Myrtle Mae's cheeks reddened and she let out another giggle. All across the churchyard, folks quieted their conversations and turned in rapt attention.

Ida couldn't help but laugh, too. Her papa looked his bride-to-be in the eye as he spoke tenderly. "Myrtle Mae, I love you. I'd shout it from the treetops, if I thought it wouldn't embarrass you."

"It wouldn't." She gave him a wink.

He nodded then finished up his little speech. "I'm askin' you to be my bride. Will you marry me, Myrtle Mae? Put me out of my misery once and for all. Say you'll be mine."

She nodded and whispered a tearful, "Yes." A roar of applause rose up from the crowd.

Myrtle Mae got her ring.

Papa got his bride-to-be.

And Ida...well, from where she sat, the only thing more appealing than the scene before her was the look in the eye of the man who reached over and took hold of her hand, giving it a squeeze.

With joy flooding her heart, she squeezed back.

Chapter Thirty

"**D**id you save room for cobbler, Mr. Bradley?"

Emma Gertsch's words certainly got Mick's attention. He opened his eyes and looked at the older woman in curiosity.

"Cobbler?"

"Yes indeed." She rose to her feet and brushed the dirt from her dress. "It's our annual cobbler bakeoff and we'll be needing judges."

Though he wanted to groan, his stomach already painfully full from the meal he'd just consumed, Mick thought better of it. "Am I to assume you've entered a cobbler in the bakeoff?"

"Well, now that you mention it…" She fanned herself. "But I would never stoop to persuading you to vote for mine. That would be wrong. Though I must say the dewberries from my property are the juiciest in the county and I do spend hours collecting them each spring."

"I see."

From behind him, Ida laughed. "You have nothing to fear, Mick. None of the entries are marked, so you won't have any idea whose is whose. I've entered a cobbler myself."

Mick looked over at Johnsey and patted his full stomach. With a laugh, Johnsey stood and helped Mick to his feet.

Fifteen minutes and a dozen bites later, Mick and Johnsey declared a tasty peach cobbler the winner. Truly, Mick didn't know when he'd ever tasted anything so fine. He prayed the flavorful concoction belonged to Ida. A blue ribbon would go a long way toward winning her heart. Unfortunately, Myrtle Mae bounded to the front of the crowd to claim her ribbon, a tenacious smile on her face.

"Looks like it's been your day," Reverend Langford said, handing her the ribbon. "Not quite sure how you're going to top this one!"

"Oh, we'll top it, all right." She turned her attention to the crowd. "We'll be having the weddin' soon, and I'll bake up the tastiest cake you ever did see. We'll celebrate together." She turned to face her husband-to-be as she asked, "How does an autumn ceremony sound to you?"

"If I can wait that long." He winked and reached for her hand.

"We look forward to that," Reverend Langford said.

As Mick moved back in Ida's direction, he thought about the upcoming wedding. He wondered what it would be like to settle here, marry Ida and raise a family.

The longer he thought about those things, the more plausible they became. Within minutes, he felt as though his heart might spring from his chest. Could he really do it? Live here in Texas? Maybe he'd been right when he compared Spring Creek to the Promised Land, especially in light of the new plan that now consumed his thoughts. Perhaps that's what the Lord had had in mind all along.

Ida worked alongside Dinah, packing her aunt's wagon. With so many things to return to the mercantile, she thought it best to offer a hand. Besides, a ride into town meant a few more minutes with Mick, something she dearly craved—even if he hadn't voted for her apple cobbler.

Still, in spite of her growing feelings, Ida knew better than to give her heart just yet. She sensed that the Lord had quite a bit of work to do in Mick's life, and she certainly didn't want to get in the way of that. Too much too fast could have devastating consequences. To put the cart ahead of the horse—especially in matters of the heart—was never a good idea.

A short time later they arrived at the mercantile, and Ida looked on with a smile as Johnsey helped Dinah down from the wagon. After all the sadness Dinah had endured, she deserved the kind of happiness a man like Johnsey could bring.

Ida turned and looked at the empty lot next door. Though she didn't want to see it used for a gambling hall, she had to admit that the charred ruins made her sad. And the look in Mick's eyes every time he gazed at the property nearly broke her heart. *Lord, lead the way. Show him what to do. Show us all what to do.*

"A penny for your thoughts."

Ida swung around, unable to hide her grin as she saw Mick standing close by. "Oh, I was just thinking about Dinah and Johnsey."

He glanced up to see them disappear into the store. "They make quite the couple, don't they?"

"Yes," Ida agreed, "though I never saw it coming, if you want to know the truth of it. They seem so different. And he's nothing like Larson, in any respect." In fact, Ida didn't know when she'd seen two more different men. Larson had been older than his years, an average-looking man with a heart as big as Texas. Johnsey's wide smile invited others in, and almost made them forget about his wholesome good looks and boyish face.

"I've always heard that opposites attract." Mick drew a bit closer, and Ida felt her breath catch in her throat.

"True," she whispered, "though I cannot help but think that any romantic union would be unduly strained if the parties were vastly different."

"Different, as in a big-city gambling-hall man and a small-town girl who is more at home on a church pew than a bar stool?" His eyes twinkled with mischief, but Ida struggled to find the humor in his words.

"I thought you'd laid the idea of a gambling hall to rest, Mick."

"I'm not saying otherwise. It's just interesting to think I've come all the way to Texas looking for one thing," he said with a pensive look, brushing a loose hair out of her face, "and ended up with another."

"Another?" *Is he referring to...me?*

He looked toward the empty lot. "My original plans lie in ruins."

Ida followed his gaze. No doubt, giving up on his dream had come at a cost, but he needed to let go of that altogether, or she could never consider marrying him.

Marrying him? Where had such a notion come from? Mick Bradley had never even asked to court her, let alone offer a marriage proposal. Surely the heat must be playing with her thoughts today. She took a step backward.

Mick gave her a curious look. "What did you think of that sermon this morning?"

"I enjoyed it immensely. Reverend Langford always manages to tie his messages in to the holidays, and I thought his liberty theme was quite brilliant. Of course, I always love to hear his testimony. He is quite a changed man. Gives me hope."

"For me?"

She smiled. "For people in general, I mean. Myself included."

"I guess it's going to take a while for the Almighty to convince me He's got a grandiose plan for my life. Seems like the only thing He's shown me so far is, well, ashes."

"There's a wonderful scripture about God's ability to bring beauty from ashes," Ida said. "And I've no doubt He will do that for you, if you ask Him to."

"He's already brought one good thing from the rubble," Mick said. "I never would have known you—really known you—if not for the attack I've come under."

"True."

After a pause, he added, "But don't you see? That's my dilemma. I'm having a hard time trusting in a God who allowed something like that to happen. He could have stopped it. For that matter, He could've stopped Brewster and his men from burning down my business. A lot of money went into that lumber, and the money I paid the workers, too. Just doesn't make sense to me. If the Lord wanted to stop me in my tracks he should have done it before I made the investment." Mick shrugged.

"There are so many things about God's timing—and His will—that elude me," Ida confessed. "He could have stopped Larson's death. And the death of my mother." She drew in a deep breath. "We cannot comprehend why things happen like they do, but we trust anyway."

Mick shrugged. "That might make sense to you, but from where I stand it seems mighty impractical to put my trust in a God who's liable to derail me. Brewster's men nearly took my life, Ida. That's enough to make me angry. And even angrier that they still haven't been brought to justice."

"Our system of justice is vastly different from the Lord's," she countered. "'Vengeance is mine, saith the Lord. I will repay.'"

"It might be His," Mick agreed, "but that doesn't stop me from wanting to take matters into my own hands sometimes."

"You must trust me when I say that I understand all too well," she said. "I've always been one to rush out ahead of God. To take things into my own hands when they belong in His. But if I've learned one thing over the past couple of months it is that we're sometimes called to give God the reins. Even when it doesn't make sense."

Mick shook his head. "Sounds easy enough, but hearing it and doing it are two different things."

"Of course." Ida gave him a concerned look. "I do hope you will allow the Lord to continue to work in your heart, Mick. You've made such headway, and I know what a strong man you are. You will be stronger still if you make your peace with God."

"I suppose." He pulled her close. "But why do we need to talk about all of that right now? Isn't it enough that we're together?" He leaned in and whispered gently in her ear, "You've stolen my heart, Ida. Do you understand what I'm saying? I'm undone."

Ida felt a lump rise in her throat and she dreaded speaking her next words. "My feelings for you are very strong, as well. But it's not enough, Mick, though I'm sure this won't make much sense to you. I cannot give my heart to a man who has not given *his* heart to the Lord."

"I'm trying to figure all that out, but it's going to take some time. I'm on the right track, don't you think?" He gave her a pleading look. "I'm plenty willing to admit I've got a ways to go before I get things all figured out. But I don't see why that has to keep us from being together."

"It's a matter of wholly submitting your will. Asking Him to be Lord of your life."

"I'm just not sure what that entails."

She smiled. "It means He takes control. And it means you have to be willing to trade in your dreams for His, if that makes sense. Once that takes place, I'm more than happy to—" she felt her cheeks flush "—consider courting you. If that's what you're asking."

"Yes, that's what I'm asking." Mick rested against his crutches. "But I wonder if you're hesitant for another reason."

"What do you mean?"

"Maybe you don't want a man who's crippled. Is that the real issue here?"

Her heart broke at his painful words. Clearly, he did not understand. "You're not crippled in the usual way," Ida said. "It's not your bones that haven't mended—it's your heart. And until it does, until you've made your peace with God, I cannot…"

"Cannot what?"

"Cannot allow myself to consider the possibility. It's not enough that you care for me."

"You care for me, too."

"I do care for you." She swallowed the growing lump in her throat. "But God's plan is bigger than what I'm feeling. Or what you're feeling, for that matter."

"How do you know that?"

"Because I know that it will bring a peace that passes all understanding, and I don't have that. Not yet." She gave him an imploring look. "I want to have it, and I'm praying for God's perfect will in this situation."

A defiant look came into Mick's eyes and he pulled back, his jaw tightening. "Well, when you figure that out, come and tell me, because I can honestly say I don't have a clue what all the fuss is about. I'm crazy about you, and I know you love me, too." He paused and seemed to be collecting his thoughts. "You're a stubborn girl."

"What?"

"You've got a backbone of steel, like those railroad tracks over there. No bending, no concessions. And yet you would have me concede all my plans, my dreams." He shook his head. "Where is the fairness in that?"

Tears sprang to Ida's eyes as she spoke. "This isn't about what's fair, Mick. It's about what's right."

"I only know one thing that's right." He turned back toward the mercantile, stumbling on his crutches as he mumbled, "And you're about to let it slip right through your fingers."

Chapter Thirty-One

The following afternoon Mick called for Ida to meet him upstairs in the kitchen. He needed her assistance with a project, one he could not unveil just yet. He knew his unusual request would upset her, but figured it would be worth the risk, especially if everything went as planned. She entered the room cautiously.

"Did you want me, Mick?" She wiped her hands on her apron.

More than you know.

"The shop is full of customers and Dinah needs my help," she said.

Indeed, something about Dinah seemed amiss today. He'd noticed it early on. Her eyes had a misty glow about them, a sure sign that she'd been crying. And a somber expression replaced her usually bright countenance. Something felt wrong.

"Nellie's gone for the day," Ida continued. "She took the morning train to Houston to fetch her mother."

"I see." After a brief pause, he continued. "Well, I am sorry to interrupt, but this will only take a moment.

I wonder if you would be so kind as to call for your father. I have a business matter to discuss with him."

"Papa?"

"Yes."

"Is this about lumber?" The expression on her face hardened as she spoke the words.

"Perhaps." Mick offered up a smile as he thought about his new plans. A visit from Mr. Mueller would prove to be essential, as would some private time with Johnsey and Dinah. And the local banker. Yes, with the help of others, his dream of a new building would become a reality.

Ida crossed her arms. "I could call for Papa if you like, but it hurts my heart to do so."

"I beg your pardon?"

"I suspect that you are reconsidering the gambling hall. Hoping to acquire funds to rebuild?"

"Well, to be honest…" How much should he tell her?

"Mick, I just think it's a bad idea, especially now." Her eyes misted over and he wondered at her sudden outburst of emotion.

How could he begin to explain his motives if she resorted to tears? Standing up to a tearful woman had never been his forte.

Ida's features hardened before he could say a word. "Mick Bradley, I'm ashamed of you."

"Excuse me?" Would she not even let him get a word in edgewise?

Her cheeks now flamed. "The Lord has spared your life. Given you a second chance. And you're going to take advantage of that by returning to the very thing that drove you from Him in the first place? Don't you see? Building that place will be your ruin."

He was more frustrated than ever. Obviously, she didn't care to listen to his explanation, though he had carefully planned just how he would break the news. "Apparently, speaking with you about this is useless, at least right now. Maybe we can talk again later."

"I'm begging you to reconsider. This is not the direction you should be headed. Remember what you said about the Promised Land?"

He nodded. "Of course."

"Only good things await people in the promised land," she emphasized.

"But how do you know what I'm contemplating?" he asked. "What makes you think it's bad?" Honestly, if she would just slow down, he would convince her that his motives and his actions were anything but.

"I can't see into your heart."

"Well, that's a shame." He shook his head. "I'm convinced you would change your mind if you could." Indeed, she would put an end to this arguing right away.

Mick tried to stand, but lost his balance as the bad leg gave way beneath him. She rushed to his side, and caught him as he started to go down. They stood in a tight embrace, her flushed cheeks now at his shoulder level.

He glanced down into her tear-filled eyes and for a brief moment wanted to draw her close, wanted to trace a tear down her cheek with his fingertip, wanted to run his hands through that beautiful blond hair. If he told her everything would work out fine in the end, would she believe it? He had the urge to kiss her on the spot—surely that would leave a much better memory than bickering.

He managed a few words, whispering into her ear. "It seems you're always saving me from falling."

"I'd like to save you again," she whispered back. "But only the Lord can do that. And I pray you will open your heart to Him and allow it. You must see that building the gambling hall is in direct opposition to His will. Please don't do this, Mick."

"Ida, calm yourself." He eased back down onto the chair once again, dejected. "Just call for your papa and I will fill you in on the details later. In the meantime, I'm just going to have to ask you to trust me. Can you do that? I know I haven't given you much reason to do so in the past, but you will find that I am trustworthy, I assure you."

She stood in strained silence, her cheeks flushed. Ida's emotional response had shaken him to his core. Why would she respond in such a way? Had she really noticed no change in his life—his attitude—at all?

She went back downstairs to the store, and within an hour, Mr. Mueller arrived. Mick gave the best presentation he could manage, speaking animatedly about the revenue his new building would bring to the community. If Mr. Mueller would just see fit to front him the lumber, that was.

"Young feller, I don't see as you're in any shape to be building anything. Looks to me like you should be recuperating, not working."

"I can do both," Mick argued. "And I plan to stay put in Spring Creek. If you'll do me the favor of trusting me with the lumber up front, that is. If you don't..." Mick couldn't finish the statement. He had no idea what he'd do if this plan fell through.

Mr. Mueller's face softened and the crinkles around

his eyes deepened as a smile lit his face. "You're doing this for my girl, aren't you?"

"I am, sir." Mick did his best not to let the grin spread too far. He wanted Ida's father to take his request seriously, after all.

"I take that to mean you love her." Dirk Mueller's mustache twitched.

"I do, sir."

"Well, in that case, how could I possibly say no?" The older man gave Mick a bear hug, and patted him on the back. "If you love her half as much as I think you do, she's going to be one happy woman. Now let's get busy and build that building!"

Ida made the journey toward home as the sun began to set. She drew in one deep breath after another, trying to remain calm and levelheaded. Only one problem— she didn't want to remain calm. She wanted to scream. To kick something. To shout to the skies, "Once a wolf, always a wolf!"

Mick Bradley. What had she ever seen in the man? And whatever made her think he'd change, just to make her happy? Had he been toying with her emotions all along? Did he own a host of gambling halls from North to South? Was there an Ida in every town between here and Chicago?

Just the thought of it sent a shiver down her spine. "I should have heeded my own warnings," she muttered under her breath as she drew near the tracks. Yes, dressed in sheep's clothing he'd somehow wormed his way into her heart. And she'd let him. Simple as that. She had no one but herself to blame. Somehow, knowing that made her even more angry.

"Ida!"

Ida turned and saw Sophie coming toward her.

"I missed you at the mercantile. Dinah told me you'd just left," Sophie said, trying to catch her breath. "Is Dinah all right? She looked quite sad."

"Yes, something is not right with Dinah today. She wouldn't talk about it, however."

"I see."

They continued on in silence for a moment.

"Did you enjoy the picnic yesterday?" Sophie asked.

"I did. I'm sorry we didn't get a chance to speak," Ida said. "I was…"

Sophie waited for her to continue. When Ida didn't, Sophie smiled.

"Ida, I want to talk to you about Mick."

Ida was surprised by the rush of jealousy that came over her. The words flew out of her mouth before she could stop them. "Sophie, I know that you think Mick is very handsome. You've made no secret of that. But you must know that he is not the man we would wish him to be. He is planning—"

Sophie put her hand on her friend's arm. "I think you've misinterpreted my feelings. Yes, he is a handsome man, but I'm not interested in him. I never have been. Ida, I've known you a very long time. Almost our entire lives. And I feel I must tell you that I have never seen you look at a man the way you look at Mick Bradley. All those comments I made about him were just my way of trying to get you to see him, Ida. To truly see him. To look beyond his gambling hall and see the way he looks at you. He's never had eyes for anyone in this town but you, Ida. Don't doubt that for a minute."

Ida was so stunned by her friend's words that she couldn't come up with a reply.

"Please, Ida, don't let this chance pass you by. Mick is a good man. Even if he is a bit misguided at times." Sophie pulled Ida into a hug. "Life is full of wonderful opportunities but you have to recognize them in order to take advantage. Do not miss this one because you've got blinders on."

Ida wiped a tear from her cheek as Sophie released her. Sophie gave her hand a final squeeze and headed toward her home. Ida stood frozen in place, speechless. What a fool she'd been. Her best friend had probably known how she felt about Mick long before she herself did. And to think that Sophie would try to win Mick for herself was absurd. Had Ida no faith in their friendship? She felt she scarcely knew herself anymore.

She began to walk. As she came upon the railroad tracks, she had a sudden realization and a wave of guilt washed over her. July 5. Larson had died two years ago today in this very spot. No wonder Dinah had looked so somber today. That one night had changed everything for Dinah—for all of them. These tracks served as an ever-present reminder. And yet, Dinah was falling in love. She was allowing herself to fall for Johnsey Fischer—she was moving forward and taking a chance, trusting in her feelings.

Can I not do the same? Is God showing me a path, showing me His will—and I'm ignoring the signs?

Ida looked down at the tracks in front of her. With a deep breath, she lifted her foot and took a step across.

As soon as Dirk Mueller left the mercantile, Mick started putting together a plan for how—and when—

the new building would come together. And just how he would let Ida know. Sooner was probably better than later, given her earlier response.

He summoned Dinah to his room. Mick smiled at the look of hopeful expectation in her eyes when he gave her the particulars of his new plan, and her excitement seemed to grow when he asked if she would send word for the reverend to come tomorrow. She scurried off with a smile on her face—the first he'd seen all day.

Ida's words came rushing back to him after Dinah left. *"It's not your bones that haven't mended—it's your heart. And until it does, until you've made your peace with God..."*

The words had felt like an accusation at the time, but now they blanketed him, bringing hope. In spite of his failings, Mick wanted to believe the Lord could change things, turn things around. Could God do that... for him? For his relationship with Ida?

Maybe his train needed to be on a different track, headed off in a completely different direction.

The words to the hymn Mick had sung last Sunday came back, stirring his heart to action.

Tell me the story, as to a little child,
For I am weak and weary, and helpless and de-filed.

Mick looked down at his leg, and then shifted his gaze to the crutches leaning up against the chair. He believed now that his leg would mend in time. Someday he would look back on all this as nothing more than a distant memory.

Oh, but when he thought of Ida—when he remembered the way she'd felt in his arms, heard again the sound of her voice as she chided him, thought about the sparkle in her blue eyes, the determination in her voice—he could hardly contain himself. This was a girl sent straight from heaven. What was the word Johnsey had used? Manna. Yes, manna from heaven. And he would win her over with this new plan, for he'd placed her in the very center of it.

He'd made other plans in the past, and things had ended badly. When he'd been in charge, the situation had spiraled out of control.

What could he do to prevent that from happening this time around? Only one thing came to mind—the one thing he'd avoided most of his adult life. With a heavy but hopeful heart, Mick Bradley bowed his head and began to pray.

Chapter Thirty-Two

Ida arrived at the mercantile at exactly two o'clock for once. She found the place busier than usual. There seemed to be an excitement in the air—something she couldn't put her finger on, exactly. For one thing, Dinah looked surprisingly happy today. More so than usual, in light of her sober countenance yesterday.

"What's happening here?" Ida asked as she reached for her apron. "Papa's been whistling all afternoon, and you've got a smile that would light up the town."

"Do I?"

"You do. So fess up. What's going on?"

Dinah shrugged. "I don't know what you mean."

Ida fussed with her apron strings. "I figured you'd be overwhelmed, what with Nellie and Johnsey both being gone."

Ida glanced out the window at the throng of people passing by. Sure, the train from up North had brought in newcomers. Likely they'd venture into the store before heading on to their final destinations. "What time do you expect Nellie and her mama?"

"Any time now. I've got their room ready upstairs.

And Johnsey will be in on the afternoon train with his father. I'm looking forward to meeting him in person— I've heard so much about him."

Ida nodded, her gaze shifting toward the stairs. She longed to ask about Mick, but didn't want to appear anxious. What in the world had Mick said to her father to put such a spring in his step and song in his heart?

"Yes, he's still here."

"What?" Ida turned to face her aunt.

"I'm guessing you were thinking of Mick," Dinah whispered, "and he's still here for another few days."

"And then?"

"I'm not sure of his plans, only that he said he will stay through the end of the week. And in the meantime, he's holding court with someone up there."

Ida felt her stomach knot up. "Papa?"

"Your father is expected to return any moment," Dinah explained, "but right now Mick is busy talking to—"

"Excuse me, miss, I wonder if you could point me toward the soda crackers." An unfamiliar railroad worker interrupted their conversation. Ida led him to the aisle with the soda crackers, wondering about Mick's visitor.

Papa soon arrived and headed up the stairs. If Ida hadn't been so busy, she would have been tempted to march up there and find out what was going on.

Nellie and her mother arrived at two-thirty, and were welcomed at once. Dinah ushered them up the stairs, taking the frail woman's bags and offering encouraging smiles. Nellie looked hopeful and nervous. Ida imagined she was longing for her mother to be well and whole, for this new venture to work.

After getting them settled in, Dinah returned with a shimmer in her eyes. Very rarely did Ida see her aunt cry.

"Is everything all right?" she whispered.

Her aunt turned back with a shrug. "I don't know how long Nellie will have her mother with her on this earth, is all. And it put me in mind of my mama. And yours." She brushed away a tear and went back to work. Ida did her best to pay attention to the customers, but Dinah's words had touched a deep place in her heart, one she hadn't visited for some time.

She did long for her mother, more than she'd admitted. Somehow it helped to know that Dinah—a spiritual giant in Ida's eyes—struggled with the same feelings. Together, they would help Nellie through this. Whatever time the dear girl had with her mother would be spent happily.

At quarter till three, a voice at the front door rang out in exaggerated volume, causing everyone in the place to look up in surprise.

"Dinah Mueller."

Ida looked across the room and noticed Johnsey standing there alongside an older man. Carter, who sat on the floor playing with his marbles, scrambled to his feet and ran to Johnsey, leaping into his arms with joy written all over his face.

"Well, hello there, son." Johnsey gave him a warm hug then placed the youngster back on the ground. "I'd spend more time saying hello, but I've got some business to take care of with your mother." Johnsey eased his way through the heavy crowd and drew near the register.

"You cut in line, sir," Dinah said with an embarrassed smile.

"Mmm-hmm."

"Can I help you?"

"You can. Come on around here to this side of the register."

She looked at the crowd of people and shook her head. "I have customers to wait on."

The folks in line all eased their way back, likely curious to see what Johnsey would do next. He strode behind the register and met her face-to-face.

She looked up at him with whimsy in her eyes. "You're up to something."

"I am." He put his hands around her slender waist and lifted her to sit on the heavy glass showcase.

Dinah gasped and her cheeks pinked. "Put me down from here," she said in a whisper. "What are you doing?"

"Exactly what the Lord placed on my heart to do." Reaching into his pocket, he took out a ring.

Several in the room began to chuckle and the color in Dinah's cheeks deepened.

Johnsey cleared his throat to quiet the crowd. "I'm glad you could all join us today," he announced. "Want to make this news public. All good news should be." He turned to face Dinah, his voice softening. "You have the best heart of any woman I've ever known, and I'm asking you—no, I'm begging you—to share it with me. I promise to take care of it, to the best of my ability. I will love you till the day I die, Dinah."

Ida swallowed hard at those words, remembering Larson. Just as quickly, she reminded herself that this was a new day, a new opportunity for happiness for Dinah.

"I will care for you and for Carter," Johnsey added, "if you'll have me. Will you, Dinah? Will you marry me?"

Dinah threw her arms around his neck and planted a kiss on each of his cheeks, then uttered a resounding, "Yes!"

Johnsey slipped the ring on her finger and kissed her squarely on the lips. The crowd let forth a roar, along with a round of applause.

Carter raced to his mother's side, jumping up and down. The elderly man who'd entered with Johnsey stood with a smile on his face, watching the scene. Johnsey quickly made the introductions, and everyone was pleased to meet his father at last. Ida found him to be an amiable man, the twinkle in his eye resembling his son's and his smile nearly as broad as his thick mustache.

Just as the crowd thinned, Ida noticed a group coming down the stairs. Her heart seemed to lodge in her throat. Papa led the way, assisting Mick. Intrigue set in as Reverend Langford's smiling face appeared after Mick's. As they moved her way, she heard one thing that stopped her in her tracks.

"Thank you so much for your help, Mr. Mueller." Mick released his hold on one of the crutches and slipped his hand into Papa's for a firm shake.

"Well, son." Mr. Mueller gave him a nod. "How could I turn you down, especially now that the reverend's on board? If he says this is a good idea, it's a good idea. Plain and simple."

Ida's thoughts whirled 'round in her head. Off to her right, her aunt Dinah stood arm in arm with her new fiancé. To her left, the good reverend offered a hand of congratulations to Mick Bradley for building…a gambling hall?

Could the day possibly get any more peculiar?

Chapter Thirty-Three

Mick did his best to hide a smile as Mr. Mueller crossed the room ahead of him. He sensed Ida's gaze, but didn't look her in the eye, afraid he would give away too much. Instead, he turned his attention to Dinah and Johnsey, asking for a private conversation outside. With Reverend Langford, of course.

After curious glances from Ida, the four headed out to the boardwalk, where Mick gave Johnsey a slap on the back, nearly losing a crutch in the process. He congratulated the happy couple on their engagement.

Then he got down to business. If he could talk the soon-to-be newlyweds into working with him, the final piece to the puzzle would be firmly locked into place.

With anticipation building, Mick turned to Dinah and the questions began.

"Whatever are they doing out there?" Ida paced the floor in front of the register.

Nellie, who had come bounding down the stairs at the earlier uproar, shrugged. "I haven't got a clue, but if Reverend Langford is involved, it can't be bad."

"I don't know." Ida allowed herself a brief glimpse outside. Mick and Johnsey exchanged a firm handshake, and the reverend looked on with a smile. What shenanigans did they have up their sleeves?

Her question was answered in short order, at least in part. They all entered the store and Dinah cleared her throat, garnering the attention of everyone present.

"We're going to close up shop for a few minutes."

"Excuse me?" Ida gave her a curious look. "In the middle of the day?"

Johnsey nodded. "It's all right. We will return soon. Ida, will you come with us?"

Ida looked back and forth between Mick—whose eyes twinkled merrily—and Dinah, who maintained a straight face. None of this made any sense at all.

Tagging along behind them, Ida made her way out to the boardwalk, half the town of Spring Creek now following. Her heart thumped in anticipation as Mick made his way toward the empty lot.

Sure enough, they stopped directly in front of his property, and he turned to her with a smile on his face. Her heart melted at once, even before he spoke a word.

Mick signaled for her to join him at the front of the crowd. He gently took her hand and gave her a wink. "You're probably wondering what all of this is about."

"I am."

"Well, I don't blame you. But let me put any fears to rest. I am not now—nor ever, for that matter—building a gambling hall."

A wave of relief flooded Ida's soul. She nodded, doing her best not to cry at the news.

"I wanted to tell you yesterday, but didn't have the

chance. I've had an idea brewing for a few days now, one I think—I hope—you will approve of."

"What sort of idea?"

"Let me ask you a question first. What do you think of when you hear the words *German sausage sauerkraut balls?*"

"My kitchen? The workers I feed every day?" Ida said.

He nodded. "And when you hear the words *Wiener schnitzel?*"

Ida couldn't help but smile as she responded. "Something I'm known for around these parts?"

"Yes, you are known for your cooking," he said. "And I knew from the minute I tasted your food that you needed your own place to cook for others."

She stared at the property, absorbing his meaning. "Are you saying…?"

"I'm saying that you're looking at the property for Ida's, the newest restaurant in town, one that's going to rival The Harvey House and any other place that dares to call itself an eating establishment. One that—with all of us pitching in—will turn a nice profit."

A boyish grin spread across his face. "This will be a place the locals and railroad men alike can call their own. What do you think about that, Miss Mueller?"

Ida felt her cheeks warm as she turned to face him with a smile. "Are you serious, Mick? Because if you're teasing me…"

"I can assure you, he is quite serious," Reverend Langford interrupted. "This is a man who refuses to put his boots in the oven."

"I beg your pardon?"

"He's trying to say that I was never meant to be a gambling-hall owner," Mick said. "And that I'm not the man I used to be." As if to prove the point, Mick pointed to his feet. Ida stared at the worn cowboy boots.

"Where in the world did you get those?" she whispered.

"Reverend Langford brought them over. Told me to try 'em on for size. To plant my feet in Texas soil and stay put. So I think I'll do just that."

"A new man needs a new pair of boots," the reverend added, giving Mick a slap on the back.

Mick turned to face Ida and her heart quickened. "There's not a thing about me that's the same," he explained. "I can tell you more about that later, but you've got to trust me when I say that I've crossed over into the Promised Land, and I want you right there with me, by my side." After staring into her eyes for a few seconds, he added, "What do you say?"

"I'm overcome." She shifted her gaze, afraid the tears would come. "The restaurant is a marvelous idea, and I'm so grateful, but…"

"But?"

"But what about the mercantile? Who's going to help Dinah?"

"As quick as she'll marry me, I'll be there," Johnsey said.

"I'll do whatever you need," Sophie called from the back of the crowd. The sight of her best friend overwhelmed Ida as she thought of their recent conversation.

"I'll go on helping, too," Nellie added. "At the mercantile or the restaurant."

"Don't fret, Ida," Dinah encouraged with a smile. "Chase after your dream."

"My dream?" Ida looked at the burned-out lot for a few seconds. She'd always been most comfortable in the kitchen, but how had Mick known? He'd rarely seen her in that role, after all. Did he know her heart even better than she did?

She turned back to him. "I can't do something of this magnitude on my own," she whispered.

He pulled her close. "Exactly. Which is why I'm going to manage the restaurant. I'm going to walk right next to you every step of the way."

"You are?"

"Sure. I've had a few years of experience. In a different field, of course, but still."

The gathered crowd laughed. She looked up into his eyes—warm, loving eyes. Eyes that convinced her this was a man to be trusted. A man who refused to put his boots—new or otherwise—in the oven. Whatever that meant.

Another familiar voice rang out from the back of the crowd. "What's all this I hear about a new restaurant?"

Myrtle Mae.

The older woman pushed her way to the front of the group, and Ida smiled as she noticed her father also standing nearby.

"There you are, girl. Come here and give me a hug," Myrtle Mae said.

After a slight chuckle, Mick released his hold on Ida and she eased her way in Myrtle Mae's direction.

"Now, here's what we're going to do." Myrtle Mae looked at the lot with a wrinkled brow. "Do you think you can handle the breakfast crowd by yourself?"

"With a little help from Nellie, maybe."

"Good girl." Myrtle Mae's voice was all business. "Then I'll take care of the lumber-mill workers until noon. After that I'll come to town to help you. Together we'll whip out some of the best meals folks around these-here parts have ever tasted."

"Are you sure?" Ida could scarcely believe it. To have Myrtle Mae working for her would be an answer to prayer. "But what about your job at The Harvey House? And what about you, Papa? Won't you need her at home?"

"I will come to town for my evening meals," he said. "That way I'll get the best of both worlds."

"And don't let me hear you mentioning The Harvey House again," Myrtle Mae said with a scolding look on her face. "They're our competition now." Ida grinned at Myrtle Mae and thanked her with all her heart.

Ida made her way back to Mick and he wrapped his arms around her, pressing gentle kisses into her hair. She felt him take a deep breath.

"Will you be mine, Ida? Will you take me, broken as I am?"

Ida's heart swelled with joy and she reached up, touching his cheek, whispering, "Broken no more."

Epilogue

Mick paced the aisle of the church, ready to get the day's events under way. He looked over the congregation, smiling at those who'd come out to offer their support—again. The past couple of months, the townspeople had rushed to help build the new restaurant, offering support of every kind.

He couldn't help but smile as he thought about how happy his bride-to-be looked each morning as she prepared breakfast. How she smiled as folks complimented her favorite dishes. What a success the place had become, and how they'd celebrated together when Mick was able to send his investors their payment in full.

Yes, the good people of Spring Creek were certainly more than friends. They were his staunchest supporters, his prayer partners and his family.

Most of them, anyway. To date, the sheriff hadn't been able to get the necessary witnesses to come forward regarding Mick's attack, but Mick had reconciled himself to that fact. As Ida so often said, "Justice is in the hands of the Lord." He'd wanted to take it into his

own hands a time or two, but the Almighty had somehow given him peace in the middle of that storm.

"What do you suppose is taking so long?" he asked
the reverend.

His good friend let out a laugh, one that echoed
across the crowded room. "Taking so long?" He slapped
Mick on the back. "I've performed over thirty weddings
and they always run late, even with only one bride involved. But three?" He pulled out his pocket watch and
took a look. "I'd say we're doing well if we get this shin-
dig started by one o'clock."

Mick let out a groan. This was supposed to be a
noon affair, with a huge meal following. If they didn't
get things started—and soon—the flowers would be
wilted and the food ruined.

He turned to the two other grooms. From what Mick
could tell, Dirk appeared the most anxious. He occasionally pulled out his watch for a cursory glance, but
most of his time was spent staring at the double doors
in anticipation.

Johnsey remained calm, greeting guests and making
small talk. As the minutes ticked by, he eventually made
his way up the aisle to the front of the church, where
he took a seat next to his father and Emma Gertsch.
Interesting, how the two had been spending so much
time together.

No, Mick wouldn't think about anyone else's love
life today but his own.

And Johnsey's.

And Dirk's.

Now, if they could just locate their brides, they'd
have a wedding—one the folks in Spring Creek, Texas,
wouldn't soon forget.

* * *

"Are you almost ready?"

Ida looked up as she heard Sophie's voice. "Nearly. I'm just trying to get these wayward hairs tucked away." She fidgeted with her up-do, adjusted her veil and pinched her cheeks to give them a rosy appearance. Turning back to her friend, she asked, "How do I look? And be perfectly honest."

"Honestly, Ida. You're the prettiest bride I've ever seen."

Ida took her by the hand. "Bless you for that."

From the back of the room, Myrtle Mae cleared her throat. Loudly. Turning to her, Sophie chuckled then added, "You are an exquisite bride, as well, Myrtle Mae." She then turned her attentions to Dinah, who stood in front of the mirror, fussing with her delicate pearl necklace. With a smile, Sophie said, "Dinah, you are absolutely beautiful in that dress."

Dinah made a graceful turn, showing off the gown that Emma Gertsch had sewn by hand. "I can't believe I actually own a dress I didn't make myself."

"Yes, but look at the great sacrifice on your part. You had to promise Emma a lifetime supply of dime novels in exchange for her work."

Everyone erupted in laughter, and for a moment, all nerves were set aside.

"We are late, ladies. Likely our menfolk are getting anxious," Ida said.

"I don't know about yours," Myrtle Mae said as she moved toward the door of the tiny classroom, "but my man is probably having a fit by now."

"Well, of course he is." Ida drew near and gave her

mother-to-be a kiss on the cheek. "This is going to be the happiest day of his life."

"Aw, don't make me cry, Ida." Myrtle Mae glanced in the mirror one last time at her reflection. "I've already done the best I could with what God gave me. I don't want red-rimmed eyes to spoil the effect."

"Nothing could spoil the effect," Dinah added. "You look radiant."

Nellie, who stood nearby holding the bridal bouquets, let out a little sniffle. "This is such a happy day!"

All the ladies gathered together in a hug, smiles on every face. Ida looked at her aunt and Myrtle Mae with a full heart. Together they made their way to the back doors of the church. From inside, Ida heard the familiar strains of the wedding march. Reverend Langford's wife wasn't half-bad on the piano, though Myrtle Mae might disagree. And the dear woman had been practicing for months in preparation for this special day.

"Are you ready?" Dinah whispered, giving Ida's hand a gentle squeeze.

Ida gave a nod and the doors swung wide. Nellie and Sophie—the loveliest of bridesmaids—made their entrance first, fall flowers in hand. Myrtle Mae followed, her wide girth even wider with her full skirt swishing this way and that. Then it was Dinah's turn. She turned to give Ida one last loving glance before heading off to meet her man.

Ida watched it all with hands trembling. Up at the front of the church, she caught her first glimpse of Mick. He stood tall and straight in his suit, crutches no longer necessary. On his feet, as always now, the worn cowboy boots. On his face, an anxious smile.

As their eyes met from across the crowded room,

Ida's heart raced in anticipation. She'd no sooner taken her first step toward him than Dinah's words, spoken months earlier, came rushing back at her. *'I predict you will one day look a man directly in the eye—and slapping him will be the furthest thing from your mind."*

A smile played at the edges of Ida's lips. Yes, she had to conclude. Looking at her Mick from where she now stood, watching the twinkle in those smoky gray eyes, slapping him was indeed the very last thing on her mind.

* * * * *

Ida's German Sausage Sauerkraut Balls

(Makes 24—30 balls)

1/2 pound bulk sausage
1/4 cup chopped onion
16 ounce can sauerkraut
2 tablespoons dry bread crumbs (fine)
4 ounces softened cream cheese
2 tablespoons snipped parsley
1 tablespoon sweet hot mustard
dash garlic salt
dash pepper
1/3 to 1/2 cup all-purpose flour
2 eggs
2 tablespoons water
1/3 to 1/2 cup fine dry bread crumbs
cooking oil for deep fat frying

Cook sausage and onion in a large skillet until the sausage is cooked thoroughly (meat broken into small pieces). Drain sauerkraut, then combine it in a mixing bowl with the sausage mixture, as well as the bread crumbs, cream cheese, parsley, mustard, garlic salt and pepper. Cover and allow this mixture to chill overnight. Shape into balls (approximately 2 tablespoons each). Beat eggs and water together. Roll balls in flour, then egg mixture, then bread crumbs. Fry a few balls at a time in hot oil (365 degrees) about two minutes or until golden brown. Remove and drain on paper towels. Place on baking sheet and put in a 275-degree oven to keep warm.

SPECIAL EXCERPT FROM

Love Inspired.
SUSPENSE

*When a guide-dog trainer becomes a target of a
dangerous crime ring, a K-9 cop and his loyal
partner will work together to keep her safe.*

Read on for a sneak preview of
Blind Trust *by Laura Scott,*
the next exciting installment in the
True Blue K-9 Unit miniseries, available
June 2019 from Love Inspired Suspense.

Eva Kendall slowed her pace as she approached the training facility where she worked training guide dogs.

Using her key, she entered the training center, thinking about the male chocolate Lab named Cocoa that she would work with this morning. Cocoa was a ten-week-old puppy born to Stella, a gift from the Czech Republic to the NYC K-9 Command Unit located in Queens. Most of Stella's pups were being trained as police dogs, but not Cocoa. In less than a month after basic puppy training, Cocoa would be able to go home with Eva to be fostered during his initial first-year training to become a full-fledged guide dog. Once that year passed, guide dogs like Cocoa would return to the center to train with their new owners.

A few steps into the building, Eva frowned at the loud thumps interspersed between a cacophony of barking. The raucous noise from the various canines contained a level of panic and fear rather than excitement.

Concerned, she moved quickly through the dimly lit training center to the back hallway, where the kennels were located. Normally she was the first one in every morning, but maybe one of the other trainers had gotten an early start.

Rounding the corner, she paused in the doorway when she saw a tall, heavyset stranger scooping Cocoa out of his kennel. Panic squeezed her chest. "Hey! What are you doing?"

The ferocious barking increased in volume, echoing off the walls and ceiling. The stranger must have heard her. He turned to look at her, then roughly tucked Cocoa under his arm like a football.

"No! Stop!" Panicked, Eva charged toward the man, desperately wishing she had a weapon of some sort.

"Get out of my way," he said in a guttural voice.

"No. Put that puppy down right now!" Eva stopped and stood her ground.

"Last chance," he taunted, coming closer.

Don't miss
Blind Trust *by Laura Scott,*
available June 2019 wherever
Love Inspired® *Suspense books and ebooks are sold.*

www.LoveInspired.com

WE HOPE YOU
ENJOYED THIS
LOVE INSPIRED® SUSPENSE BOOK.

Discover more **heart-pounding** romances of **danger** and **faith** from the Love Inspired Suspense series.

Be sure to look for all six Love Inspired Suspense books every month.

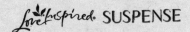

Looking for inspiration in tales
of hope, faith and heartfelt romance?

Check out **Love Inspired**® and
Love Inspired® **Suspense** books!

New books available every month!

CONNECT WITH US AT:

Facebook.com/groups/HarlequinConnection

Facebook.com/HarlequinBooks

Twitter.com/HarlequinBooks

Instagram.com/HarlequinBooks

Pinterest.com/HarlequinBooks

ReaderService.com

SPECIAL EXCERPT FROM

Love Inspired®

When a young Amish man needs help finding a wife, his beautiful matchmaker agrees to give him dating lessons…

Read on for a sneak preview of
A Perfect Amish Match *by Vannetta Chapman, available May 2019 from Love Inspired!*

"Dating is so complicated."

"People are complicated, Noah. Every single person you meet is dealing with something."

He asked, "How did you get so wise?"

"Never said I was."

"I'm being serious. How did you learn to navigate so seamlessly through these kinds of interactions, and why aren't you married?"

Olivia Mae thought her eyes were going to pop out of her head. "Did you really just ask me that?"

"I did."

"A little intrusive."

"Meaning you don't want to answer?"

"Meaning it's none of your business."

"Fair enough, though it's like asking a horse salesman why he doesn't own a horse."

"My family situation is…unique."

"You mean with your grandparents?"

She nodded instead of answering.

"I've got it." Noah resettled his hat, looking quite pleased with himself.

"Got what?"

"The solution to my dating disasters."

He leaned forward, close enough that she could smell the shampoo he'd used that morning.

"You need to give me dating lessons."

"What do you mean?"

"You and me. We'll go on a few dates…say, three. You can learn how to do anything if you do it three times."

"That's a ridiculous suggestion."

"Why? I learn better from doing."

"Do you?"

"I've already learned not to take a girl to a gas station, but who knows how many more dating traps are waiting for me."

"So this would be…a learning experience."

"It's a perfect solution." He tugged on her *kapp* string, something no one had done to her since she'd been a young teen.

"I can tell by the shock on your face that I've made you uncomfortable. It's a *gut* idea, though. We'd keep it businesslike—nothing personal."

Olivia Mae had no idea why the thought of sitting through three dates with Noah Graber made her stomach twirl like she'd been on a merry-go-round. Maybe she was catching a stomach bug.

"Wait a minute. Are you trying to get out of your third date? Because you promised your *mamm* that you would give this thing three solid attempts."

"And I'll keep my word on that," Noah assured her. "After you've tutored me, you can throw another poor unsuspecting girl my way."

Olivia Mae stood, brushed off the back of her dress and pointed a finger at Noah, who still sat in the grass as if he didn't have a care in the world.

"All right. I'll do it."

Don't miss
A Perfect Amish Match *by Vannetta Chapman,*
available May 2019 wherever
Love Inspired® books and ebooks are sold.

www.LoveInspired.com

LIEXP0419

Inspirational Romance to Warm Your Heart and Soul

Join our social communities to connect with other readers who share your love!

Sign up for the Love Inspired newsletter at **www.LoveInspired.com** to be the first to find out about upcoming titles, special promotions and exclusive content.

CONNECT WITH US AT:

Facebook.com/groups/HarlequinConnection

 Facebook.com/LoveInspiredBooks

 Twitter.com/LoveInspiredBks

LISOCIAL2018